ENDGAME

A MAX AUSTIN THRILLER - BOOK SIX OF THE RUSSIAN ASSASSIN SERIES

JACK ARBOR

For Yuki Nomura, friend, mentor, sake-drinking partner

"If you wait by the river long enough, the bodies of your enemies will float by."

~Sun Tzu

PROLOGUE

Sysmä, Finland

"*Blyad!* I can't see it."

Max dug a foil-wrapped package of nicotine gum from his pocket, snapped out a piece, and popped it in his mouth. "I can't bloody see it." He wadded the gum wrapper and hurled it into the corner where it landed among a pile of its cousins. The recently renovated cabin had been in Max's family for two generations. The smallish room where Max stood consisted of a slanted ceiling of cedar planks peppered with recessed lights. The walls, also constructed of cedar planks, were punctuated by broad floor-to-ceiling windows which overlooked snow-covered fields and hills with spruce and pines. A small wood fire crackled in a fireplace with a steel pipe for a chimney. Smells of fresh-cut wood mingled with the tinge of smoke. The room was modern and fitted with Scandinavian furnishings and fixtures. The white oak floor was covered with thick wool rugs in Kashmir patterns.

Max paced along a wall hidden beneath a wallpaper of printouts tacked and taped to the cedar planks. Thousands of images, diagrams, headshots, and surveillance photos were arranged haphazardly on every available surface. Handwritten notes on yellow stickies were peppered over the documents, and a rainbow of colored yarn was strung out from picture to picture. The yarn rose and fell over the sea of images and from pushpin to pushpin. Yellow and blue highlighters called emphasis to certain typewritten passages and thick black ink circled various pictures of men and women. The floor was littered with more printouts, dozens of which were crumpled like the nicotine gum wrappers, while others were strewn randomly.

"I like your Russian cursing, sugar. Better than that British slang." A woman entered from the sauna room and shrugged on a brief kimono. She was tall and willowy and flowed into the room in a flourish of billowing silk. Long bare legs were covered in a sheen of perspiration, as was her pale but sculpted face. Waist-length white hair was held back with a lacquered barrette. The woman went by the name Goshawk, after the large raptor known as the *gentle hawk*. Her vocation was that of accomplished computer hacker, and she usually lived in a reclusive compound in Paris's warehouse district. She secured the kimono with a silk sash and sidled over to Max. "Take a break. You've been staring at this mess for a week."

Max threw up his arms. "How can he have stolen all these files, gathered all this information and"—Max swept an arm around the room—"not have identified the man who heads the kommissariat?" The *he* was Max's late father, Andrei Asimov.

"Even your father was not infallible. If the answer was

in here, he would have acted on the information and you wouldn't be in this mess."

"You keep saying. I refuse to believe there isn't a clue in all this." Max stepped to the wall and jabbed his index finger at pictures. "Many of the oligarchs are in here. The Arkady brothers. Boris Rotenberg. Timchenko. Kovalchuk. Hundreds of files and dozens of paper trails that show how money flows between the Russian president and these men. It shows how they launder and hide a lot of his money." Max walked to the wall next to the fireplace and pointed at more pictures. "He's got in-depth dossiers on all the consortium members, including Nikita Ivanov, Ruslan Stepanov, Andrey Pavlov, Lik Wang, and even Zhao Zheng. Their finances, notes on their family, their backgrounds, and secrets that can be used for blackmail."

Goshawk snorted. "How KGB of him."

"Like Pavlov's preference for men." Max shrugged.

"Not that there's anything wrong with that." Goshawk's eyebrows went up.

"Homosexuality in Russia is still taboo." Max shook his head. "It can ruin careers." He strode across the room to where a walnut table sat piled with cardboard file boxes. Hundreds of colored tabs helped organize the thousands of documents. He rested a hand on one of the boxes. "Decades of financial transactions that show money flowing out of state-run Russian businesses and into the coffers of the Russian president's cronies. Also payments to consortium members. It's the largest transfer of wealth, I mean theft, from a country to individuals since the Marcoses pillaged the Central Bank of the Philippines."

Goshawk's hand drifted to her chin. "Logically, I agree. There should be a clue in there. You've been through all of the files?"

"Most of them." Max threw up his hands. "It's like the kommissar's identity didn't matter to the KGB. If I can't find him, how am I going to shut him down?"

"Makes me think the kommissariat is sanctioned by the KGB."

Max swept files from a low-slung sofa and plopped down. "I thought of that. But my father was senior in the KGB. He would have known."

"That's my point. Your father was also a member of the kommissariat."

"Which was viewed by the Russians as treason. I refuse to believe there was a connection. My father grew disillusioned with the KGB, which is why he stole all these documents in the first place. If he knew about a connection between the KGB and the kommissariat, he would have told us about it in Vienna. It's possible the KGB simply didn't know the kommissar's identity."

"Your father couldn't have stolen every KGB file, so this is probably only a subset of the KGB's intelligence on the kommissariat. Maybe his identity is buried somewhere your father couldn't get to." Goshawk raised a finger. "I know what you need." She strode into the small kitchen area where the sounds of whisking were followed by the whistle of a teapot. When she returned, she held out a mug made of glazed pottery. "Take a break. The neural networks in your brain need rest."

The mug was filled with a frothy green tea called *matcha*. Notes of lawn cuttings and loam filled his nose as he blew on it to cool it. "As long as these kommissariat people are allowed to walk the earth, my nephew, Alex, and my sister are in danger. I don't have time for damn neuron networks."

"Neural."

"What?"

"Neural networks. It's how your mind forms connections and draws conclusions from disparate facts. You have to build them up, nurture them. It's like a garden. You can't rush nature."

"Right." Max stood and carried his matcha out a side door and onto a porch built from treated lumber. The snow was cleared but the planks were icy under his boots. Two inches of fresh snow rested on the wooden railing, but the sun warmed his skin. Beyond the porch was a sea of pillowy snow interspersed with green conifer and Norway spruce. Undulating hills and vales of the same white and green textures stretched into the distance. The wilderness was silent and still.

On the railing, where the board connected to the cabin's siding, sat a six-inch wood carving of a bear. The bear sat up on its haunches and gazed out over the snowy field. As children, when Max and Arina visited the cabin with their father, Andrei would remind them of the bear's significance in Finnish mythology. *This is Otso.* Andrei would touch the bear's head. *He's the king of the forest, king of the animals. A spirit who is our friend and brother. He is our long-lost relative who fled the family and was transformed into a bear by the power of the forest.* Now Max touched the bear's head. Had his father been referring to himself? Old Andrei's nickname in the KGB was the Bear. Was fleeing the family a reference to when Andrei defected from the KGB? Did he flee his KGB family? A sinking sensation hit Max's gut as he turned his back on the bear and stood at the railing.

He sensed Goshawk's presence before her hand slipped across his chest from behind and her chin rested on his shoulder.

"Patience, darling. It will come."

Max's thoughts returned to the riddle of the Vienna Archive and the mysterious man who went by the title of the kommissar. *If you wait by the river long enough, the bodies of your enemies will float by.* Max's father liked that quote. Sun Tzu, if he remembered correctly. The saying appeared in Max's mind alongside a jumble of memories of his father. Larger than life, Andrei Asimov was one of Belarus's most famous spies. At an early age, Andrei had trained Max in spycraft while Max's friends played hockey on frozen lakes. Now Max was grateful for the skills his father taught him as he fought to keep what remained of his family safe.

Even if this is all my father's fault. It's the enigma that is the Asimov family.

Max let out a deep sigh and bowed his head before he took a sip of the matcha. "You're right. It's just... I'm so close. I can feel it. The information is there. It's on the tip of my tongue, but I can't see it."

"That doesn't make any sense." She snorted.

Max shrugged and put up his hands. He was still learning the English idioms. "You know what I mean."

Goshawk's hand drifted south to his belt. "You know what else helps your neural networks?"

With a chuckle, Max turned and found her standing with her robe open. She took his hand and pulled him into the cabin.

ONE

London, England

The team tailing Max were professionals. They were good enough to toy with his mind. Ever since he and Goshawk uncovered the Vienna Archive, a trickle of anxiety teased his thoughts like an encroaching sandstorm. The disquiet was there, hiding in the shadows, and it showed itself during Max's darkest moments. Moments when he was tired or under stress. Like now. The appearance of the silver sports coupe for the second time that night triggered a flash of dread. Max shoved the emotion aside, but the niggling remained.

The silver sports car was a two-door hatchback and it sat along the dark street with its lights off, but a trickle of exhaust escaped the rear pipes. From where Max stood a block down and across the street, two shadows were visible in the front seats. The street was lined with two- story brick warehouses circa 1940, but lately the neighborhood had become rave central. Close behind the ravers followed the gentrifiers, and it wouldn't be long before the Harringay neighborhood was home to hipster tech execs and the warehouses were converted to lofts and trendy coffee shops sprouted like weeds. But now the streets were dark and clear of pedestrians. The silver car had appeared twenty minutes ago on a different block in a different neighborhood.

Or had it?

Don't be paranoid, damn it.

In art as in love, instinct is enough.

His father's quotes popped into his mind often, a welcome reminder of his old man. Now that old Andrei was dead, perhaps the quotes would fade into the patina of memory. That one, a favorite of his father's from a French novelist, applied as much to spycraft as it did to art or love. When Max's mind crept into his work, he ignored it and relied on his instincts. Instincts that were honed over decades of field operations where the outcome was either the target's life or Max's own. Now in his late forties, his instincts hadn't failed him yet. And instinct told him the silver car was a tail.

Max ambled along a sidewalk slick with moisture. Springtime in London was fickle, with flowers in bloom but also with damp air that clung to his skin. The sidewalks were wet, although there was no rain. A wool peacoat warded off the frigid dank, a scarf hid his bearded face, and a black watch cap was pulled tight over his shaved head. Fog swirled around the amber gas lamps. From the corner of his eye, the two men still sat in the coupe. He walked closer to get a better view of the vehicle and the men inside it. Asian. Bald heads. Square jaws. *What are they doing?* Max strolled another block and turned left onto a narrow street that angled up a slight hill.

So far the short surveillance detection route had turned into an hour, and he was in danger of missing his flight. His sister, Arina, hospitalized for two months, was awake from her coma, and Max was headed to Colorado to bring her to London. There were a dozen moves he might make to lose the tail, but he wanted to know who followed him. And how did they find him? The skin on the back of his neck prickled.

He hastened up an incline and made two quick left turns into an alley and jogged past piles of refuse and a broken-down scooter. After another turn, he was back on the street with the silver sports coupe.

Except the car was gone.

Max crossed Eade Road and ducked down a ramp that led to a walking path that ran along the New River. He strode west with his hands shoved deep in his pockets and wished he carried a pistol. The walking path was deserted save for a homeless man sleeping under a large sheet of cardboard. Or was he part of the surveillance team? *Is my mind playing tricks?* He took stairs up two at a time and emerged onto Green Lanes, a busy road during the day. Tonight the only vehicle was a lorry that tossed up a gentle spray on the wet road. And a dark panel van.

The van, clean of any markings, drove north at a slow pace. A sensation crawled in Max's gut as he followed the van's path. The windows were blacked out, and the taillights were covered. The van appeared new, but the lights illuminating the rear license plate were out. The tickle on his neck grew into an itch.

To the south was the Manor House underground station, and to the north was a hotel with a taxi stand. The van drove north, so Max turned south. The silver coupe was parked along the street between two cars.

Shit.

All second-guessing evaporated. This was a problem.

Green Lanes Road was lined with shops and pubs with residential flats above the commercial establishments. This late at night the windows were dark. Two men turned onto the deserted street fifty meters away. They walked toward Max.

Max jaywalked across the street and beelined south toward the safety of the underground stop. Followers on foot in the subway would have to stick close and, at this late hour, might reveal themselves. Movement reflected from a barbershop window revealed two men in dark clothing at Max's six o'clock position. They walked with purpose in Max's direction. Ahead, two men exited the silver coupe.

Tires screeched as the dark van bounced onto the curb to Max's right. To his left was a pub, where a red neon light flickered in a tiny window. Ahead were two men and behind were two men.

The van's sliding door latch pinged and the door rolled open. Two dark shadows jumped from the vehicle as Max pivoted and yanked on the pub's door handle.

The door didn't budge.

Max gave another fruitless pull before he whirled to face his attackers. Something cold and metallic poked his neck. A click, electricity pulsed, and his body spasmed. His knees buckled and he pitched to the cobblestones.

"Hit him again." The words were in Mandarin, which Max understood. He had a passing comprehension of spoken Mandarin. There was no time to consider his attacker's nationality as another jolt of electricity coursed through his spine. As Max fell, strong hands jerked him up by the back of his jacket and a black hood turned out the lights. Stunned from the pain of the electricity, his limbs were frozen. He was tossed and landed hard on a metal floor, where his wrists and ankles were bound by plastic cuffs.

Sorry, Arina. I'm going to miss my flight.

The van lurched off the sidewalk and into the street.

A man in the van started to speak but was shushed by another. A knee jabbed into Max's back and stayed there. As if he could move. He was numb from the two bursts of electricity. The van's wheels hissed along the wet roads, and they turned right and picked up speed.

Something was fastened to Max's head and all sound disappeared. Noise-canceling headphones. Everything was removed from his pockets, including his grandfather's lighter and the specially modified Blackphone.

These guys were professionals. There had been six men on the street and another driving the van. He didn't know how many accompanied him in the vehicle, but presumably two drove the silver sports car, which left maybe four in the van. A big team. Well organized. Strong, capable guys. *How did they find me?*

The only sensory information available was the motion of the van. It swayed around several curves and made two more turns before it settled into a steady pace. The vehicle stayed that way as Max tried to mark time by counting, but he soon gave up. They were on a long trip.

His thoughts turned to his nephew. While Alex's mother convalesced in a Colorado hospital, the boy was sequestered at the cherry orchard outside Bath, England, where Max lived under the protection of the British government. Now eleven, Alex was subjected to long days of homeschooling by a matronly taskmaster supplied by the

British. The teacher, an old battle-ax of a woman with leathered skin and a faint mustache, sternly reminded Max how far Alex was behind other students his age. Alex had first rebelled against the assignments, but recently he warmed to the work and now earned solid marks. Max was proud.

Thoughts of Alex distracted him as the van slowed and executed a series of turns before it increased speed on a winding road. It stayed on that road for what Max guessed was a half hour before it lurched onto a dirt road, where it bounced over ruts and holes until it ground to a halt. Four unyielding hands grabbed him, propelled him from the van, and carried him horizontally. Rain dampened the cloth hood and stopped when he assumed they entered a building. The breath went out of him when he was dropped on a dirt floor. While he gasped for air, the headphones and hood were removed, and the door clanged shut, leaving him in darkness.

TWO

Undisclosed Location

An ache began in his shoulders and migrated along his arms to his wrists and hands where the plastic cuffs dug into his skin. The dark room took shape as his eyes grew accustomed to a pale light glowing from under the door. After he waited a spell to ensure the men did not return, he shifted his weight and rolled in the dirt onto his back. He wormed to a sitting position against the wall opposite a stout wooden door. The small room's walls were built from oversized stones set in mortar. A ceiling of wooden rafters was overhead. There were no windows. The stale odor of rotting vegetables was strong. Probably a root cellar.

All sense of time departed him. Occasional footsteps squeaked overhead and eventually the glow from under the door clicked off and he was left in darkness. There was only one reason he was still alive. Whoever was behind the abduction wanted the Vienna Archive.

Good luck.

The enormous trove of KGB documents stolen by his father was protected in such a way that even if he wanted to, Max was unable to give it up. The downside of this little plan was that once they determined this, they might as well kill him. The security scheme for the Vienna Archive he and Goshawk devised was about to be tested.

His stomach growled, and the air grew chilly. Eventually, he drifted off.

The door banged open and Max jolted awake. Through a bright light that pierced his eyeballs, four dark shapes materialized. He was pulled upright, and someone snipped the cuffs holding his ankles. The men were all Asian with hard stares and grim lips pressed tight. None carried visible weapons. They hustled him out the cell door and into a basement, where four men in T-shirts and cargo pants played cards. Eight men so far.

Calloused hands held him in a cast-iron grip, maneuvered him to the opposite end of the basement, and shoved him into a stout wooden chair. The chair was constructed of two-by-fours and secured to a concrete pad in the dirt floor. A row of halogen lights and a video camera were in front of the chair. A standard interrogation setup. Almost a cliché.

Plastic cuffs secured each ankle to a chair leg. The zip tie holding his wrists was cut, and two strong men held his arms while another man used two zip ties around each wrist to bind him to the chair's arms. His hands went numb. Two of the guards shifted to a ready position in front while the other two disappeared behind him. Maybe they stood guard at his rear. That's how he would do it.

"Is he ready?"

The voice in Mandarin floated down the wooden steps. It was soft but commanding and was familiar.

One of the guards, a man with wrinkles at the corners of his eyes and gray at his temples, replied in the affirmative. Measured footsteps navigated the stairs, and a man in a light gray suit appeared. His gaunt face was puckered in a frown and sparse brows furrowed over eyes that glittered. The newcomer clasped one wrist in the other hand as if protecting himself, but Max knew the head of China's Ministry of State Security feared no one.

"Hello, Zheng." Max flexed his wrists in a futile attempt to gain blood flow to his hands.

A woman descended the stairs and leaned on a wall. Despite the dim light, she wore dark Wayfarer sunglasses. The newcomer produced a cigarette and lit it with a match, inhaled deeply, and let smoke trickle from her nose and mouth. Max recognized the woman. She was the same woman who appeared on the foredeck of a fishing trawler in the Adriatic Sea to pick up a raven-haired killer who had once saved Max's life.

Is she friend or foe?

The crinkle of a plastic bag sounded behind Max, and it was yanked onto his head and held in place by strong hands. He heaved in a breath but only sucked plastic into his mouth while the lack of oxygen surged panic up his spine. He clamped his mouth shut, closed his eyes, and held his breath. *Fight the panic. Stay calm. Conserve oxygen.* He held his breath until his eyes watered. Right when he needed to open his mouth and heave for air, the bag was removed.

Max gulped in fresh oxygen.

Zhao Zheng, the director who oversaw the secretive Chinese ministry charged with spying and counterespionage, took a step closer. The director's eyes were narrow, and his brow was furrowed. "We meet at last, Mikhail Asimov."

The director used English in a soft and melodious tenor with perfect diction. Harvard educated, if Max's recall of Zheng's file was correct. One arm crossed Zheng's chest while the other rested there to allow delicate fingers to toy with his lip. "I knew your father well, but you and I have never met. Despite our differences, I am sorry to hear about your father. He was a worthy adversary. Fair, ruthless, cunning. But like most Russians, he was a blunt instrument. I enjoyed pitting my team against his. A pity it was cancer that took him out of the game. We all want to go while in the heat of battle, do we not?"

"We're Belarusian." Max sneered. "And he was killed by a bullet."

"How does the saying go?" Zheng shrugged. "Die by the sword?"

How does Zheng know about his father's cancer?

Zheng clucked with his tongue. "I see surprise on your face. I know many things, Mikhail. It's my business to know the intricate details of my adversary's comings and goings. I wouldn't be good at my job if I didn't. I know, for example, that your father staged his death six months ago and went into hiding in Vienna. I know he was afflicted with horrible lung cancer, and it was only a matter of time. I know he was shot in the chest and died in your arms before the cancer took him."

Max's mind raced. His father's exile was a tightly controlled secret. So tight that even Max hadn't known his father remained alive. Only a few people in Andrei's inner circle were aware.

"I see the wheels turning, Mikhail. You're wondering

how I know these things. You're wondering who betrayed you or what network might be compromised. Do not waste your energy. Our network is everywhere. We have people and technology under every rock and in every corner. I also know, like many, that Andrei squirreled away thousands of files that document the inner workings of the Russian government, the kommissariat, and the various subcouncils. These documents outline kommissariat membership, the flow of funds, how money is hidden. Where the dead bodies lie, so to speak. We also know that this dossier contains intricate details of how the Russian president hides his money."

Max attempted to slide his arms back to relieve the tension and allow blood flow back into his hands. He managed slight relief. "And yet, with your people and technology, you do not know where the Vienna Archive is."

Zheng's hard face remained stoic but there was a brief flare of light in his eyes, which disappeared as soon as it showed. "They say you are a chip off the old block, as the Americans like to say. It's true, we do not know where the Vienna Archive is. But we know who has it, and we have the man who has it." Zheng raised his hands. "All is not lost."

Throughout their conversation, Zheng was rooted in place. The halogen lights remained off. The woman in the Wayfarers still leaned against the far wall, although she had finished her first cigarette and lit another. Now Zheng took a step closer, within kicking range if Max's legs were free. "Do you know why I am on the Council for Petroleum and Natural Gas?"

Max did his best to shrug while secured to the chair. "China needs oil and natural gas to fuel its economy. Russia has it. You're there to protect China's interests and make sure your energy supply is secured."

"You're not wrong." Zheng's eyebrows went up. "China has many legitimate oil and gas pacts with Russia. Why must I subject myself to the indignities and inconveniences of such a secretive charade?"

"Protect your own interests," Max said. "Your personal wealth has no doubt increased as a result of your inclusion on the council."

Zheng shook his head. "Maybe you're not as smart as they say you are. So the record is clear, my allegiance is to the People's Republic of China." His gaze shifted to the woman standing next to the wall and back to Max. "My dividends from the council, all of them derived from illicit operations by the kommissariat, are funneled into my agency's official accounts. Every single ruble, and I have detailed documents that prove it. The same cannot be said of the late Mr. Lik Wang, which is one reason it was necessary to... ahem... send him into retirement."

Max snorted. "Your hands are clean. You're there as a watchdog. To protect China's interests and nothing more."

Zheng snapped his fingers. "That is partially correct, Mikhail. As the Vienna Archive no doubt documents, Chinese monies generated by legitimate oil and gas transactions funnel out of Russia, either into the Russian president's pockets or through the various subcouncils. The optics aren't good for China. We are not a well-understood country by outsiders. That is partly by design. It's also our nature as a people. Throughout history, we've been ostracized, invaded, and controlled. The Mongols, the Japanese, Russians, French..." Zheng's fists clenched and relaxed. "Our nation's security drives our nationalism, our secrecy, and influences much of our foreign policy. But lining our lacquer box is a sense of fairness and pride. If payments from China were traced to the bank accounts of criminals, it would be a national embarrassment and taint us on the world stage."

"And you think the Vienna Archive shows evidence of that. That payments from China for oil and natural gas are routed into the bank accounts of oligarchs."

Zheng signaled with a long finger and the plastic bag was shoved over Max's head.

He managed a quick breath. Through the cloudy plastic, Zheng's arms were crossed, and he peered at his watch as the seconds ticked by. The bag was left in place until something in Max's prehistoric brain overrode his conditioning. He gaped open his mouth to suck in air, but the plastic filled his mouth. Panic took over and his arms strained at the plastic restraints, and he thrashed his head to free himself, but vice-like hands held him in place. The bag sucked in and out of his mouth as he struggled. Blackness appeared at the edges of his mind. Right as the dark threatened to overwhelm him, the bag was removed.

"Impressive," Zheng said as Max heaved his chest to get as much oxygen as possible. "Did you know that brain damage can begin after only two minutes of being deprived of oxygen? That was a full three minutes. I wonder how many cells in that big brain of yours just died?"

Max gulped air and glared at Zheng.

The head of China's secret service took out his phone, tapped a few times, and put it back into his pocket. "Let's get to business, shall we? As you know, there are a lot of interested parties looking for your father's so-called Vienna Archive. The Americans. The Germans. Yes, I see the surprise in your eyes. Despite your mother's failure, the BND still seeks the archive. The Russians perhaps covet the archive more than any other." Zheng slapped his thighs with his hands. "But here we are. In the middle of nowhere.

Only you and us, Mikhail. Why don't you save yourself the pain and agony of the coming days and weeks and give us the archive?"

"What archive?"

There was no mirth on Zheng's face as he turned to gesture at the woman next to the wall. "Let me introduce you to my colleague, Colonel Wu. Extracting information is her specialty. Don't worry, Mikhail. It will be a slow process. There will be moderate pain, but she'll get into your mind, and by the end you'll beg her to let you talk. It might take a week or two or longer. But eventually you'll tell us what we want to know. It is a certainty. Do me a favor and relent now. Or do Colonel Wu a favor and hold out for as long as you can." Zheng shrugged. "It matters not to us." He strode to the foot of the stairs. "I wish you a good day. It is unlikely you and I will ever see each other again." Zheng snapped his fingers.

The plastic bag was stuffed over Max's head as Zheng walked up the stairs. The halogen spotlights snapped on and Max's world disappeared in an impenetrable brightness as he struggled for breath.

THREE

Undisclosed Location

Max blacked out right as the bag was lifted from his head. Someone slapped him across the face and his eyes shot open to blinding lights and he squeezed them shut.

His wrists and ankles burst free from the plastic ties. Before Max was able to flex his muscles, he was yanked to his feet and his arms were wrenched behind his back so his shoulders strained and almost popped from their sockets. His eyes opened in time to see Colonel Wu holding a cigarette. It was the only detail Max noticed before he was force-marched into the root cellar. He was secured so his arms were overhead and attached to a large hook high on the wall. Two men lifted him as a third ensured his wrists were on the hook. When the men let go, Max dangled so his toes were off the ground. If he angled his toes down, he was barely able to touch the floor.

Headphones were placed over his ears and heavy metal music blared.

"Are you ready for our little talk?"

Max understood some Mandarin, but his mind was addled, and it took time to make sense of the words. He was slammed onto the wooden chair and more zip ties were used to hold his arms. The silence was blessed, but it was hard to form a coherent thought. Four men, all Chinese with practiced and efficient movements, took positions around the basement's perimeter. No amount of flexing of his arms and legs helped loosen the bindings.

Where were the other four men? Did they leave with Zheng, or were they upstairs?

Colonel Wu appeared like an apparition, with her wiry gray hair in disarray and Wayfarer sunglasses pushed on top of her head. Her skin was the same color as her hair, and her teeth were a dull yellow. A cigarette was clutched in a claw-like hand adorned with cracked fingernails, and she reeked of tobacco smoke and body odor. Thin lips sucked on the butt like it was nourishment, and she blew a cloud of smoke into Max's face as she straddled a chair backward.

"We meet again." The woman's voice was husky, and if Max's eyes were closed, he would swear it was a man talking to him. "I don't like talk, unlike Mr. Zheng. Tell me what I want to know and you'll get a rest."

"Water," Max managed. His throat was barren, and it was hard to form words. He had no idea how long he was in the room with his arms trussed over his head and subjected to an endless loop of the screaming music. At first he tried to shut it out. Mind over matter and all that. His training, as good as it was, didn't prepare him for this kind of torment, and eventually the screaming overwhelmed him and his mind went numb. Madness might be next.

The woman signaled, and one of the guards cranked open a bottle of water and poured it into Max's upturned mouth. He drank until he gagged and spit out a mouthful. Drops landed on the woman's boot. The guard tossed the bottle and pummeled a fist into Max's nose, which burst, and warm blood mixed with the water on his face.

Colonel Wu puffed on a new cigarette. "Tell me. Where is the Vienna Archive?"

The cold water helped clear his mind, and he dredged up a memory of one of the thousands of files in his father's archive. The file had caught his eye when he realized it was a dossier on the same woman from the boat in the Aegean Sea just a couple months ago. "Ru Shi Wu." Max's voice was sandpaper, but he got the words out. "Born 1955 in Hong Kong out of wedlock to a Chinese mother who was a maid to your British father. Your mother lived in the slums, your father was minor aristocracy and a wealthy financier. You ran away at sixteen and disappeared for a decade, after which you reappeared as a low-ranking officer in China's Ministry of State Security. You moved up in the ranks and are now Zheng's right-hand woman. You're thought to be only one of a few level-four black belts in open hand Wing Chun. You're slowly trying to kill yourself one cigarette at a time. How am I doing?"

As Max spoke, Wu's coal-black irises blazed. She sucked on the butt, blew out a haze of smoke at Max's face, and flicked the butt into a corner in a shower of sparks. "Are you done?"

"Just getting started."

Wu lit another cigarette. "Give us the archive or go back to your cell."

Max smirked. "Don't you want to know what else I know? What else may be in that archive about you? If I hand it over, someone might see something you don't want—"

The palm strike was faster than a blur. Max's head rocked back, and more blood spattered onto the woman's arm. The blow landed on his nose, which added to the pain from the earlier hit. Wu backed away from the chair and issued a command in Mandarin. One man shoved the plastic bag over Max's head as another released his arms from their bindings, and he was dragged into the root cellar. He struggled for breath as he was resecured on the wall, his aching arms overhead. Mercifully the bag was removed, but the headphones were replaced. Hate metal blared into his head as he gasped for oxygen.

Max was barely sentient when he was removed from the cell and secured to the wooden chair. Blob-like shapes floated around him. He formed an image of his nephew in his mind, the towheaded boy who had become the center of Max's world. Alex was the sole purpose behind Max's fight with the kommissariat. He wanted everything for Alex that Max didn't have growing up. A normal childhood and the chance to become a doctor or a business owner. Meet a beautiful girl, settle into a nice house, and raise a family. The ordinary life Max never got. Was Max compensating for his own shortcomings? Did it matter?

The image of Alex wavered in and out of his hazy mind.

A shot of ammonium carbonate surged through his brain as a guard snapped smelling salts under his nose and the room appeared in stark focus. Pain centered on his nose and radiated through his skull. Maybe his nose was broken. Dark humanoid shapes bobbed in his periphery, and Wu's chair was empty. Cigarette smoke wafted from somewhere, which meant she was nearby.

As if in confirmation, her guttural voice rang in his right ear. "Where's the archive?"

Max couldn't move his jaw, and his tongue was stuck to the roof of his mouth. A young and smooth-faced guard dressed in a gray T-shirt approached and squirted a bottle of water onto his face. He lapped at the liquid and got a mouthful. It wet his tongue so he was able to form words. "You don't want these men to hear what I'm going to say."

Wu appeared from out of the shadows. The ubiquitous cigarette hung from a corner of her mouth, and her hands were shoved into her pant pockets. "Where is it?"

"Even if I wanted to give it to you, I can't. Access to the files requires dual factor authentication. That means—"

"I know what it means. What are the two factors?"

Max snorted. "That's going to take more work on your part."

Wu signaled to the men standing to the side.

"Wait." Max raised a finger, which was awkward with his arms bound to the chair. "I can tell you a few things." He nodded his head at the men near the wall. "But you don't want them to hear what I have to say."

Wu crossed her arms.

Max rattled his arms against the bindings holding him to the chair. "I'm not going anywhere. No tricks up my sleeve. Besides, from what I read, you wouldn't have a problem handling me by yourself."

"Speak or you're going back to your cell."

Max raised his eyebrows and lowered his voice. "Department 82."

The result was like someone opened a shade. Wu snapped her fingers and issued a command in Mandarin.

When none of the guards moved, her voice boomed. "Out. All of you." She pointed at the stairs.

The four men walked to the steps. The last man, the one with wrinkles at the edges of his eyes, squinted at her as he walked, but they all disappeared up the stairs.

A knife appeared in Wu's hand. "What do you know?" She shoved the tip into the underside of Max's chin, and it drew blood.

"Hey, easy with that thing—"

Smoke curled into Max's nostrils from Wu's cigarette as she drove the tip further into his skin. A craving for nicotine surged in his mind.

Wu turned the knife so the tip gouged out a chunk of skin.

"Okay, okay." Max forced his dry tongue to form words. "You're funneling intel to Japan's Department 82. You're Japan's agent, and if that comes out, you're a dead woman. The ministry will make you disappear."

"How do you know this? Department 82 is so secretive that the emperor doesn't even know it exists."

A grin appeared on Max's face, which he quickly smothered. "There is a dossier on Department 82 in the Vienna Archive, along with a file on you personally."

The knife tip wavered until Wu's eyes narrowed and she shifted the blade so it pushed against his jugular. "What's to keep me from slitting your neck right now? Maybe the archive should stay buried forever."

The Chinese agent was close enough for Max to smell her body odor. It was a fruity, onion-like smell that reminded him of the liver and onions his mother use to make when he was a kid. "I don't think your boss would be happy if I died without giving up the archive's location. You might survive that. But it's my life insurance policy that you should be concerned about."

"What life insurance?"

"I've made arrangements in the case of my untimely death. A thick file of secrets will be automatically released to an organization called the International Consortium of Investigative Journalists and simultaneously sent to an editor at *The Guardian* in London."

Wu removed the knife from Max's throat, wiped the blade on his pant leg, slipped it into her pocket, and lit a cigarette. She paced while she smoked. "How do I know you're not bluffing?"

Max tipped his head to the side. "I guess you don't. Are you willing to take that risk?"

A puff of smoke escaped her nose. "If we spend enough time together, you'll tell me everything, including your security protocols and who holds this insurance. If it even exists."

A trickle of something warm dripped along Max's neck. "Don't you think I know that every spy agency in the world wants the archive? Do you think I'd let myself be the weakest link to a cache of information my father so painstakingly compiled? You think you and Zheng are the only ones who thought of the idea of torturing me? Trust me, there is a lot of intel in the archive. Do you think I'd make it so anyone might torture it out of me? I'm almost offended."

"You're bluffing."

The trickle of blood was now more like a flow. A desire overcame him to check his chest for blood, but Max forced his eyes to remain on her face. *No weakness. Not now.* "You want to believe I'm bluffing because it allows you to keep the upper hand. You don't want to have to live with the idea that I know your secret and it might get out into the world. Your biggest fear is being found out by the Chinese. For whatever reason, you're giving their secrets to the Japanese. That's your business, but that ends if what I know comes out."

Wu walked and smoked but never once took her gaze off Max. She paced a long time. One of her men stuck his head down the stairs, and she waved him off.

When the door banged shut, she whirled. "What now? If I let you go, I'm dead."

"There is only one way out of this I can think of." Max narrowed his eyes at her. "But you're going to have to trust me."

In a low voice, he told her what they needed to do.

FOUR

Undisclosed Location

"Help! Help!" Colonel Wu's voice rang out in Mandarin.

The scurry of feet and scraping of chairs on the floorboards overhead were followed by the banging of a door. Boots pounded on the stairs, and when the four Chinese commandos arrived in the basement, pistols up, the wooden chair where the prisoner sat was empty, and severed plastic zip ties lay on the floor.

Wu stood in the center of the room. The prisoner was behind her, his forearm around her windpipe and a knife blade poised at her jugular. Blood seeped along her neck from a shallow cut. Her cigarette lay smoking on the dirt floor.

Max used her body to shield himself from the four men and used his best Mandarin. "Drop the weapons or she dies." Don't give the team time to consider how he might have gotten the drop on Wu. Use the chaos and intensity to blur the men's perspective. "Do it now!" Max dug the knife into Wu's throat and more blood flowed.

The Chinese soldiers hesitated and glanced at the oldest among them. The soldier with gray temples, who Max pegged as the team leader, put his free hand out while his gun hand remained steady. "Stay calm." His English was excellent. "Put the knife on the ground and no one will get hurt."

Max was counting on the psychology of the situation. With Wu tight in the crook of his arm, Max circled in the direction of the stairs as he kept his back to the wall. Colonel Wu, their senior officer, was a barrier. "Drop the guns," Max yelled. "Do it now."

Three of the Chinese soldiers lowered their pistols onto the ground while the team leader held steady.

"Do it, Chen." Wu's voice was panicked.

"He's going to kill you anyway." Chen's teeth were clenched.

"He won't," Wu said. "He knows if he does, he will be chased by the Chinese to the ends of the earth. You don't want that, do you, Mr. Asimov?"

Was that a subliminal message? "Drop it, Chen," Max yelled. "I'll kill her if I have to. I'm out of options." Max pulled Wu another step.

Chen lowered his pistol to the dirt floor.

Max dragged Wu another step so they were positioned at the foot of the wooden stairs. "Kick the weapons this way." Max pushed the blade tight against Wu's throat. If things went wrong, he had no qualms about killing his new partner. One swipe with the knife and a push to send her at the four men before he bounded up the stairs.

Chen kicked the pistols across the floor one by one.

Now comes the delicate part. "All four of you. Back up to the rear wall and get on your stomachs."

Again, the men hesitated, so Max yelled and made his hand quiver like he was going to jab the knife into her throat. "Do it!"

In unison, the Chinese commandos laid on the floor at the rear of the room.

Max removed the knife from Wu's throat, and she let out an audible breath. With a fluid movement, he swiped the blade across her left deltoid and shoved her hard, so she stumbled across the room. He shifted the now bloody blade to his left hand and snatched a pistol from the floor. It was a Chinese-manufactured QSZ-92 with a star on the grip. If Max remembered right, the gun was chambered for 9mm ammunition and the magazine held fifteen rounds.

Wu held a hand to her shoulder while blood seeped through her fingers. Her eyes were hooded. The knife wound was not part of the plan, but Max wanted her occupied with managing the cut and used it to send a signal to her men.

He slipped a second pistol into his waistband next to the small of his back, and he dropped the magazines from the other two and cleared their chambers. A pile of zip ties was on the table, and Max waved the gun at Wu. "Secure their hands and feet."

He leveled the gun at her as Wu used the plastic cuffs to tie their hands. That's when she veered off course from their plan. Wu produced a switchblade from her boot, stood over one of the men, grabbed his hair, and dragged the blade across his throat. A gush of blood spurted onto the dirt floor.

Max danced out of the way of the blood. "What are you—"

She straddled the next man and cut his throat, which

added more blood to the growing puddle in the middle of the basement floor. "Get out of here. I'll take care of this." As if to punctuate her message, she killed the third man, whose scream ended in a gurgle.

"What will you do?"

Wu snatched a pistol from the ground, banged home a magazine, and pointed the gun at Chen.

"You don't have to do this." Chen's voice was a whimper.

Wu racked the slide and pointed the pistol at the back of his skull. "I'm sorry, Chen. You're in the wrong place at the wrong time. I'll spare you the blade." She pulled the trigger twice and two bullets ripped into Chen's head and blood spattered on the wall. He slumped, and Wu slid the gun into her waist. "We better go. Zheng and his men may return at any time."

"I hope he does." Max held on to the railing as he walked up the stairs. In the kitchen, he found his boots, shirt, his grandfather's Zippo with the burnished Belarusian flag, and his wallet with identification and a wad of cash. His secure Blackphone was missing.

Wu used the stove to light a cigarette. "You didn't have to cut me, you know." She shrugged out of her jacket and stripped to her bra. A four-inch cut on her deltoid oozed blood.

"I wanted it to be authentic. If I knew you were going to kill those men, I wouldn't have bothered. Zheng will think it was me."

While Max dressed, she disappeared and reappeared with a shoulder bag and a bottle of hydrogen peroxide, which she handed to Max. He doused her wound, which she endured with stoic resolve, and used a kitchen towel to make a bandage, which she taped to her shoulder using duct tape. She rummaged in her shoulder bag and withdrew a new shirt.

"No, he won't. That little charade would have unraveled fast. I'd have been interrogated for weeks and probably die in a cell somewhere near the border of Mongolia." Wu snorted. "I can't stick around the Guoanbu. It's time for me to disappear." *Guoanbu* was the Chinese name for the Ministry of State Security.

"Where will you go?"

"Doesn't matter. Let's get out of here. I'll drop you at a train station."

The Chinese safe house turned out to be a farmhouse on a dozen acres two hours west of London. Wu drove the van and they wove through the backroads of Swindon, a large town in Wiltshire, before she dropped Max at Swindon Station.

Max hesitated before he left the van. "Mind telling me how you guys found me?"

"Sources and methods." Wu's face was stoic.

Max raised his eyebrows.

"The cherry orchard," Wu said. "It's the worst-kept secret at MI6. Like Zheng said, we have sources everywhere. We've been watching the orchard and followed as you left."

Max nodded. "Thanks. How do I get in touch with you?"

Wu stared through the windshield. A pedestrian dragged a rolling suitcase along the sidewalk in front of the van. "You don't."

Max considered bumming a cigarette, but he exited the van, ducked into the train station, and bought a ticket for Bath.

FIVE

Bath, England

Chaos erupted at the cherry orchard when Max straggled down the driveway resembling a carcass dragged from the woods. Tom, the ex-Special Air Service soldier and now the farm's live-in groundskeeper, saw him first and raised a shout. Tom's wife rushed out and fussed over Max before she disappeared into the kitchen to warm up a pot of soup. Alex sprinted into the living room and was followed by Spike the dog. Alex smothered Max with hugs while Spike licked Max's face.

There wasn't much physical damage. Only bruising around his wrists and ankles and the swelling around his eyes from when Wu broke his nose. But exhaustion set in, and he fell onto the sofa near the fireplace while Tom built a roaring fire and Alex fetched him a glass and the bottle of the Irish whiskey Tom let him keep in the house. A diehard scotch enthusiast, Tom forbade American whiskey on the premises, but he endured the lone bottle of Irish whiskey after Max showed him on the internet where the Irish purportedly distilled their whiskey 89 years before the Scots.

After Max finished his soup, gulped two fingers of the alcohol, and allowed Tom's wife to clean and dress his nose, he admitted to Alex that he didn't make his flight and had not been able to see Arina, Alex's mother.

The boy's face fell until Max placed a hand on his arm. "Don't worry. As soon as I rest up, I'll catch the next flight out, okay? Your mom is fine, she's recuperating. She'll be here in no time."

Spike jumped onto the couch and curled up next to Max while he sipped whiskey and listened as Alex filled him in on his studies. The matronly tutor supplied by MI6 was a taskmaster, and Alex complained bitterly. As if to bolster the boy's complaints, his teacher poked her head in and snapped her fingers. Alex groaned, but Max prodded him off the couch and back to his schooling as a commotion arose from the front of the farmhouse.

A racing-green Range Rover pulled into the circle drive and three people alighted as Tom and his wife rushed out to greet the newcomers. C, Britain's sage chief of MI6, Great Britain's foreign intelligence service, disembarked from the front passenger seat. Callum Baxter, MI6's dogged senior officer, exited from the rear passenger seat while Cindy, Baxter's shrewd senior analyst, hurried around from the opposite door.

Why is C here?

He expected Baxter and Cindy to show up for a debrief, but C's appearance added gravity. Max walked out to the porch as the three intelligence officers strode up the walk. C wore a gray mackintosh overcoat that billowed in the breeze. Known only by the first initial of his title, C was a former field operative and case officer and held the respect of every man and woman who worked under him, Max included. When he reached Max, he held out a bony hand, which Max took in his own. "The helicopter in for service, sir?"

Matching Max's height at six foot four, C was bony where Max was muscular. C's hand was long and thin, and a prominent Adam's apple bounced as C chuckled. "Indeed, it was on another assignment. With an escort, we made the two-and-a-half-hour trip in two hours. These two were forced to endure my phone calls the whole way."

When Callum Baxter shook Max's hand, Max looked at him askance. There was a marked change in Callum's appearance. Where usually the senior MI6 man carried crumbs and other foodstuffs in his unkempt goatee, today the facial hair was trimmed and clean. His eyebrows and ear hair were tamed, and his white shirt and tweed jacket were pressed and devoid of stains.

Max caught Cindy's eye as Baxter tromped into the farmhouse.

The star analyst shrugged. "Don't ask me." She handed Max a sealed and padded envelope. "A gift from Goshawk."

When Max opened it, a heavy mobile phone dropped into his hand. It was black with rounded corners and was almost as heavy as a brick. Called a Blackphone, the device was made in the UK and its circuitry and software was heavily modified by Goshawk to prevent bad actors from hacking it or tracking its location. "I assume you tried to hack into it." Max chuckled.

"I'll neither confirm nor deny." Cindy winked and strode up the two steps and into the farmhouse.

Max's incarceration had been seventy-two hours in duration, during which time Callum Baxter and the MI6 team worked night and day to search for any trace of him.

Max's failure to check in when the flight from Heathrow to Denver landed set off a tidal wave of frantic searching, and Baxter, Cindy, and the team were almost as weary as Max. Ordinarily based in London at MI6's Lego brick-like headquarters, the MI6 team had established an operations annex in the stone barn that was a dozen paces from the farmhouse's kitchen door. This is where the debrief took place.

Max lounged in a chair, nursing the whiskey and longing for a cigarette, while Baxter asked the questions. Cindy, who wore a smart suit jacket with its sleeves rolled up, typed on a laptop. C sat in a corner and listened, his only movements the periodic cleaning of his wireless spectacles.

Max told the story, albeit with a few key modifications.

"You sure it was Zhao Zheng? Director of China's secret service?" Baxter rose and paced. His hand dug in his jacket's side pocket and emerged with a pipe, which he held but did not light.

"Absolutely." Max tapped his finger on the chair arm. "Zheng and a team of Chinese commandos. Young men, all highly capable."

"The idea that the head of China's secret service was here on the ground in London without us knowing is alarming," Baxter said. "Tell me again what Zheng said."

"The endless death metal rattled my brain, so it's difficult to remember details. But he explained his role on the council and that they killed Lik Wang, their own man, for siphoning off funds to his own account. Zheng was protective of Chinese resources. He doesn't want Chinese investments landing in the hands of oligarchs or criminals. He knew I found the Vienna Archive and wanted me to hand it over."

Baxter tugged at his goatee. "Go over your escape one more time?"

Standard interrogation techniques were to ask random questions to keep the subject off guard and to get the subject to repeat their story multiple times. It allowed investigators to dig into inconsistencies, which helped illuminate deception. Max knew this, of course, and his counter-technique was to be as vague as possible. There was a lot he didn't remember, or at least that's what he told Baxter. Things would get interesting when the MI6 team discovered the four bodies at the Chinese safe house, so Max stayed light on the details. "I wiggled the hook free from the wall in my cell. It was set in old concrete. When they came for me, I overpowered the two guards and got out of there. My mind was addled, so I'm hazy on the details, but that's the gist." There was little rationality for why he protected Colonel Wu, but his instinct guided him to buy her enough time to get out of the country.

The debrief took two hours, during which time Max repeated the story several times. When they were done, the three men retired to the farmhouse's spacious kitchen and left Cindy to direct the search for the Chinese safe house from the operations room in the stone barn.

"I'm glad you arrived back in one piece." C took Max by the elbow and guided him to the table in the kitchen. "You must recover your strength."

That's an odd comment. "Thank you, sir. I intend to."

A fire in the kitchen's hearth was stoked to life, and Tom set out a bottle that had been left behind months ago by C after his last visit to the farmhouse. The alcohol in the bottle was clear and there was no label. "Something more dignified than that rotgut whiskey you two like to drink," C said. The three men sat around the kitchen table as C did the honors. "I'm surprised to see this much gin left in the bottle."

Max held his glass as C poured a finger. There was the smell of juniper and a few spices he didn't recognize. He dreaded the first sip of the warm gin. "We wanted to ensure there was enough of your brother's gin left for you, sir." He avoided looking at Baxter, for fear he might burst out laughing.

"You can't fib to an old fibber." C raised his glass and the three men clinked and sipped. "My brother has won awards with this gin, you know."

The first taste was exactly as Max remembered it. The floral alcohol burned his throat and he almost burped. "This is why you Brits take tonic and citrus in here."

C laughed, and Baxter hid a grin behind another sip. "That's surprising coming from a Russian."

Max set the glass on the wood table and rummaged in a satchel and removed a thick file encased in a sealed envelope. He slid it to Baxter on the table. "I promised you intelligence from the Vienna Archive. Consider this the first of many."

Baxter put his hand on the file. His nails were manicured. "What is it?"

Max smiled. "In there is a detailed file of a certain Russian national living in London. I believe you gave him political asylum."

Baxter looked over sharply. "Who is the Russian?"

"Konstantin Zaitsev."

"Zaitsev?" Baxter rolled his eyes. "He's retired. The Russian president forced him to sell his car rental business, and when he balked, Zaitsev was tossed in prison on trumped-up charges of embezzlement. He was released when he agreed to sell to the Russian president's cronies. He left Moscow and settled here twelve years ago, but he lives a quiet life in Knightsbridge. We check on him occasionally, but—"

"He's selling weapons." Max tapped his finger on the file. "Zaitsev and a couple other exiled Russian oligarchs are stealing guns from former Soviet states and selling them to hot spots in Africa and the Middle East."

"Preposterous." Baxter rolled his eyes. "Never happen under our noses."

"It's all in the file." Max pointed at the dossier. "Transactions, dates, buyers, sellers, and even the banks they're using to route and launder funds. Account numbers. Bills of lading. Been going on for a decade. This is probably more MI5's territory but figured you'd want to know what one of your asylum seekers is doing right under your nose." While MI6 performed the spying on behalf of the British government, MI5 was the department responsible for security internal to Great Britain. Max eyed C, who polished his glasses.

Baxter slipped the file into an attaché case. "We'll look into it, but don't get too excited."

"If I'm wrong, I'm wrong." Max refreshed their glasses. Baxter's reticence didn't bother him. He had an ulterior motive for exposing Zaitsev. Clinking glasses with the three men, Max sipped and glanced at C. "What brings you all the way out here to our humble cherry orchard if not for a taste of these exalted spirits? Callum and Cindy are more than capable of handling a small debrief."

"Indeed." C took a mouthful and allowed the liquid to

swirl in his mouth. "Something happened that I find too odd not to discuss in person."

"Odd, sir?" Max asked.

C nodded. "Someone in the Russian president's close organization reached out to us. Through the Russian ambassador."

"The Russian ambassador is still in the UK?" Max leaned his arms on the table. Calls for the Russian ambassador to be dismissed had coursed through the UK government as the Russian war ground away in Ukraine.

C nodded. "For now."

Max poured another splash of the gin into each of their glasses.

"Does the name Dmitry Kozov ring a bell?" C asked.

"Vaguely." Max nodded. "He's close to the president, right?"

"Correct. His title is first deputy chief, which is a meaningless title. In reality, he is the Russian president's closest strategist. His nickname is the Red Cleaner because he's thought to be the president's fixer."

Baxter emptied his glass. "Too bad he couldn't fix the Russian president before he invaded Ukraine." On February 24th, Russian tanks rolled into Ukraine in what is being called "the Russian president's war." By this time in the conflict, thousands of Ukrainian civilians and tens of thousands of Russian soldiers had died, and while the Ukrainians were putting up an unprecedented fight, there was no end in sight to the war.

"What about him?" Max set his empty tumbler on the table.

"It seems"—C shrugged out of his jacket and hung it on the back of his chair before pouring all three men another measure of the gin—"that Kozov wants a discussion. Off the record."

"What does Kozov possibly want to talk about while they're in the middle of a war?" Baxter leaned back in his chair.

"He didn't say about what." The chief hid a bemused grin behind his glass as he emptied it. "He was specific, however, about who."

A sinking feeling took over Max's stomach as he tossed back the gin. It hit his throat with an angry fire. "Lay it out, sir."

C made no attempt to hide his smile. "Kozov wants to meet with you, Max. In person, and alone."

———

"Goal! Goal! Goal!" Alex jogged around the small field with his arms in the air. He had kicked a soccer ball past Max's outstretched fingers and between two cherry trees.

Max retrieved the ball and cleaned mud from its shiny surface as he joined Alex in the middle of the field. He dropped the ball, and Alex nudged it past Max using fancy footwork. "Where'd you learn to do that?" Max took a swipe at the ball, but the eleven-year-old deftly kept it away from him. The ball was a gift from the MI6 team for Alex's birthday, which, of course, Max had missed when he was in Vienna.

A cool sun peeked through heavy clouds. The two were taking advantage of a break in the ubiquitous English spring rains to get some air. Alex easily dribbled the ball around Max, who was recovering from the interrogation at the hands of Zheng's team.

"A couple of the SAS guys have been teaching me."

Alex wound up and drilled a perfect shot between two cherry trees.

They gave each other high fives. Alex was noticeably taller now. Max didn't have to reach down as far when their palms connected. The eleven-year-old wore his hair longer, and he looked more mature. Max put his arm around the boy, and they walked together to retrieve the ball.

"I have to go away again soon, Alex."

"I know." Alex tossed the ball in the air.

"And I have to delay going to see your mother."

"I know." Alex dropped the ball and took a shot at the goal formed by the two trees. The ball curved wide.

"It's a quick trip. As soon as I'm done, I'll fly to Colorado and bring her back." Max took the boy by the shoulders. "She's in good hands and recovering."

Alex pushed his hair out of his eyes. "I get it, okay? Choices are a bitch." He took off after the ball.

Max watched as Alex jogged away with his long hair flopping.

Eleven going on forty.

From Parliament Hill in Hampstead Heath, the largest green space in London proper, one has a panoramic view south over the city. The tip of the Gherkin, the oblong, spaceship-like office tower, pokes above the tree line. St Paul's Cathedral, the Shard, the London Eye, and BT Tower all jut over the jagged skyline. There is also an athletic field and running track which holds the annual National Cross Country Championship, where thousands tromp through the mud for personal glory. On this spring evening, however, the course was dry and the evening uncharacteristically warm. A woman in a light overcoat sat on a bench near the oval track and watched an obese man walk his French bulldog. Odd how dogs resemble their owners, the woman thought as the pair waddled along a pathway.

The woman's mission was a furtive one. She was surprised she suffered no guilt as a result of her actions, despite the fact that at least one man's career would be ruined. There was only the astringent taste of revenge. The purpose sustained her, however, a single-minded determination to get even. That was all the emotion she was able to muster.

When the man and dog had disappeared over a hill and the athletic field was empty of people, the woman rose and found a lightly worn trail through tall grasses, holly, and rowan that led into a forest of sessile oak and beech. She counted her paces and made an abrupt left turn away from the trail and followed a zigzagging route among the dense forest. After two turns, she illuminated a tiny notebook with her iPhone to make sure the pacing was accurate. She made another turn and counted five paces and stopped, knelt, and used a small trowel to dig a hole. In the hole she buried a small film canister that contained a Ziplock bag-enclosed thumb drive. After she covered the film canister with dirt and brushed twigs and leaves over the spot, she recounted her pacing back to the trail, exited the park, and hopped a train at the Gospel Oak Overground station.

SIX

The Finnish-Russian border

"By the power vested in me, kommissar for the Preservation of the State, presider over the council of three, I hereby promote you, Demetrius Sokolov, to the chancellorship of the Council of Petroleum and Natural Gas, subcouncil to the Kommissariat for Preservation of the State. This appointment is effective at once." The man in the suit of chainmail armor raised the heavy metal gauntlet and banged on the oak table. He glared through the almond-shaped eyeholes cut into the metal helmet at the man standing before him.

The subject, Demetrius Sokolov, who stood naked on the plush crimson carpet, was sixty-something, a bit shy of obese, pink-skinned, and bristle-haired. The wiry hair covered his back and chest like a shirt. He bowed on spindly legs. "Thank you, and I humbly accept."

The kommissar hid a smirk behind his helmet. This appointment was a coup. Sokolov, one of the Russian president's right-hand men, was also chairman of Sberbank of Russia, located in Moscow. Sokolov had earned a reputation as the Russian president's personal banker but recently fell into disapproval. Sokolov sought safe harbor with the kommissariat, while the kommissariat valued the banker's connections and knowledge of the inner workings of the Russian government's finances. Sokolov also possessed the skills to get around the pesky sanctions imposed by the Americans thanks to Russia's recent invasion of Ukraine.

But can Sokolov stay alive long enough to be of use?

"Comrade Demetrius Sokolov," the kommissar bellowed. "I congratulate you on your appointment. As you've been briefed, the Council on Petroleum and Natural Gas has descended into disarray under the errant leadership of Ruslan Stepanov. The body needs a strong hand on the rudder to reestablish our dominance over the oil and gas pipelines in and out of Russia. I trust that you are the right man to lead us back to our former glory."

"I accept the challenge, but with one question. May I speak freely?"

"You may."

"From my review of the documents and meeting minutes of the prior... um... regimes, it appears as if the rabid pursuit of a single man and his family have led to the council's disarray. It has distracted the team and depleted precious resources. From what I can tell, the vendetta has been fruitless and arguably destructive to the council's operations. My strong recommendation is for the council to move on, circle the wagons, and focus on petroleum and economics to rebuild our portfolio. Without the distraction, I can put us back on a path to profitability in twelve months' time. I believe this is why you appointed me."

Anger washed over the kommissar, but he controlled

the emotion and let it dissipate. The banker was, of course, correct. The expectation that the council would be able to take care of the Asimov problem was a miscalculation. "You distinguish yourself, Comrade Sokolov. I absolve the council from its sworn duty to assassinate the Asimov family."

The banker blanched at the word *assassinate*, but his gaze remained steady. The kommissar appreciated Sokolov's fortitude.

"Sir, with respect." Sokolov raised his hand. "My efforts to repopulate the council with an effective team to help us reclaim our economic position is hampered by the... er... history of the group. To be blunt, sir, council members are dying like flies. If we're to regain our former economic position, that threat needs to—"

The kommissar put up a gauntleted fist. "Enough. I will take care of Asimov myself. I promise, he will not be a problem for you or the council. You are excused."

The kommissar shuffled through the great hall and cursed the stuffy helmet and the heavy chainmail. The two-handed broadsword dragged behind him and left a furrow in the plush crimson carpet. Years of alcohol and rich Western foods had done their damage and carrying the weight of a knight's armor for hours was almost beyond his ability. At an immense gilded door, he swiped a card and the portal permitted him access to a lesser hallway, at the end of which he stopped to put his eye to a retina scanner. The lock chunked open, and he pushed into a luxurious room with modern furnishings. Only a handful of people were allowed through this door, and when the portal locked behind him, the man wrenched off the helmet and let it fall to the silk rug with a *clank*. He shrugged off the chainmail and heaped it on the floor next to the sword and stripped off his underrobes and kicked off the ridiculous clown shoes.

This charade is getting old.

Nude, the man stepped into a small but well-equipped bathroom, turned on the shower, and let the steaming water scald his pink skin before he switched to icy water. When he was done, he toweled off and grimaced at a glimpse of himself in a tall mirror. While not exactly fat, by Western standards anyway, a paunch hung over his waist and his pectorals sagged. Alcohol had wreaked havoc on the capillaries in his face, and he vowed again to quit the stuff. As he did most days when faced with the reality of his life, he consoled himself with the power and wealth he accumulated, a feat which allowed him to live as he desired. At least when he wasn't wearing the ridiculous knight's outfit.

With the towel around his waist, the kommissar retrieved a small wooden box from under the bed. Hand-carved engravings adorned the top and it was locked with a brass padlock. He used a tiny key that hung on a chain around his neck to open the lock, and he rummaged through the contents and removed a picture. It was aged to yellow and depicted a man and a woman who stood close to each other. Mixed emotions of longing and despair surged as the kommissar gazed at the woman in the photo. The viewing was a ritual, one which the kommissar performed every time he was alone in the room. *Soon I can rest. As soon as I kill Asimov.* He replaced the image, locked the box, and shoved it under the bed.

When he was dressed in a tailored dark gray suit, crisp white shirt, and bright red tie, the kommissar entered the antechamber and was greeted by a tall young man in a midnight-blue suit. His black hair was short and parted on the side. "Everything go all right, sir?"

The kommissar thought his favorite bodyguard's heritage might be a mixture of Caucasian and Asian, but he had never asked. "Yes, Miko. It went as well as expected." He breathed a deep sigh and helped his most trusted assistant heave the chainmail armor onto its stand. The sword was stored in a scabbard that leaned against the chainmail. The helmet capped the armor so the whole thing resembled a big scarecrow. When he was done, Miko held the kommissar's greatcoat and handed him a scarf and Russian-style fur ushanka, which he put on his head. The kommissar despised the ratty hat, but when in Rome, as his ex-wife used to say. Before they exited the room, Miko gave him an off-white masquerade mask, which he put on. It was an extra precaution in case he was seen leaving the building.

Upon leaving the inner sanctum, they turned left, away from the castle's main hall, and took a narrow staircase to an elevator, which whisked them to a private helipad on the castle's roof. The rotors of a Sikorsky S-92 swung lazily. Miko followed the kommissar into the passenger compartment, where he strapped into a plush leather seat.

Miko wore a holster with a Beretta handgun, and concealed in the bulletproofed chopper were three weapons at the kommissar's disposal. His assistant was trained in several hand-to-hand combat techniques, was a crack shot, and like the POTUS's Secret Service, sworn to sacrifice his life for the kommissar's. Unlike the Secret Service, Miko was paid handsomely for the risks he took. The helicopter was routinely swept for tracking and listening devices, as were all the kommissar's vehicles.

The helicopter rose into the pale afternoon light that

would soon disappear, even though they were past the spring equinox. This far north, the days were always shorter. As they angled on a western vector, the kommissar surveyed the sweeping property below and marveled at its significance. Close to the Finnish-Russian boarder, the sprawling castle was constructed in the fifteenth century to defend the Finns' border from the Grand Duchy of Moscow. Located on several hundred acres, the hulking stone keep was fenced with thick stone walls and wrought iron barricades and patrolled by guard teams with dogs. Motion sensors, heat signature readers, and motion-activated cameras were hidden throughout the property. It was one of a half dozen such installations throughout the world owned and operated by the kommissar's organization, the legitimate operations of which were called the Halo Group.

As the bird soared over the stone wall that served as the property's southern boundary, he removed the mask, tossed it on the seat beside him, and dialed a number on his mobile.

His partner, an executive and former US Army Ranger named Alden Ashe, answered. "I trust it went well?"

"It was fine," the kommissar said. "He's scared of the Ferret." *Ferret* was code for Mikhail Asimov.

"He should be. So far, the Ferret is winning. He's caused enough damage—"

"Enough. I know what he's done. It's no longer the council's job. Assemble the team tonight. We're taking over the Ferret problem."

Ashe was silent for a beat. "That's risky. Is this the wisest decision?"

"Listen—" He almost used his partner's name on the mobile phone but caught himself in time. "It's not up for discussion. My job is the unpleasant stuff. Your job is to run the company. Go run the company and let me take care of the stuff you don't want to know about."

"What if we feed Ferret the rest of the council and then call a truce? Give him his retribution and call off the contract on his family."

"No!"

Miko's eyes narrowed as the kommissar took a breath. Outside, the ground was a carpet of green trees. Patches of melting snow flashed beneath the tree canopy. "We'll discuss it when I get back. Assemble the team."

There was a long silence on the line before his partner spoke. "It will be done."

The kommissar ended the call. Were the benefits of tolerating his so-called legitimate business partner worth it? He glanced at Miko, who gazed out the window. *One order is all it would take.* Miko turned and caught his eye, and the kommissar looked away.

The kommissar occupied himself with phone calls until they landed at a small airfield, where they stepped into a rickety hangar at the end of a row of decrepit buildings. The airfield's shabby condition was a carefully orchestrated disguise. The facility was also owned by the Halo Group, and behind the scenes, it operated as a well-honed machine.

Inside the dilapidated hangar was a Cessna Citation X+. With a top speed of almost Mach 1, the airplane was coveted by the superrich even though the model was no longer in production. The kommissar's organization owned four of them. He and Miko boarded.

Five minutes later they were airborne and westbound.

As the Cessna Citation X+ taxied, Miko excused himself for a trip to the lavatory. Once the bathroom door was locked, he removed his phone, activated an encrypted messaging application called Signal, typed a quick message, and hit send. By the time he was back at his seat for takeoff, Signal had deleted the message from his phone, leaving no trace.

SEVEN

Alexandria, Virginia

"You seem distracted."

Kate Shaw hid a flare of annoyance by taking a swallow of wine, her third glass, and refrained from checking her phone. It had already buzzed once in her pocket. Her therapist said dating was good for her, so she redoubled her efforts to pay attention to the man in front of her.

The restaurant advertised itself as farm-to-table, whatever that was, and it was packed with middle-aged up-and-comers. Back in the eighties, when Kate grew up, the pack of well-healed thirty-somethings were referred to as yuppies. What's the word now? Metro? Hipster? Gen Y? Millennial? Whatever it was, Kate was too old to be here.

Over her wineglass, which she used to block the lower half of her face, she focused on her date. The young banker was annoyingly handsome and wore his sleeves rolled and a thin silk tie tight against his neck in perhaps a careful attempt to portray success and easy confidence. Strong jaw, full lips, and a sculpted nose. Smooth, coifed, and cultured. *The anti-Max*. Her date had already flashed a platinum Amex card and picked her up in a Porsche.

Help me.

Her phone, located in a side pocket of her sport coat, vibrated again. It was the double pulse buzz she programmed to alert her when Kaamil Marafi, the star analyst who worked for her at the CIA, sent her a message. She took another sip and held the glass in both hands. "Do I? I'm sorry. Work is troubling right now."

His smile was lopsided in a way that probably appealed to half the women in the room. "And what is it that you said you did?"

"I didn't." Kate set the glass on the table and picked at her food. It was a plate of roasted vegetables, some kind of soy product meant to replace meat, and a sauce. It was the most appetizing thing on the menu. The restaurant called itself *plant-based*. "It's a government kind of thing, and the politics are thick, that's all." She forced a grin before she took a bite of a roasted pepper. "Thinking about getting out of the game and opening a flower shop." *Where did that come from?*

The banker's eyes lit up. "Flowers, huh? Lots of margin in flowers, but also a lot of breakage."

"What's breakage?"

"Flowers have a short shelf life." The banker forked a piece of veggie burger that had escaped the bun. "If you don't sell them fast, you'll toss a lot of cost of goods." He popped the bite into his mouth.

"You really know how to sweet talk a girl." Kate laughed. Her phone double buzzed a third time. *Kaamil was working it.*

Her date, someone named Beckett or Bennett or something, held out his palms. "Sorry, I analyze every business idea. Can't help it." White teeth sparkled and a fancy diver's watch—*but do you actually dive*—clanked on the table as he touched her hand. "This place is boring. What do you say we get out of here?"

Good idea. She hid her revulsion by pulling her hand away to take another gulp of wine. "What do you have in mind?"

"My place. I've got *Four Weddings and a Funeral* on Blu-ray." He waggled an eyebrow. "Hugh Grant."

She faked a broad smile. "Sounds perfect." *Who is Hugh Grant?*

The banker put a finger in the air to summon the bill.

"Let me check my phone and powder my nose." She removed the phone from her handbag and waved it at her date. "That's the third time my boss has pinged me." She rose from the table, offered him what she hoped was a conspiratorial wink, grabbed her bag, and dropped the cloth napkin over the full plate of food. Beckett or Bennett surprised her by also rising in an unexpected show of grace. It almost made her feel bad for what she was about to do.

Kate threaded her way through the tables and glanced back to see her date hunched over and signing the check. *Probably thinks he's getting laid.* Instead of turning left into the lady's room, she ducked into a service hallway, pushed through a swinging door into the kitchen, ignored the glances from the kitchen staff, and exited the rear door into the alley. A left and then a right along Alexandria's Old Town streets took her away from the restaurant.

While she walked, she consulted her messages. Now there were four texts and two voicemails, all from Kaamil. The text messages were all emojis in the shape of a telephone and the little yellow laughing hysterically faces. At a hotel, she poached a cab from the back of the line.

"Where to, miss?"

Where to? Nowhere to go. There was a half-empty bottle of white wine in her fridge, and that was it.

"Langley. And step on it."

———

"Thanks for rescuing me." Kate held her CIA-issued phone to her ear. Kaamil was on the other end. They had a prearranged signal: If Kate sent him an emoji of a banana, he was to call and text several times with a fake emergency. She had sent the banana before Beckett or Bennett had picked her up.

"Another hot date, huh?"

"It's getting old," Kate said. The cab sped north and followed the Potomac River through Reagan National airport before they curled around the Pentagon and past Arlington National Cemetery. Across the river was the tidal basin, and the Lincoln Memorial was lit with yellow spotlights. The symbols of America's democracy served as reminders of her precarious position as a tiny cog in the mighty machinery of American imperialism. She had given it her life, and it had chewed her up and spit her out before once again embracing her in its unyielding bosom. *What a mind-fuck.* Yet here she was. *Really? A flower store?*

"Happy to help." Kaamil's voice was clipped, which is how he spoke when he was excited. "I have something for you."

"Okay." A sinking feeling crept into her stomach. "Is this related to Operation Wormhole?" Wormhole referred to the ongoing interview of a source in Beirut who claimed to have information on the Assad regime's use of chemical weapons. So far it was turning out to be a dry hole.

"Nope."

"What then?"

"Bobcat made a drop."

Kate's pulse quickened. Bobcat was a source she had recently developed in London. A source with access to MI6's intel on the Vienna Archive. Visions of Max Austin, also known as Mikhail Asimov, scrolled alongside images of Asimov's father, Andrei. Anger pulsed. A surge of anxiety washed over a need for retribution. Outside the cab, yellow and white lights streamed by in a blurred streak as she tried to find her bearings.

"You there?"

Kate rubbed the bridge of her nose. "Did we pick it up yet?"

"Yes. The team in London grabbed it. Memory stick. They sent the contents over. I called you as soon as—"

"I'll be in the office in a few minutes." Kate hung up and stared through the window. All the pain and suffering she endured at the hands of the Asimov family flooded her. Would bringing the Vienna Archive back to the agency erase all that? Mixed emotions coursed through her mind. A surge of vengeance. Hesitation at the prospect of getting involved in the Asimovs' mess again. A need for retribution. Reticence at the prospect of seeing Max, a man who once triggered desire in her loins but who now just made her angry. A career instinct to do good for her agency, a place that was her entire career. Her whole life, for that matter. Bobcat was Kate's best shot at finding the Vienna Archive, the prospect of which shot a surge of adrenaline through her blood stream. Out the cab's window to her left, pale lights winked across Arlington National Cemetery.

Recovering the Vienna Archive on behalf of the CIA would be the ultimate fuck you to the entire Asimov family.

Despite the swirl of emotions, a smile crept across her face.

After badging through Langley's security checkpoint, she took the elevator to the fifth floor and entered the bullpen, an open space with a dozen dark gray cubicles. Monitors lined the perimeter walls while whiteboards on wheels were parked haphazardly throughout the space. Her office was at one edge of the bullpen, and it contained a large desk and two mid-century modern black leather couches along with a small conference table. One wall was lined with windows that overlooked Langley's interior courtyard. The other walls were glass and looked out over the bullpen.

One floor above her sat the director of the CIA, Chester Wodehouse. As Deputy Director of Counterintelligence, Kate rated the plush office and a large staff. During working hours, twelve analysts filled the bullpen with a boisterous chatter. On that Friday night at 9:00 p.m., one light was on over the largest cubicle. Kaamil's well-coifed head popped up and he followed Kate into her office.

At somewhere north of thirty years old, Kaamil was fit, tall, and darkly handsome. His coal-black hair was slicked back and held in place with gel. A silver tie with a large knot was snugged against his neck over a crisp blue shirt that stretched over his biceps. The only evidence that it was late on a Friday night were his sleeves, which were unclasped from their cuff links and rolled partway up to reveal muscular arms covered in a thatch of dark hair. Kate often thought Kaamil was the proprietor of a five-star boutique hotel in a former life. She tossed her bag on a leather couch and plopped next to it.

Kaamil remained by the door, arms crossed, and leaned a shoulder on the glass. "Man, you clean up well for a date."

"What did Bobcat's intel contain?"

"Details from a debrief MI6 did on Asimov. Apparently he was kidnapped by the Chinese and escaped. I sent the documents to you."

"Anything about where the Vienna Archive is located?" Kate rose and rummaged through a small fridge and emerged with a half full bottle of rosé. She twisted open the screw top and filled a coffee mug. Kaamil didn't drink, so she didn't offer him any.

"Unfortunately not."

Disappointment washed over her. "All right, I'll read through it." Kate returned to the couch with bottle and mug in hand.

"I'm going to head out. Let me know if you need anything." He stepped out of her office.

"And Kaamil." The analyst turned back as Kate gulped wine. "Keep this on the down low for now. Let me read through what Bobcat sent before Wodehouse gets wind."

"Copy that, boss."

Kaamil left her office and the light snapped out over his cube, and Kate was left with her laptop and wine bottle. "Let's see what you have to say, Ms. Bobcat."

EIGHT

Washington, DC

It was a gray stone building among many gray stone buildings located in a nondescript section of Dupont Circle. On one side of the building was a law firm; on the other side was a bank. The only indication that a business of any sort resided in the building was a street address plaque attached to the gray stone that read 277. As in 277 P Street NW. French doors in the front were opaque and locked twenty-four hours a day. High above the door was a ribbon of decorative millwork. The millwork's sole purpose was to conceal high-powered video cameras. Windows, equally opaque as the front doors, lined the front of the building on floors two through five. Most who strolled by on any given day either took no notice of the building or assumed it was a secretive embassy of a foreign government or perhaps a chapter of the Freemasons.

The only way into 277 P Street NW was through the rear. To gain entrance, a visitor was required to type in a nine-digit code that changed weekly, which uncovered a retina scanner. Once past the retina scanner and inside the first antechamber, the visitor was required to put all electronics and weapons in a locker and walk through a scanner. The scanning system was manned by a team behind one-way glass. Once through the security gauntlet, the visitor was buzzed through into the inner sanctum.

The kommissar preferred meeting in this building when he had other commitments at government offices in the District. He maintained a small but secure and lavish brownstone in Georgetown, and 277 P Street NW was convenient to the White House and the Capitol Building. His firm, the Halo Group, maintained three other facilities in greater Washington, DC. One was concealed in a sea of beige warehouses near Leesburg that stored all manner of tactical gear, including vehicles, motorcycles, weapons, and electronics. A ten-bedroom home on six acres was in the Berkley neighborhood, two and a half miles northwest from Georgetown. That home was used for meetings and operational planning. The firm's primary offices, which housed a hundred personnel who managed the Halo Group's legitimate military contracting business, was in a sterile office park in Reston, not too far from Dulles Airport.

If a homeless person were lounging in the alleyway behind 277 P Street NW on that chilly Sunday morning, they might see several vehicles arrive and a variety of occupants disembark. There was the tall silver-haired gentleman in a wool overcoat and cashmere scarf who got out of a chauffeured Audi sedan. There was a slight woman with skin the color of caramel wearing a leather jacket who parked her motorcycle near the dumpster. The last two men arrived in a black SUV. One wore a fedora pulled low and a scarf around his face, while the second wore a midnight-blue suit and followed the man with the fedora.

All four utilized the keypad and retina scanner before they disappeared inside the building.

The interior of the gray stone building was plush by office standards. The walls were hung with all manner of original artwork, including a dozen selections from the kommissar's personal collection. Walnut floors were covered in endless Persian-style rugs, and the modern office furniture was sleek and minimalistic. The kommissar and his partner, Alden Ashe, surrendered their mobile phones, watches, and fountain pens. Miko set his Beretta pistol in a locker. The caramel-skinned woman, who went by the name Cora, had brought nothing offensive.

They gathered in a large open room that served as a kitchen, dining room, and event space. The young woman, whose wild hair was held off her forehead with a pastel-colored hairband, operated the espresso machine as Miko positioned himself along one wall. A man of few words, Miko was never far from his boss, the kommissar, who received a cup of espresso from the young woman. Ashe draped his suit coat over a chair back and stood with his arms crossed.

"It ends here," said the kommissar after he sipped his coffee. "The Asimov problem ends now."

While he paused to finish the espresso, no one spoke. "I can admit when I'm wrong." He raised a hand. "Hindsight is twenty-twenty, and it was wrong to expect the council to take care of the Asimov problem. Nathan Abrams was incompetent. Nikita Ivanov was an imbecile. Ruslan

Stepanov... well, he was blinded by his ego. It was a distraction, and now... Well, now we're paying the price."

Alden Ashe rocked on his heels. The kommissar had worked with Ashe long enough to know this was a sign of agitation. A dashingly handsome man in his fifties with crystal-white teeth and movie-star cheekbones, Ashe was a former Army Ranger turned business executive who was now the public face of the company's legitimate operations. While he preferred limited knowledge of the firm's black operations unit to maintain plausible deniability, his presence lent gravity to the situation. When Ashe spoke, his voice was gravelly and projected in a way that expected compliance with his command. "Isn't it true that our problem is a Vienna Archive problem, not an Asimov problem?"

The kommissar accepted a second cup of espresso from Cora. "We solve the Asimov problem, we solve the Vienna Archive problem, Alden." The kommissar paced. "Asimov is a threat to this organization's very existence. A threat—"

"A threat we created." The former Army Ranger's eyes were gray steel.

"A threat"—the kommissar sneered at Ashe—"that we did not create. Andrei Asimov betrayed us, just as he betrayed his own country, when he stole from us." The kommissar banged his fist on the table. "It cannot go unpunished."

"Your old feud with Andrei is fueling your need for vengeance." Ashe's voice was calm. "And that's blinding you to the damage—"

"Enough!" The kommissar thrust out his hand. "The past is the past. What's done is done. I'm happy to continue this in private." *Had Ashe passed his useful life? Was there a future for the Halo Group without Ashe at its helm?* He asked himself this often, and the answer was always complicated.

Ashe crossed his arms.

The kommissar's voice crept up an octave. "The Asimov family must die. The archive must be recovered." He resumed pacing and his voice assumed its normal baritone. "Let us focus on the task at hand." His eyes flicked to the woman at the other end of the table, who sipped her third espresso. Cora LeRoux was the Halo Group's utility player, the undercover chameleon who blended in everywhere and was equally adept with a computer as she was with a variety of weapons. Cora was a black belt in so many martial arts that the kommissar lost track, and he knew she itched to get a shot at the so-called Russian Assassin.

The kommissar pointed his chin at Cora. "Give us your report. Is our source at the CIA still productive? And what's the latest on Shaw's movements?"

"Affirmative. Still productive." Cora grinned. "According to our source, Kate Shaw is hesitant to use her past relationship with Asimov to gain access to the Vienna Archive. The CIA are instead pursuing a more... um... indirect route."

"That works to our advantage," the kommissar said. "How are preparations going to turn up the heat on Shaw?"

"On track." Cora raised her eyebrows. "We're a go for tomorrow night's operation."

"And where are we with our leverage on her?"

"A team is enroute to Colorado as we speak."

The kommissar glanced at Ashe, who was rocking on his heals again. He turned his attention back to his star operative. "Cora, where are we on tracking Asimov's movements?"

Ashe cleared his throat. "Is our CIA source passing

along information from their source in MI6?"

The kommissar chuckled. "What a tangled web. The CIA has a source at MI6. We have a source at the CIA."

"That's an affirmative." Cora stared at Ashe. "Anything the CIA team gets through their MI6 source we see almost immediately. We know Asimov was picked up by Zhao Zheng and interrogated by the Chinese in a farmhouse outside London for three days. We know he also somehow escaped, although we don't yet know the details. Four of the Chinese team were killed after Zheng left the interrogation to his lieutenant, one Ru Shi Wu. Wu holds rank of colonel. Intel has it she carries out Zheng's dirty work. Now Colonel Wu has disappeared. Asimov probably killed her. Asimov claims to have not given up any information on the Vienna Archive to the Chinese, although I'm skeptical. How is that possible?"

"How is it possible Asimov is still alive?" Ashe spoke through gritted teeth. "He's got the nine lives of a cat."

The kommissar frowned. "We're going to put an end to his nine lives. Do we know where he is now?"

"Sequestered at the farm in Bath under a British Special Air Service guard," Cora said.

"Is a direct assault out of the question?" Ashe asked.

"It may come to that." The kommissar paced. "But right now we're going to let Cora's operation play out. Kate Shaw is our key to nailing Asimov. She is emotionally scarred from the trauma of her recent captivity, and she blames the Asimovs, both Andrei and Mikhail. She's alone in the world with no one but her CIA family. She wants retribution and we're going to enable that."

Ashe twisted his wedding ring. "If true, why would she betray the only family she has?"

Cora smirked. "She'll have no choice."

NINE

Washington, DC

"How'd it go with the stockbroker?" Chester Wodehouse leaned against his massive glass-topped desk with his arms crossed. The CIA director's oversized head sat on broad shoulders, and he wore his standard black T-shirt under a black sport coat and jeans. Gleaming black alligator-skin cowboy boots were crossed. He conducted many of his meetings in that posture.

"He's a banker, and it was boring." Kate Shaw sat on one of the low-slung black leather sofas at the far end of Wodehouse's office and nursed a strong coffee. Outside the floor-to-ceiling windows was a view of the Memorial Garden, where gold-, pearl-, and coral-colored koi swam languidly in a glistening pond. The courtyard was empty this early on a Saturday morning.

"I hope you were nice to him. He's a close friend of my sister."

"She can date him then." Kate held her coffee in two hands.

Wodehouse groaned. "I went to a lot of trouble to make that happen."

Kate shrugged. "I didn't ask to be set up. He drives a Porsche, for Pete's sake. He might as well have been wearing a white turtleneck." Kate fluffed her hair with her fingers. The previous evening, after Kaamil left and she finished the bottle of rosé, she pulled a blanket from a cupboard and dozed on the couch in her office. This morning, she shrugged on a fresh blouse from the closet in her office.

Wodehouse hung his extra-large head. "There was a day when a Porsche guaranteed a guy was going to get laid."

"This isn't the eighties, Chester. Coke and Porsches are out. If he had picked me up in a Tesla and brought some weed, maybe I'd have blown him in the back seat."

Wodehouse put out his hands in a defensive gesture. "Fine. No more setups. Sit home every night and knit a sweater." He strode over to the credenza where a box of donuts sat next to an extra-large urn of coffee. The director lived off a steady diet of both, and Kate didn't know how he avoided a heart attack.

When the director turned holding a jelly-filled, Kate greeted him with her middle finger up. "You're a sexual harassment suit waiting to happen."

Wodehouse burst into a deep laughter. "That would be the least of my problems." He shoved the donut into his mouth, ripped off a big chunk, and chewed as red jelly dripped to the floor. "Speaking of problems, how is the Vienna Archive operation going?"

Kate averted her gaze from the gluttony. An off-white koi meandered in the pond below the window. Despite Wodehouse's crass behavior, she liked the big man. A twenty-year veteran of the agency, Chester Wodehouse had hundreds of successful field operations under his belt. He was an agency insider and a Beltway outsider, which meant his staff trusted him, but Congress, who the agency relied on for funding, mistrusted him. His meetings with the president were few and far between. These days he spent more time on the Hill testifying about his predecessor's illegal activities and begging for money than he did in an operations room. It ate at him, and the dark bags under his eyes gave his fatigue away. His Senate confirmation was a narrow vote, and the current administration discounted the CIA as old-fashioned and tainted by scandal.

Kate crossed her leg and bounced it on her knee. "It's going."

Wodehouse frowned. "We had a deal, Kate. I assume Kaamil is enjoying his newfound freedom here in America. Why do I get the sense you're not taking our deal seriously?"

"I'm aware of the deal." Kate rose and walked to the window while she cradled her coffee in both hands. "And yes, Kaamil is settling back into normal life after he was illegally imprisoned for six months and subjected to inhumane treatment in his own home country because the agency tipped off the gestapo in the UAE."

Wodehouse cleared his throat. "That was Piper Montgomery, not us. We did what we could to make it right." Chester Wodehouse had reinstated Kaamil with full tenure and a hefty raise. "I held up my end of the bargain. What are we doing to find the Vienna Archive? We need a win right about now."

There was a rap on the door before it cracked open. "You wanted me?" The man who entered was once muscular and tall but had turned soft and stooped in his senior years. A fleshy face and a red-veined nose hinted at heavy alcohol consumption.

Wodehouse spoke through a mouthful of donut. "Stephen, yes. Join us. Kate here was about to brief us on the Vienna Archive thing."

Stephen MacCulloch, former director of the Counterintelligence Center Analysis Group and now Wodehouse's deputy director, stooped to pour himself a coffee from the urn. When MacCulloch was promoted, Kate took his former position after her reinstatement.

"Any progress on bringing that sucker home?" MacCulloch took a chair at the conference table and plucked at a crease in his pants as he crossed a leg.

Kate filled her own coffee mug and strolled to the window, where she leaned her back against the glass, as far away from MacCulloch as possible. "We know that since uncovering the Vienna Archive, Max, Mikhail Asimov, has been sequestered at the MI6 safe house outside London. From what we can tell, he hasn't traveled except to Colorado once to see his sister. Arina Asimov, you may recall, is lying in a coma in an Aspen hospital. Max took his nephew, Alex, there once to see her, but they didn't remain. It was a quick trip, in and out on an MI6 jet. Otherwise, he's been sequestered at the cherry farm in Bath."

Wodehouse licked his fingers and brushed crumbs from his shirt. "Is your source inside MI6 producing any intel? Bobcat?"

"Affirmative." Kate nodded once. The identity of Kate's source was a closely held secret among her, Kaamil, and two other staffers. Not even Wodehouse or MacCulloch was privy to the details of the operation.

"And what about the archive?" MacCulloch sat with his fingers steepled.

Kate directed her comments to Wodehouse, although MacCulloch was technically her direct superior. "We know the elder Asimov, Andrei, accumulated thousands, if not hundreds of thousands of documents while he served as the Belarusian assistant director of that country's KGB. We believe he secreted them away in a bunker located on the Asimov compound property outside Minsk. We know Mikhail uncovered the archive after Andrei's death last month. We think Asimov has digitized the Vienna Archive. We base this on his relationship with the hacker known as Goshawk, who he trusts. She likely has helped him lock away the archive behind a dozen firewalls."

"Can Kaamil hack through her defenses?" MacCulloch drained his coffee.

Kate refrained from snorting. "We have to know where it is to hack into it, Stephen. Even if it's digitized, they probably have it in cold storage."

"Cold storage?" Wodehouse started in on a chocolate glazed.

"A server not connected to the internet," Kate said.

MacCulloch groaned. "So this cold server might be anywhere on the planet under lock and key?"

"Cold storage. And yes, that's the issue."

MacCulloch spread his hands with his palms up. "You've told us all the problems. What's the plan here?"

Kate sipped her coffee to hide an eye roll. MacCulloch represented all that was wrong with the CIA. The old guard who failed to grasp the most rudimentary concepts of the internet and the Information Age, but who thought they could direct the agency into the twenty-first century. "Without intel on the archive's location, we can't go kicking in doors and taking names. Right now we're waiting for Bobcat to yield results."

A silence filled the office, and Wodehouse crossed his arms.

MacCulloch tapped his forefinger on the table. "I thought you said you know this Asimov fellow. You developed him as an asset. And his father too, yes?"

Kate nodded but avoided looking at MacCulloch. *Don't go there.*

MacCulloch leaned his elbows on his knees. "It should be a simple matter to get back into his good graces. He trusts you." He slapped his thighs and leaned back in his chair and looked at Wodehouse. "Am I missing something here?"

Wodehouse looked at her with raised eyebrows.

"It's not that simple." Kate sat up and set down her coffee mug. "He's not going to let me into his inner circle and tell me where the archive is. He's too smart for that. He's been burned too many times."

MacCulloch snorted and crossed his arms. "That's bullshit. Chester, are you going to—"

Kate walked to the coffee urn, which was right next to the door. Her instincts screamed at her to run.

Wodehouse put out a hand. "Kate, Stephen is right. We need to exhaust all our options here. And that includes you reinvigorating your prior relationship with Asimov. We can't just sit back and wait on the off chance Bobcat reveals actionable intel. Other agencies are out there pounding the bushes to find this thing."

Instead of refilling her coffee, Kate set the mug on the credenza and walked out of Wodehouse's office.

As the door slammed behind her, MacCulloch cried out, "The insolent little bitch."

TEN

Davos, Switzerland

For one week in January of every year, this town of 11,000 people located in the Landwasser Valley of the Swiss Alps shuts down to host the annual World Economic Forum. During that time, the mountain village is inaccessible to all but those with an invitation to the three-day event. Helicopters and limousines descend on the tiny town and converge on the Steigenberger Hotel, where world leaders and billionaires are sequestered in what one journalist called the most secure hotel in the world. Snipers are seen on rooftops. Bomb-sniffing dogs patrol alongside an undisclosed number of Swiss military. Bunkers in the mountains are fortified, and even tanks have been known to make an appearance.

On this bright April day, however, the town was practically in remission. A few skiers straggled down the thinning snowpack, and Davos residents had begun the off-season task of cleaning up from a long winter. The hotels were at half occupancy, if that, and the residents who were not preparing for a bustling summer season had departed for much-needed vacations to warm climates. The meeting between Max and the Russian president's emissary was scheduled to take place the following evening at the Steigenberger. Naturally, that's where Max booked rooms for the MI6 team, much to Baxter's annoyance, who complained about the stiff room rates.

The meeting was to be a formal and above-board affair and was designed that way by C in order to protect Max from being kidnapped, or worse, by the Russian FSB. As with any event conducted by an intelligence service, there was always the specter of a kidnapping or other devious plots, especially where the Russians were involved. Indeed, the Russian president was on record saying that treason was the most egregious crime possible in Russia and that Russians "never forget." Andrei Asimov's betrayal was legendary. Max's practical defection to Great Britain was fresher in the Russians' memory. The Russians' track record of killing or attempting to kill dissidents like Skripal, Navalny, and others reinforced the implicit threats, and so Kozov's meeting request raised serious questions of intent. C and MI6 suspected foul play and therefore planned on it.

Max thought otherwise, for his own reasons.

MI6 and the FSB negotiated and agreed to, through the Swiss Federal Intelligence Service, a single one-hour meeting between Kozov and Max in a private suite. No aides were to be present. As intermediaries, the Swiss were to provide Kozov and Max each a room key to the suite only five minutes before the allotted meeting time to prevent anyone from hiding a listening device or otherwise tampering with the space. Rooms on either side, across the hallway and beneath and above the suite were locked and unoccupied. The curtains would be closed. Members of the capable Swiss Special Forces patrolled the building, secured the floor where the meeting was to occur, and prevented anyone from getting anywhere near the meeting. Max and Kozov were to walk through metal detectors and were prohibited from bringing anything into the room, including mobile phones, watches, pens, jewelry, or laptops. Max was briefed and cautioned to always stay at least six feet from Kozov in order to prevent poisoning, which was Moscow's favored method of assassination.

Max wasn't worried about being killed by Kozov. The Vienna Archive, which contained many details of the Russian president's family, personal life, and finances, was his protection. Max suspected the Russian president was after the Vienna Archive, and the meeting with Kozov might be the initial offer, or more likely, the first threat.

Max and the MI6 team arrived in Zurich via an MI6 Lear before they separated to make the 150-kilometer journey to Davos. Because they were probably under surveillance, MI6 wanted to conceal the number of people in their arrival party. Max paired with Cindy to travel the three-hour distance by train while Baxter and two blue-suited MI6 muscle made the trip via an MI6 BMW sourced from the Zurich field office. Harris, the young utility field operative under Baxter's command, drove the BMW. A local MI6 officer from the Zurich office liaised with the London team at the hotel and handed out burner phones and weapons. Max was handed a Beretta 92X Compact 9mm. He dropped the magazine, cleared the chamber, worked the action, and reloaded before he proclaimed it suitable. The British team set up a command post in a suite located as close to the meeting location as the Swiss allowed while Max went alone to his room to brief Goshawk via a secure connection on his Blackphone. The hacker was safe in her Paris compound, where she operated from behind a secure network of firewalls and remote proxies.

"Our security protocols for the archive are about to be tested again." Max made an inch-wide gap in the curtain with a finger to allow a view of the street below but remained behind the wall. He didn't want to be a sniper target.

Goshawk's fingers clacked on a keyboard in the background. "I'm confident, sugar. Except, of course, for the physical copies you kept."

Max grunted. "We've been over this. What if the cloud blows a gasket or someone hacks the system or the servers overheat?"

"And I've told you. We're redundantly backed up and secure enough where those are not problems."

"Every system is vulnerable. There is no such thing as perfect digital security." Outside on the street below, a family trudged along a sidewalk through snow melt and mud.

"So you keep saying, and yet the banking system stays afloat." Goshawk snapped her gum.

"We have as much data security as the banking system?" The argument was always the same, and it always ended in a stalemate. They agreed to disagree. Max thought Goshawk was too enamored with her digital security, and she viewed Max as a dinosaur for deciding to keep a physical copy of the archive. "The failsafe is still in place?"

"Affirmative. Nothing has changed."

"The test with the Chinese last week was child's play compared to what's about to happen."

"I don't know why you agreed to take this meeting." Goshawk's voice was low.

"I have my reasons. Soon this will all be over."

"I hope you escape with your skin intact. When are you coming to visit me?"

"Let me get through this with my skin intact first."

He hung up as a vehicle drove through a puddle in a spray of water. After he braced a chair under the doorknob and double-checked the deadbolt and chain, he took the gun with him into the bathroom.

When he finished with a fast cold shower, he shaved his neck and trimmed the beard he had grown to hide the scar on his cheek. His full black beard contrasted with his shaved pate. The long cut on his cheek was given to him by Egor Dikov three months prior in Stockholm. Dikov got the worst of it with a stovetop-shaped burn on his own face.

Max dressed in jeans, boots, a black T-shirt, a black turtleneck sweater, and a black café racer leather jacket. Davos was 5,000 feet above sea level and April evenings were chilly. As he laid out a dark gray wool scarf and a black watch cap, scratching sounded from behind the suite door. When he turned, there was an envelope on the carpet that someone had shoved under the door.

Max thumbed the envelope open to find a single card of thick and luxurious stock. By habit, he sniffed and caught a hint of fruity cologne. A note was written in scrawling Cyrillic. *White SUV, out front, forty-five minutes. Tell no one. Come alone.*

Although Max quit smoking, he still carried his grandfather's Zippo lighter that dated back to World War II, made from tarnished silver with the Belarusian flag burnished into one side. The flag was worn from spending decades in men's pockets. Max *pinged* it open and held a flame to the note as he carried it into the bathroom and dumped the burning paper into the sink.

There was a knock at his door thirty minutes before Max was to be picked up by the white SUV and an hour before the scheduled meeting with Kozov. Max opened the door to find Baxter standing in the hallway.

Baxter stared at the ground. The MI6 officer's eyebrows, although neatly trimmed, were furrowed.

"What is it?" Max held the door as Baxter entered his suite. Max glanced along the hallway and saw no one before he shut the door.

Baxter sniffed. "Is something burning?"

Max held out the lighter. "Caught my sweater on something and had to singe some threads to keep it from unraveling. Damn annoying."

Baxter harrumphed and crossed his arms.

"Spit it out." Max gripped Baxter's elbow. "What's going on?"

"Ow, for bollocks' sake." Baxter pried his arm from Max's grip. "She disappeared."

"Who disappeared?"

"Arina. Your sister. She's gone. Overnight. She was in her hospital bed when the nurse made her last rounds. In the morning"—Baxter spread his arms—"gone."

"Taken?" Max's voice went up a few decibels. "Someone took her?"

Baxter shook his head. "We don't think so. There was a sheriff's deputy on duty outside her room. Around midnight, he took a coffee break and used the loo. He was gone for ten minutes, give or take."

"Does the hospital have security cameras?" Max paced to the window. *Great timing as always, Arina.*

"A few." Baxter nodded. "Outside, but not in the hallways. That's the other reason we don't think she was taken. At 12:02 a.m. a woman about her height exited the hospital through a side entrance and got into the front passenger seat of a dark sedan."

"Plates?"

The MI6 officer shook his head. "Not visible on the camera footage."

"What about CCTV? Can we track her vehicle—"

"Negative." Baxter shook his head again. "The US doesn't have the same kind of camera network we have here. Aspen is in the mountains, off the beaten path. The car could have gone anywhere. Utah, Denver, or north to Wyoming."

Max paced. It wasn't the first time Arina had disappeared since this whole thing started. That time, she was seeing Victor Dedov. Arina clearly lived a secret life she didn't want to share with her brother. "What's the state of her health?" Arina had been in a coma for six weeks following an attack on Spencer White's cabin outside Aspen. She was gut shot, and Max was forced to leave her behind while he chased Alex's kidnappers.

Baxter joined him near the window. "From the reports, she had recovered from the gunshot wounds to her abdomen. Physically, she is thin and weak. Her short-term memory was spotty, but it was returning. The doctors said that with continued physical therapy and counseling she will make a mostly complete recovery."

Max's initial panic receded, but concern clouded his thinking. "Mostly complete." He said it under his breath. *What are you doing, Arina?* "I should go there."

Baxter shoved his hands into his jacket pockets. "I knew you would want to do that. But you'll be searching for a needle in a haystack. We have our men looking into it in partnership with their sheriff's office. What more can you do?" Baxter checked his watch. "Besides, you have a meeting in forty minutes. I wasn't sure I should tell you before your meeting with Kozov, but figured you'd want to know as soon as I knew."

Max bumped his fist against the wall three times. Baxter was right. If he flew to Colorado, there wouldn't be much to be done. By then Arina might be anywhere. "If the daughter of a master spy doesn't want to be found..." Max turned to Baxter. "Thank you for telling me."

Alex was right. Decisions are a bitch.

After Baxter left, Max took out his secure Blackphone, a heavy and nearly indestructible mobile phone modified by Goshawk with custom encryption, and dialed a number by heart.

The voice that answered was gruff but familiar. "Let me guess. You're coming out here to help me with the Sheetrock?"

Max chuckled. "Since when do you use Sheetrock in a log cabin? How's it coming along, Spencer?"

"About like you might expect. Slow, but satisfying."

"Good to hear. I need a favor."

Spencer White, former CIA black ops officer, cleared his throat. "What do you need?"

At the appointed time of 4:00 p.m., neither Max nor Kozov showed up for the arranged meeting at the Steigenberger hotel. The Swiss team made frantic calls to both the British and Russian congregations. Baxter threw his Blackberry against the wall while Cindy smothered a smirk behind her hand.

Kaamil's head appeared in her doorway. "Guess what?" There was a wide grin on his face.

Kate set the confidential report she was reading onto her desk and crossed her arms. "You found the archive?"

The analyst's face fell. "Nothing that good. But we heard from Bobcat again. A request to meet."

"In person?" Kate's eyebrows went up.

"Yes. Bobcat will be at location number one tomorrow afternoon and location number two the next day, according to protocol. I sent you the decoded transcript."

Location number one was the Smithsonian Museum of Natural History. Location number two was the Smithsonian Air and Space Museum. Bobcat would rotate between those two meeting locations twice over two days, at noon and then again at 3:00 p.m. If Kate couldn't make any of those prescheduled appointments, they would try again the following week. All of this was arranged in advance. Normal protocol was a dead drop, where Bobcat would leave a thumb drive with whatever intel was gathered at one of three locations across the London metropolitan area, including the Hampstead Heath location. The in-person meetings in DC were reserved for something of significance, intel that Bobcat didn't feel safe leaving in a dead drop.

Kate forgot all about the document she was reading. "Let's put a team on location number one at noon and make sure she isn't followed. If things are good, we can do the second meeting."

"Roger that. I'll get it set up." He stepped out of her office.

ELEVEN

Davos, Switzerland

Out of sight from the MI6 team, who were gathered in the hotel suite, a snow-white Range Rover with darkened windows pulled under the Steigenberger portico. The vehicle ignored the team of valets and drove to where Max waited with his hands shoved into his jacket pockets. Three beefy Caucasian men dressed in black were in the vehicle. The rear door popped open, Max stepped inside, and they were underway. The interior of the vehicle smelled of cigar smoke. No one spoke.

The white Range Rover wound its way along a mountain road as dusk lengthened the shadows. At one point, the hulking man in the rear seat next to Max held out his hand and Max put his palms in the air. "Left my phone at the hotel." The gorilla patted him down anyway. The woods on either side of the road were silent, but Max figured there were invisible patrols lurking in the darkness.

The vehicle stopped at a checkpoint where the undercarriage was sniffed by a bomb dog and four armed paramilitary types examined identifications. Another man circled the SUV with a handheld device that Max assumed scanned for tracking devices and radio transmissions. After they were released, the vehicle continued up the winding road and endured another checkpoint at a gate. The gate area resembled those at embassies in war zones with concrete barriers and armed guards. The sun was behind a mountain by the time they passed a four-car garage and curved around a circular drive with a massive fountain at its center.

The level of security was enough to indicate a VIP was in residence. Rumor was the Russian president sequestered himself in a residential compound in the Moscow suburb of Novo-Ogaryovo and only communicated with his administration via Zoom. He maintained offices in three locations: the Kremlin where he rarely visited, the one in Novo-Ogaryovo, and one in the Black Sea city of Sochi. His offices in the last two locations were built to appear identical to keep people guessing as to which location he was in. With war raging in Ukraine, it was unlikely the Russian president was here in Davos, Switzerland. But you never know.

Two commandos flanked the entryway's double doors. The home was one level, but it sprawled in all directions. Atop a small mountain, the compound was larger than a beach resort. To the left was a circular pad where an armored Mil Mi-17 helicopter sat quiet and dark. The men from the Range Rover led him through the front doors and into a cavernous atrium filled with brightly colored tapestries. A sculpture of two nude, intertwined maidens was on a pedestal in the center of the entryway.

They walked through the lobby and along a gilded hallway adorned with a bewildering variety of art. There were several dark and stormy oils from the Romantic period interspersed with a few Cubists and the colored squares of Rothko. A spattered Pollock was opposite a hazy Monet. Max stopped in front of a painting filled with various shades of tan along with rectangles and other squared off shapes. The word *Café* was painted in the upper right corner, and if you didn't look too closely, the visage of a long-nosed face was evident in the picture's center. "Wait. Is that—"

One of the guards prodded him ahead. "Never mind that. Keep moving."

"Hold on." Max shook off the man and studied the painting. "This is a Picasso."

Two bodyguards grabbed his arms and propelled Max down the hall. He craned his neck to get another view of the painting. "Wasn't that stolen? Damn, the picture's name escapes me. It's on the tip of my tongue."

The four men passed through an expansive living room with a sunken fireplace in the center surrounded by leather furniture. A kitchen was to the left, and enormous two-story windows lined the far wall, where a sunset glowed over a far mountain range. The twinkling lights of Davos spread over the valley below. He was directed through a double door to a room off the main living area. The three bodyguards remained near the fireplace while the double doors were shut behind Max, leaving him alone in the study with one man.

The den was oblong with a vaulted ceiling held in place by stout wooden beams. The furniture was Scandinavian, with a lot of black leather, chrome, and teak. Fur throws were tossed strategically on the furniture, and the walls were covered with eclectic works of art like in the entryway. A bearskin covered the floor, and stuffed animal heads were mounted in the spots that were free of art.

Along one wall stood a youthful man of average height in a blue suit. A large mole was on his left cheek. His small mouth was centered between two pudgy cheeks, which was incongruous with the man's diminutive build. Pale skin, dark circles under his eyes, and a black shock of hair gave the man a cuckolded air. It was Dmitry Kozov.

The room was otherwise empty. "Where's your boss?" Max strode to a wall covered with stuffed animal heads. "Thought he'd be here."

Kozov said nothing.

Max half turned to the door and pointed. "That painting. On the wall back there. The title is something about pigeons. Didn't the thief say he dumped the painting in the trash?"

Dmitry Kozov crossed his arms. "You are, of course, correct, Mikhail Asimov. On one of those statements, anyway."

"Which one?" Max raised his eyebrows.

"The painting in the hallway." Kozov's voice had a slight nasal tone. "It is indeed a Picasso. It's called *Le Pigeon Aux Petits Pois*." His French was atrocious.

Max snapped his fingers. "The Pigeon with Green Peas. It disappeared from Musée d'Art Moderne de la Ville de Paris." Max, who lived in Paris for a decade, enunciated the beautiful French language with ease. "The thief was arrested, but he said he threw the painting into a trash can."

Kozov raised his palms to the sky. "And yet somehow it found its way here to this humble chalet."

Max laughed and nodded. "You'll excuse me if I don't shake your hand. I've been advised to keep my distance. You Russians like your poisons."

"And yet you agreed to ride in a vehicle with three men, each of whom could kill you with their bare hands. You must trust me a little, Mikhail Asimov."

Since he wasn't invited to sit, Max fell back on a creamy leather sofa that faced Kozov, who remained standing. "Don't worry, I've left a trail of breadcrumbs."

Kozov snorted. "Birds eat breadcrumbs."

Max shrugged. "I've got something you want. Your boss wants, actually. If you kill me, you won't get it."

"You should not feel safe, Mikhail." Kozov jabbed a finger in the air at Max. "Your family has committed the most grievous sin against Russia. An unforgivable, egregious error that has sealed the Asimov fate. Maybe not today, but you will die."

"We all die someday." Max leaned so his elbows rested on his knees. "How's your little invasion going?" Since Russian tanks invaded Ukraine in February, depending on whose propaganda you believed, the Ukrainians had shown remarkable resistance and had pushed the Russians back.

Kozov strode to the center of the room, where he leaned on the arm of a throne-sized chair. "It's simply a matter of time. We control their ports. Their economy is ruined. We can hold out longer than they can."

"The West will provide an endless supply of heavy weapons." Max grinned. "They'll mount a counter offensive with those Western guns and retake their ports. They'll never give up. And meanwhile, you continue to lose the battle of public sentiment."

Kozov smiled. "Have you heard the story about the two Russian soldiers taking a smoke break as they sit on top of their tank in Poland?"

Max pursed his lips. He had, but he wasn't going to admit it.

"One soldier says to the other, 'Twitter says we lost the war.'" Kozov chuckled. "Get it?"

Max shook his head. "You may not care about public sentiment, but your country is being bled dry—"

"By Western thugs!" Kozov's face turned red. "They'll use any excuse they can to beat us down." He thrust his finger at Max. "And you! You and your father have done nothing but help them. You're both traitors." Kozov turned and strode to the wall, and when he faced Max, he had regained his composure.

Max rose to his feet. Better to also be standing if Kozov was going to lose his temper. "It's more than just the West who are stealing from you. Dozens of your own countrymen are siphoning money and resources away from Mother Russia. You need my help, or should I say your boss needs my help. Isn't that why we're here right now?" *Poke the bear first, then ease up.*

"You're right, Mikhail Asimov." Kozov's face softened. "The kommissariat has operated in Russia for decades with a maddening impunity. It's a shadow government that meddles in the affairs of a sovereign nation and bites at our ankles like a stray dog. It hides behind a veil of cowardice and operates in the murky corners of the darkest criminal enterprises. The men who make up the various councils are the scum of the earth." Kozov paced and banged his knuckles on a table. "Like the West, they milk Russia of its vast resources and rob our citizens of their welfare and prosperity."

The pot calling the kettle black. Max grinned. "The kommissariat put your boss in power. He profited from that personally. And now you guys want the kommissariat gone."

Kozov's blue eyes flashed, and he fixed Max with a stony gaze.

Too far?

"There is only one way out of your predicament, Mikhail Asimov," Kozov said.

"What makes you think I have a predicament? I like where I sit."

Kozov chuckled and shook his head. "You are but one man, and we know many things. For example, we know where your friend, the... er... woman with the bird name..."

Alarm prickled Max's skin.

"What is her name? Goshawk?" Kozov spit the word out like it was rancid meat. "Let's say we have a long conversation with her. I bet we convince her to tell us a few things. I imagine we'd get to the bottom of this business."

Perspiration broke out on Max's forehead. "I assure you, she can't help you. Our security requires both of us to be alive. If either one of us is harmed, the files are automatically released to the Western media."

Kozov raised a single eyebrow. "How about that cute little nephew of yours? He can't hide behind MI6 on that cherry orchard his whole life."

Did Zhao Zheng share the Chinese intel with Moscow? A pit formed in Max's stomach, but his expression remained placid. "A dozen intelligence agencies are looking for the archive. Any one of them have endless interrogation and torture techniques at their disposal. I was just acquainted with a few of those on behalf of Mr. Zheng, and I'm still here. The archive is well hidden, with multi-factor access controls and a dozen fail-safes." Max put his palms in the air. "Go ahead and test it. But it will not go well for you."

When Kozov said nothing, Max crossed his arms. "You

called this meeting. You must have a proposal. Why don't you spit it out instead of making baseless threats? I'm a reasonable man. I'm sure we can work something out."

Kozov's blue eyes twinkled. "It's simple. Hand over the Vienna Archive. That's it."

"The whole archive?" Max nodded as if the idea were the most profound notion in the world. "And in return? What do I get?"

"A lifetime pardon for you, Alex, and your sister," Kozov said. "The Asimov family's problems are behind you. Arina can raise Alex without fear of harm. Isn't that what you want?"

Ten beats ticked by. *It is indeed what I want.* An entire year on the run, fighting for Alex and Arina. The last twelve months had taken a toll. The fight to stay alive and find their pursuers prevented him from building the relationship he wanted with Alex and mending fences with Arina. In fact, it had done the opposite. Just like a father who works too many hours, Max's fight had driven them further apart.

"There is one more thing." Kozov held up a finger. "You must retire from your work with the British. Live wherever you want, go back home if you'd like. But we can't have one of Russia's best-trained operatives on the payroll of our enemy."

Max pursed his lips. "Just like that. Hand it over and all my troubles go away."

Kozov held out his hands. "Simple as that."

"How much do you know about the kommissariat?" Max's finger tapped on the back of a chair until he forced it to stop.

Kozov's smile vanished.

Max nodded. "See, what I think is that you need the Vienna Archive to learn enough about the kommissariat to put them out of business. You view the archive as your way out from under the kommissariat's thumb, and you think my information will give you enough intel to do that."

Thin lips pressed together as Kozov's face turned pink. "We need nothing from you." He banged a fist on a table. "This is a one-time offer, and it expires in one minute. Decide."

While the Vienna Archive was chock-full of information implicating various council members and providing reams of data on illegal transactions, it was silent on the identity of the man who runs the kommissariat, and Max still hadn't figured it out. The Russian president didn't know this, of course. Max's play involved half bluff, half good cards. It was like holding two pair in Texas hold 'em. He didn't have a busted hand, but he wasn't going all in either. A card might turn up to make a full house. Max spread his hands. "Here is a counter proposal."

Kozov's eyebrows stitched together and deep creases appeared on his forehead. "I'm not here to—"

"I'll give you enough information to eliminate the four councils." Max counted on his fingers. "I have names, rosters, financial records, meeting minutes—enough for you to wipe them out. In exchange, I want the pardons. Meanwhile—"

"Nyet!" Kozov cut his hand through the air like a knife.

Max took a step forward.

Kozov put his hand out. "Stay put."

The Russian disappeared through a door.

TWELVE

Washington, DC

Kaamil and a small team sat in a van parked on Independence Ave SW, one block from the Smithsonian Air and Space Museum while Kate Shaw approached the museum on foot from the National Mall side. The Capitol Building was to her left, and to her right the Washington Monument glinted off the Reflecting Pool. A warm breeze ruffled the wisps of her curly hair that escaped a black ball cap. A tiny receiver was stuck in her ear, hidden by the curls.

Kaamil's voice appeared in her ear. "No sign of Bobcat yet."

A surveillance team on foot roamed both outside and inside the museum and reported back to the van at regular intervals. According to the chunky Breitling watch on Kate's wrist, there were ten minutes before the appointed meeting time. Bobcat was nowhere to be seen.

Kate entered the museum, glanced up at the Spirit of

St. Louis flown by Charles Lindbergh from New York to Paris in 1927 as the first solo nonstop transatlantic flight, and kept moving. She dodged a class of schoolchildren and skirted a Japanese tour group and headed for the Space Hangar, where the space shuttle Discovery dominated. There she meandered as if browsing the various plaques and displays. The appointed time came and went, with each roving footman reporting in without sighting Bobcat.

Kate gave it an additional fifteen minutes, which is how long it took her to read each of the displays. She texted a note to Kaamil. *Abort*.

As she turned to exit the hangar, a tall woman with bright red hair walked over and touched Kate's arm. "*Pardonnez-moi*. Do you know where I may get a coffee?" She spoke the code phrase in French, but with an American accent.

"I believe there's a restaurant by the main entrance." Kate's coded reply was in English. Without staring, Kate attempted to penetrate the disguise. The bright red hair flowed from under a felt spring hat. A gauzy scarf in pastels was wound around the woman's neck and movie star-sized sunglasses covered her eyes. Kate pointed at the Smithsonian's front door. "I can show you."

"*Merci beaucoup*." The woman fell in beside Kate as they walked from the Space Hangar and into the cafe. When they both had coffees and faced each other over a table in the corner of the busy restaurant, the woman slipped a memory stick under a napkin and slid it to Kate, who palmed it and stuck it into a pocket.

"It's all there in my report." The woman dropped the French and spoke in English. The American-accented French was developed over many years working in the field while stationed in Paris.

"Anything that might indicate where the archive is located?" Kate sipped her coffee.

The woman's eyes shifted. "Perhaps."

"There must be a reason you called the in-person."

The woman, code-named Bobcat, glanced around. There was a suitable din in the cafe, and no one was close enough to hear their conversation. Two girlfriends enjoying a coffee together. "Asimov has started to provide MI6 with intel. Something about a Russian national living in London who is involved in illegal weapons sales."

"Okay." Kate sipped and waited. There must be more.

Bobcat lowered her voice. "Asimov mentioned that he kept a physical copy of the archive. Apparently, there is some disagreement between him and the woman who helped him secure the digital version."

"A physical copy, huh?" Kate pictured stacks of file boxes in a basement. It was an intriguing detail, but this information did little to help.

Bobcat nodded. "Seems odd in this day and age. And one more thing."

Kate had agonized about using this woman for the assignment, given what Bobcat endured in the past. But the woman, a former CIA field officer, had volunteered. She begged to be involved. Ordinarily, Kate would never use someone like Bobcat with this big of an axe to grind, except Kate identified with the woman's sentiment. Sometimes vengeance was a powerful motivator. "Go ahead."

"MI6 uncovered communications between Mikhail Asimov and someone else that referenced a location called Riverside."

"Riverside?"

"Yes, it was a reference to a cabin. I'm told the cabin was used by the elder Asimov to meet with Julia Meier years ago. The cabin has been in the Asimov family for generations. MI6 believes the context of the communication was in relation to the Vienna Archive, and they believe perhaps this Riverside is a hiding place. Does it mean anything to you? Any idea where this Riverside place is?"

Kate tossed back her coffee and shook her head. "No."

Bobcat's eyes clouded and she hung her head. "Okay."

Kate touched the woman's hand. "But I know who might."

McLean, Virginia

"Thanks for meeting me out here." Wodehouse's pockmarked face was drawn. He wore the same black sport coat over black T-shirt and blue jeans that was his trademark. The only time he wore a real suit is when he visited the Hill or the White House, which was often of late.

"Nice to get some air." To Kate's right was the koi pond. The green water was murkier than the other day when she watched the fish from Wodehouse's office. Thunder cracked far off, and a gust of wind ruffled her suit coat. She pulled it around her and waited for Chester Wodehouse to speak.

"We had a deal, Kate." The director's voice had a hard edge.

"I'm working on my end of it." She shrugged.

"Are you?" The director shoved his mitt-sized hands in his pockets. His brow furrowed and a frown appeared. "Frankly, I think you're sandbagging."

A shot of heat prickled her neck. "The fuck I am. How about that deal in Beirut? That was a coup. I watched the president's speech last night on Syria. That was a direct result of Operation Wormhole. It was classic spy shit and just the kind of thing you need to be taking to the White House."

"I get fifteen minutes with the president a week. Every time I do, he wants to know where we are on the archive. My tenure, short as it may be—heck, our tenure—will be defined on whether we find that archive and nothing less."

"You better get a team on it then." The sky had turned dark, and wind whipped at the trees in the courtyard.

"You're the team, damn it." Wodehouse spread his arms but lowered his voice. "If anyone can find it, it's you. You know the Asimovs better than anyone. You ran Andrei as a source for years. You operated with his son, and he trusts you. You probably slept with—"

"Fuck you, Chester." Kate crossed her arms.

Wodehouse let out a breath. "Sorry. But there's no one else, Kate. You're our best shot."

"Well, then we're screwed. I suggest you work your magic over at the NSA and get them to up their game."

Wodehouse spun so his back was to Kate, and he ran his hand over his face. A drop of rain pattered onto his shoulder. When he turned, his eyes were narrowed. "I hate to do this, but if you don't get focused on the Vienna Archive, I'll have no choice."

Kate crossed her arms. "No choice?"

"You're out. Off the team. And it won't be a simple firing. There will be an investigation. You'll get raked over the coals. Who knows what they'll dredge up?"

"You wouldn't!"

"Who do you think is protecting you from all of that?" Wodehouse spread his arms again as another fat raindrop hit his jacket. "With everything you've been through, there are plenty of people who want your head on a platter. People who will question your loyalties and your operational readiness."

"MacCulloch?"

"Among others."

Kate turned her shoulder to Wodehouse. The fish meandered through the murky water. "That geezer shouldn't even be in the agency."

Wodehouse touched her arm. "Look, I'm the only one standing between you and the entire CIA's investigative apparatus. And if you don't increase the intensity on this archive thing, I'm going to be included in that witch hunt. What do you think will happen to you?"

Kate slumped. To her right, a neon-orange koi slid through the murky pond water. "It's such a long shot."

"I read Kaamil's latest report on Bobcat. What are you doing about this Riverside lead?"

Kate tapped her toe on the slate tile of the koi pond courtyard. *Is Kaamil funneling his reports to Wodehouse now?*

"Don't blame Kaamil," Wodehouse said. "I told him to send me the writeup." A drop hit Wodehouse's forehead. "What about getting back into Asimov's good graces? We structure an operation where you're kicked out of the agency. At least that's what we'll leak to the public. You pair up with him again, gain his trust. When you uncover the archive, you can steal it. It'll be the ultimate betrayal. You'll finally even the score." Wodehouse chuckled.

Kate's eyebrows rose. "I suppose you want me to sleep with him, too?"

Wodehouse shrugged. "Whatever it takes."

"Well, fuck you, Chester." Kate whirled and walked away.

"Kate."

She stopped and turned.

"Look, I'm sorry." The director's face was drawn. "You're my only hope."

Her shoulders collapsed. The rain fell hard now and Wodehouse's face glistened. She eyed the ground. The image of her former boss at the agency flashed in her mind. William Blackwood, former director of Special Operations, was a man of integrity. A man whose personal life was exploited by his enemies within the agency. Blackwood had supported Kate's ascension before he was betrayed by Piper Montgomery, the agency's former director. Now Bill was dead. The idea that Wodehouse might be run out of the agency for her failure to uncover the Vienna Archive weighed on her. She sighed. "I think I know who can tell me where Riverside is. Our intel suggests it's the location of the physical copy of the Vienna Archive. If that lead doesn't pan out, we'll go with your idea."

The clouds opened and big drops pattered on the pavers. Wodehouse smiled. "I'm counting on you, Kate."

THIRTEEN

London, England

Max consented to meet in the austere and keep-like building that housed MI6 at Vauxhall Cross because C requested it. The spy chief had back-to-back budget meetings and wasn't able to escape the office. On a sunny day, the green and beige MI6 building resembled a cross between a Transformer robot toy and a dystopian castle. Today, under overcast skies that spit rain, the oppressive building was a monster that threatened to come to life.

Max brushed water from his flat-billed cap as Baxter ushered him through the main entrance, where he was subjected to a security check that involved an x-ray image, a hand wand, and scrutiny of his identification. The security guard hesitated as he peered first at the identification picture of a clean-shaven Max and then at Max's face with a full beard.

As he and Baxter exited the security area and ascended

a long escalator, Max tugged Baxter's coat arm. "Do they know this ID I'm using is fake and made by you?"

Baxter stared ahead and didn't answer. Dozens of suited administrators hustled to and fro with briefcase and jacket in hand. The marble interior was full of green plants, all of which appeared fake until a trio of uniformed gardeners trooped by with tools and watering cans. The entire place was like the interior lobby of a mid-rate law firm.

"You get the irony, don't you?" Max plucked at Baxter's sleeve again. "You snuck me through your own security using fake identification from your office."

There was no response from Baxter as they stepped off the escalator and walked to a bank of elevators.

"You can't give me the cold shoulder forever, you know." Max talked to Baxter's back.

When they entered the empty elevator car and the door closed, Baxter turned on him. "You know how much time we wasted on that little deal in Davos? How bad it makes us look? How much money we and the Swiss spent? We have other cases we're working on, you know. We're not here to be your bloody lackey. When will you get it through your head that the world doesn't revolve around you? You may have even pushed C too far this time."

Max stifled a grin. "You realize that—"

Baxter held up a hand. "Save it for C. You have some explaining to do. Maybe he'll care. I don't."

The two men rode the rest of the way to the top floor in silence. Max stood behind Baxter so the MI6 man couldn't see Max's smirk.

When the doors hissed open, they stepped into a plush antechamber where three administrative assistants sat at desks. The desks were clean and tidy. It was Max's first time in C's inner sanctum, and one feature made him point at the door at the end of the room. "Seriously?"

Baxter ignored him and approached one of the desks where a tailored young man sat wearing a headset. The other two desks were each occupied by a beautiful but austere woman. They resembled librarians. One of the librarians rose and accepted their coats and stowed them in a closet.

Baxter and Max were directed to a waiting area furnished with three plush sofas in a U shape. Baxter went to a credenza and helped himself to tea while Max walked around the room and stopped outside the door at the far end of the room. His mouth dropped open. The door was covered in a green felt-like material, called baize, and above the doorframe was a red and a green light. At the moment, the red light glowed bright.

Max turned to Baxter and pointed at the door. "Are you guys for real?"

Baxter eased into a couch and set his tea on a glass side table. "Don't ever say MI6 doesn't have a sense of humor."

The green felt door and the lights over the transom were straight out of the early James Bond novels. Books which Max had read as part of his Western indoctrination training. Max ran a finger along the smooth baize surface. It was the same material used on billiard tables.

The red light above the door winked out, and the green light blazed on. A moment later, the assistant with the headset indicated they should enter.

The inside of the office of the chief of MI6, Britain's Secret Intelligence Service, was nothing like how M's office was depicted in the novels. Instead of stuffy mahogany-paneled walls, broad floor-to-ceiling windows offered a view of the River Thames. The view was distorted by what Max assumed was bullet-proof glass. An enormous glass table that served as a desk sat in the middle of the room. More leather sofas sat in one corner, and a wall was covered with photos of C during various field operations and with dozens of heads of state.

C stood behind his desk, arms crossed, in his shirt sleeves, tie loose at the neck. "That was the director of the Swiss Federal Intelligence Service. He was too polite to chew me a new asshole, but it's what he was thinking. Intelligence relations between our two countries just took a big step backwards." C's eyes were hooded as he glared at Max. There was no offer to sit or any other pleasantries. "Care to explain why you wasted hundreds of thousands of our taxpayers' pounds and the time of dozens of men and women across three agencies?"

Max spread his hands. "Kozov had no intention of meeting me at the Steigenberger. He wasn't even at the hotel, something that your so-called Swiss friends failed to confirm. I didn't know that in advance. It was only when they reached out to me at the last minute that I realized he wasn't at the hotel. By then"—Max let his hands fall—"it was too late."

"You might have at least notified Callum."

Baxter cleared his throat from his position near the window.

"It was a delicate situation," Max said. "The note had explicit instructions. I didn't want to take the chance that anyone might jeopardize the meeting." Max shrugged. "If I notified you, no telling what you'd have done. A single misstep might have buggered the whole thing."

C crossed his arms. "You had no advance knowledge that Kozov wasn't at the hotel?"

Max shook his head. "How could I? Until I got the note,

I was ready to meet Kozov at the hotel, like we planned."

C collapsed into a massive leather desk chair and pointed to two chairs in front of his desk. Max sat. After a moment, Baxter also sat.

Max crossed a leg. "Seems like an intelligence failure on the part of the Swiss. They didn't even know Kozov wasn't in the building."

C fussed with an ornate pen on his desk and let out a breath. "As I told you, you're entitled to do what you want with the Vienna Archive, despite the time and money invested by the British government in keeping you and Alex safe. England has stuck her neck out on your family's behalf, which is a dangerous position to be in."

"You're continuing to weigh the risk/reward equation," Max said. "Does it continue to benefit England and MI6 to help me? Or is the cost too high?"

C nodded.

"Too high." Baxter stared straight ahead.

Max shrugged. "You guys have to make your own decision. If you're out, I understand. Say the word and I'll make other arrangements for Alex."

The chief put up a palm. "Let's not be hasty. It probably goes without saying that we're open to any intelligence you might want to pass along."

Quid pro quo. You give us something, we're happy to keep you in the family.

"You guys find anything on Zaitsev?"

C's eyes narrowed at Baxter. "Do we have an update on Zaitsev from MI5?"

Baxter let out a deep sigh. "Not yet. I'll make a call."

Max pursed his lips. "I'm confident the intel I handed over on Zaitsev will yield results. There's more where that came from."

C nodded and steepled his fingers. "Indeed. Do you want to tell us about your meeting with Kozov?"

"He told me that I needed to stop working for you."

C snorted. "That's not what I expected you to say."

"I didn't tell him anything." Max relayed much of his conversation with Dmitry Kozov, including Kozov's offer. A pardon in exchange for the entire Vienna Archive.

"You should have taken the deal," Baxter growled.

"I can't." Max shook his head. "The archive is my entire leverage. And I'm going to share with you something that I didn't share with him. It stays in this room. Do I have your word?"

"Of course." C nodded once.

A few beats went by.

Max raised his eyebrows at Baxter. "Callum?"

"Yes, yes." The older intelligence officer waved his hand. "You don't need to ask."

"While I have the names and dossiers on each of the forty-eight members of the four councils, I do not have the identity of the man who runs the kommissariat. The archive is silent on his name. The man who runs the whole thing is a mystery. He's a ghost, and until I uncover who it is, I can't put this whole thing behind us."

"So..." C rubbed his cheek with a bony hand.

"So Kozov can't guarantee Max's safety." Baxter smiled. "And it was the kommissariat who put the Russian president into power in the first place, and he must believe they can take him out of power. Both of you are still under their thumb."

"Exactly." Max frowned. "But the Russian president doesn't know that. He thinks I hold all the keys to his safety and security."

"High stakes game you're playing here," Baxter muttered. "Why did he let you go?"

"Same reason the Chinese let me go. I have intel that will go public if I'm incapacitated or killed. Or he believes I do." Max shrugged and grinned. "Besides, it was only his opening salvo. He's testing me. They want to gauge where I'm weakest."

C's hand moved from his cheek to his forehead, which he rubbed. "What is Kozov's next move? He and his boss won't sit idle."

Max raised his eyebrows. "He threatened Goshawk and Alex, so it's possible he may go after either one of them. But I doubt it. He stands to lose more than he gains if he goes one of those routes. My guess is they'll attack our cyber defenses and try to take the archive that way." Max frowned. "He won't be successful."

"Goshawk should relocate to be safe," Baxter said. "What about the cherry orchard? It's as safe a place as any."

Max shrugged. "I'll talk to her about it." The cherry orchard is the last place he wanted Goshawk to be. Best to keep her and Alex separated.

C steepled his fingers. "Okay, so what's next?"

Max rose and paced as he talked. "If the Russian president were to put the four councils out of business, that leaves only the kommissariat. The councils are how the kommissariat acts. They develop policy, make business deals, siphon money, and engage in acts of terrorism and intimidation on behalf of the kommissariat. The kommissariat would be powerless and vulnerable."

"How is the Russian president supposed to put the councils out of business?"

"What he always does. The Russians who sit on those councils, traitors in the Russian president's eyes, will be jailed on trumped-up charges or exiled. They'll be stripped of their titles and their assets will be sold to either the Russian president or his cronies at bargain prices. Any of the Russians in the government who are betraying the president will probably be sent to the gulag. The non-Russian council members will be banned from the country or also arrested. Maybe a couple of them would be killed. It's the secrecy that protects the council members. Without that, it's open season for the Russian president."

C chuckled. "So you're going to supply Kozov with the identities of all the council members."

Baxter snapped his fingers. "But the Russian president wants the kommissariat. They're the ones that enabled his presidency. He believes they can take it away from him. How do you intend to convince him to go after the four councils without also going after the kommissariat?"

Max smiled. "That's where you guys come in. We're going to run an operation to enlist the help of our old friend Erich Stasko. Stasko will help us get at the Russian president where he's most vulnerable. Once I show him how powerful the information is in the archive, he'll take my offer seriously." Max grinned. "Are you guys in or are you kicking me to the curb?"

"The curb," Baxter grumbled.

C narrowed his eyes. "Before we commit, I'd like to know what you have in mind."

"We're going to hit the Russian president where it hurts the most. We're going to convince him that we mean business." Max walked C and Baxter through his plan to recruit Erich Stasko and force the Latvian banker to roll over on the Russian president.

When Max was done, even Baxter grudgingly agreed to the plan. The three men shook hands.

FOURTEEN

London, England

"Callum, listen—"

Baxter whirled and put up a palm. "Don't say a word. C may be falling for your crap, but I'm past it. You can pound sand, for all I care." He turned and stalked down the busy hallway.

The two men received several looks from MI6 staffers as Max chased after him. "Are you saying you don't want to be in on the Stasko operation? This is the intelligence opportunity of a lifetime."

The senior MI6 officer swiped his badge and banged open a door. Max slipped through before the door snapped shut. Gone was the splendor of the upper floors and the agency's executive suites. This was a large beige and gray cavern with a drop ceiling and endless cubicles. A long row of file cabinets lined one wall while windows lined another. Each cubicle was occupied by an earnest young woman or man in a smart outfit typing on a keyboard or talking into a headset. There were no personal effects or artwork in sight. Max slowed his pace and took in the spectacle. *Is this where office workers go to die?*

Max glanced around for coffee. Before he spotted a coffee urn or break room, Cindy's blonde head popped over a shoulder-height cube wall. "There you are. Ready?" She darted from the cube and waved them into a conference room.

Max entered to see a man's face on a large LCD. The face he recognized, and he wasn't surprised to see it. The conference room was another matter. *How can these people work in this environment?* The room's walls were painted battleship gray, the table was dark gray, and the wheeled chairs were light gray plastic with holes in the backs. There weren't even any plants, fake or otherwise. "What did you guys do with all the color around here?"

Cindy rolled up her white blouse sleeves and tapped on a tablet. "Presenting our old friend Erich Stasko, the Latvian banker." The image on the large screen showed a trim and well-tailored man in his mid-forties with thinning white hair and rimless glasses. It was a close-up surveillance image of the subject walking across a crowded plaza.

Baxter collapsed into one of the chairs and glared at Max. "Cindy already knows your plan?"

Max hoisted himself to sit on a credenza with his back against the wall. "I didn't want to lose any time, so I asked her to get started." When neither Baxter nor Cindy spoke, Max pointed at the screen. "As you know, Erich Stasko is also Number Twelve on the consortium... er... the Council for Petroleum and Natural Gas. He's their banker. Launders the money, distributes the proceeds, makes it all happen among his Latvian banks and a bunch of offshore accounts that range from Panama to the Caymans to Switzerland." Max tried to catch Baxter's eye when he mentioned the Swiss, but the MI6 man was studying the screen.

Cindy crossed her arms. "But that's not Stasko's only job."

"Right." Max scanned the room for coffee. Ever since he had quit smoking, Max's coffee consumption had skyrocketed. "Is there any coffee?"

Cindy hit a button on an intercom. "Charles, can you please bring black coffee and an Earl Gray with milk to the Moonraker conference room?"

Max slapped his knee. "Wait. Your conference rooms are named for Ian Fleming novels?"

"Ignore him." Baxter shook his head. "Continue with your briefing, please."

Cindy tapped on the tablet, and the picture of Stasko was replaced with a rotating group of documents that showed a bewildering series of financial transactions. "Stasko's banking empire, in addition to washing money on behalf of the kommissariat, is also a key part of the Russian president's financial empire."

"He's playing both sides of the fence?" Baxter leaned over to get a closer view of the documents on the screen. "That's a dangerous game."

"It only works if the Russian president doesn't know Stasko is on the consortium," Max said. "All consortium members' identities are secret."

They were interrupted by a young man wearing an apron and pushing a trolly. A carafe of coffee was placed on the table next to China cups and saucers and coffee service.

A tray of finger sandwiches and biscuits accompanied the coffee. A teacup and a small kettle were placed near Baxter's elbow. Max poured two cups of coffee and handed one to Cindy before he resumed his position on the credenza.

Cindy tapped and a picture of a paunchy-faced Caucasian male appeared. The subject's gray hair was awry, and dark bags were under his eyes. He appeared next to an image showing the interior of an office. The desk drawers were pulled out and the contents were dumped on the floor. Papers were everywhere. "Meet Konstantin Zaitsev, former Russian oligarch, current British subject and, according to Max's archive, a large-scale weapons dealer."

"Zaitsev?" Baxter set his teacup down with a bang. "I thought we gave that file over to MI5?"

"We did." Cindy smiled at Max. "Based on the information Max provided, MI5 raided his house while we were in Davos and uncovered a trove of evidence, which they shared with us." She sipped coffee and tapped the tablet to make a document appear on screen. An ornate seal was at the top along with the embossed name and address of a bank. From Max's vantage point, he couldn't make out the print or see the bank's name. There were five items on the document, four of which were seven-figure numbers in the debit column. One line included an eight-figure number in the credit column. The denominations were in dollars.

Cindy took another sip before she talked. "This is a memorandum of a wire transfer that shows what we believe is a remittance for one of Zaitsev's weapons transactions. The four seven-figure debits are transfers out to four numbered accounts. We're tracing the account numbers, but it's difficult with the opaque international banking laws. The account number which sent the money, however, belongs to Erich Stasko's bank." Cindy used a laser pointer to highlight the eight-figure credit. "We know that account from our prior dealings with Mr. Stasko." A few months ago, Max had pressured Erich Stasko into helping him figure out who masterminded a bombing in London's West Brompton neighborhood that killed fifty-six.

Baxter looked at Max for the first time since they entered the room. His eyes blazed. "Did you know this would happen when you put us onto Zaitsev?"

Max shrugged. "I thought it might, but I wasn't certain. Can we implicate Stasko in this weapons deal?"

Baxter harrumphed. "Even if we got a conviction, we'd have to petition Latvia for extradition, which might take years and there is no guarantee it will be successful. Stasko will hide behind lawyers, and we may never get him on British soil."

Cindy beamed. "We figured you'd say that."

"We?" Baxter furrowed his brow.

Max tasted the coffee. It was no better than a brown crayon dipped in hot water. "What if Stasko comes to London voluntarily?"

Baxter scoffed. "The man never travels. Stasko is a workaholic and shuttles between his home outside Riga and his office in downtown Riga via helicopter or armored SUV. He never leaves Latvia. How are you going to make him visit London?"

Max caught Cindy's eye and they both laughed. "We thought you'd never ask."

"What do we know about Stasko? His personal life, his habits?" Max refreshed his coffee from the carafe.

"Quite a bit." Cindy paced at the front of the room. "Most of it is intel from our operation last fall. Two daughters, one at King's College, who you've met, and one at Cambridge. One studies economics, the other is in medicine, which I believe you know. Both are excellent students and the pride of their respective classes.

"At age forty-four, Erich Stasko is young to have earned so much wealth. He owns and runs one of the largest banking networks outside Switzerland. His banks are more secretive than the Swiss, especially after the rollback of Swiss banking privacy regulations in 2012."

"Which didn't amount to much," Baxter grumbled.

"He's the richest man in Latvia." Cindy pointed at a screen that showed a variety of bank statements. "He has no known vices except he's a workaholic, and he likes to collect priceless antiquities. He keeps a warehouse of them outside Riga and, our sources tell us, he has a private curated museum of artifacts in his main residence, a walled compound in Old Riga.

"There is one part of his life that's interesting." Cindy clicked a few times and an image of a statuesque blonde woman appeared. "Meet Mrs. Stasko. His wife, a former model named Inge Doré, stays in their London flat much of the time and has been seen on the social circuit with various men who are not her husband. She goes by her given name and drops the Stasko."

Max walked to the front of the room to examine the image. The surveillance shot showed Mrs. Stasko walking on London's famed Oxford Street with several shopping bags on the crook of her arm. Her skin was pale, her cheekbones prominent, and her wavy blonde hair billowed around her as she walked. She was taller than most of the pedestrians. "French and Norse. Quite a combination."

"Her father was the French ambassador to Norway, where he met Inga's mother." A click by Cindy and another image of Inge Doré appeared. This showed her in eveningwear standing close to a man in a tuxedo. She stood eye to eye with her date, and her curves filled out her black gown. "At a fundraiser. The man is Piers Preston, a rear admiral in the Navy and a minor peer. A viscount, I think."

"Viscount Hereford," corrected Baxter.

"And a very eligible bachelor." Cindy's eyes sparkled as she clicked. The screen showed a collage of images, each of Inge Doré in various modeling poses, and all in various stages of undress or skimpy lingerie or bikinis. Many of the images were covers of high-profile fashion magazines. "In her time, Doré was a sought-after cover model with contracts with a few cosmetics and fashion brands."

Max sipped his coffee. "How did she and Stasko meet?"

"Rumor has it that Doré went through a rough patch. All her modeling proceeds were stolen by her manager, and anything left disappeared up her nose. She hit rock bottom and did a stint at Kusnacht, an exclusive rehab clinic in Zurich, which is, apparently, where she met Stasko."

"Stasko was in rehab?"

"Yes, when he was in his late twenties. It's why he doesn't drink or anything. He's been clean ever since."

"He replaced whatever addiction he had with an addiction to work. Why are they estranged?"

"We don't know. But there's only one recorded visit of Stasko to London, which was two years ago. According to immigration records, he stayed for forty-eight hours, listed his lodging as a brownstone he owns, and that's about it."

"So the way to get Stasko onto British soil is through his wife. But how?" Baxter pawed at his goatee, a sign the officer had forgotten his anger at the mishap in Davos and his interest was piqued by the operation.

Max set his coffee on the table and folded his arms. "You're going to turn me into minor British royalty, and I'm going to seduce Mrs. Stasko and convince her to bring Erich to London."

FIFTEEN

London, England

"Max, we have a problem."

Cindy's voice appeared in Max's earpiece, which was a microscopic speaker invisible to the naked eye. The flesh-colored device was the latest from MI6's technical team, and it contained a small microphone and enough technology to eliminate ambient noise. It was tuned to Max's voice. Gone were the days of talking into one's sleeve. "Tell me."

The blonde analyst sat in a van along with Harris and Baxter. The van was parked on a side street a block over from the Victoria & Albert Museum, where Max had left his car, a BMW borrowed from the MI6 motor pool. Max buttoned his tuxedo jacket and ascended the short stairs leading to the museum. The team had surveilled Inge Doré for the past forty-eight hours as she shopped, lunched with girlfriends, and sent an assistant out at the last minute to rent a strand of green Tahitian pearls for this evening's gala.

"She has company," Cindy said into Max's ear.

"Well, may the best man win." Max laughed and checked his watch. In keeping with the MI6 office theme, Max had chosen a Rolex Submariner, which everyone knows is the true James Bond watch. There wasn't time to procure the vintage reference model 6538 worn by Bond in *Dr. No*, so he settled for the more modern ref. 16610 on a NATO strap, which is how Sean Connery wore it. The gala opened thirty minutes ago, and Max was fashionably late.

"Not that kind of company," Cindy said into his ear. "Two people. I think it's another surveillance team."

That caused Max's step to falter as he reached the door, which was held open by a regal-looking attendant with a full plume on a helmet designed to resemble a palace guard. During the prep for the operation, Cindy told him the gala's theme was *Deconstructed Royalty*. It struck Max as disrespectful, but the fundraiser for the British Heart Foundation was to be attended by the city's A-listers. MI6 provided the hefty per-plate contribution and finagled Max an invite.

The mission was simple: Meet and secure a date with Inge Doré. To facilitate that, MI6 kitted Max out with a fake identity as minor royalty. Max made a show of looking at his watch, nodded to the doorman, and waited to the right of the doors while he watched dozens of London's elite arrive. "You sure they're watching her and not me?"

"Mostly sure. There is another van. We recorded the license plate earlier in the day outside Doré's place, and the same van showed up here tonight. A couple just stepped out of the rear of the van and headed to the museum. Red-haired woman in a pale-yellow overcoat and a Caucasian male wearing a tux and a paisley-blue bow tie."

"I've got them." The couple in question approached the museum from the northwest side, opposite from where Max waited. *Wish I had a cigarette.* He removed his secure Blackphone and pretended to scroll. "Any idea who they are?"

"We're running facial recognition right now, but so far nothing."

"What makes you think they're surveillance on Doré?"

"Harris scrolled through CCTV footage from her street, and that van has been there for the past week. Can't imagine why a couple would emerge from the back of the van and attend the gala if it wasn't surveillance. Ran the van's tags and they show as recently stolen from a florist. I'm debating calling the bobbies on them." Cindy used slang to refer to the Metropolitan Police.

"Hold off on that for now. I'm going in." Max put his phone away and followed the couple through a security checkpoint and into the museum. He waited as the red-haired woman checked her spring-weight overcoat. Underneath she wore flowing black pants and a gauzy backless top that showed off a smooth, muscular back of porcelain skin. With a clutch in hand, the woman took her man's arm and glided into the crowd.

The main event was a cocktail reception in the museum's sculpture gallery. When Max entered, the immense room was full of gentlemen in black tuxedos and their beautiful dates in black cocktail dresses. MI6 had scrubbed the guest list and found it was minor peerage, business executives, a few high-profile artists, the occasional British government administrator, and one or two actors. *How had they missed these two intruders?*

Doré had paid for her plate and that of a girlfriend, and the two women arrived in long black gowns, sequined clutches, and muted makeup. Max had no trouble spotting the towering blonde among the silver-haired patrons. The rented pearl necklace glowed in the ambient light.

The sculpture gallery was designed in pale creams and whites. The tile was white with thin black outlines, the walls were cream, the overhead arched ceiling was white, and even the pedestals holding the sculptures were off-white. The gala attendees milled among the statues and three fountains while holding flutes of champagne. Max found the bar, thought about ordering a shaken martini, but opted for an Irish whiskey poured over a chunk of ice. Glass in hand, he wandered in Doré's general direction and scanned for the woman in the backless top and the man with the paisley-blue bow tie.

"Max, we got a hit on facial recognition." Cindy's voice was urgent.

Max put his phone to his ear and pretended to have a whispered phone conversation. "Go ahead."

"Nothing on the guy, but the woman is in Interpol's database. Last name Petrova. Suspected member of an elite Latvian kill squad." As Cindy finished, the couple in question appeared off to Inge Doré's left, where they sipped drinks and admired a sculpture.

Max eyed the couple while pressing the phone to his ear. "You don't say." The Latvian couple were five feet from Doré.

Inge Doré and her girlfriend stood around a tiny cocktail table and sipped champagne. Their eyes roamed the crowd as they talked, like people more interested in being seen than having an intimate conversation. The long strand of rented pearls was around Doré's neck and knotted so it hung in the center of her ample cleavage. Doré's girlfriend leaned close, said something, and left her drink on the table before walking off in the direction of the toilet.

The red-haired Latvian woman in the backless top sidled close to her date and the two talked in hushed tones like two intimates. When they parted, Max recognized something in the woman's hand that made him put his phone away. "I gotta go."

"What's happening?" Cindy's voice was in his ear, but he didn't answer. His attention was focused on the pale-skinned Latvian, who had parted from her date. The man in the paisley-blue bow tie was now walking to a side exit, where a security guard let people out but not in. The woman slid through the crowd on a route aimed to take her near Doré. Hidden in the Latvian's hand was a small, pointed instrument that resembled a pen. It was not a pen. Max had employed such a weapon himself; it was a carbon-fiber blade disguised as a writing instrument. A weapon that had gone undetected by the event's low-quality security. The killer was almost upon Doré.

"Inga!" Max shouted and put his hand in the air. "Inge Doré, is that you?" Several people glanced in annoyance at the gauche outburst, including Inge Doré, but not the assassin. *She's a pro.* Max cut through the crowd in Doré's direction. The Latvian was at Doré's back and a sudden shift of her arm projected her intention to shove the razor-thin blade into Inge Doré's kidney in an attack known as the *renal strike*. Requiring a thin but strong blade, the renal strike was a favorite technique of assassins in close quarters. It yielded almost instant death with little blood. In the chaos of the victim's collapse, the killer could exit before the event was identified as a killing. Max had used the technique himself.

He stuck out his foot.

As the Latvian slid through the crowd and jerked her arm back to perform the strike, she bumped into Max's leg.

Max let his drink slip from his hand as he shoved the killer's shoulder. At the same time, he used his hip to jostle Inge Doré out of harm's way and took hold of the would-be killer's wrist that held the weapon. He wasn't quick enough to prevent the blade from slicing Inge Doré's tricep, and she sucked in her breath from the pain. As the Latvian tripped, Max bent her arm back and up, and the carbon knife fell from her grip and into Max's hand. He slipped it into his jacket pocket while the woman tangled in Max's legs and hit the floor. To the outside observer, it appeared like an ordinary collision where one person inadvertently bumped into another.

"Oh, God. I'm so sorry." Max bent to help the red-haired woman to her feet. "I'm such a klutz." Their eyes met and there was the fire of hatred there before she pushed off through the crowd.

"She's exiting to the west," Max muttered. "Might want to grab her."

"Copy that," Cindy said.

"What did you say?" It was Inge Doré. She held her arm while a trickle of blood seeped through her fingers. Her eyes turned glassy, and she swayed on her feet.

Max whipped out a handkerchief and gently removed Inge's hand and replaced it with the white cloth, which he tied around her arm. The knife wound was shallow. After shrugging off his tuxedo jacket, he put it around her shoulders. The crowd around them resumed their party; no one seemed to notice the tall blonde woman's wound. Max put his arm around her. "Inge, I can't believe it's you."

"I don't think I..."

Max put his lips close to her ear. "Don't talk. We need to get this arm looked at, but let's not make a scene."

"Okaayy... Lesss go." Her words were slurred, but she

permitted Max to lead her to the front entrance. As they walked, Inge Doré became more and more disoriented and heavy on his arm. When they pushed through the museum's main lobby, he nodded to the doorman and muttered something about too much drink. The doorman helped them into a cab, and the cabbie asked for an address.

"Nearest hospital, and step on it."

SIXTEEN

London, England

"Who are you?" Inge Doré's voice was rough with sleep.

Max set down his book, a dogeared copy of *1984* by George Orwell, and inched open the velour blinds so early morning sunlight streamed in through the window. Doré lay cocooned in her king-sized bed surrounded by a dozen pillows and covered by a thick duvet. A well-groomed gray and white shih tzu lay curled on the end of the bed. A pink ribbon held long hair out of the dog's big eyes.

Max sat in a Victorian-style upholstered wing chair at her bedside. His tuxedo jacket lay on a satin settee along the wall, which is where he had caught a few hours of sleep. He sipped coffee brewed in her kitchen. "You were drugged."

In the cab the previous evening, Doré lost consciousness but remained breathing. An MI6 doctor met them at the hospital, where tests were conducted, treatment was administered, and the arm wound was sutured. After a heated discussion, where Baxter insisted she remain at the hospital, Max convinced him to have her transported to her home. Max wasn't about to let a plum opportunity slip by. The intimacy of her home would help Max to make a connection with the former model. Now Cindy, Harris, and Baxter sat in the van parked outside Doré's flat. The tiny earpiece remained in Max's ear.

The news didn't seem to surprise her. "Did you drug me?"

Max shook his head. "How well did you know the woman you were with at the gala?"

"Are you the police?" She pronounced the words deliberately.

Max shook his head again. "I'm a friend."

Her eyes narrowed. "I don't recognize you."

"Do you remember me from last night?"

She turned her head. "I don't remember much from last night."

Max helped her sit up and handed her a glass of water. "Someone gave you xylazine, which is commonly used to sedate horses. I'm guessing it was in your champagne. It'll be a couple of days before you're back to normal. Who was the woman you were with?"

In fact, Max already knew. Through facial recognition, Cindy had determined Doré's companion was another Latvian who held an administrative role at the Latvian Consulate in London. The woman disappeared and never returned to the gala after pretending to visit the toilet. Max guessed she was sequestered in the Latvian Embassy and would soon be on her way out of the country.

"You sound like the police."

"Some might take that as a compliment." He grinned.

"The woman's name is Elina Linde. She works at the Latvian Consulate."

At the woman's name, Inge squeezed her eyes shut. "She told me her name was Rita. Said she works for an equity firm on Canary Wharf."

Max shook his head. "You two met recently. At a fundraiser, or maybe a museum. It was casual. You had a few things in common. She offered you access to exclusive social events or parties."

A tear appeared on Inge's cheek. "She has two shih tzus, I have one. We met in the park. We belong to the same fitness club. She got me into the Cirque Le Soir."

Cindy's voice appeared in Max's ear. "That's an exclusive club, members only. Leonardo DiCaprio goes there a lot."

Max rubbed his chin. "She was a friendly face in a big city."

Inge brushed at a tear and screwed her face into a mask. "I guess." She examined the bandage on her arm. It took a dozen stitches to close the wound. "Do you know what happened last night?"

As Max explained the events of the previous evening, he watched her face for any kind of emotion. There was none. He kept the details vague. "You were the target of an assassination attempt."

Her eyes went wide. "And you prevented it?"

Max raised his eyebrows. "Do you know who might want you harmed?"

She averted her gaze.

"Was it your husband?"

Her mouth dropped open, and she peered at Max with wide eyes that filled with water. "What do you know about that?"

Overnight, while Inge Doré slept off the sedative, an MI6 team interrogated the pale-skinned woman who had attempted to kill her. They got nowhere, and now the woman sat in a cell and refused to talk. An official from the Latvian embassy would soon visit MI6 headquarters with paperwork that showed the woman was a member of the embassy's staff and protected by diplomatic immunity. Besides, where was the evidence? Max handed over the knife to Baxter, but there were no prints. Surveillance footage from the museum showed nothing other than a simple collision between Max and the woman. Soon the would-be assassin would disappear back to Latvia along with Elina Linde.

"We know plenty." Max used the plural pronoun on purpose. "We know you haven't seen your husband in years. We know he's a workaholic, and when your daughters left for college, he buried himself in his work. You were bored and spent more time here in London to, as you told him, see your daughters more. In fact, you established a life here and enjoyed the shopping, restaurants, and social life in London more so than Riga. Over time, you two grew apart. Except recently you decided you wanted to make it official, didn't you?" Max rose and dug in his jacket pocket, where he removed an envelope, which he handed to Inge.

"What's this?"

"Open it."

She removed two four-by-six-inch glossy images. Both showed surveillance images of her on the arm of a taller man. Inge flung them to the floor. "This is extortion?"

"We don't care who you're with. That's your business."

"Then what? What do you want?"

Max shrugged. "Our guess is that your husband would rather you be dead than divorced. Maybe it's financial, maybe it's his pride. But he tried to have you killed last night."

Inge averted her eyes.

Max put his hand on her forearm. "We want you to stay alive."

She touched the bandage on her arm. "How do you intend to do that?"

"There is a lot we don't know, Inge. You told Erich that you want a divorce. Erich doesn't want a divorce. We guess it's because that makes it financially messy for him. What you don't know is that Erich works with lots of unsavory people. People he can use to make problems go away. You've become a problem for him, and if you were to die, his problem goes away. He failed this time, but next time..."

The tears flowed now, and Max handed her a box of tissues. Her hand crumpled the tissue and held it to her mouth. "What do I do?"

"We can help you, Inge."

"In exchange for what?"

"We need you to get Erich to come to London."

She balled up a tissue and tore it in half. "How am I supposed to do that?"

Max shrugged. "That part is up to you. We'll help if we can, but you know him better than we do. What would make him want to visit?"

The shredded tissue fluttered to the floor, and she took another one and started the process all over again. "How do you intend to keep me alive? If he comes here, he might try to kill me."

"Erich is a banker. He isn't going to kill anyone. He may hire someone else, but that kind of thing takes time. Organizing that team took months and a lot of money. It will take him several months to make another attempt. If you can get him on British soil, we will take him off the game board before that happens."

Inge sniffled. "You have something on him, don't you? You need him here in London to arrest him."

Max shrugged. "Are you on our team, Inge?"

———

"You lied to her." Baxter stalked the gray carpet in the Moonraker conference room.

"I didn't lie to her, but I may have omitted some information." Max glanced at Cindy, who was bent over her laptop.

"The moment Stasko is in our custody, we freeze his assets." Baxter's hands were shoved in his pockets. "She'll have nothing."

Max held up a finger. "First, we are not going to freeze his assets. Remember that we're going to trade him his freedom for his help. He's going to help us ensnare the Russian president. To do that, he'll need his assets. Let's keep the prize in mind." Max raised two fingers. "Second, if you try to freeze his assets, you won't get them all. You might be able to freeze the assets that you know about, but you can't freeze his entire banking system. If he has half the intelligence we believe he has, Erich and Inge have dozens of offshore accounts between them, and probably half of those, or more, are in her name. Their London townhouse is in her name. This is why he wants her dead instead of getting a divorce. There are too many accounts and assets that he's put in her name to keep them protected. If she dies, those assets revert to him."

"If we screw this up, she's dead," Baxter muttered.

"She'd already be dead if it weren't for us."

Cindy twirled her finger in the air. Her head was bent over a laptop where she monitored the reports from the surveillance team attached to Inge Doré. "She's dialing."

"Put it on speaker."

Cindy clicked a button.

"You son of a bitch." The voice was Inge's.

"Honey, what are you saying?" The voice was Stasko's.

"You think you can kill me off and your problems go away?"

Max put a hand on his forehead. "Subtle, Inge. Real subtle."

Erich Stasko's voice was strained. "What are you talking about?"

"I know you sent people to kill me, you coward. Well, they failed. The bitch with the little knife missed me. How do you like that, you cocksucker?"

"I don't know where you get these ideas from—"

"It's over, Erich. I'm filing the papers tomorrow, first thing."

"Honey, Inge. My sweets. Can we talk about this? You know how much I love you. I'd never hurt you like you're saying. Where did you get these notions?"

"All you care about is money. You've never cared about me or our daughters. You never even visit us."

"That's not true. Don't do anything until we talk about it. I'll hop on the jet and be there before you know it. We can work this out without courts or anything."

Five beats ticked by, and the three in the gray conference room peered at each other. No one breathed.

"Okay," Inge said. "I'm sorry. I was upset. I know you'd

never do anything to hurt me, Erich. Let's talk about it and figure out what to do. I can't live like this anymore."

"Of course, of course. I understand. I'll be there in three hours, and we'll figure something out."

The call ended.

Max spread his hands. "We're on."

SEVENTEEN

Building 311, Moscow, Russia

It was one of those ubiquitous cinder block buildings on the outskirts of Moscow identical to all the others. Brown and dingy, the building's windows were grimed over, and rust marks ran down from the flat roof. The four-story building was long, narrow, and sandwiched between a low-rent apartment building and an oil refinery that belched dark smoke. On this spring day, a pewter-gray sky was low overhead and dirty snow had melted to reveal mud and dead grass underneath. The building's parking lot was filled with rusted Lada hatchbacks from the 1980s. The building's only remarkable features were the security cameras that bristled on the exterior and the barbed wire fence that surrounded the grounds.

No one knew what went on in the building, and no one asked. In Russian government circles that were aware of its existence, the building and the operation contained within were referred to only as *Building 311*.

If any of the neighbors who lived near Building 311 managed to gain entry, they might be disappointed. If they made it over the electrified fence, past the armed guards, in between the metal detectors, and through several doors secured by retina scanners, they would stumble upon the most benign office. It was a vast room filled with desks, computers, monitors, and young women and men furiously clicking their mice. Other than the clacking of keyboards and the occasional command barked by the man sitting at the desk on the pedestal at the front of the room, the facility was silent.

Once the intruder was escorted from the room and sent to the nearest gulag, the room would get back to its business of searching for the famous hacker known by her online handle: Goshawk.

The man at the front of the room was Gleb Semenov, a colonel in Russia's Unit 90750 of the Russian Main Intelligence Directorate (GRU). While there was no military action among his otherwise distinguished pedigree, he possessed advanced degrees in computer science and mathematics from Tsinghua University in Beijing and the National University of Singapore. Through decades in the trenches, he had distinguished himself by leading a handful of high-profile hacks on Ukraine's power grid, petroleum pipelines in the US, and software firms around the world. Now Semenov's docket was clear, and he was assigned a team of the country's best computer hacking talent and given a mandate: Find Goshawk, find the Vienna Archive, and find them fast.

The colonel had lived and worked in the Soviet and Russian government apparatus long enough to know the bureaucracy's guiding principle: What have you done for me lately? The medal board on his chest, the warm and comfortable apartment in Moscow's Golden Mile neighborhood, and his mother's cancer care would all be forfeited if he didn't achieve this latest mission.

The young team under his command were incented differently. Each knew that if he or she were the one to discover the Vienna Archive or find the elusive and secretive hacker code-named Goshawk, that their family would reap the rewards that included a luxury apartment, guaranteed retirement benefits, and access to better education for their children.

The yellowed phone on Semenov's desk rang, and he answered. "Da?"

"Comrade Semenov."

The colonel recognized the voice on the other end of the phone. He needed no introduction, and Semenov's pulse quickened. Dmitry Kozov, the man with the president's ear. Said to be the president's fixer. "Da."

"A car is waiting outside. You are to brief him in twenty minutes' time. Are you prepared?"

The colonel pulled at his collar. Somehow the temperature in the room had risen a few degrees. "Of course, Comrade Kozov." The line went dead, and the clacking of keyboards filled the room.

London, England

The capture of Erich Stasko on British soil was a quiet operation performed by MI6 staff with assistance from UK Visas and Immigration. Ordinarily, the capture of an international fugitive like Stasko, wanted for international money laundering and illegal weapons sales, required a joint task force involving MI5, Scotland Yard, and Immigration. A law enforcement salad, as Baxter called it. Because MI6 had no intention of remanding Stasko to custody, they used a skeleton crew of Harris and two MI6 muscle along with Baxter, Cindy, and Max. The head immigration official at London's City Airport was brought in on the operation just as Stasko's Bombardier Global 7500 touched the tarmac.

The rest was a formality. Stasko was separated from the two staffers who accompanied him on the private jet, cuffed, searched, relieved of his electronics and pocket contents, and led to a waiting SUV with dark windows. He protested, yelled for his embassy, threatened lawsuits, and his two aides busied themselves with futile phone calls. The two MI6 muscle put him in the rear seat of the SUV, where he came face-to-face with Max.

"Hello, Erich."

Stasko's face drained. "You. You'll never get away with this."

Baxter got in the front seat, and the vehicle took off with one of the MI6 men driving. They were followed by a large black Jaguar sedan with Harris, Cindy, and the other muscle. The caravan took the A13 East at a high rate of speed with lights flashing.

Max patted Stasko's thigh. "I just did."

―――

The MI6 Westcliff-on-Sea safe house was chosen for its relative proximity to London's City airport and MI6 headquarters, and because of the property's size at over twenty acres, which meant they were hidden from neighbors' prying eyes. An MI6 advance technology team had already visited the property and installed a video feed, monitors, and other gear. One video camera was in a basement room that served as Stasko's cell, and another was in the living room which was converted to an interrogation room. The monitors were in a side bedroom, which is where Cindy and Harris were posted.

While the MI6 muscle relieved Stasko of his shoes, tie, belt, and jacket and secured him in the cell, Max and Baxter strolled the outdoor gardens that offered a view of where the Thames reached the English Channel. A cold spring breeze blew off the ocean and the men were bundled up. Max wore a scarf around his neck and a flat cap. "You look almost English," Baxter told him. "But the beard gives you an Irish flair." They followed a path of steps through brown and green knolls and hedges in the direction of the water.

"Remember our deal," Baxter said.

"I remember." Max shoved his gloved hands deep into his jacket pockets.

Baxter's hands were also in the pockets of his thick overcoat. "He gives us the names of the account holders of the funds transferred from the weapons sale."

"I got it." Max wanted a cigarette. It was something about the cold ocean, the overcast skies, and the fact he was about to interrogate an adversary. The nicotine craving surged, and he patted his pockets for a box of smokes.

"And he will not be mistreated," Baxter said. "Not here on British soil. Not on my watch."

"No more than he already has been?"

Baxter stopped and grabbed Max's arm. "I'm serious. You will not beat him, poke him with lit cigarettes, or cut off any of his fingers. Got it?"

"Lit cigarettes? I've never done that in my life. Jesus. You must think I'm a monster."

"I know what I've seen. I know what you're capable of. Now let's get started. The sooner we get through this, the better." The two men turned onto a pea gravel walkway and returned to the house.

The captive was placed in a chair and given a bottle of water and left to sit for an hour. Baxter called this *letting him marinate*. The items in the room were the chair Stasko sat in, a small table, a wooden kitchen chair, the video camera on a tripod, and a bright halogen lamp. The captive was left unbound, but all the windows and doors in the living room were sealed with boards save for one metal door that was locked. The team observed via the video camera as Stasko sipped his water and wandered around the room. The banker tapped at the wood covering the windows and half-heartedly tested the plywood before he sat in the chair.

"He's remarkably calm." Cindy sipped from a water bottle.

"He knows he has something to trade." Max tasted his coffee, grimaced, and took another drink.

After an hour, Baxter opened the metal door accompanied by one of the muscle, who stood near the wall as the MI6 officer took the second chair. The first thing he did was to hand Stasko the sheet of paper showing the electronic funds transfer, to which the banker shrugged before handing it back.

"This is going to take a while," Harris mumbled. Over the course of an hour, Callum walked Stasko through an orchestrated rundown of the evidence against him, which included the link to his bank account and dozens of documents uncovered in the Zaitsev arrest.

By the end, Stasko remained nonplussed. "So arrest me.

Why am I here talking to British Intelligence? I'll take my chances in the courts." He refused to provide Baxter with any information about the weapons deal. "I get a lawyer, my embassy, and I want both now. What you're doing here is illegal."

The banker was taken back to his cell, which consisted of a mattress on the floor, and was left a plate of fish and chips from a local take-out joint and a bottle of water. The door was shut to his protests and appeals for a lawyer.

"We're going to need more leverage." Baxter collapsed into a chair and dug for his pipe. Cindy was hunched over her laptop. Harris archived the video footage and uploaded the interview to the MI6 servers at Vauxhall.

Max sat on a table and sipped coffee. "Is it my turn yet?"

EIGHTEEN

Westcliff-on-Sea, England

"I may have something." Cindy turned her laptop so her screen was visible to Max, Baxter, and Harris. "Since Inge's phone call to Erich, I've been digging into her finances. What did she mean when she said she drained the bank accounts? So far, we know of two bank accounts in her name, and we know the London flat is in her name. But check this out."

Max hunched close to the screen. It showed a bewildering array of legal documents, spreadsheets of figures, webpages of numbered accounts, and handwritten ledgers. "What is all this?"

Cindy pointed a manicured nail at her computer. "If I'm right, and I think I am, a substantial portion of Stasko's banking empire is owned by Inge Doré."

"A controlling interest?" Baxter paced at the rear of the tiny room. "If she holds that much control over his banking empire, it explains why they're still married and why he ignores her... ahem... indiscretions."

"I'm still digging," Cindy said as she typed. "The actual ownership records of Stasko's banking empire are a morass of a legal structure that would take a phalanx of lawyers to untangle."

"We might have enough here for me to do a little bluffing." Max held his fist out to Cindy. "Nice work."

Cindy beamed and bumped his fist.

They let the banker marinate as they dug further into the legal structure of Stasko's companies. After wading through hundreds of documents, Max pushed his chair back and pinched his eyes. "He's not stupid enough to give her controlling interest. But it looks like she has a substantial share of the business and enough voting rights to make trouble."

"If she were to align with another owner and pool their interests, Erich might lose his control over the entire shebang." Baxter tapped his finger on the table.

When Erich Stasko was brought into the interrogation room, he was met by Max alone. The banker's face was drawn, and the sparkle was gone from his eyes. He slumped in the chair and gazed at Max. "I see you've graduated from terrorizing college girls to hiding behind intelligence tossers."

Max's eyebrows rose. "For the record, I was very polite to your daughter. She helped me find my way on that bewildering campus. She's a smart young lady with a bright future."

"What do you want, Asimov? I know you're behind this whole thing. That ancient professor that was in here before was the warmup round."

Max crossed a leg over the other. "How's your council

on... what's it called? Council on Oil and Gas? How's that going, Erich? I hear that council members keep dying off."

Stasko shifted in his chair.

Max grinned. "It's more like the council on death and dismemberment. It's an unhealthy place to be these days."

Stasko swallowed on a dry throat. "I'm still here, so you must want something."

Max rose and paced behind Stasko's chair and put his hands on the banker's shoulders as he spoke in Stasko's ear. "That ancient professor, as you call him, is the only thing standing between you and serious pain. If it were up to me, we'd see how attached you are to your fingernails."

The fear of pain is more effective than the actual pain itself. It was one of his father's many mantras.

"I like them fine." But the banker closed his hands into fists and crossed his arms.

Max strode around to face Stasko and put a foot on the empty chair seat. "You're going to do a couple things for us, Erich. First, you're going to provide the ancient professor with the names attached to those numbered accounts he wants."

"Forget it. I'd rather take my chances with a lawyer."

Max nodded. "There's not going to be a lawyer, Erich. I'm going to guess that you're afraid your money laundering business would dry up if it became known you were working for British Intelligence."

Stasko's blank face belied nothing, but his eyes shifted before they met Max's gaze.

"You have a choice, Erich. It's not a choice I'd want, but it's all the choice you're going to get today. Your decision will be difficult. You'll need to weigh the risks against the rewards of each. But you're a banker, Erich, and that's what bankers do."

"What are you talking about?"

"What is the one thing you fear most, Erich?"

When the banker didn't respond, Max took a seat. "Of course, you fear death. Most everyone does. You fear that harm might come to your daughters, which is natural. But beyond that?"

Stasko shrugged but said nothing.

"It's funny what fear will do to a man. It can make you do the most outlandish things. In this case, you hired a hit team to kill your wife to eliminate your deepest anxiety."

Blood drained from the banker's face.

"Yes, we know about the Latvian hit squad you sent after Inge. That's some cold shit, Erich. Kill your own wife? And why? Not because she's been screwing around on you. That's been going on for years and you ignored it. Too busy working to care, I guess. But the moment she threatened divorce, your biggest fear kicked in, didn't it?"

The banker looked at the floor.

"Your biggest fear is being broke. You don't want to lose everything you've worked for. You know that if Inge divorces you, she takes all the assets and bank accounts that are in her name, which includes almost half of your company."

Stasko rubbed a palm over his face.

"I get it." Max shrugged. "It's early days. You're young and full of love for your beautiful bride. You buy a bank using Doré's family's money. A loan from her father. In the moment, it's a family affair. No one thinks you'll grow to be one of the largest banks in Eastern Europe. No one thinks you'll get involved with the Russians and start laundering money. You don't intend to break laws, but it happens. You can't turn away the money. Maybe they have something on you. What's the phrase? Too big to fail. How am I doing so far?"

Stasko's head sagged.

"Every man at one time or another has been blinded by a sexy piece of ass, Erich." Max smiled as if it had happened to him. "Meanwhile, Inge owns a large portion of the bank. Not fifty percent, but enough where she exerts influence. Inge was beautiful and sexy, I get it. Inge was into it also. She was in love with her beau. In love with the money. Maybe she knew about the money laundering and looked the other way because the money was too good. It paid for her dalliances. Then things turned sour. You exchanged your substance addictions for a work addiction. She got bored with Riga and found ways to amuse herself in London. Eventually you grew apart. She fell in love with someone else and wanted a divorce."

Stasko rubbed his face with two palms. "How do you know all this?"

"It's what we do, Erich." Max lifted his hands with his palms up. "A divorce might rip it all open. It might expose the fact that she owns such a large portion of your banking empire. Her family might get involved. You can't risk exposing your money-laundering operations. So you decide to dispose of your own wife."

"Oh, God."

"Except you failed. Now she's angry, Erich. A woman scorned. She doesn't care about your money. She wants to hurt you. The only thing standing between you and complete ruin and a probable death is me. I'm your only hope."

The banker hung his head, his shoulders dropped, and a tear rolled down his cheek. "I need to protect my daughters."

"I can help you, Erich."

Stasko began to wail. Years of stress and a dysfunctional marriage bursting out all at once. The tears flowed freely, and Stasko's body was wracked with sobs. Max let him cry. He left the room and returned with a bottle of water and roll of toilet paper. After the banker blew his nose, wiped his face, and regained control, he took a deep breath. "What do we do?"

"For starters, our ancient professor wants the names attached to those bank accounts."

Stasko nodded. "What else?"

"You work for MI6 now. You're going to move your base of operations to London, where you'll be safe from the kommissariat. We will help you salvage the parts of your empire that you can."

"I can't move to London."

"Sure, you can. Just think, you can work things out with Inge."

"That ship has sailed."

"There is one additional thing I need your help with, Erich."

"Shit. What else?"

Max whispered in the banker's ear.

NINETEEN

Langley, Virginia

"I found Julia Meier." Kaamil's head popped up from his cubicle.

"Where?" Kate stepped out of her office. This late in the evening, she and Kaamil were the only ones in the bullpen.

"Germany, but barely."

"What's that mean?" An image appeared in Kate's mind. It was of the silver-haired spy who tried to destroy Kate's life. Proud, regal, and highly skilled, Julia Meier was a senior officer in Germany's BND, that country's intelligence service. As part of Julia's pursuit of the Vienna Archive, Julia had betrayed Kate. She was also Max Austin's birth mother, a fact Kate wanted to ignore.

The images of Julia Meier were replaced by a flood of emotions. A hunger for vengeance. Hesitation at the prospect of getting involved in the Asimovs' mess. A need for retribution. Reluctance to see Max. A maternal desire to succeed for her agency, the agency that was her entire life, and to protect Chester Wodehouse. Julia Meier was her best shot at finding the Vienna Archive, the prospect of which shot a surge of adrenaline through her blood stream.

What would Max do once he found out she'd recovered the Vienna Archive? A smile crept across her face, and all her emotions were replaced by the familiar operational focus. A calm amidst the roiling turmoil of her mind. It's a place she went to when there was a job to do. It was home, the only peace she knew.

Kate walked around to peer at Kaamil's screen, which showed a blue and green map of the North Sea, Germany, and Denmark.

"She's living on an island out in the North Sea." Kaamil pointed at a tiny finger of land jutting into the North Sea. "About as far north in Germany as you can go before you hit Denmark."

"How did you find her?"

"Sources and methods."

"Tell me."

"I may have hacked into a certain someone's server." Kaamil grinned. The smile appeared slowly, like the Cheshire Cat in *Alice in Wonderland*.

"The BND?"

"Negative." He shook his head.

"Kaamil, damn it. Tell me."

"Rhymes with mäs-hawk."

Shit. Goshawk. Max's hacker. A mysterious woman known by one of her many online hacker personas, Goshawk had an uncanny loyalty to Max. She was also a wickedly good computer hacker known to take few risks and deploy dozens of layers of security. "Are you sure she didn't detect you?"

"I got through three firewalls and two proxies undetected. It's not my first rodeo, you know."

Kate laughed. Kaamil, born in the United Arab Emirates, attended university in the US. He liked to westernize his English by binge-watching Netflix and incorporating American idioms into his vernacular.

"Did you get your NSA girlfriend to help you?" Kate poured herself a glass of water from the carafe on the sideboard.

"How do you know about her?" Kaamil's eyes sparkled.

"There isn't much goes on around here I don't know about."

Kaamil shrugged. "May have. Does it make you feel better if I told you I did?"

Yes, but no need to tell him that. "Any sign of the Vienna Archive?"

"Unfortunately not. There are vast portions of her server network that are impenetrable. But we got into this one."

"What did you learn?"

Kaamil clicked to zoom in on the map and expose a scythe-shaped island off the coast of Northern Germany called Sylt.

"Wow, that's up there," Kate said.

Kaamil zoomed further in. "Like I said, it's on the northern border of Germany. She lives in a tiny house along the peninsula here." He pointed at a thin arm of the island that jutted south into the North Sea. "Not much there except sand, houses, and a few World War II bunkers."

"You sure about this?" Julia Meier was known to have

several personal safe houses located around Europe. "How do you know she's there?"

"According to the email traffic between her and Goshawk, after Julia's ordeal at the hands of the Russians, she retired from the BND and has been convalescing in her home on Sylt. Her official status with the Germans is retired. She's no longer on their active officer roster."

"Yeah, right." Kate rolled her eyes.

"What's the next move?" Kaamil said.

"Get the listening devices ready and book me a flight tonight. I'm going to pay her a visit and bait the hook. Let's see if she bites."

Kate Shaw backed in her Tesla for better access to the charger, wiggled the plug so it fit tight, and grabbed her stuff from the back seat. Along with a leather shoulder bag, there was a plastic sack with Thai curry takeout. Eating this late made her sleep restless, but she was famished and wouldn't sleep tonight anyway. At least not without help from a bottle of wine. With the bags in hand, she walked through the darkened parking structure under her building and into the concrete stairwell, where she trudged up five flights.

The idea of a redeye flight over the pond was tiring. Despite her fatigue, the need for justice burned like an ever-present flame. It fueled her and kept the fatigue at bay. Finding Julia Meier energized her.

She used a key to crank open the deadbolt, pushed the door open with her foot, and entered her flat. Light from the city outside cast a glow through the tall windows over the wide-open kitchen and living area.

She sensed the presence before the intruder materialized. It was the thinnest of scents, a deodorant smell that didn't belong. A chill crawled along her spine, and she dropped her purse and the food and whipped the pistol out from the small of her back.

A standing light clicked on to illuminate a form sitting in a chair.

Kate swung the gun and pointed it at the intruder using a two-handed stance. "Why are you in my house?"

The person in the chair was unfamiliar. Her face was young, her skin was the color of caramel, and wild, frizzy hair sprang out from a headband. A pug nose was centered above full lips, and long lashes surrounded big eyes. A fawn-colored leather jacket was tight over a thin turtleneck. Jeans and boots completed the outfit. They were the clothes of an Alexandria hipster who belonged in a coffee shop. A hipster who might be a model. Her hands sat on her lap, and a business card was trapped in her fingers. "Hello, Kate."

"You have five seconds to get the fuck out of my house before you're sucking air through two holes in your chest."

The intruder put her palms up. "Don't shoot the messenger, Kate."

"One."

"We know a lot about you. We know you used to be a rising star in the agency. We know Piper Montgomery ruined your career, put you in a black-site prison, tortured you. We know you were kidnapped—"

"Two."

"—by Victor Dedov and you were rescued by Mikhail Asimov. We also know Andrei Asimov used you, and Julia Meier had you arrested by the German secret service. You've been burned too many times by the Asimov family.

You're back at the agency alongside Chester Wodehouse. You're his confidant and might be his heir apparent. You're not sure whether you can trust him or the agency, but it's all you've got."

"Three." *How does she know all this?*

"We also know Wodehouse has tasked you to find the Vienna Archive. You're hesitant but deep down, you know it's your ticket to retribution for everything the Asimovs have done to you. If you want that vengeance, call this number and meet with us." The woman held out the card.

"Get your hands up and kneel on the floor." Kate waved the pistol. "Do it now." *Whoever this woman is, she must have knowledge of a leak at the agency. How else could she know all this?*

The woman stood and dropped the card on the chair and put her palms up. "Shooting me accomplishes nothing, except it leaves you with a mess on your hands. By now you're wondering who we are and how we know so much about you and Mikhail Asimov. If you shoot me, you'll never know. If you try to arrest me, it will end badly for you."

"Four."

The woman with the fawn-colored leather jacket sidled toward the door with her hands in plain view. "Call the number, Kate. We can help each other. We share the same goals. You'll be glad you did."

Kate tracked the woman with the muzzle of her pistol.

When the woman got to the door, she paused. "Sorry about your dinner. That curry smells delish." The door opened and she disappeared.

As the door slammed shut, Kate darted to the door and slid the deadbolt in place. The Thai curry had spilled out of the container and spread across the wood floor. Tears filled her eyes. As she fell into the chair, the gun slid to her lap.

When her nerves calmed, she pulled the card out from under her. A 10-digit number was handwritten in neat print and nothing else.

What the hell?

TWENTY

Langley, Virginia

It was 10:00 p.m., and her flight was in two hours. The bullpen was empty, although Kaamil was en route with her favorite coffee drink, an oat milk latte with an extra shot of espresso. She wrote out as accurate a description as possible of the woman in the fawn-colored leather jacket and her recollection of the dialog. Slight build, African American or perhaps Latin mix. Gorgeous enough to have been a model. Self-confident enough to not flinch with a weapon pointed at her. Obviously an operative. Foreign government? Who was she? And how did she know so much about Kate's background?

Kate sent the description to Kaamil's inbox so he could run it through the agency's various databases to find an identity.

When Kaamil strode in, he set her coffee on the desk. Despite the late hour, her star analyst was impeccably dressed in a dark blue shirt and silver tie.

"Are you okay?" Kaamil sipped from his own coffee cup.

Kate had already filled Kaamil in via telephone. "I'm fine. I need you to find out who this woman is. All I have is this phone number and a description." She held out the card left behind by the intruder.

Kaamil took the card. He snapped a photo of the front and back with his phone and read through her written description. "Sounds kinda hot."

"Kaamil."

He shrugged. "Sorry."

Kate sipped the coffee. "Keep this under your hat. The stuff she knows is spooky. There must be a connection to the kommissariat, and she knows a lot about me." Kate lowered her voice. "She might be connected to our agency leak."

"Copy that." Kaamil nodded and sat down with a tablet and a pen to operate an application designed to sketch an image.

Kate did her best to describe the details of the woman's features as Kaamil drew the woman's face.

"Like this?" He turned the tablet to show a young woman's face.

"No, her face was thinner. Softer cheekbones. Smaller nose—"

"Hold up. Jeez." He worked the application and showed her another version. "Like this?"

"Yeah, closer. Fuller lips. And the hair isn't an Afro. It was a frizzy jumble. Like she wanted dreadlocks but wasn't there yet." Kate drained her cup and refilled it with hot black coffee from the machine in the break room.

When she returned, Kaamil showed her an updated

image with fuller lips and dreadlocks. "There is no setting for almost-dreads. This will have to do."

"That's closer."

"Let's do a facial recognition search in the database and see what we find."

"How long?"

"I'll set the accuracy coefficient wide, so it generates a lot of hits. We will have to sort through hundreds of false positives. Might be a while. I'm sure the number is untraceable, but we'll give it a shot. Are you going to call it?"

"Not sure yet." She glanced at her watch. "I have to get to the airport."

"Roger that."

"And Kaamil..."

"Yes, ma'am."

"This stuff is in the vault, right?"

"Tighter than a nun's—"

She held up a palm and Kaamil laughed. "Let's walk through this Julia Meier operation one more time before I go. I'm dubbing it Operation Bunker Hill."

"After the old war bunkers on the island of Sylt. I like it." Kaamil bobbed his head as a wide grin spread across his face.

"Bring your laptop in here and let's get to work. We have a few minutes before I have to go."

Time to see an old enemy.

———

Kate's destination was a scythe-shaped island in the North Sea called Sylt that was so far north in Germany, one needed to drive into Denmark first before crossing over to the island. After she decided to push Wodehouse's expense budget, she rented a big white BMW, merged onto the autobahn, and set the speedometer on 200 kph, about 120 mph for Americans. She stayed to the left, flicked her lights at slower vehicles, and relished the meditative state required to operate the car at a high rate of speed. Her mind cleared, and her focus was on the road. Lights flashed in her rearview mirror once, and she pulled over to let a Porsche fly by. By the time she reached Flensburg to cross into Denmark, her armpits were damp, but the exhilaration and concentration had its intended effect. A renewed focus set in.

I'm going to find this damn Vienna Archive.

Getting there required crossing a bridge to an island called Rømø, where she would catch a ferry south to the island of Sylt. With its rolling dunes and empty beaches, the island was an ideal location for a spy's retirement. The island teemed with visitors during the summer, but it was desolate nine months of the year and painfully cold when the damp winter winds swept off the North Sea. On this spring day, a pale sun hinted at the summer to come, but the breeze was crisp with the reminder of winter. Salt was heavy in the air and a flock of sea birds circled overhead. Kate took a winding road through dunes capped with reeds waving in the wind and parked near a tiny house.

The home was newly built in the Scandinavian style popular in Denmark. It was about the size and shape of two shipping containers, with a metal corrugated roof and dark brown exterior. A cedar-colored deck ran the length of the side facing the ocean, where two chairs sat overlooking a placid surf. Off the far side was a small greenhouse filled with plants and flowers. The structure was made with a metal frame and plastic sides that rolled up to expose the plants to fresh air. This is where she found the home's sole occupant.

The woman straightened from a tomato plant. "If you're here to kill me, get on with it." Thick silver hair was pulled back with a lacquer barrette and she wore a dirt-soiled apron over a light cotton jacket.

Kate was on a wooden walkway outside the greenhouse. For the occasion, she wore an olive-green army-style jacket by a New York designer, and her hands were shoved deep in the jacket's pockets, where she grasped a compact 9mm. "Hello, Julia. I'm sure you have three pistols hidden in your garden and were warned by people watching the ferry terminal that I was on my way. There's probably a BND sniper watching me through a rifle scope."

Julia Meier bent over the plant and snipped. "The BND can't be bothered to spare any expense on my behalf. How did you find me?"

"We have our ways." Kate put a hand on her hip.

Julia Meier shifted to another plant. Her movements were sharp, and the sheers cut branches with angry thrusts. "So you're back with the CIA then."

Kate stepped left to get a better view of Julia's hands. "I thought we might help each other."

Julia snorted. "Those days are over for me. Besides, I can't imagine how I might possibly be of use."

The old intelligence officer put out to pasture. Unneeded. Kate cringed. *Is this my fate? Destined to an old age of loneliness on a desolate island with nothing but plants to keep me company?* Her heart strings twanged, despite Julia's betrayal. "We have intel about the Vienna Archive. I think you might find it interesting."

The older woman straightened and shifted to another

plant and resumed trimming. Green branches fell to the ground.

When there was no reaction from Julia, Kate took a step up to the wooden deck where the greenhouse was constructed. Her hand grasped the gun's handle. "We believe Max has the Vienna Archive. Our intel suggests the archive was stored by Andrei in physical files. Andrei didn't trust the internet. We think Max created electronic files and secured those with layers of encryption and authentication." Kate stopped to gauge Julia's reaction.

With her back to Kate, Julia's face remained hidden. The sheers snipped in a blur as green stems and leaves dropped to the ground.

"We also think Max kept a physical copy of the archive." Kate took another step to her left. "We have intelligence on the location where we think he's storing the Vienna Archive, and we think you can help us find the spot. We believe it's a location that's been in the Asimov family for generations. You knew Andrei better than anyone. If anyone can help us, it's you. If we can find the archive, the agency proposes to share it with the BND. It would offer you—"

"What intel?"

"What?"

"What intel do you have on the location?"

Kate spun a lie to protect her source. It was one she rehearsed on the airplane. "We've been gathering signals intel from online chatter between Max and his hacker, and a word keeps turning up. The word is Riverside. It's in the context of an estate or a house that has been in the Asimov family."

The old BND officer said nothing.

Julia's face was angled away from Kate, so Kate couldn't

judge the old woman's reaction. "Does Riverside mean anything to you?"

When Julia straightened, a gun was pointed at Kate. "Out."

Damn, she's still got it. Kate removed her hands from her pockets and put her palms out. "Julia, put the gun down. I'm not here to—"

"Get out, and don't come back." Julia's eyes blazed and her finger was tight on the trigger.

"Okay, I'm leaving." Kate lowered her hand. "I'm going to remove a card from my jacket pocket and set it here, okay? Don't shoot." Kate slowly dipped into her pocket and set a business card on the wooden railing. "That's my mobile. Think about it and call me if you change your mind. We need your help. We can help each other."

The gun wavered, and Julia turned to look at the clipped greenery. It was as if air had escaped a balloon. Julia slumped to sit on a bench, the gun pointed at the ground. A half-dozen plants were stripped of their leaves and branches. "I can't do it anymore." Julia's voice was strained. "I've left all that behind."

Kate nodded and ensured her hands remained visible. "I understand. Believe me, I do. Do you mind... It's been a long drive. Can I use your bathroom before I go?"

Julia waved the gun in the direction of the house. "It's open." Her shoulders sagged, and her back was bent. Deep wrinkles surrounded her eyes. Age had crept in since the last time Kate saw her. *The price of uselessness?*

Kate entered the tiny house through a sliding glass door from the deck facing the ocean. The inside was spotless and obsessively organized. A narrow door stood open to a bathroom. To be prepared, Kate had brought three listening devices and immediately saw options to use two of them.

On the counter was Julia's mobile phone plugged into a wall socket. Kate put her hand into her pocket, glanced around to ensure Julia hadn't followed her into the house, and retrieved a tiny memory device. She unplugged Julia's mobile phone and plugged the device into the phone's dual data and charging port.

While the software downloaded to Julia's mobile phone, she removed a tiny microphone the size of a pencil eraser from her pocket. The device had a strong adhesive on one end. Kate affixed it to the underside of a barstool. A few taps on her own mobile phone and the bug connected to the home's Wi-Fi. The bug was designed to piggyback the Wi-Fi and download an audio feed from the mic to one of Kaamil's servers in DC.

Kate turned back to Julia's mobile phone. The download was still in progress. Kate glanced at the door. No one was there. After what felt like an eternity, the screen on Julia's phone flickered green and returned to its normal state. She removed the device, stuck it into her pocket, plugged the phone back into the cord attached to the wall socket, and stepped into the bathroom.

There, she flushed the toilet and washed her hands and walked into the living room. Julia stood in the open sliding door, gun in her hand, muzzle pointed at the floor.

A chill crawled along Kate's neck. *Did she see me? Was she watching?*

Julia waved the gun. "Don't come back here. If you do, I'll shoot you on sight."

Kate put her hands up with the palms out. In her peripheral vision, the phone was out of place. It was on the counter, but six inches from where it was previously. *Did Julia notice?* "I understand. If you change your mind, call me."

Julia backed out of the doorway and Kate eased by her. Once in the car, she dialed Kaamil. "Did you get them?"

"Affirmative. We own her phone, and the bug is active."

Kate let out a breath. "Let's hope I piqued her interest and she doesn't suspect I did anything with her phone."

TWENTY-ONE

London, England

"How do you get the attention of the world's most powerful man?" Max sipped his coffee as his audience found their seats. "And a man who is in the middle of a war?"

The gray Moonraker conference room smelled of burnt coffee and Harris's beef and horseradish sandwich. Baxter fiddled with his phone and Cindy, for once, abandoned her laptop and sat with rapt attention as Max addressed the room. Today she wore a smart gray pantsuit with a pale-blue blouse open at the neck, where a sapphire pendant hung.

"Steal something from him." Cindy scrunched her nose.

"He's the richest man in the world," Harris said between bites. "What can we steal that he can't replace?"

"There's no evidence he's the richest person in the world," Baxter scoffed.

"No public evidence." Max nursed the cup of tepid brown beverage that passed for MI6 coffee. "The Russian president has siphoned billions from the country and parked them in offshore accounts and shell companies, and he holds controlling interests in dozens of businesses through cutouts."

Harris licked his fingers. "What's a cutout?"

Max nodded at Cindy, who answered. "Let's say you want a pint of beer, but your bride frowns on it and is known to prowl around the local to catch you in the act. You're sitting at the bar with your best friend, someone you trust not to drink your pint. When the pints arrive you give yours to your friend, who sits there with two pints you bought. There's a glass of water in front of you. Once in a while, after looking around to ensure your ball and chain isn't skulking around, you reach over and take a big drink of your beer. If your bride appears, it looks like your best friend has two pints and you're drinking water. That's a cutout."

Harris swallowed a bite of sandwich. "Yikes. That's a lot of trouble to go through for a pint."

Max laughed. "It's plausible deniability. Except think in terms of billions of dollars. A small circle of close friends owns controlling interests in the businesses. Periodically these businesses, think oil and gas, or banking, or ski resorts, gives the owner a loan. The loan is unsecured and has a super low interest rate. The loan is never paid back, and the funds end up in an offshore account controlled by a shell company with layers of insulation, so no one knows who owns the shell company."

"Is that legal?" Harris popped a chip into his mouth.

Baxter snorted.

"Legality is relative when you control the business laws in your own country," Cindy said. "Anyway, there is nothing illegal about keeping money in a foreign or offshore bank account."

Max drained the dregs in the coffee cup. "The loans are meant to give the appearance of propriety. Plausible deniability. Some estimates are that the Russian president controls at least a hundred billion dollars using his friends as cutouts."

"Do you know the details?" Cindy's eyes were bright. "From your father's—"

"I know a bit. I've seen documents that paint a complex scheme of ownership through various shell companies, but they are way beyond my level of comprehension. But I doubt it's everything."

Baxter held out his hand. "Hand it over, and we'll have our experts sort it out."

Max shook his head. "It might come to that. But for now, I have another idea."

"How do you steal from the richest man in the world?" Cindy tapped a pencil on the table. "If you try to shut down one of his entities or drain one of his bank accounts, he will replace it tomorrow or pivot to a new one."

"That's right." Max poured coffee from the urn. "So how do we get his attention?" He sipped his coffee.

The room grew silent except for the smacking of Harris's lips.

"Let me walk you through my idea." Max attached a small laptop to a cable so the screen showed on the wall monitor. He clicked to show an image of a woman in her early twenties with straight, shoulder-length blonde hair and a bemused expression. She wore a designer jacket open to the waist to reveal porcelain-white skin, and she posed for the camera with a hand on a hip. Her hair was pulled back tight in a small bun. Max clicked to show a picture of the same woman, except this time she was dressed in riding gear, and she held a helmet and a crop. The woman posed next to a tall black horse with a coat that shimmered in the sunlight. In the background was a paddock surrounded by a white fence. Beyond the paddock was a line of trees and a white overcast sky.

"Meet Paulina Petrauskas, fashionista and world champion dressage rider who spends her time living and training in Germany." Max clicked a few more times to scroll through various images of the woman. There were surveillance images of the woman eating at a restaurant or strolling along the street with shopping bags on each arm. Dozens of pictures included Paulina riding horses while wearing tall riding boots, gray breeches, and a black tailcoat. "Paulina Petrauskas is the Russian president's secret illegitimate daughter. The media has published rumors, but I have evidence in my father's files. She lives and works in Germany and takes a Lithuanian name. Paulina doesn't have ties to the Russian president. No public ties, that is."

Baxter groaned and banged his phone on the table. "No, no, no! I forbid it. You're going to far!"

Max put his palms up. "What are you talking about?"

"You want to kill the Russian president's illegitimate daughter? I can't—"

Cindy yelped, and Harris set his sandwich down.

"Who said anything about killing her?" Max spread his arms. "What's wrong with you?"

Baxter sat and put up his hands.

Max shook his head. "Anyway, until recently, Paulina Petrauskas flew under the radar until a Russian tabloid claimed that she is the Russian president's illegitimate daughter, an allegation which he, of course, denied." Another image flashed on the screen. This one showed a young woman in a red singlet holding a Russian flag. The woman's arms were muscular, and her shoulders and traps were well defined. "This is Paulina's mother, famed Olympic wrestler Valeria Koblova, who won gold at the 1984 Olympic Games in the seventy-two-kilogram freestyle. Koblova and the Russian president were linked romantically for several years."

"Besides this tabloid, what evidence do you have that the Russian president is the father?" Baxter asked.

Max clicked a few more times and images of documents flashed. "Working with Stasko, we were able to marry documents from the Vienna Archive with bank records from Stasko's banking empire and draw a few conclusions. Paulina owns five properties sprinkled around Europe, each worth tens of millions of dollars. She owns them through a bewildering maze of shell companies and offshore bank accounts. The residences have been known to be used by the Russian president." More documents flashed. "We also have evidence that hundreds of millions of dollars of medical equipment purchased by the Russian government was sold to shell companies owned by Paulina, after which the equipment was then resold back to Russia at twice their value. This had the effect of draining millions from Russian coffers into Paulina's bank accounts. There is evidence of these kinds of transactions in a dozen other industries. Because of all these shady deals, Paulina is one of the richest women in the world." Max fished a thick folder of documents from his satchel and plopped it on the table. "It's all there."

Harris grinned. "She's a cutout."

"Very good." Max nodded once.

"Why does she live in Germany?" Cindy tapped a pen on her palm.

"The Germans are the best in the world at dressage." Max smirked and clicked, and another image opened that showed the profile of a shimmering oxblood-colored horse with white socks and a white nose standing on ivory gravel. A stone wall surrounded by greenery was in the background. "Meet Misty Blues. Bred and trained in Denmark, this Danish Warmblood has the dressage world in a lather. Reviewers claim he's the smartest and best-looking horse to appear on the dressage scene since Totilas sold for eleven million euros back in 2010, which was the single highest amount ever paid for a dressage horse. Misty Blues is expected to go for twice that amount."

Baxter set his phone on the table. "Twenty million for a bloody horse?"

"Yes, Callum. And guess who one of the bidders is?"

Harris finished his sandwich and crumpled the paper into a ball. "Paulina."

"Exactly. Paulina Petrauskas." Max clicked, and a photo of a bank ledger appeared. "I've been studying auctions, and they are tricky business. One can't simply show up to the auction of a dressage horse and make a bid. The auction is by invitation only, and funds must be deposited into escrow. It's a whole dog and pony show." Max chuckled at his own joke while Harris groaned.

"I don't understand the play." Cindy knitted her eyebrows. "Sure, Paulina wants the horse. But anyone can outbid her. It's a public auction, right?"

Baxter muttered under his breath. "The auction is rigged."

Max grinned. "Callum is right. Like I said, it's a private auction, invitation only. These horse communities are extremely small with a dozen people in the world willing to pay millions for a horse. The Russian president has rigged the auction so his daughter will win. She might not even know it."

"Why rig it? Why not just buy it?"

"It's all a facade to maintain deniability that he is her father."

"How has it been rigged?"

"There are only ten parties invited to the auction. The Russian president has placed five people in the auction, all of whom have no intention of winning the bid. The other five have either been threatened or paid off. It's his birthday gift to his daughter. The thrill of winning an auction for the most expensive dressage horse in history. She probably doesn't know the bidding has been rigged."

"You got this all from Stasko?" Cindy's eyes were wide.

Max nodded.

"So Stasko is going to enter the bidding?" Harris asked.

"Oh no." Max waved his hand sideways through the air. "That would take all the fun out of it."

Cindy grinned. "You're going to enter the bidding with Stasko's money."

"C would never give me twenty million euros. But Stasko can help get me into the auction. Stasko's bank provides the escrow account and holds the contract with the auction company. All I need is the MI6-provided identity and an airplane ticket to Berlin." Max's smile was ear to ear. "And I need a brand-new custom-tailored suit. And one of those James Bond gizmo watches."

Baxter shook his head. "The Russian president isn't going to like it. He might try to dissuade you."

Max rubbed his palms together. "I'm counting on it."

The secure Blackphone buzzed in his pocket and Max removed it to see a familiar caller ID. *Magnolia Massage*

Parlor. He walked out of the conference room and into the hall before he hit the button to answer. "Hello, Spencer. Any word on Arina?"

"About all I can do is confirm the MI6 story," Spencer White said. "The sheriff here is a friend. I talked to the deputy who was on duty outside her hospital room. Earnest kind of guy. Feels terrible about what happened. But not much else to report."

"Better men than he have been bested by my sister."

"I told him that he was dealing with a pro. Anyway, he was gone from the door for ten minutes. Enough time to get a coffee from the machine and stretch his legs. I saw the footage from the camera over the side entrance. The camera is one of those motion sensor jobs that only fires when it needs to. Decent visibility in the darkness. But it was overhead, so it showed her walk from the side door right as an SUV arrived. She got in and the vehicle took off before her door was shut. I think it's her, but I can't be a hundred percent sure. She didn't appear to be under any kind of duress."

Max grunted. "Any markers on the SUV?"

"It was a late model Chevy Tahoe. Silver. There are a million of those out here in Colorado."

Max was silent.

"There is one more thing," Spencer said.

"Tell me."

"I got the sheriff to help me interview the nurse who was in charge of the floor Arina was on. The only thing that stands out is Arina received a package a few days ago. Addressed to her at the hospital. For security reasons, it was opened by the deputy on duty. A different guy. He indicated it was a mobile phone. There didn't seem to be anything wrong with it, so they gave it to Arina and tossed the packaging."

"That's like giving candy to a toddler. What kind of phone was it?"

"Samsung, I think. Didn't look like a burner. No one remembers if there was a return address on the package. At the time, they didn't think anything of it. She might call you."

"Right. Thanks, Spencer. I owe you."

"You missed the drywall, but I'm about to put in an oak flooring if you can get here."

"Soon, my friend. Soon." Max ended the call and stuck the phone in his pocket. If Arina was going to call, she would have already.

Retired Lieutenant General Vincent Brown Found Murdered

The news article was buried on the third page of *The Washington Post* and generated little comment among those inside the Beltway. Most of the harried government and private sector workers on their commute via automobile or Washington, DC's Metro system consumed their news via a social media feed or scrolled the newspaper's website on a tiny screen. Few public eyeballs found the article and those that did kept scrolling.

However, the headline triggered alerts on two analysts' computers. Kaamil Marafi was distracted by the alert and scanned the article before routing it to Kate's phone. Goshawk, who also had configured an alert to be notified whenever Lieutenant General Brown's name appeared in the news, read the article with more interest. Details were sketchy, but Brown, who was a lieutenant general in the Marine Corps and the deputy commander of the United States Cyber Command, was found facedown in the Potomac River on the banks of the Red Rock Wilderness Overlook outside Leesburg, Virginia. The cause of death was reported as suspicious, but no other details were provided. Brown had a clandestine life as the hacker who called himself Bluefish and who pursued Goshawk and Max until Max took him off the playing field, so to speak.

But why did General Brown end up dead?

Before she routed the article to Max, Goshawk hacked into the Leesburg Police Department servers, where she found a report of the general's death that included pictures of the body along with a detailed description of the body's condition and the coroner's report. The general appeared to have been beaten to death and had sustained wounds consistent with walling, a torture technique where the victim is slammed repeatedly into a wall. The investigation was taken over by NCIS, the Naval Criminal Investigative Service, who maintained jurisdiction over USMC Lieutenant General Vincent Brown.

Goshawk packaged up the various news articles and police reports and sent them to Max's phone.

TWENTY-TWO

Berlin, Germany

They checked into the Rocco Forte, a baroque five-star luxury hotel, under assumed names. Max posed as a wealthy American from Kentucky and strolled in with custom-stitched cowboy boots under his tailored suit. He dispensed with the cowboy hat and chose to let the boots talk for themselves. Understated cowboy, he called it. He presented the manager at hotel reception with an American Express Black Card and was delighted when the manager upgraded him to a suite. "My assistant's room goes on my card as well." He pointed his chin at Cindy.

Cindy handed over an American passport under the name Cynthia Smith and kept a frown on her pretty face. Her hair was pulled back in a severe shoulder-length ponytail, and her charcoal pantsuit was pressed. A set of pearls hung around her neck, and she had applied skin tanning cream to transform her pale neck into a sun-drenched tan. Everyone knew Americans got too much sun. She carried a leather case and was all business. She was awarded a smaller suite adjoining her boss's palatial five-room apartment. When they got to their rooms, they both walked out to the shared balcony, which overlooked the Bebelplatz, a public square bordered by the State Opera, St Hedwig's Cathedral, and Humboldt University. The buildings around the square were of neoclassical architecture, and the distinct green dome of St Hedwig's Cathedral dominated the skyline. The cathedral was damaged by Allied bombing in World War II but was restored in the 1960s in the postmodern style.

Max put his hands on the marble railing. The old Max would have lit a cigarette during moments like this. Instead, he ignored the craving. "This is where the SS and Hitler Youth groups burned 20,000 books in 1933. Some of them were by Karl Marx and Albert Einstein."

Cindy sucked in her breath. "Why did they do that?"

"It was a symbolic effort aimed at free thinkers and intellectuals. Like any authoritarian movement, the Nazis were threatened by the intelligentsia. In order to take and hold power, autocratic regimes need gullible masses who are willing to believe any propaganda told to them by men in power. The educated classes, including university professors, writers, doctors, and even lawyers were a threat to the Nazis. By burning the books, the Nazis signaled that the teachings of Marx were wrong." Max shrugged. "Such subversion techniques have worked for hundreds of years, especially in Russia."

The square was filled with a display of 200 colorful bear sculptures, each over six feet in height and designed by different artists. "I like the bears better," Cindy said.

Once they were settled, Max and Cindy convened in Max's room to go over their plans. A secure video link was established from Cindy's laptop to the Moonraker conference room, where Baxter and Harris sat. Baxter fiddled with an unlit pipe as the team walked through the operation for the tenth time.

Cindy's addition to the field team was fought against by Baxter, who suggested they send one of MI6's more experienced field operatives. After an hour-long debate that threatened to turn into a row, Max explained that he needed Cindy's skills with her computer. When Harris signaled that he couldn't travel because his dog was ill, Cindy's fate was sealed, and Baxter grudgingly gave in.

The plan was simple. Max, using the false American identity provided by MI6 and funds provided by Erich Stasko, had bought his way into the auction. One of the previous attendees took ill after an MI6 team tainted his wine, making him unable to participate in the in-person-only auction. Coincidentally, Max was made available as a last-minute attendee by Erich Stasko's bank, who provided the escrow and financial bona fides on behalf of Max's fake identity.

Max paced in the hotel suite as Cindy banged away on her laptop. "It's only a matter of time," Max said. "When they catch wind of me, the Russian president's team will be in contact to ensure Paulina wins the bidding. What do you think it'll be? A threat or a payoff?"

"Payoff." Cindy nodded her head. "Definitely. They won't threaten an American."

After the afternoon-long teleconference with London to iron out the details of the operation, Cindy folded her laptop and the two assumed their identities. The spring evening was chilly, so they took jackets and accepted a black car ride from their hotel to the Mandala Hotel, where they had secured a reservation at Restaurant Facil, a

Michelin two-star rated spot frequented by Berlin's nouveau riche.

During transit, and while they ate, Max watched for anyone who might be watching them. It was difficult to pick out any tail in the heavy Berlin traffic on the short drive over. But in the Mandala hotel lobby were two men who eyed them from near the bar. Although the men wore sport coats, their demeanor and attire were rougher than the rest of the diners, all of whom were chic and stylish. Max noted gun bulges under their jackets, and he took a chair positioned to keep them in eyesight.

When the waiter appeared, Max chose the gourmet menu and enjoyed sunchoke and yellow beetroot salad, trout caviar, oysters with imperial caviar, pork belly, breast of pigeon, and wagyu flank steak, and finished with a poppy seed and hazelnut pear. Cindy, giddy at the experience, chose the vegetarian option and exclaimed with delight as the parade of waiters brought gazpacho of elderberry, miso green beans, lemon risotto, artichokes with watermelon and a green called *lovage*. A serving of baked eggplant with seaweed, fennel, and cream of stewed vegetables followed, and she finished with a dessert made of cherry, pistachio, and shiso. They ate with reverence, surrounded by a bamboo garden, and sipped a French burgundy. By dessert, the two burley men had disappeared.

When the last plates were cleared, Max ordered an espresso, and when the bill came, he paid with the Black Card.

"Callum will have a heart attack." Cindy hid a laugh behind her hand. Her voice was a little slurred, and her eyes were glassy. Max had taken it easy on the wine as he kept an eye on the two men.

Max shrugged. "You can thank Erich Stasko." He held

Cindy's chair and she leaned on him as they walked to the door. The waiter held their coats, and Cindy took his arm as they strode through the hotel's lobby.

"Byron? Byron, is that you?" The voice projected across the lobby and belonged to one of the men who watched them in the restaurant. "I can't believe it's you. Byron!"

Here we go. To Cindy he whispered, "This is it. I'm going to put you into a taxi, okay?" They stopped in the hotel's transom as Max reacted to the voice hailing them. A uniformed doorman held the exterior door open.

Cindy held on to his arm. "Don't leave me."

"You'll be all right." Max spoke into Cindy's ear. "Better for me to have this conversation myself. They want to buy me off. Let's meet back at the hotel." Max addressed the doorman in German. "Get this woman a taxi please. The Rocco Forte."

"Right away, sir." The young man took Cindy's arm and directed her through the door. A yellow cab door opened and Cindy stepped into the car.

Max turned to walk back into the lobby as a broad-chested man waving a cigar in the air clapped him on the shoulders. He towered over Max's six-foot-four frame. A colossal head was set on immense shoulders and his suit jacket and shirt stretched over a broad chest. His free hand clenched a rocks glass with a brown liquid. Cigar smoke puffed from his mouth as he talked. "Byron! Of all the gin joints! Do you remember me?"

"I can't say I do." Max feigned disinterest.

"It's Ivan Babić!" The large man spoke loud enough to hurt Max's ear. "From that safari in Kenya last year!" Pulling Max close, he huffed into his ear. "Let's go have a chat, shall we?"

Max let himself be guided into the hotel's bar, a modern

pink-hued affair with long yellow floor-to-ceiling wall sconces. Ivan steered him to where another imposing man leaned against the bar, who wore a coat and turtleneck pulled up into a fleshy chin. Both men were about forty and in that stage where muscular men turn to fat. Strong, but slow. Blunt instruments sent to intimidate.

The only other occupants of the bar were a couple huddled in a booth where they held an intimate conversation. A waitress delivered a round of martinis and cleared glasses from their table.

Ivan maneuvered Max so he was between the two men and waved over the bartender. The woman behind the bar was dressed in a white shirt and black apron, and her hair was shaved on one side and long on the other. A nose ring sparkled in the overhead lights. "What will it be, gentlemen?"

"Mila here was telling me about the bourbon scene here in Berlin, weren't you, Mila?" Ivan put a meaty paw on the bar.

Mila smiled. "That's right. We have over 250 whiskey producers here in the State of Brandenburg, more than twice as many as Scotland."

"Which do you recommend, Mila?" Max was dwarfed by the large men on either side of him.

The bartender grabbed a squat bottle adorned with a black stallion wearing a German Pickelhaube, the spiked helmet worn in the nineteenth and twentieth centuries by Prussian and German armies. The black label read "Preussischer Whiskey."

Ivan roared with laughter and put his arm around Max's shoulder. "The bottle has a horse! How perfect! One for each of us, Mila."

When three whiskeys were delivered, the bear of a man

pulled Max close. "We know your name isn't Byron." Ivan laughed loud enough to startle the bartender before he lowered his voice. "Isn't that right, Mikhail Asimov?"

Something jabbed into his side, down low, beneath the level of the bar, out of sight of the bartender. It was on the side of Ivan's friend. Max stiffened as he tipped his glass to his mouth.

"My friend has a stiletto poked into your side. One wrong move and he'll shove that thing so far into you that it will go through your lung and into your heart. Understand?"

"You're not going to kill me," Max said. "Tell your friend to put the knife away before it ends up in his jugular. I'm happy to talk, which is why I let you find me."

Ivan appeared to consider this before he nodded to the other man. The pressure at Max's side disappeared.

"Now what do you want?"

The larger man threw back the last of his drink, faced Max, and leaned an elbow on the bar. "A message from our friend. You know who I mean?"

Max raised his eyebrows in feigned pretense at surprise. "He sent you guys all the way to Berlin with a note? Why didn't he just call?"

"Funny guy. Isn't he a funny guy, Yuri?" Ivan roared with pretend laughter. He took the cigar from where it rested on an ashtray and took a puff. When he turned, he blew smoke into Max's face. "He wants you to leave town tonight. There is a redeye to London, and there are two seats in business class, one for you and one for your cute little assistant. You're out of here."

The mention of Cindy made Max stiffen, and he hid his discomfort with a sip of the whiskey. A vision of the heavy glass slamming against Ivan's temple appeared and went.

"I'm here on business, which is none of his business. Twenty-four hours, then we're leaving. Tell your friend that we appreciate his generosity, but that we'll take our flight tomorrow night."

Ivan jabbed at Max's chest with a sausage-shaped finger. "You're not listening. The boss wants you gone. Tonight. It's not a request."

Max considered grabbing the finger and bending it back and putting the man on his knees. Might result in a stiletto to the kidney. But he brushed the finger to the side. "Remind your boss that he's not my boss. I'm here to buy a horse, and when that's done, we'll be on our way." He pushed away from the bar and walked in the direction of the entryway.

"Mikhail Asimov," Ivan called out in a mocking tone. "He might not be the boss of you, but he's the boss of your cute little assistant."

TWENTY-THREE

Berlin, Germany

Max spun around to see Ivan smiling. The table of martini drinkers rose to their feet and stumbled past, leaving the three men and the bartender alone in the cramped room.

"What did you say?" Max clenched his fists.

The massive Russian leered and sucked in his breath. "It's an insurance policy. The boss doesn't need his business disturbed by whatever you're planning." He shrugged his massive shoulders. "He figured you might need a little, uh..." He turned to his friend, who piped in.

"Persuasion." Yuri beamed.

"Yeah, persuasion." Ivan leaned one arm on the bar and sucked on his cigar.

Max took two steps and slammed the palm of his hand into Ivan's face, which crumpled the cigar and broke the big man's nose.

Ivan grunted at the strike, swayed on his feet, but remained upright. His eyes narrowed.

In a fluid motion, Max grabbed Ivan by the head and brought his face down into his knee, which connected with the broken nose with a crunch. Ivan crashed to the floor. *The bigger they are, the harder they fall.*

Yuri reacted faster than Max calculated, but the Russian's hand got caught in his pocket. As Ivan knelt on the floor on all fours, Max headbutted Yuri while the thug fumbled with something in his pocket.

"Let me help you with that." Max yanked at Yuri's arm and the stiletto clattered to the tile. Dazed from the head strike, Yuri fumbled on the floor, but Max raised his knee and crushed it into the thug's mouth. A white chunk of something fell to the floor. One of Yuri's teeth.

The thin knife lay near Max's shoe. He snatched the stiletto, grabbed Yuri by the back of his jacket, and shoved the tip into his neck far enough to draw a bead of blood. "Tell me where she is. Now. Or this knife goes into Yuri's neck."

Yuri mumbled something through his bloody mouth.

"Can't hear you. Speak louder, Yuri." Max shifted the knife tip from his neck to under his chin and pushed the blade in and blood flowed freely. Yuri yelped. "Oh, you can talk. Tell me what you did with her."

Ivan rose to a knee, stumbled, and caught himself on the bar. Max gripped the knife handle in his fist and hit Ivan in the side of his jaw, sending the big man crashing back to the floor. Max grabbed Yuri around the neck so he had the man's collar in his left fist and showed the Russian thug the stiletto blade. It was an inch from the man's eye. "If you don't want to walk around wearing a patch for the rest of your days, tell me where she is. You have three seconds. One..."

Yuri struggled in Max's grip, so Max thrust the blade

until it touched the man's eye. The Russian thug clenched his lids tight, and the blade wavered in the struggle.

"Two..." Max poked the knife tip a millimeter into Yuri's eyelid.

The Russian thug moaned and went limp. "House... safe house..."

There was a commotion and shouts in German behind them. Max, his fist tight on Yuri's collar, whipped Yuri around to see a single hotel security guard standing in the bar's entryway. The guard's eyes were wide.

"Back, stand back," Max shouted in German at the guard while he brandished the blade against the Russian's neck. The bartender gripped the bar at the far end, her eyes wide.

"Ivan, empty your pockets." When the big man stayed motionless, Max kicked him in the ribs. "Empty your pockets."

A phone, a wallet, a pistol, and a roll of cash tumbled to the ground. Max pushed Yuri against the bar, shoved the items in his pockets, and grabbed Yuri's jacket collar. "Okay, Yuri, we're going for a drive." Max yanked the thug from the bar, and while holding the knife to his neck, force-marched him at the hotel security guard.

The guard, a young blond man in a uniform with a curled cord running to his ear, talked into his sleeve. He carried no weapon and moved aside as Max and Yuri approached. Max thrust Yuri through the bar's entrance and into the lobby. As Max strode past the security guard, Max tipped his head at the bar. "Take that man into custody. He's a Russian killer on Interpol's most wanted list."

The security guard's mouth opened. He stopped talking into his sleeve and stepped over to Ivan as the big man writhed on the ground. When Max looked back, the guard had trussed him with plastic cuffs.

Max propelled Yuri into the lobby and hustled him through the double doors and out under the hotel's portico. A black BMW sat idle, where a white-haired gentleman helped a lady from the passenger seat. The valet stood near the driver's side door while he jotted a note on a ticket. As the lady stepped away from the car, Max shoved Yuri into the passenger seat, slammed his fist into Yuri's jaw, kicked the door closed, and ran around to the driver's side.

As the valet yelled and the white-haired gentleman gasped, Max jammed the car into gear and hurtled out onto Potsdamer Straße. Wheels screeched and horns blared as Max gunned the engine, fishtailed, fought for control, and sped east. Yuri wiped his bloody face and hung on. When the car was under control, Max hit Yuri in the temple with a closed fist. *Can't have him getting his bearings.*

"Toss your phone, Yuri." Max opened his window and threw out Ivan's mobile.

Yuri's movements were slow, so Max reached over and patted him down, reached into his jacket pocket, and tossed his mobile out onto the busy road.

"Where's the safe house, Yuri?"

Blood and saliva dripped from Yuri's face. He rode in the passenger seat in a daze.

Max merged left and took a hard left at Ebertstraße. To their left was the massive Grober Tiergarten, Berlin's largest park at 520 acres, and the Victory Column, always lit at night, that celebrated the Prussian victory in the Danish-Prussian War of 1864. Yuri scrabbled at the door handle. With his left hand on the wheel, Max grabbed Yuri by the back of the neck and slammed his face into the dash. The Brandenburg Gate appeared ahead, and Max fought with the wheel to navigate the curve. Another left put them on a wide three-lane boulevard with the park on both sides. Max hit the brakes and screeched into a parallel parking spot.

He was out and yanking Yuri by the collar before his captive was able to react. The occasional car sped by, but there were no pedestrians as Max manhandled the Russian into a stand of trees. Moonlight filtered through the tree branches that held spring buds but no mature leaves. At the base of a tree trunk, Max took Yuri by the collar and rammed his face repeatedly into the course bark of a thick oak. "Where, damn it? Where is the safe house?"

Yuri said something Max was unable to hear.

Max dropped the thug onto his stomach and wrenched the man's right hand behind him and pushed, and Yuri yelped in pain. Max pressed the knife against the index finger of Yuri's right hand. "Are you right-handed, Yuri? Is this your trigger finger?" Max sawed at the skin with the blade.

"Okay, okay," Yuri panted. "I'll tell you. Don't. Please don't. It's close to here. I can show you where it is."

"The address. Give me the address."

Yuri spat out four numbers and a street name.

Max yanked his captive to his feet and hustled him back to the car, where he used the BMW's fob to pop the trunk. After frisking Yuri one more time, Max pushed him into the trunk and slammed the lid.

TWENTY-FOUR

Berlin, Germany

Haste mattered. Once the Russian team learned of Ivan's incarceration and Yuri's disappearance, there was no telling what might become of Cindy. As he pulled out into traffic, he considered alerting MI6. He yanked his phone out, put his thumb over the speed dial to Baxter, decided against it, and tapped the address Yuri gave him into the BMW's GPS system.

The location was in a neighborhood south of his position called Kreuzberg. It was a gentrified district once popular with squatters and artists that had grown into a multicultural hub of nightlife, cafes, and countercultural life-sized artwork. Max cared about none of that as he flipped a left to go around the Victory Column and made another left to skirt the southern edge of the park.

The safe house was on a narrow street barely wide enough for two cars to pass. No pedestrians were in sight. Both sides of the street were lined with row homes, the majority of which were run-down with cracked stairs and shattered exterior light bulbs. The vehicles that were parked bumper to bumper were dented and several were missing side mirrors. MI6 put their safe houses in upscale neighborhoods. The Russians chose squalor.

Max knew from experience that any Russian safe house was well monitored with closed circuit cameras on the front and rear and would have at least four well-armed and capable men inside. The Russians keep a low profile, and the neighbors would be clueless as to the activities going on next door. Max did a circuit around the block and took the rear alleyway. The three-story row home roofs were steeply pitched, and there was no easy access through the windows. A garage was all that was visible in the rear. After he motored past the garage, Max found a parking spot on the street.

There is only one way in. Through the front door.

At the touch of a button, the trunk popped open, and Max grabbed Yuri by the lapels and dragged him from the car. The Russian thug was dazed, and he had dried blood on his face, but he was conscious. "We're going for a walk. One false move and this stiletto goes into your kidney. Do you understand?"

When Yuri nodded, Max thumped the trunk closed and pushed Yuri ahead. "There is a camera over the door." Yuri coughed up mucus. "It's how we check on visitors. Anyone not on our list shows and we ignore them."

"I'm counting on that." Max gripped Yuri's collar as they marched along the street. "How many are there?"

"Four."

"If you're lying to me, Yuri..."

When they got to the address, Yuri walked up the steps

with Max hidden behind him. "Bang on the door." Max kept his head low.

The front doors on the row house were narrow doubles, with one side for opening and the other for seeing through. A vestibule was on the other side of the window, and an interior door was beyond the vestibule. The home was dark, and the exterior light bulb was smashed. Dark curtains or sheets were over the front windows.

Yuri rapped on the door.

"Pound harder."

After tilting his head to the camera, Yuri banged his fist on the wood.

"Did you look at the camera?"

"Da."

Is this going to work?

It took another round of pounding before footsteps rang out behind the door. A voice appeared as the door cracked open. "Yuri, what are you—"

When Max heaved and pushed Yuri through the door, there was a tangle of arms and legs as Yuri and a man inside crashed to the vestibule floor. Stiletto in hand, Max stepped over Yuri and drove the blade into the second man's stomach under the ribcage and angled the strike upward so the knife tip found the heart. After he removed the knife, Max searched the man and found a Makarov in a shoulder holster. He slipped the knife into his pocket and grabbed Yuri by the collar and jerked him to his feet. "Want to live?"

"Da."

"If there is one hair out of place on her head, you're going to suffer a long and agonizing death." Max kicked the dying Russian's legs so the body was fully in the vestibule and pulled the front door shut. With Yuri held in front, Max pushed through the door into the main level.

The living area was separated by walls from the kitchen and dining room. Wallpaper peeled from the walls, and the carpet was stained. Furniture from the 1980s was scattered through the room. A Caucasian man sat at a card table with a vodka bottle, cards, and Styrofoam food containers on top of it. The room smelled like fried potatoes. At the commotion in the entryway, he rose to his feet.

Max shot him twice with the Makarov. The shots rang out in the small room and the man pinwheeled his arms as he fell. His leg kicked out, the card table fell, and the bottle crashed to the floor.

"That's two. Were you lying to me, Yuri?"

"Viktor! Viktor! Kill the—"

Max rapped the gun's handle against Yuri's temple and the Russian thug collapsed. A standing lamp was against the wall, and Max yanked out the cord and used it to bind Yuri's wrists. With a yank, he pulled the cord tight. A quick check of Yuri's neck indicated a weak pulse, but the man was out cold. Max left him there.

Pistol out, he went in search of Viktor.

He found Viktor in the basement, where the thug stood behind Cindy. It wasn't clear who was more scared, Viktor or Viktor's captive. Cindy was tied to a chair and wore the same clothes they dined in earlier. Her eyes were frozen wide open, her breath came in rapid bursts, and her chest heaved. Viktor was tall and skinny with dark hair cut short and stubble-covered cheeks. Perspiration beaded on the thug's forehead. A gold chain was around his neck, and a tan leather jacket was over a white T-shirt. The gun was held to Cindy's temple with a shaking hand, and the Russian's eyes were as wide as Cindy's. The thug's finger was curled around the trigger. At the rate his hand trembled, the gun might go off at any second.

"Cindy, are you hurt?"

Cindy shook her head with a jerky movement.

"Viktor, put the gun on the ground."

"Nyet! I shoot her if you come closer." Viktor shifted to put the bulk of his body behind Cindy.

Max stopped but held the Makarov on Viktor, who was ten meters away. The basement was lit by several bare bulbs that hung from a low ceiling, and they stood on a dirt floor. A rusty washing machine and dryer with its door open sat to the left, while dusty boxes were stacked along the far wall. A dark furnace with octopus-like ductwork sat in a corner. A vision of Max's incarceration in the basement of a KGB safe house in Lukow, Poland, flashed in his mind. Nathan Abrams had been in the process of relieving Max of his fingernails when Spencer White appeared with an automatic rifle.

A sob burst from Cindy, she shifted her head, and for a split second, Viktor's pistol barrel slipped from her sweat-covered temple.

Max shot Viktor in the forehead, and Cindy screamed at the report.

A tiny hole appeared between Viktor's eyes and the Russian tipped over backwards. The pistol clattered to the floor.

Max rushed to kick the pistol away, but the thug was dead.

Cindy's scream faded as she ran out of air. She fought for breath and let loose a scream that pierced Max's eardrums. After checking Viktor's vitals to ensure he was dead, he used the stiletto to free Cindy, who threw her arms around him.

"Some lungs you have there." Max patted her back. "We have to go. Can you walk?"

"I think... so..."

With his arm around her back and under her shoulder, he helped her to her feet. After a stumble, she gathered herself and followed Max from the basement, up the wooden stairs, and into the main room, where they found Yuri struggling.

Max kicked him and squatted next to him. "Yuri, even though you lied to me, I'm going to leave you alive. I want you to give our friend a message. Can you do that for me?"

The Russian's face was a mess of blood and mucus. When he opened his mouth and sputtered, there were gaps where his teeth should be.

"Tell him that if he ever tries a stunt like this again, I'm going to hunt him down and cut his balls off and shove them in his mouth." He looked at Cindy, who leaned against the wall between where the living room led to the foyer. Her eyes were glazed and she swayed on her feet. Max shook Yuri. "Repeat the message."

When the Russian spoke, his words were slurred. "If he trith it again, you're going to hunt him down and cut hith ballth off and shove them in his mouf."

"You got it."

Yuri wiggled on the ground. "Can't feel my hands."

Max loosened the cord but left Yuri's hands tied. "You might want to get outta here soon, Yuri. I'm going to call in an anonymous tip to the polizei and blow this safe house."

Max stood, took Cindy's arm, and helped her out the door and into the fresh air. "I'm sorry you had to see that."

Cindy leaned her weight on his shoulder. "He deserved it."

―――

On the way back to the Rocco Forte hotel, Max introduced Cindy to the countersurveillance method called the surveillance detection route, or SDR for short. It was after midnight, and traffic was sparse, which made spotting a tail easier.

"I thought that stood for Software Defined Radio." Cindy's voice was hoarse.

Max led her to the nearest hotel, a Sheraton, where Cindy detoured into a bathroom. "Don't dally." He did his best to wash the blood from his knuckles and splashed cold water on his face.

She emerged a few minutes later with her hair somewhat under control and her face washed. The doorman hailed them a cab, which they took to a Radisson Blu hotel, where they walked through the property, cut through a rear door, and walked two blocks over to the Capri Hotel, which resembled a cross between an ancient Mayan temple and a Soviet prison.

"This is exhausting," Cindy said as they stepped into another taxi.

"Tell me about it. I spend too much of my time doing this shit." Max craned his neck to watch behind them. There were no cars behind them.

Two taxicabs later, they arrived at the Rocco Forte hotel to find an empty lobby and a single night manager behind the reception desk. There were no authorities waiting to ask questions about the row at the bar. Max asked the manager for a bottle of their best bourbon to be sent to the room and hustled Cindy to his suite. By that time, Cindy was practically sleepwalking. He helped her into his king-sized bed, where she burrowed into the sheets and fell asleep. It was a simple matter to move her belongings to his room, after which he wedged a chair under the door to his suite and another to the connecting door and went on a search for a cigarette. When he realized there were none in the hotel suite, he collapsed into a couch.

Cindy lay on her side, blonde hair spread on a pillow, shoulders rising and falling in slumber. *What a trooper.* When the room service knock came, Max gripped the Makarov pistol and stood next to the door. One way to get shot through a door is to use the eye hole. The shooter sees the movement behind the peephole and knows your location. Max had employed the trick on occasion himself.

"Who is it?"

"Room service, sir."

"Wait there."

"Aye, sir."

Gun up, Max removed the chair from the connecting door, crossed through Cindy's room, and listened at the door to the hallway. Silence. He cracked the door and glanced into the hallway. Empty, except for the night manager, a cart with a bottle of brown liquid, an ice bucket, and two crystal glasses.

"Bring it here." Max lowered his voice, but it startled the man.

The night manager wheeled the cart to Max, who handed him a one hundred euro note from Yuri's money clip and pulled the cart into the room. He replaced the chairs under each door and wheeled the cart into his suite where Cindy slumbered.

He did a double take at the bottle. It was the same

brand he was served at the bar with the two Russians. Squat bottle with the horse head on the cap. Preussischer Whiskey. *Has to be a coincidence.*

Max dropped an ice cube into a glass and splashed a measure of the whiskey over the ice cube. He was about to sink into a chair when he noticed a package on the cart next to a row of folded napkins.

It was a small envelope with a lump in the middle.

The envelope started ringing.

TWENTY-FIVE

Berlin, Germany

The trolly brought by the night manager sat in the center of Max's hotel suite. It was draped with a cloth that covered all four sides to hide the industrial underpinnings of the metal cart. An ice bucket was on top of the cart, next to the bottle of German bourbon. Two ornately folded napkins were arranged next to a pair of ice tongs. A thin vase with a single flower stood in the center. Everything was ordinary about the room service delivery except for the envelope.

The envelope was ringing.

Max eased aside the cloth to look under the cart. No blinking lights appeared, but it was too dark to see whether anything, a bomb maybe, was secured to the underside of the metal cart. He removed the bottle, the glass, the envelope, and the ice bucket and slid the cloth from the cart.

Don't let there be a bomb.

The cart had a handle on each end and a single steel

shelf under the main platform. It was empty. There was no bomb.

The ringing stopped.

A glance at the bed revealed Cindy still lay on her side snoring gently.

Max poured himself a whiskey, took a gulp, and poured another measure before he fell into a chair along with the envelope. When he ripped it open, a mobile phone tumbled out. It was thin and small, like a burner. He flipped it open.

The writing on the screen was in German, which he was able to read. The phone was indeed a burner, a disposable mobile phone charged with a set amount of time and difficult to trace. As he examined the number in the recent call list, the phone rang again.

Max thumbed the answer button. "Hello."

Two beats went by. "Mikhail Asimov, I presume."

The voice was familiar. "Dmitry Kozov. If you're calling about your boys, don't waste your breath."

A chuckle. "Lots more where I got those from."

"You might want to recruit better if you want to play in the big leagues."

"The sports clichés. They told me that you'd westernized after all that time in the West. Gone native. Soft."

"Ask Yuri who's gone soft." Max took a chug of the whiskey. "What do you want? I need sleep before I go shopping for a new dressage horse."

"That's why I'm calling."

"If you're going to threaten me, don't bother. Judging by those goons you sent, my odds are good. Besides, I've been meaning to get into dressage. The women are cute in those little outfits."

"The boss has an offer."

"I'm listening."

"Not on the phone. In person."

"Love to. I'm booked through tomorrow. Available after that."

"Now."

Max snorted. "That's not happening. Like I said, I have an auction tomorrow afternoon. After that—"

"We both know you have no need for a horse, Mikhail Asimov. Your little gambit worked. You have his attention. I suggest you not squander it."

Don't over close. It was another one of his father's admonishments. It means that once the decision is made or the conclusion reached, move on. Drop it. Let it go. "With your little war going on over there in Ukraine, I assume he's in Moscow."

"I will neither confirm nor deny his location."

Max stood and paced. "Fine. Tomorrow morning, the Gendarmenmarkt." The Gendarmenmarkt is a public square in Berlin near the Berlin concert hall.

Kozov chuckled. "The location will be of our choosing."

Max splashed more bourbon into his glass. "Okay, Dmitry. It's your barrel of monkeys."

"The Hellmann Schlosshotel. Do you know it?"

"I can find it."

"Be there at 8:00 a.m. We have the whole hotel, so when you arrive, pull up like a normal guest and you will be directed."

The transmission ended.

The entryway to the Schlosshotel Berlin was a narrow but tall wrought iron gate set into off-white stone walls topped with ornate lanterns and gargoyle carvings. The building itself was two stories of white stone capped with a third story in orange tile. The briefing email provided by MI6 indicated there were fifty-three rooms in the former mansion, and that Chanel's Karl Lagerfeld designed the interior. Max wasn't sure who Karl Lagerfeld was, but Cindy was impressed and disappointed she wasn't able to see it.

After a sleepless night on the settee with the Makarov balanced on his chest while Cindy snoozed, Max got her to Berlin's executive airport and bustled her onto the waiting MI6 jet. She would arrive safe in London before Max set foot in the Schlosshotel. She protested but was overruled by both Baxter and Max.

A variety of luxury vehicles were parked in the hotel's front drive. Two Bentleys, a Lamborghini, and a handful of more pedestrian BMWs. The portico was opulent but tiny, and Max ignored the uniformed valet and backed his rental Mercedes between a stretch Bentley and a two-seat roadster of a make he didn't place. He locked the car, pocketed the fob, and waved off the valet on his way through the two-story-high doors and into the lobby.

A handful of uniformed men wearing paramilitary gear and toting automatic rifles were stationed around the perimeter of what might be the most opulent hotel lobby Max had ever seen. Three-story windows towered overhead, dwarfing the massive faux-candle chandeliers. An eclectic mixture of leather and upholstered furniture was gathered in pods on a floor tiled in taupes and muted golds. The far wall was red, which was off-putting, and a staircase with an ornately carved railing was to the right. The bodyguards eyed him as he strode into the center of the lobby where he was stopped. A guard waved a wand over Max's body before he patted Max down. The only thing he found was the BMW's key fob, which he removed. "Phone? Weapons?"

Max shrugged. His pockets were empty. His phone, his grandfather's lighter, and even Yuri's money clip had gone on the MI6 jet along with Cindy.

"Mikhail Asimov." The voice arose from the staircase where a statuesque woman stood in a crisp blue suit. Her hair flowed over her shoulder, but her blouse was fastened at the neck. "This way, please."

Max followed the woman up the stairs and into an event space with cathedral ceilings. Their heels clicked on the tile as they strode through the cavernous room and up another sweeping staircase. His escort turned her head as she walked. "Can I get you anything? Coffee, water perhaps?"

"I've been warned not to consume anything, nor touch anything while I'm here."

The woman nodded. More guards were stationed along the way, and two immense men flanked a pair of double doors.

The woman stopped and put her hand on one of the double doors. "Are you ready?"

"Mikhail Asimov. We meet again."

The voice was Dmitry Kozov's. The Russian president's right-hand man leaned against a regal-looking wooden chair at the end of a long conference table. The chair was upholstered with red velvet and an ornate carving of birds topped the back. A dozen identical chairs were positioned around the table but were empty. Kozov was impeccably dressed in a tailored suit and crisp white shirt, but the bags under his eyes were heavy.

"Let's make this quick. I've got a horse to buy." He winked at Kozov.

"I see you more as a racehorse kind of man." Kozov opened his suit jacket, where a pistol was trapped in his waistband.

"I like seeing the ladies dressed in their dressage outfits."

"Don't we all." Kozov's face was more pallid than the last time Max met him. The dark mole popped in contrast to his white skin.

The room was a tall-ceilinged drawing room that someone had converted into a boardroom. It was probably that Lagerfeld fellow. A wall of windows behind Kozov overlooked a garden in bloom. The walls were covered with impressionist artwork. "Since you rented the entire place, maybe they'll let you take home the paintings." Max stroked his chin while he admired an oil. "I always confuse Manet and Monet. Now which one married his mistress?" When Kozov said nothing, Max turned and put out his hands. "Danny Ocean? *Ocean's Eleven?*"

Kozov stared at him.

Max shook his head. "So where is your boss?"

"Like I said, we won't reveal that information."

"I'm here to make a deal." Max strode to the table, selected a chair at random, and sat. "We can help each other, your boss and me. Are you able to make a deal on his behalf?"

Kozov remained standing. "All he cares about is you not bidding on a horse."

"Somehow I doubt that's all he cares about."

"What else does he care about?"

"Besides his invasion of Ukraine?" Max drummed his fingers on the table.

"Goading us will not get you far."

Max frowned. "As you both know, the four councils of the kommissariat operate with impunity in Russia and Ukraine. They control a significant amount of the oil and natural gas transactions and they're bleeding your country dry. They're stealing from your boss at a time when he can't afford it."

"You mean the Russian people." Kozov ran a finger along the leather back of a sofa.

Max shrugged. "Whatever story you want to tell yourself. The men who sit on the four councils are anonymous. Their names are a closely guarded secret. Your boss needs those names, and I have them. I have records of the transactions, bank account numbers, and contracts. I have their identities. I have everything you need to destroy the councils."

Kozov folded his arms and leaned his hip against the back of a couch. "If you have this information, why don't you use it to your benefit?"

Max shrugged his left shoulder. "I have no interest in money or business. I could eliminate each of the council members, those that are left, but that would take a while. My interest is in ending the nightmare for my family as quickly as possible."

"What do you suggest we do with those names?"

Max rolled his eyes. "I don't need to explain your business to you."

Kozov stroked his chin with a finger and was silent for a moment. "Assuming we take action to put an end to the councils, that leaves the kommissariat. What is your plan?"

Max spread his hands. "There is a plan in motion." *Bluff.*

"You don't know who the kommissar is, do you?" Kozov's eyes narrowed. "He might be the Russian president, for all you know."

Max shook his head. "The kommissar is a lot taller."

Kozov frowned.

"If the councils are out of business, the kommissar is neutered." Max smiled. "While the kommissar might live, the councils are how he executes his strategy. Sure, he may restart the councils, but that will take years. Meanwhile, I'm going to find him. And kill him."

Kozov pursed his lips and was silent for a few beats. "And what do you want in return for all the names?"

"Simple. A pardon for my father, myself, Alex, and Arina."

"Your father? He's dead."

Max nodded. "I want his good name restored."

Kozov shook his head. "And the Vienna Archive?"

"What about it?"

"We want it."

Max shook his head. "Not happening. It's my insurance. It's how I stay alive."

The Russian president's fixer paced, and when he turned, the pistol was trained on Max.

Max furrowed his brow as he raised his hands. "I thought we were making progress here."

Kozov barked an order. The doors opened and two men in military garb entered. One man placed the muzzle of a pistol against Max's neck while the other bound Max's wrists behind his back with plastic cuffs.

As he was led from the room, Kozov's voice was in his ear. "We're going to see just how good your insurance is."

TWENTY-SIX

Building 311, Moscow, Russia

A needle in a haystack. Wasn't that what the Americans said? Colonel Semenov adjusted his tie. Somewhere among the one hundred million servers in the world were the group of files described as the Vienna Archive. The existence of the files was no longer in doubt. Asimov had proven he had access to intimate information regarding the Russian president's deals, both personal and governmental, and Asimov had shown that he wasn't afraid to use the information.

First, there was the arrest of Konstantin Zaitsev by Britain's MI5, the exposure of which was made possible when Asimov provided that agency with secret intel from the Vienna Archive. After that, there was the appearance of Asimov at the private dressage horse auction, which was also a result of using materials in the archive. What else did Asimov have up his sleeve?

Colonel Semenov's strategy was to find Asimov's partner, the hacker known as Goshawk, and trick her or force her to divulge the archive's location. The name Goshawk was well-known among the hacking elite. No one knew what she looked like, but she was widely regarded as a *she*, as evidenced by computer forensics on the limited communications known to be attributed to her. There was also evidence she resided in Europe, likely Western Europe, although there was also speculation that she was in Eastern Europe.

To find her, Semenov had activated several operations. Yes, he enjoyed access to the room full of Russia's best and brightest hacker elite. But he had no intention of letting one of these kids best him. If one of the kids in the room unearthed either her location or the location of the Vienna Archive, it would be the end of Colonel Semenov's career. To keep the kids occupied, he doled out an endless stream of wild goose chase assignments.

Semenov was seasoned enough to know that most hacking successes rested on social engineering rather than brute force computer work. Even though zero-day exploits happen, they are few and far between and are often mitigated by software companies before they can be exploited. Instead, successful hacks involved persuading a human to do something they shouldn't, either through force or trickery. Granny calls a phone number where the person talks her into allowing them access to her computer. A witless employee clicks on a phishing link. Heck, even the Stuxnet worm that disrupted Iran's nuclear program was introduced to a closed system by a human.

When the young hackers in front of him watched Colonel Semenov, they all assumed he was filling out paperwork or reviewing reports, but he was in direct contact with a remote team of operatives on the ground in an upscale neighborhood in Montenegro.

To find Goshawk, Semenov intended to find someone acquainted with her and apply pressure. Semenov knew who that person was and where he was located.

Hamburg, Germany

"Hello, Kate."

The voice was familiar, and Kate spun around. Her hand darted for her gun until she remembered they were in an airport. "Are you following me?"

The woman's outfit was the same: A tan formfitting leather jacket over a light sweater and black jeans, boots that laced over her ankles, frizzy hair held out of her face by a wide headband over her forehead. Eyes that sparkled when she smiled. *This woman enjoyed her job.* The woman put her hands out. "Nothing to be afraid of. We're in a safe place. Airports are designed that way. Nowhere safer to have a nice chat. You've got your coffee. How about I get a cup and we go for a stroll?"

Despite her best judgement, Kate waited as the woman got a small coffee. It was something called a flat white with oat milk. *Hipster.* "No pour-over for you?"

The woman's eyebrows arched, and she sipped. "Unfortunately, they don't do that sort of coffee here."

Kate studied her out of the corner of her eye. Young, late twenties or early thirties. Graceful movements. Dancer, maybe, or a martial artist? *Watch your step, Shaw.* So far, Kaamil's database search had proved fruitless. "You got a name? What do I call you?"

"Let's walk." The two women strolled along the concourse amidst the flurry of civilians. "Call me Cora."

"Cora what?"

After another sip, Cora chuckled. "Just Cora. Have you thought about our offer?"

"What offer? You haven't made an offer yet. What do you want, access to our intel?"

The woman laughed. "Negative. We have access to your intel already. Our people are everywhere."

A pang of anxiety hit Kate. *The mole?* "Then what?"

"We want the same thing, Kate. We can help each other."

"I doubt that. You don't know what I want."

The woman *tsked*. "You want your old life back, Kate. A secure position at the CIA. Enough autonomy to run your operations. You want to make a difference. You're married to the agency, Kate."

Kate snorted. "I have that."

"Do you?"

"What does that mean?"

"Why do you think Wodehouse brought you back?"

The two women strolled through the busy concourse like two traveling friends. Kate shrugged. "He needs a confidant. Someone he can trust."

"You mean because of the leak."

Shit. How much does this woman know? "I don't know what you're talking about." This line of discussion threatened to rock her off the stable foundation she thought was reestablished.

"Okay. But really. Why do you think Wodehouse brought you back?"

She couldn't bring herself to say it. "Get to the point."

The frizzy-haired woman sipped her coffee. "He wants

the Vienna Archive. He needs it to solidify his position. He thinks you have a shot of finding it, and he's a man who likes to hedge his bets. If you fail, do you think he'll keep you around? You're damaged goods, Kate. The agency thinks you're washed up with psychological scars from your captivity. I've seen the reports. Every psychologist and personnel staffer at the agency recommended against bringing you back. Wodehouse's balls are hanging out in the wind. You're there for one thing—that's to bring back the Vienna Archive. If you fail at that, Wodehouse will cut you quicker than... Well, fast anyway. To save himself."

They reached the end of the concourse, where a tall window overlooked the runway. A line of wide-bodies waited for takeoff while a regional jet landed in a plume of vapor as the tires hit the tarmac. *Is she right?* Kate's stomach roiled at the prospect. *What else do I have? Nothing.* "State your offer."

"It's simple. We work together to procure the Vienna Archive. You need our firm's services. We have an array of people and resources around the globe."

"I already have access to that through the CIA."

The woman who called herself Cora turned so her back was to the window. She crossed her arms over her chest while holding her coffee. "We have resources you can use without tapping official agency resources."

"Off the books." Through the window, a train of baggage carts trundled by.

"Right. Off the books. Blank check. No requisitions. No budgets. No politics."

"And what about Asimov?"

The woman shrugged. "What about him? Once we get the Vienna Archive, he's expendable."

Kate stared at the line of airplanes.

Cora touched Kate's arm. "We get the Vienna Archive and share its intel with the agency. Wodehouse secures his position. Your job with Wodehouse is safe. Everyone wins. It's what you want, no?"

Kate crossed her arms. *It is what I want.* "I'll think about it."

"Don't think too long, Kate." Cora pushed away from the window before she turned. In her hand was a small tablet. "If you're still wavering, have a look at this."

Kate's mind clouded, but she took the device. *What now?*

The woman disappeared into the throngs of travelers as Kate eyed the small tablet. It was about the size of a large mobile phone. She tossed her empty cup into a trashcan and tapped the tablet's screen. It was an Android device, and its screen showed a single icon. Her heart thumped in her chest as she tapped the icon.

A video appeared showing blue sky, green pinyon trees, and splotches of snow on the ground. In the distance was a home construction site with a newly built log cabin, a large roll-off dumpster, and stacks of construction materials. Her stomach turned over as a man she recognized emerged from the front door. Tall, gangly, and sporting a craggy face covered with a white beard, Spencer White rummaged among a pile of two-by-fours, selected one, eyed its length, and carried it into the house. The video ended.

On weak legs, Kate found a bench and collapsed onto it.

Montenegro

. . .

The team of three men used the cover of darkness to slip into the modern home on the blue-water coast of the Adriatic Sea. The house was a low-slung one-story affair with a row of windows along the back that overlooked a small pool. The facade was white, and cedar slats covered the windows from the inside. No lights were on, and the team's radiant heat sensors indicated one stationary human-shaped lifeform was inside. It looked to be prone, which led the men to believe the shape was asleep.

If any of the three men noticed the tiny surveillance cameras on the exterior of the building, no one spoke up. How dangerous was it to apprehend a single retired computer hacker?

One of the men issued a command into a hidden mic. A moment later he received confirmation that power to the house was cut. Any alarm system or cameras were now dysfunctional. Entry was gained through the rear glass sliders after one of the men picked the lock. The three men raised their pistols and slipped into the home.

A moment after they entered, a series of muffled whomps were heard from underfoot and the floor shook. Lights clicked on throughout the house, and the intruders froze. A burning smell accompanied smoke that wafted from the furnace vents. The team leader held up a fist, which commanded his men to hold fast. *What just happened?*

The three men were in a sparsely furnished living area. What furniture was in the room was of the mid-century modern design, lots of teak and clean lines. Nothing cluttered the tabletops. A phonograph and speakers were along one wall, while crates of vinyl records were stacked on the floor.

A voice rang out from deeper in the house. "You fellas want coffee?"

The three men glanced at each other.

A moment later, a small man wrapped in a robe popped his head into the living room. "Coffee? Black or with sugar?"

The team leader, unsure how to act, raised his gun.

The tiny man raised his hands. "No weapons here. I figure you want to chat about something, so we might as well have coffee."

The team leader found his voice. "How do you have power?"

But the short man was gone. The three intruders walked through the living area and into a tidy kitchen and dining area. The sole appliance on the white counters was an elaborate coffee machine, which is where the homeowner busied himself. The team leader sent one of his men through the rest of the house. By the time the operative returned and pronounced it clear, the man in the robe had set out three mugs with black coffee and cradled one in his hand. "There's no one else here."

"How do you have power?" the team leader repeated.

"Solar. I have a Tesla Powerwall as a backup with two batteries. I can get four days of juice from one battery." The homeowner was small in stature and his oversized head was shaved clean. He wore large black plastic glasses with thick lenses.

"What's the smoke from downstairs?" The team leader sipped his coffee. It was an involuntary act born of habit. When you hold coffee, you sip it. And it was excellent.

"You tripped my self-destruct mode. All the servers downstairs are fried. Nothing left. Whatever you're here for isn't here." The small man shrugged his shoulders.

"We're not here for your servers."

"What then?"

"Will you confirm you are the computer hacker known as the Monk?"

"I will do nothing of the sort until you tell me why you're here."

While he held his coffee in his left hand, the team leader pointed his pistol at the tiny man's left kneecap and fired. The bullet entered his patella, tore through the femur, and exited in a shower of blood, cartilage, and bone. The red material spattered against the white cabinet as the homeowner screamed. The mug smashed to the ground and sent black coffee splashing over a gray tile floor. "Nikolay, wrap up that wound, get Mr. Monk a painkiller, and get him over to that chair."

While his men did their best to bandage their prisoner, the team leader helped himself to more coffee. It was turning into a long night, and the hot black coffee was welcomed. Once the famous computer hacker was snug in a chair with his knee bandaged, the team leader snapped smelling salts under the Monk's nose. The tiny man sputtered to consciousness.

The team leader stood in front of the sobbing man and sipped his coffee. "We're here to find a friend of yours. She calls herself Goshawk."

TWENTY-SEVEN

Washington, DC

Fatigue and despair took over and dulled Kate's senses. During the return flight over the pond, she had medicated with an endless stream of tiny vodka bottles. Now the cab ride home was a blur through the watery lights of the city, like traveling through a kaleidoscope. Thoughts fluttered like butterflies, no one idea settling on her mind. Her carry-on bag thumped against the stairs behind her as she trudged to the top floor. An intruder might easily have snuck up on her. She didn't care. All she wanted was the cold bottle of white wine in her fridge, her bed, and a long sleep.

They had threatened Spencer White, her longtime friend and colleague. Spencer was a father figure to her, a man who watched out for her and counseled her. A former black ops CIA officer who performed dozens of operations under Kate's command, now Spencer wanted to be left alone to rebuild his cabin.

What choice did she have but to play along?

When she walked into her flat to find the frizzy-haired operative sitting in the leather chair, Kate fell into the couch opposite and didn't bother hunting for her gun. As she sat there studying the woman, she remembered the bottle in the fridge, so she rose on wobbly legs and retrieved it. The screw cap clattered to the wood floor, and she returned to the couch and took a long pull right from the bottle.

"Did you watch the video, Kate?"

By way of an answer, Kate took another swig. The buttery chardonnay warmed her bones, and she crossed one leg over the other. "How did you beat me here?"

Cora smirked. "We have multiple private jets. All our travel is done without the pesky immigration requirements. We have people in immigration departments in most countries we operate in and a few we don't." Blue neon light from outside glinted off the barrel of a small pistol that rested on the woman's leg.

Kate guzzled the wine. "What do you want?"

"I want an answer, Kate. We're running out of time." Cora shrugged. "We need each other. You bring the archive back to the nest and your status is solidified. Heck, they may let you take over the CIA after Wodehouse rides off into the sunset."

The refrigerator's ice maker interrupted the silence before Kate spoke. "I need Kaamil."

"Of course, you do. But you can't bring him into this. Use him for what he's good at but tell him nothing of our partnership."

Cora rose to her feet, slid the gun into a pocket of her leather jacket, and removed a smartphone, which she tossed to Kate. "This phone has an encrypted chat app so we can communicate." Cora strode to the door, put her hand on the knob, and pivoted. "Oh. And one thing. It probably goes without saying, but don't fuck with us. We have people everywhere. We know things—"

"Yeah, yeah. I get it."

Cora disappeared through the door as Kate guzzled from the bottle of wine.

A bee buzzed through Kate's semiconsciousness, which was joined by another bee, and another, and soon a swarm of the black-and-yellow insects swirled around her head.

With a heavy arm, she attempted to swat at them. *Go away.*

More bees joined the cloud, darting and weaving through the air around her ear. The buzzing became incessant, and this time she used two arms to wave them away. Light pierced her eyeballs, and she stifled a yelp and clenched her lids back together.

The buzzing remained. *My phone.* It was wedged between the pillows and her head.

She pawed at it and cracked one eye. There was a dozen missed calls, all from Kaamil. While she held the phone, it vibrated with another incoming call from her analyst. She hit the answer button and put it on speaker, and her head dropped back into the pillows. A pounding ache in her temples replaced the buzzing.

"She's on the move." Kaamil was breathless.

"What?" Her voice was thick through a dry mouth. "Who?"

"Are you sick?" Kaamil's voice turned concerned. "You don't sound so good."

Kate clenched her eyes and forced them to open.

Sunlight streamed through the open blinds. "What time is it?"

"Ten. Did I wake you?"

"Hold on." Kate levered herself onto one elbow, scanned the bedroom, and saw the empty bottle of chardonnay next to a half-empty bottle of vodka. "Ugh."

"What is it, Kate. Are you all right?"

She put one bare foot on the floor, then the other, and sat up. Nausea swam through her head, and she almost fell back into the bed. "Call you back." She ended the call, stumbled into the bathroom, stripped out of her clothes, and stepped into the shower. She put the water on cold and endured the frigid jabs of icy water. Her stomach heaved and a stream of clear liquid erupted from her throat and disappeared down the drain. Dry heaves ensued, and she sank to her knees and coughed up bile and spit it onto the shower tile, where it was washed away. When her stomach was empty and the heaves dissipated, she turned the water on hot, and washed her body and her hair with shaking hands. With a towel tied around her hair, she padded to the kitchen, prepared a fried egg on dry toast and ate it standing at the kitchen island. Her hands stopped shaking.

After the dishes were cleaned, she poured out the remaining vodka. A thorough search of the house uncovered two more vodka bottles and three bottles of wine. They all went down the sink. Her mobile phone rang.

"You sure everything is okay?" Kaamil's voice was thick with concern.

"I'm fine. Julia's on the move?" At each stop on her reverse trip from Hamburg to Washington, DC, Kaamil had reported via text that Julia's mobile phone hadn't moved, and there were no calls or data transmissions. No conversations were picked up from the bug Kate had left in the house. Kate feared Julia suspected something and perhaps switched phones or scanned her house for listening devices.

"She's in Denmark." Kaamil's voice brightened. "Rather, her phone is in Denmark. Heading east on the E20. Probably to Copenhagen."

"She make any calls?"

"One. Any guesses?"

Bingo. "Wolf." Kate hurried to her bedroom with the phone plastered to her ear. Frederick Wolf was Julia's superior at the BND.

"You got it. I think the first part of the conversation was some kind of code. Random pleasantries exchanged. They agreed to meet in person."

"Where?"

"Helsinki."

"Helsinki? As in Finland?" Her carry-on bag was on the bedroom floor with dirty laundry spilling out of it. She tossed the soiled clothing into the corner and yanked a few clean items from hangers. "Book me a flight."

"You want me to put together a team from the Helsinki field office?"

The idea stopped her in her tracks. After a moment of thought, Kate resumed her packing. "Negative. It's too early. Let's see where this goes before we roust everyone."

"Copy that."

London, England

The woman lied about her age. She lied about a good many things, that much became evident later. Such is the underlying psychology of vulnerability and victimhood.

The inside of the stately Tudor with the ivy-covered brick and stone glowed from the fading embers of the fireplace and a bottle of French Bordeaux. A trail of clothing, starting with a pair of patent leather pumps, meandering to a corduroy jacket with patched sleeves and a short black dress, and ending with a skimpy thong and a pair of rather frayed boxer shorts, led to a tufted leather couch. On the couch, a naked and paunchy man past sixty was intertwined with a long-legged woman of forty-something. Or at least that's the age she claimed.

The evening began innocently enough. Dinner was at the Ledbury, a Michelin two-star restaurant in Notting Hill that required Callum Baxter to cash in a favor to secure a late seating. His date had sat demurely with a throw over her shoulders and hung on his every word. Drinks after dinner, at her suggestion, were at the nearby Royal Lancaster with a view over Hyde Park. Things got interesting when her throw came off to reveal a deep décolletage. The temperature went up when her hand caressed his thigh over martinis with a wave of vermouth and three olives.

Later, as he stumbled around the living room looking for his glasses, he searched his memory for what happened after the martinis and only recalled hazy images. A cab ride with her hand deep in his lap. A fumbling romp to the couch. The woman's naked skin against his, a sensation so foreign to him that he gave in and succumbed to her lead, which she took with gusto. Fuzzy memories of the night swirled. Was it good for her? Was there urgent ascendancy to an apex of pleasure? Could he hold his head up? Had he proudly represented the Baxter family name by honoring her needs like a gentleman?

He hoped, but try as he might, he didn't remember. And there was no evidence. No condom, although he would never engage in intercourse without one. Or would he? An image of her nude breasts undulating over him swam into view for a moment but swept away before panic crested over him. His privates were clean, and there was no evidence of the prophylactic. So maybe they hadn't. And where was she? Why did she disappear in the middle of the night? And what should he do about this headache?

At the time, none of it was untoward, even her disappearance, for the woman was prone to odd behavior. The two met weeks ago at the Tate Modern, a museum so full of dreck that Callum had a hard time getting through the door, but his housekeeper proclaimed the temporary Warhol exhibit spectacular. So he went, intending to dash through until he met the beautiful woman in the form-fitting pant suit who professed to be the newest member of the curation staff fresh from Luxembourg. Black hair laced with silver fell over bony shoulders and framed an olive-complected face punctuated with sparkling blue eyes. Aside from the gray-laced locks and tiny crinkles emanating from her eyes, her taut skin indicated youth. Under the duress of an afternoon rosé, she professed her age to be in the early forties.

Several dates followed, whereby the two argued, debated, and cheerily fought over the merits of modern art versus the classics. Prior to the night at the Ledbury, there was such a heated exchange over Yayoi Kusama's infinity mirror rooms that the bartender had cut them off, at which point the two burst into spontaneous laughter before Baxter helped her into a cab. It was only a matter of time before they consummated the affair.

It was during these weeks of courting when his officemates at Vauxhall Cross, the location of Britain's Secret Intelligence Service, took notice of the spring in his step. Their boss's shirts were starched. Management, including C, wondered about the lack of foodstuffs in Callum's chin beard. And was the goatee trimmed and the ear hair waxed away?

Was Callum Baxter actually seeing someone?

———

As Callum slept, and as spring rain pounded the leaded glass, the naked woman disentangled her legs and rose from the couch, found her clothing, and dressed, except for the shoes. Those she placed by the front door while she finished her other preparations. Latex gloves appeared from a hidden pocket in her purse and snapped onto her hands. Also from her bag came moist towelettes and a tiny spray bottle, which she used to clean the man's private parts, hands, and face. As she swabbed and disinfected, the soiled cleaning products disappeared into her bag. She plucked a microfiber towel from the bag, which she scrubbed over every surface she touched. In the middle of the carpet, she bent to pluck the used condom and seal it in a small Ziplock bag, which she also stored in her purse.

Satisfied the area and the man were sanitized of any of her DNA, she slung the leather bag over her shoulder, darted through the kitchen and out the back slider and across the lawn through the spring rain. A small outbuilding stood among budding rose bushes in the back yard. At the stout door to the outbuilding, she bent and worked a pair of lock picks and a moment later she was inside, where she found a home office brimming with stacks of papers. She took her time and used a tiny camera to snap hundreds of images of the files, all marked with the distinctive CLASSIFIED red tape, all of which she put back exactly where she found them.

With the latex gloves on, she locked the office door and retraced her steps. Back in the warm living room, she checked on her date. The man lay nude on his side on the leather cushions, out cold, a result of the half tab of Rohypnol she slipped into his Manhattan. A melancholy sensation flickered—she enjoyed his company, and he was a better lay than she expected—before the emotion winked out in the back of her heart. After she draped a wool blanket over his legs and torso, the woman looked around the room one last time before snatching her shoes, covering her face and head with the throw, and exiting through the front door.

TWENTY-EIGHT

Undisclosed Location

Almost forty-eight hours. No word from Max.

Goshawk stalked around the spacious apartment in bare feet, while a tiny Bluetooth earbud was lodged in one ear. Her jean cuffs had been frayed by the designer, and she wore a simple silk top.

There was no contact since Max walked into the hotel to meet Kozov in Berlin. According to an obscure news clipping on the internet that popped up in one of her alerts, the auction of Misty Blues had proceeded without interruption, and the horse was sold to an anonymous buyer. There were no Russian press releases, and the news media in that country didn't cover the auction. Goshawk distracted herself while she waited. Online games of Go. Scrub the kitchen. Cook a batch of pot brownies. Watch an episode of *FBI: Most Wanted.*

The ding of an alert yanked her from the sumptuous

living area where she scrolled through various streaming services looking for something to watch. The tone of the alert was configured by Goshawk to indicate it was a message from Cindy at MI6.

She might have news.

Goshawk padded across the polished concrete floor and down the hall to the command center. Four monitors were in a grid over her desk while four additional screens were affixed to the walls, where various news feeds from CNN, Al Jazeera, the BBC, and TASS streamed. TASS, the Russian News Agency, was all propaganda, but Goshawk liked to monitor it for any news of the Russian Presidency, fake or otherwise.

She tapped a key and one of her desk monitors woke. A chat window flashed with a message from Cindy. *Any news on your end?*

Goshawk's stomach sank. Her acrylic-clad fingernails clacked on the keys. *None. I take it MI6 hasn't heard from him since D-Day?"* D-Day was their code phrase that indicated the time and date of Max's meeting with Kozov in Berlin.

No word.

A bubble with three dots appeared, which indicated Cindy was typing. Goshawk checked the time on a digital wall clock and did a quick calculation. The forty-eight-hour window was almost up. It was the window of time she and Max agreed upon before she was to commence Operation Defcon.

Operation Defcon was a specific set of protocols designed to exert escalating pressure on the Russian president. If Max were alive, Defcon was his way out of captivity. If Max was dead, it was Goshawk's vengeance.

Cindy's message appeared. *What should we do? I'm worried.*

"I'm worried too, darling," Goshawk whispered to herself as she typed into the chat window. *I'm on it. Don't worry.*

I want to help.

"I know you do, sugar." Goshawk typed a message. *Sit tight. I got this.*

She minimized the chat window and brought up a command window before she reached to the back of her desk and grabbed a different keyboard. This one had a row of twelve function keys across the top row labeled F1 through F12. Each key was programmed specifically for Operation Defcon. She caressed the F1 key with a fingernail.

She glanced at the clock on the wall.

It hit the forty-eight-hour mark.

Here we go.

She pushed the F1 key.

———

Hamburg, Germany

Lights twinkled over the seventy-square-kilometers of land and water that encompassed the Port of Hamburg. Even two hours past midnight, Europe's third busiest port bustled with activity. Cranes that towered over the water hummed and groaned as they unloaded forty million metric tons of cargo per year. Across the port's seventeen terminals sprawled endless rows of containers, warehouses, and football pitch-sized container ships.

Nestled in a big slip deep in the Blohm+Voss shipyard rested an eighty-two-meter-long super yacht named *Exquisite*. No one knew who owned her, but there were plenty of rumors. Her white hull reflected the winking lights of the port around her. The massive cruiser was powered by two water jet propulsion engines that made eighteen knots. Her range was more than 4,000 nautical miles. Inside, she boasted a fifteen-meter indoor pool that was convertible into a dance floor, and her berths accommodated twelve guests and fourteen crew members. The yacht reportedly cost its owner $100 million to build. All the ship builders had gone home for the night, and the yacht was dark and locked. Her crew was nestled in for the night at the Westin in downtown Hamburg.

Also on that night, the night shift security guard called in sick, which forced the supervisor to call in a temp. The temp guard clocked in and started his rounds. No one noticed his sleeves of arm tattoos, his toothless grin, or his ruddy cheeks. It was common for guards to carry food and equipment on their rounds, so no one commented on his knapsack. And no one snickered about his bowlegged walk or his long gray ponytail. Later, everyone would have difficulty describing the temporary guard to authorities. The agency who supplied the guard had no record of the man, and the guard who was supposed to work that night was found much later, bound, gagged, and unconscious on his living room couch.

At 2:00 a.m. that night, a muffled explosion sent shock waves through the Blohm+Voss shipyard. The waves pitched the docks and rained water and ship parts on the metal roofs of the shipyard's buildings.

When the smoke cloud dissipated, *Exquisite* rested on the bottom of the bay. Water lapped at the blown-out windows on the second deck, and she listed to starboard. Later, investigators found that the ship's entire hull below the water line was destroyed in the explosion. The fifteen-meter pool was gone, as was the dance floor.

The temporary security guard was never located.

TWENTY-NINE

Washington, DC

"Three calls in the last twenty minutes, sir," Miko said.

The kommissar's heels clicked on the concrete corridor and echoed off the arched ceiling high overhead. Conduit and copper pipes lined the walls at shoulder height and fluorescent lights gave off a harsh blue-yellow glow. Miko walked slightly behind him with a mobile phone in his outstretched hand.

A meeting with the president of the United States, even if the man was the kommissar's childhood friend, required all the kommissar's attention. Whatever frivolous problem Ashe had could wait. "Ignore it. I'll call him back when we're done here."

The kommissar dreaded these all too frequent in-person meetings with the president, which were always held in the bunker far below the White House and away from prying eyes. The kommissar's position in the federal government was senior enough to explain away a chance sighting, but it might raise eyebrows if the wrong Congress member were to happen along the tunnels.

The bunker consisted of a series of concrete rooms and tunnels with various secret access points within the White House and other government buildings surrounding the grounds of the president's residence. At least two ramps allowed vehicles to deposit and pick up visitors in anonymity. It was one of these ramps where the kommissar had entered the buried warren.

Built in the 1950s, the concrete walls were thick enough to withstand all but a direct nuclear strike, and when the president was hustled off to an undisclosed location, depending on the state of emergency or threat level, the bunker complex was one such secret location. When not used as a secure hiding place for the president, the vice president, the joint chiefs, or high-ranking members of Congress, the vast maze of tunnels, conference rooms, and command centers were empty and sometimes used by the president for off-the-books meetings. Throughout history, it was also used for liaisons with presidential lovers. One rumor held that John F. Kennedy rendezvoused with Marilyn Monroe in a luxurious room hidden away in the tunnels.

"Sir, he's rung back twice more and there are two text messages."

"Shit." The kommissar stopped and whirled. The click of his heals died away in the tunnel. "Give me that." He touched a number on speed dial. It was answered before the first ring. "What, damn it? What is so damn urgent?"

"We got intel on Ferret." Ashe's voice was gravel.

"What intel? From where?"

"Our friends in London." It was code for their source within MI6.

"What kind of intel?"

"It's not good."

"Shit."

Footsteps approached from the other end of the hallway. The US president's heavyset form cast a long shadow along the concrete floor as he strode in the kommissar's direction. "I have to go. P street, thirty minutes." He handed the phone to Miko, who faded into the shadows as the president arrived. Two secret service agents were ten feet behind the US president.

Despite the president's weight, he wore a well-tailored suit in blue with chalk pinstripes and the US flag pin on his lapel. "And?"

There was only one thing the US president cared about when he met with the kommissar. "We're making progress, sir. We're in the middle of the operation, which I'm confident will yield the results we're after."

"The results." The president snorted. "Do I need to remind you of the stakes?"

"No, sir—"

"If that Vienna Archive gets out into the public domain, it will do irreparable harm to not only my election chances, but our entire platform. If our enemies uncover it before we do, we're sunk."

"I understand—"

The president poked his finger at the kommissar's chest. "Do not fail me. Do I need to remind you of the price of failure? For your own life? Both of our lives?" Without waiting for an answer, the US president spun on a heal and strode down the tunnel.

The plush offices in the gray stone building at 277 P Street SE smelled of caramel and roasted marshmallows. The espresso machine was in full operational mode, pumping out shot after shot for the kommissar, Alden Ashe, and Cora. Miko stood near the wall as always. The three gathered around the coffee maker and sipped as Alden gave his report.

"MI6 believes Asimov has been detained by the Russian president. In Moscow."

The news sank into the kommissar's gut as he paced. "Damn it. How did that happen?"

"Apparently Asimov and MI6 ran an operation to try to get the Russian president's cooperation. They offered a deal whereby Asimov agreed to provide him with the identities of all the council members in return for the Russian president's pardon."

"Pardon?"

"Yes. Asimov wants his family to be able to resume their ordinary life in Minsk or Moscow. His sister and his nephew."

"So Asimov provides the identities of all the council members, and the Russian president goes after them. Dumps them in the gulag or prosecutes them for tax evasion. Or outright kills them, I guess." The kommissar paced and tugged at his collar. "He will destroy the councils, everything we've worked to build over the past thirty years."

Ashe pinched the bridge of his nose. "There's more. Stasko is helping MI6."

"Damn. Stasko flipped? Wait." The kommissar held up a hand. "If Asimov proposed this deal, and now he's incarcerated in Moscow, the Russian president didn't agree." He put both hands in the air. "He's after the entire archive and thinks he can get it out of Asimov."

Ashe nodded.

"Shit." The kommissar pointed at Cora. "How is the operation with Kate Shaw proceeding?"

Cora hoisted herself to sit on the counter next to the espresso machine. "Going well. She's tracking Julia Meier, who we believe knows where the archive is kept. The physical archive."

"How does Meier know this?"

"The CIA intercepted signals intel that suggests the archive is stored in a cabin that has belonged to the Asimov family for generations. Julia Meier knows of this cabin from her years of affairs with Andrei."

Adrenaline pulsed through the kommissar's blood. It was almost as if he could smell the scent. "And our team is positioned to take the archive, once its location is divulged?"

"They better," Ashe muttered.

"Correct, sir." Cora smiled. "You have nothing to worry about."

"And Shaw and Meier? Once we have the archive?"

Cora shrugged. "They will be taken care of."

THIRTY

Helsinki, Finland

"How's she look?"

The voice in Kate's ear was Kaamil's. Kate watched Julia Meier from the driver's seat of a Škoda liftback. She used an earbud tethered to her CIA phone to talk to Kaamil. The phone provided by Cora was in a shoulder bag and turned off.

For the last three nights, Julia Meier stayed in a renovated apartment in Helsinki's trendy Kallio district. Jet-lagged but energized, Kate surveilled the apartment for those three nights, taking catnaps in the Škoda. The building was a pleasant, light beige brick affair with tiny balconies arranged around its six-story exterior. Spring flowers bloomed, and the front was littered with bicycles and picnic benches. Students and faculty of the nearby university mixed with commuters in a choreographed swarm. Until this point, Julia stayed put. There were no visitors.

When Julia finally appeared, Kate peered through the evening murk. Julia left the building and turned south. "She looks energized."

The venerable German BND operative wore an overcoat against a spring chill and a beret pulled over her silver hair. Julia was followed by a tall man in a parka. "A man is walking behind her. Probably a bodyguard," Kate said. "It's not Frederick Wolf."

Follow in a car, or get out and go on foot? Kate cursed her lack of a CIA team. A two-car team with another two men on the street was the proper way to do this. Instead, Kate chose to go it alone. After she swung a scarf around her face and hair, she exited the Škoda and followed on foot. If Julia got into a vehicle, Kaamil would be able to track her while Kate scrambled back to the car. The earbud remained in Kate's ear, connected through the private channel to Kaamil.

"Is there a spring in her step?" Kaamil's voice was loud in her ear. It was noon in Washington, DC, and Kate figured Kaamil was on his fifth espresso.

Kate shoved her hands into her overcoat pockets. "It's like she's onto something." In the cool evening light, Julia's face was alive, her eyes bright. It was a far cry from when Kate met with Julia on the island of Sylt.

"A woman on a mission."

Julia's excursion was a nonevent. The BND operative stopped into a market to get coffee, bottled water, and a takeaway meal and returned to the condominium.

Once she was certain Julia was back in the apartment, Kate did the same and scarfed a grilled sausage and herring sandwich and washed it down with a bottle of water. As darkness settled over the street, Kate rested her eyes. She left the comms channel open with Kaamil.

"Shout at me if she moves." Kate fell into a restless sleep.

Through the gloom of her slumber appeared a rugged man with a shaven head. His brown eyes sparkled as his fingers caressed her cheek. The big hand was veined and calloused but gentle. *Max.* She woke herself with an abrupt yell as panic overcame her. Darkness had settled over the neighborhood, and the pedestrians were gone.

Kaamil's voice appeared in her ear. "She's on the move."

Kate rubbed sleep out of her eyes. "What time is it?"

"Ten your time."

Adrenaline surged and Kate became alert. "This must be it." Kate gulped cold coffee from the Styrofoam cup at her elbow.

Julia exited the apartment building and disappeared into a dark panel van with tinted windows. A residential security firm logo was on the van's side. The van roared off before the sliding door was shut.

"It's time." She started the Škoda and eased out of the parking lot. A small tablet lay on the seat next to her that showed a map of Helsinki and a pulsing green dot. The green dot showed Julia's phone traveling along city streets on a northerly path. Kate removed Cora's phone, turned it on, muted her comms with Kaamil, and typed a short text message. In a rushed phone call two days prior, Kate had updated Cora on the operation to follow Julia Meier in the hopes she might lead them to the cabin known as Riverside.

The BND van meandered through the dark city streets for an hour as Julia and her team likely watched for a tail. Kate let the van out of her sight and relied on the green dot. After the text message to Cora, Kate turned off the phone and stowed it in her backpack.

After another thirty minutes, the van carrying the BND

team merged onto the E75 highway and sped north. The roads were clear, and the van stayed at the 120 kph summer speed limit. Soon the glow of the city lights was left behind and there was nothing but sparse moonlight, rows of spruce, pine, and silver birch along the road, and the periodic headlights from oncoming vehicles. Kate stayed a mile back and relied on Kaamil's tracker, and for the next two hours, the green dot sped north.

Where on earth are they going?

They skirted the medium-sized city of Lahti, where the BND team stopped for fuel. Kate took the opportunity to fuel up at a different gas station and grab coffee. When the green dot started moving, it departed the E75 and took Highway 24 northwest for thirty minutes until it angled off onto the 314. That road alternated between engineered bridges and land bridges as it routed over a large body of water. This far north, the snow was not yet melted, and snow fields glowed in the moonlight.

After traversing a series of back roads through the wilderness, the green dot stopped a half mile from the shore of an immense body of water the map called Lake Päijänne. Kate brought her car to a halt out of sight from the BND team. "Kaamil?"

"Man, you're in the boonies. Hold, please. I'm searching satellite archives for anything in that area. Also looking on Google Earth."

Kate's pulse quickened. Might this be the hiding spot? Did Max somehow secrete the Vienna Archive away in a remote cabin in the Finnish wilderness? She shrugged on a black insulated tactical jacket and slipped a black watch cap over her head. As she waited, she twirled a short silencer onto the end of a compact 9mm. Two magazines went into her pocket.

Kaamil's voice was urgent. "I can see a single cabin situated on the shore of the lake. Rectangular, small, with a deck ringing three sides. No vehicles except the BND van."

"Can you trace ownership of the cabin?"

The clacking of a keyboard came through her earpiece and Kaamil muttered to himself. "Digging, but there is an array of shell companies and legal structures. A bank in Georgia. The country. Caymans. Registration in Panama..." Silence for several beats.

"Kaamil, still there?"

"I'm looking, hold on. This is crazy." Frenzied typing. "The cabin is owned by a shell company, which is owned by another entity in the Caymans. The Cayman company is called Belvedere, and the ownership is completely shrouded. I can't see—"

"Did you say Belvedere?"

"Yeah, but I can't see the company's directors or ownership structure."

"There is a Belvedere Museum in Vienna."

Kaamil sucked in his breath. "Coincidence?"

Kate shook her head. "There are no coincidences."

Sysmä, Finland

"What's your plan?" Kaamil's voice was in her ear.

"Let's just say if the documents are here, I'm not taking any prisoners." After double- and triple-checking the pistol's magazine, Kate slipped the suppressed weapon into her jacket alongside two additional magazines. A set of night-vision specs adorned her head and tight-fitting gloves warmed her hands. For footwear, she wore light hiking boots. Waterproof and insulated. The mobile phone provided by Cora remained behind. The last update Kate sent Cora was at the gas station. If the archive was in the cabin, Kate planned to examine the stockpile before notifying Cora. Adrenaline surged. She was so close.

Better to discover it myself before I alert Cora.

She left the Škoda hidden from the road behind a snowbank, and her boots kicked through three inches of snow as she set out cross-country. The spring temperatures fell below freezing this time of year, and it was easy to walk on the frozen ground. She ducked around the hazy green jack pines and made good time. By the time she arrived at a clearing, only a cabin was visible. It was dark, and no cars were present. There was also no river, a fact she discarded, although the cabin was named Riverside. *People name cabins all kinds of weird things, right?* The luminous hands on her watch showed 3:00 a.m. Either no one was home or the occupants were asleep. "Green dot?" Her voice was a whisper.

"It's stationary, about a hundred meters from the cabin. There is a long drive from the cabin out to the road."

Aside from Julia, there might be any number of men in the van. Kate guessed four, but she needed solid intel. With the trees as cover, she darted from tree trunk to tree trunk on an arc through the woods in the direction of the road. Soon the hulking shape of the BND van materialized through the trees. From behind a thick juniper bush, she watched through the night-vision goggles.

Two silhouettes were visible through the front windshield. A tall male with an elongated head was in the driver's seat, and a feminine head wearing a beret was in the passenger seat. The distance prevented Kate from recognizing either van occupant. *What are they doing?*

It took another five minutes for an answer. A man-sized shape appeared from the woods on the far side of the van, the van's sliding door opened, and he disappeared inside. *A scout.*

After another five minutes, the van doors opened and four people emerged. Three men and a woman, all dressed in tactical gear and black puffy jackets. The woman was Julia Meier. Strands of silver hair escaped from under her beret. The man with the granite face had the distinctive squared jaw of Frederick Wolf, Julia's longtime superior at the BND. Wolf wore a thick black puffy jacket and black ball cap. Steam puffed from his lips when he breathed. The two other men wore night-vision goggles on their foreheads and toted semiautomatic tactical rifles with skeleton stocks. One went north, and another took off along the road and ducked into the trees.

Those two men will flank the cabin and provide security. *It's how I'd do it.*

Wolf and Julia Meier waited near the van's hood with their hands shoved into their pockets. Puffs of breath escaped their mouths. *Waiting for their security to get into place.*

Mindful to watch for the two security men, Kate retraced her steps, which took her between the driveway to her right and the BND man on patrol to her left, the cabin's south. When she was deeper into the woods, she turned left and crept on a vector to take her behind the sentry. After a few minutes of walking, she crossed the man's footprints in the snow and moved to position herself between the lake and a spot where she assumed the man might watch the cabin. From her many years of surveillance experience and adding in the trajectory of the man's footprints, it wasn't difficult to determine the sentry's location. It took another two minutes of sliding from tree to tree before the sentry appeared. He was hunched over, half hidden behind a tree, with a clear view of the cabin.

Right where he should be.

The sentry whispered in German. "Number one in position."

Kate crouched behind a tree and waited with a firm grasp on her pistol's polymer grip.

THIRTY-ONE

Sysmä, Finland

Kate lifted the gun so the barrel was level with the sentry's head, which was ten meters away.

"The dot is moving." Kaamil's voice was a murmur in her headset. "Slow, like she's on foot."

Kate didn't reply, but she pulled the trigger twice. The gun barrel's gases caught in the silencer's chamber, and the pistol spat twice. The sentry slumped. Kate darted through the snow to where the dead man lay. She plucked the earpiece from his ear and, after a brief pat-down, found the transmitter in his jacket pocket. When she stuck the earpiece into her ear, she heard a German voice.

"Number two in position."

She took off at a run and retraced her steps through the snowy woods to the BND van, where she stopped to check for movement. There was none. Julia and Frederick Wolf had left the van, en route, Kate guessed, to the cabin. At a normal pace, it would take them at least ten minutes to walk the length of the long driveway.

There was no radio chatter as Kate tracked the second sentry's path through the snow. She hastened along the trail and slowed when the cabin appeared through the trees. The hulking shape of the second sentry was hunched next to a tree. She raised her gun but froze when a woman's German voice appeared in her ear. "All clear?"

It was Julia.

All hell was about to break loose if each sentry was required to reply with their status. Kate gripped her weapon and held her breath.

The sentry in front of her reached into his pocket and two metallic clicks sounded in Kate's ear. Similar to a handheld radio, the transmitter was equipped with a toggle designed to communicate when using voice was too dangerous. She reached into her pocket and found the appropriate button on the transmission unit. *But do I use one click to signify sentry number one? Or does two clicks signify all clear?* Perspiration broke out on her forehead. The wrong answer would blow her cover.

"Number one?" It was Julia's voice. "Indicate your status. Do you copy?"

One click, or two? Kate swallowed on a dry throat and clicked the button on the transmitter twice. Logic told her the all-clear signal would be consistent; otherwise Julia and Frederick would have to memorize too many different signals.

"We're proceeding down the driveway," Julia said.

Kate raised her pistol and pulled the trigger. The sentry fell over into the snow, after which she hurried to the dead man and crouched. There was a clear view of the cabin, which remained dark. Cordwood was stacked high along one wall. A wooden porch ran along the side and connected with a large deck with a view of the lake. A layer of moon-lit snow covered the iced-over lake.

She pocketed the pistol and snatched the semiautomatic rifle from the ground next to the dead sentry. Braced with one knee on the wet ground, she waited. The rifle was a Heckler and Koch HK 416 A5 with a suppressor attached to the eleven-inch barrel.

It didn't take long for the two BND officers to appear. Julia strode next to Frederick Wolf.

They believe they're protected by the two sentries.

Julia and Frederick emerged from the forest into the cabin's clearing. No weapons were visible, but their hands were shoved into their pockets. Kate tracked them with the rifle barrel trained on Wolf's chest.

Kate held her breath as the two BND officers marched along the snow-covered drive and stepped onto the porch. Wolf produced a pistol and held it in two hands, while Julia remained three steps behind.

Kate braced her shoulder against the tree, took aim with the rifle, and fired two rounds. The two bullets found the tall BND agent and spun him so he thumped against the cabin. Wolf struggled to stay on his feet, raised his pistol, and managed to get off a shot that careened wide of Kate's position. He crumpled to the deck and the pistol clattered to the wood. At the shots, Julia jumped from the porch and ran for cover.

"Stop." With the gun held to her shoulder, Kate strode into the clearing and held the barrel trained on Julia, who froze and yanked her hands from her pockets. A gun was in Julia's hand.

"Drop it, Julia."

The BND operative was motionless, but her eyes flickered to the woods behind Kate.

"You tried to ruin my life, Julia," Kate shouted. "You think I'd hesitate to shoot you now?"

Julia tossed the weapon into the snow. "This is going to cause an international incident, you know. CIA kills German citizens—"

"Does the BND know you're here?"

"You won't kill me." Julia's eyes flickered to the forest. "You won't kill Max's mother. You're in love with him, dear. You think he'd ever forgive you for killing his true mother?"

"Don't tempt me, Julia. That ship sailed when Andrei used me as his mule for that fake encrypted message. And Max..." Kate snorted. "He doesn't care about anything but himself."

"Hell hath no fury like a woman scorned."

"Yeah, well whatever." Kate waved her hand like she was swatting a fly. "I assume we're both here for the same thing. Let's go inside, shall we?" Kate tipped her head at the cabin's sliding door but held the rifle barrel trained on the BND agent. "Keep your hands visible."

Julia walked through the snow with her hands in the air and stepped onto the porch and over her dead colleague.

Kate slung the rifle across her back and drew the pistol before she followed Julia onto the porch. The sparse moonlight shined on a six-inch wood carving of a bear that sat on his hind legs on the railing near the wall. Kate did a double take as a memory flashed through her mind. It only lasted a second, but it sent chills up her spine. Years ago, when Kate was Chief of Station for the CIA in Moscow, she had recruited a high-ranking officer in the Belarusian branch of the KGB. The accomplishment made her career in the CIA. That man's name was Andrei Asimov, Max's father.

Andrei's nickname was the Bear. *Does this mean I'm in the right spot?*

The memory vanished, but Julia looked at her askance. "What is it? You look like you've seen a ghost."

"Never mind." Kate pushed Julia against the wall. "Arms up." She frisked the BND officer. There was a flashlight, which she pocketed, and a mobile phone, which she ensured was off before tossing it into the snow. After she was convinced Julia held no remaining weapons, Kate motioned at the door with her pistol.

Julia jiggled the sliding door's handle. "Locked."

Kate aimed her gun and fired two shots through the glass, which spidered. Julia kicked at the safety glass and it fell inward with a shower of glass shards. With the gun trained on Julia's back, Kate followed as the older woman stepped through the opening into the living room.

After all this time and all this work, am I about to discover the Vienna Archive?

―――

The cabin's living room was dark. The outline of a fireplace was along one wall, a low leather sectional was pushed into one corner, and a small kitchen was situated off the far end. Kate flicked on the flashlight with her left hand. The gun remained in her right. The interior was tidy and spotless. No magazines or framed pictures were in evidence. There was no sign of human inhabitants.

"Lie on the floor." Kate jammed the rifle barrel into Julia's back.

Julia complied.

Kate held the mic portion of her earbuds to her mouth. "Kaamil. You there?"

The other end of the line was silent.

She checked her phone, and the connection was still open. *He's probably getting coffee.*

Using a cord she yanked from a table lamp, Kate secured Julia's arms behind her. A more thorough search of the older woman uncovered a money clip with cash. "No identification, Julia? Standard operating procedure when operating illegally on foreign soil, huh?" Kate tied Julia's ankles using a second cord.

Once Julia was immobile, Kate leaned the rifle against the table and searched the cabin with Julia's flashlight. Her pistol remained ready in case someone was hiding in the cabin. When she stepped into the bedroom, she rechecked her phone's connection. The line remained open. "Kaamil?" Her voice was a whisper. "Kaamil, you there?"

Nothing.

Shit. A tinge of panic crept along her skin, but she shook it off and gripped the pistol as she searched the rest of the cabin. Aside from the living room and kitchen, there was a sauna off the main room, a single bedroom behind the kitchen, and a tiny loft at one end of the living room. It was all empty. As she searched, a rock formed in Kate's gut and a sinking feeling washed over her. There was nothing in the cabin. No clothing, no candles, and no food in the refrigerator. A small pantry contained canned goods, but there was no evidence anyone had been in the cabin for some time. Even the fireplace was spic and span with no ashes in evidence.

Unless there is a hidden room somewhere, the Vienna Archive isn't here.

"Nothing here, Julia." Kate's voice was high-pitched. "Where is it?"

"If it's not here, your guess is as good as mine." Julia

snorted. "Your intel led us here. This is the Riverside cabin, owned by the Asimovs. Andrei and I used to stay here—" Julia's voice caught.

Kate used the blade of Julia's pocketknife to test the floorboards. She started at one end of the room and attempted to pry up each one. They were all securely fastened down.

Julia's eyes followed her movements. "If there's a secret hiding spot, Andrei never shared it with me."

Kate was testing the walls with the knife blade when she heard it. A gentle *thump thump thump* from a distance. Kate nudged Julia with her foot as she cocked her head to hear better. "Hear that?"

"Yup. I assure you it's not us. Best untie me and give me a gun."

The decibel of the rotors increased, and it was joined by the roar of large vehicles from outside.

Kate removed the phone from her pocket and examined the screen. The connection remained open. "Kaamil, Kaamil. Are you there?" Stony silence.

The living room windows burst as small charges detonated and men in black commando gear rushed into the living room. They wore balaclavas to hide their faces and moved with well-trained precision. Rifles were trained on Kate, and she put her hands in the air. More men appeared from the front door and the side slider.

The chopper rotors grew louder, and wind whipped through the broken windows as a helicopter landed in the field to the cabin's north. A small form hurried across the field with its head down and bounded up onto the porch.

Lights burst on in the room as the figure appeared in the crowded living space. The fawn-colored leather jacket had been replaced by a black tactical down jacket, and she wore black leggings instead of the black skinny jeans, but her frizzy hair was held back by the same colorful headband. Cora strode into the living room, issued a few terse commands to her team, and stopped face-to-face with Kate. "Where is it?"

Kate shrugged. "It's not here." All emotion fled her body. It was a tidal wave that drained her of all energy and emotional fortitude. She laughed. It was a high-pitched squeal, and it racked her body in spasms that lasted minutes. When she calmed, tears streamed down her face and all the energy seeped from her muscles. She collapsed onto the couch.

Montenegro

It took twenty-four hours for the Monk to break which, considering his destroyed patella, impressed the team leader. Despite the pain, the Monk first claimed ignorance. After one fingernail was removed, the Monk admitted to being acquainted with the hacker who called herself Goshawk but insisted he had no idea where she was. Since all his servers were destroyed, there was no way to contact her.

While the team leader drank coffee and interrogated his subject, the other two operatives tore the house apart. A safe was discovered under the floorboards of the master bedroom closet. One fingernail was exchanged for the combination, and a laptop computer was found nestled in the safe, along with a pile of gold bars from the Perth Mint.

After three fingernails were removed, and the Monk

stuck to his story that he had no idea where the hacker was, the team leader placed the laptop on the hacker's lap. "When we run out of fingernails, we switch to the toenails."

The Monk put his bloody fingers on the keyboard. "What do you need me to do?"

"Find her, or the next fingernails we yank will belong to your daughters. They go to school in London, do they not?"

The Monk started typing frantically.

THIRTY-TWO

Sysmä, Finland

The next twelve hours ticked away slowly for Kate Shaw.

She was held at gunpoint by two soldiers while another soldier frisked her, removed her phone and weapons, and emptied her pockets. A set of thick plastic cuffs secured her arms in the front, and she was maneuvered to sit on the couch. Julia Meier was also frisked, trussed, and placed next to Kate. Two soldiers with automatic rifles, their faces hidden by balaclavas, observed the two women through dull eyes.

Activity bustled around them as the soldiers, directed by Cora, tore apart the cabin. Wall paneling was ripped off, floorboards were torn up, and even the fireplace chimney was removed and examined. Building materials were piled in the living room until there was nothing left of the interior. The sounds of deconstruction arose from outside as well. After a thorough search that lasted several hours, Cora stepped into the living room. There was a smirk on her face.

"Unless the Vienna Archive is buried somewhere on this property, I do believe you two were played."

"By the master," Julia muttered.

Cora crossed her arms. "We may not have the Vienna Archive, but we at least have you two. You will be the little worms, the bait that we can dangle at poor unsuspecting Mikhail. When he comes running to save his two ladies, we'll snap the noose around his neck. If one plan fails, revert to plan B."

The past few weeks played through Kate's mind like a video reel. Kaamil hacked into Goshawk's computer and found the cabin name. What if Max's hacker had let Kaamil find the cabin name? Was it a plant designed to expose anyone who searched for the Vienna Archive? It would be a trick right out of Andrei Asimov's playbook.

And what of Kaamil? Where did he disappear to? The analyst had disappeared from the open comms line. Was he compromised, or was he part of Cora's team?

And how did Cora get here so fast? To coordinate a team this large, this far in the backwoods of Finland, required advance planning. Men assembled, gear deployed, and helicopters provisioned. Since Kate hadn't known where they were headed before they arrived at the cabin, either they had tapped into Julia's communications or there was a leak in Kate's team. Because Kate's team consisted of herself and Kaamil, that was unlikely.

Unless Kaamil worked for Cora.

A pit formed in her stomach.

She let the idea rumble around in her head. If Kaamil were a double agent on Cora's payroll, that explained a few things. It explained the CIA leak. And it explained how Cora's team got here so fast. It explained his disappearance from the comms line. What a depressing thought.

Cora put a hand on her hip. "Right about now you're probably wondering how we know so much about what you two have been doing. I'd tell you, but then I'd have to kill you." Her laughter pealed through the destroyed cabin. "Which can be arranged. Let's just say we have well-placed resources in both of your organizations. We'll get a team out here with metal detectors and ground-penetrating radar in case Asimov buried his archive." She turned and issued commands to the team, who began packing their gear. "But I don't expect to find anything." Two soldiers grabbed Kate and Julia and propelled them onto their feet and out the cabin door. A cold wind licked at Kate's face, but she didn't feel it.

The helicopter sat in a field twenty meters away from the cabin. Two four-wheel-drive vans were parked near the cabin's door, not too far from where Frederick Wolf lay in a pool of his own blood. Kate stepped over the body as she was directed down the steps and through the snowy field. A pilot in the helicopter's cockpit started the engines and the rotors spun lazily.

Kate and Julia were placed on a bench seat in the aircraft, which shuddered as the rotors picked up speed. Cora and a soldier joined them, and the bird took off. The lights winked out as the guard shoved a black hood over first Julia's head and then Kate's.

The helicopter ride was shorter than she expected. It was hard to judge time, but Kate's instinct told her it was an hour. When the landing gear bumped down, strong hands lifted her from the aircraft's cabin, and she was directed to walk along a series of corridors. There was no way of knowing whether Julia remained with her. Kate counted the individual footsteps of the men around her to determine how many men accompanied her. No way to tell.

When the hood was yanked from her head, she blinked hard against a white light that prevented her from seeing. Three soldiers materialized as her vision cleared. They wore dark uniforms, and each stared at her with that blank stare of a professional. They wore the same uniforms as the men who raided the cabin. The room was stark and sanitary with white tile on the floor and walls. A drain was underfoot.

One of the soldiers pointed at her and said, "Off." The accent was vaguely Eastern Slavic and could have been either Finnish or Russian. Had they crossed the border into Russia?

When Kate did nothing, he gestured with his hand. "Off."

Kate held out her hands that were secured with the plastic cuffs.

The soldier used a combat knife to slice away the cuffs. "Now, off."

She didn't move, so another soldier, a short man with a blond crew cut, smashed the butt of his rifle into her stomach. The air went out of her, and Kate doubled over and sank to her knees. A soldier grabbed her and yanked her to her feet. The first soldier waved his hand. "Clothes. Off."

She did nothing. The short soldier rammed the butt of the rifle at her stomach again, but it caught her wrist and a flare of pain shot through her arm.

"Off. Clothes off. Or we take them off."

Kate dropped her jacket onto the floor. She kicked off her boots and her tactical pants. As she removed her shirt, she held the lead soldier's eyes. He returned her look with a dull gaze. When she crossed her arms over her bra, the soldier waved a finger at her. "Off."

She stared at the floor as she removed her undergarments, and she endured a rough cavity search with her eyes closed.

A stream of frigid water hit her from behind. She wrapped her arms around herself to stay warm. The freezing water drenched her from head to foot, and her skin broke out in goose bumps. After a few minutes in the shower, she was permitted to dry herself with a thin towel, and a set of blue hospital scrubs were thrown at her, which she put on.

She was led along a narrow corridor, also clad in white tile. The ceiling was at least two stories overhead, and powerful fluorescent lights were hung the length of the hallway. The tight group of soldiers and their captive passed several metal doors with small inset windows on either side of the hallway. When they reached the fourth door on the left, it was opened, and Kate was thrust into a tiny white room.

The door slammed behind her, and the *chunk* of a bolt rattled her bones.

The monitors showed the interior of two cells, both of which were identical. White tiles on the floor and walls with harsh fluorescent overhead lights. Each cell contained one woman, each in a similar state of duress. They both wore blue hospital scrubs, and each woman's hair was an unkempt mess. One, the silver-haired German intelligence officer, sat on her cot, her knees clutched to her chest with her head on her knees. The other, the curly-haired CIA officer, lay in a fetal position. The CIA officer had chosen not to lie on the cot but on the tile floor, a fact the kommissar found curious.

He crossed his arms and peered at the monitors. "Two people you care about, Asimov. Come and get them. And bring that damn archive with you."

It was cold. It was a great many other things—dank, maddeningly quiet, and lonely—but the cold overwhelmed everything else. People die from the cold all the time. They called it "dying of exposure." Her rational mind knew the temperature in her cell wasn't cold enough to die from.

What a disappointment.

Instead, Kate went on a hunger strike and refused to eat. After three days, two large men entered and forced a chalky liquid down her throat. When a soldier placed a bowl of food at her feet, she got a better idea. There was a spoon next to the bowl. She ate the oatmeal in the bowl and slipped the spoon into her sleeve.

When the soldier appeared to remove the bowl, he summoned a second soldier, who held her arms while the first soldier searched her. He found the spoon.

The spoon became her sole obsession. If she could hide a spoon, she might succeed in sharpening it on the tile floor to a point. A point she could use to cut the skin on her wrists and bleed out before they found her.

Please. One time, forget about the spoon.

They never did.

There was nothing left. There was no Vienna Archive. Kaamil had betrayed her. Spencer was probably dead. If she escaped, or was somehow rescued, her CIA career was over.

No spoon, no way to end the suffering. The cell was concrete and tile on all sides with a drain in the middle. For what, she only imagined. They fed her, allowed her to use the toilet. All observed, of course. By square-jawed men with stern faces who spoke no words. The fluorescent lights far overhead remained on. Until they winked off, which is when she was supposed to sleep. But she didn't. Not much, anyway. Curled in a ball on the cold floor.

As the days and nights passed, she became delirious from sleep deprivation. When sleep eventually came, she dreamed of spoons, only to be jolted awake when the overhead lights snapped on. When she realized there was no spoon, the tears came.

The drawstring had been removed from the hospital scrubs. Her feet were bare, so there were no shoelaces. Even if she could tie one of the pant legs around her neck, there was nothing to hang it on. The walls were smooth tile.

There was nothing left.

If only she had a spoon.

THIRTY-THREE

Undisclosed Location in Moscow, Russia

In the old days, enemies of Mother Russia were hustled into vans and dropped off at the large neobaroque yellow brick building at 2 Bolshaya Lubyanka Street in Moscow. Colloquially known as Lubyanka, the building was built in the same spot where Catherine the Great housed her secret police. After the Russian Revolution, Lubyanka housed the Cheka, Lenin's secret police, and its famous top-floor prison became operational in 1920. Because there are no windows on the top floor, prisoners often assumed they were incarcerated in the basement. This is where Max figured he was headed.

Max was frisked, relieved of the rental car key fob, trussed with plastic cuffs, and hustled into a van. But that's where the similarity to the usual Russian snatch-and-grab ended. The van sped along Berlin's city streets, through the gate of a private air terminal, and screeched to a halt next to a private jet. The two paratrooper-type soldiers accompanied Max and Kozov onto the plane, where they held guns trained on Max while the jet took off, achieved altitude, and pointed east.

Max attempted small talk with Kozov, but the Russian president's right-hand man buried himself in a laptop and ignored any attempt at conversation. After what Max estimated as a two-hour flight, they landed at a small airstrip, where Max was herded into another van and shackled to floor grommets. They took off at a high rate of speed and were followed by two Mercedes SUVs. Max assumed each SUV contained several paratrooper-style guards. Several Moscow landmarks whizzed by, including the 340-meter-high Ostankino tower, which at one time was the tallest building in the world. There was no hood over his head, which Max interpreted one of two ways: They were planning to kill him, or they assumed Max had no hope of escape.

Max caught Kozov's eye. "Your boss staying at home during the war, or is he down in Sochi on holiday?"

Kozov glared at him before he took his phone from his pocket and thumbed the screen.

"Are the rumors of his blood cancer true?" Max smiled, but Kozov ignored him and typed rapidly into his phone using both thumbs.

Instead of pointing east toward downtown Moscow and the Lubyanka building, the procession sped south into the Odintsovsky District, where it was rumored the Russian president kept a government residence and offices. They wound through tree-lined streets and after forty-five minutes, drove through a series of gates manned by armed guards before they disappeared into an underground garage. Max was hustled out of the van, propelled along a series of corridors, and tossed into a sparsely furnished room. The plastic cuffs were removed, and one soldier held a gun on Max as another snapped a GPS bracelet around his ankle.

The soldiers departed and Kozov entered. "Escape is futile. You're surrounded by a hundred of these soldiers and at least a half dozen fences and walls. If you were to escape, you're giving off a GPS signal, so we'll find you. The only way that thing is coming off is if you chew off your own ankle."

Max spread his arms. "I have no desire to escape. You're playing right into my hands." He flipped his wrist and glanced at it as though he were wearing a watch. "What time is it?"

Kozov shook his head. "Don't worry about what time it is. Take advantage of your creature comforts. If the boss doesn't get what he wants, those comforts won't last long."

With a shrug, Max collapsed onto a fabric couch. "In that case, send caviar along with crackers and smoked salmon. Also a nice red wine." Max waved his fingers at Kozov. "Posthaste, please. I'm starving."

The door slammed as Kozov and the two guards left Max alone in his cell.

It didn't take long. Max estimated it was twelve hours before he was visited by two capable-looking soldiers, a thug in a leather vest, and an annoyed-looking Kozov.

Until this point, Max was treated like a dignified prisoner. For fun he had jiggled the door's metal knob. *Locked in.* The room was furnished with the couch where he lounged, an empty credenza, a twin-sized bed with scratchy sheets, and a small table and chairs. A low bookcase contained a row of dog-eared works of Russian literature, including most of the canons by Tolstoy, Dostoevsky, Pasternak, Bulgakov, and Grossman. The room was clean, warm, and well-lit by fluorescent lights. To nap he covered his eyes with a pillow. Max assumed the constant lighting was to make the video feed resolution clear, for high up on the walls were mounted two video cameras. Even if he were to stack the chairs on the table, he wouldn't be able to reach the cameras or the lights, not that he had any intention of doing so. Such an action invited mistreatment. He would have enough problems once they figured out what he was doing here.

Instead of the caviar and red wine, he was brought a bowl of borscht, a hunk of bread with a hard crust but soft center, and a carafe of water. The meal was served with plasticware, which could be used to slit a man's throat, but Max left the plasticware alone. Better to let his original plan unfold. The borscht and bread were excellent, and he complimented the chef when two soldiers cleared the tray. Without anything else to do, Max began reading Tolstoy's *Anna Karenina*. It was oddly satisfying to read the text in Russian, as it was meant to be, instead of an English translation, which he was forced to read during his many years of Western indoctrination at the hands of the KGB.

He was halfway into Part One, where Anna's arrival was announced to help calm the frayed nerves of a family in turmoil, when the locks chunked and the door opened. The four men crowded into the room. The two soldiers took positions on either side of the door. Each was armed with a Taser and a holstered pistol. Leather Vest, who had a crew cut and a crooked nose but no visible weapons, stood over Max.

Kozov crossed his arms. "I assume the destruction of the *Exquisite* was at your hand?"

Max rose and set the book on the table. "The exquisite what?"

Kozov said nothing but nodded at Leather Vest, who took two steps and plowed a fist the size of an anvil into Max's solar plexus.

It wasn't that Max didn't see it coming. Leather Vest fought like a street brawler and telegraphed his every move. Max simply preferred the punches to being tased. He collapsed into the strike and landed butt-first on the sofa and stayed there gasping for breath.

Leather Vest stood over him and slapped a fist into his open palm as if he was waiting for Max to stand and challenge him. The brawler slapped his fist again and a third time, and each slap reverberated in the room.

Max caught his breath. "Are you actually pounding your fist into your hand?"

The only response from Leather Vest was a glare.

"I'm not going to fight you." Max raised his hands. "I'd rather not be hit with fifty thousand volts of electricity after I put you down, so do your worst."

Leather Vest glanced at Kozov, who shook his head. "Take a rest." Leather Vest leaned on the wall where he glowered at Max.

"What's this *Exquisite* thing?" Max pursed his lips and bunched his brow. He heaved air into his lungs.

"You know what it is." Kozov's eyes narrowed. "What I don't know is how you learned of the ship's existence."

Max chuckled. "There's a lot I know. I know the ship was built by the Lurssen Group and transferred to Blohm+Voss for all the finishings. I know the boat's ownership is hidden among an elaborate structure of shell corporations. I have all the shell corporation documentation. I know Morozov, one of his cronies, paid for the boat, but

Morozov has also received at least a dozen no-interest loans from—"

"Enough." Kozov held out a hand. "You got his attention, although all you did was save the boat from being confiscated as part of these... sanctions." Kozov spit the word out like it was bad fish.

Max shrugged.

"You know what I think?" Kozov crossed his arms. "I think you don't know who the kommissar is. Your precious Vienna Archive doesn't name the kommissar."

Max raised a palm. "Maybe you're right. What difference does it make?"

"Your deal isn't so good, Asimov. Sure, we can wipe out the councils. But the kommissar is still out there. What's to stop him from doing it again?"

"You put a stop to all the funds flowing out of Russia. While you guys do that, I keep looking for the kommissar. Once I find him..." Max shrugged and spread his hands palms-up.

"You're sure his identity is not in the Vienna Archive?"

"My father told me. It's not in there. He was a member of the kommissariat and even he didn't know the identity of the kommissar."

Kozov's eyes narrowed. "Your father was a member of the kommissariat?"

Whoops. A rock sank in Max's gut. *Was that the wrong thing to say?* "I'm not sure..."

"Do you know, Mikhail Asimov, what a problem that kommissariat has been for us?" Kozov clenched his fists. "They have robbed us—our country—blind. They have siphoned off billions of dollars of natural resources. They have coerced dozens of our elected officials to work against us, against our government."

You mean they've stolen billions of dollars from the Russian president. Max shrugged. "I understand what a problem they have been for you. That's why I'm here. I want it to end. For you, and for me. My father is dead. That's ancient history—"

"You want him officially pardoned? A traitor who conspired against his own country?"

Max spread his hands wide. "Yes. That's what I want."

"Nyet!" Kozov's face was red. "You're finished, Asimov. You and your family. Done." He turned from Max and walked to the door.

"Don't you wonder why I'm here?" Max leaned forward so his elbows were on his knees.

Kozov whirled. "You're here because we brought you here."

Max spread his hands. "You don't think I'd waltz into your little hotel back there in Berlin without a backup plan. Don't you want to know what it is?"

Kozov crossed his arms.

"Every forty-eight hours"—Max examined an imaginary wristwatch—"he's going to lose something."

"Lose what?"

Max shrugged. "Wait and see."

"Until?"

Max shook his head. "Until we make our deal. He wants this, trust me. He gets the names of all the men on the councils who work against him. Everyone who plots to steal your oil, siphon money from your economy, orchestrate deals against Russia. With that knowledge, he can eliminate them all."

"In return for a pardon."

"A full pardon for me, my family, and my father's good name."

Kozov snickered. "That's a deal breaker. Andrei was a traitor. He started this whole thing. He was a member of the kommissariat. He stole thousands of the KGB's documents. You know how we treat traitors. My boss will never go for it."

Max shook his head. "Incorrect. He didn't start it. He simply exposed it. These documents will free you guys from a conspiracy that operated right under your noses. That's the deal. Take it or leave it. Every forty-eight hours."

Kozov smirked, and the four men began to file from the room.

"Take good care of Paulina's new horse," Max said to Kozov's back.

Kozov turned. "You wouldn't hurt an innocent horse."

Max shrugged.

The men filed from the room. Leather Vest was the last to depart, and he held Max's eye as he backed out and slammed the door.

THIRTY-FOUR

Undisclosed Location

A muted news report from the BBC played on a screen over Goshawk's head. It showed nighttime shots of a large yacht sitting low in the water with flames licking at the sky. A pretty reporter in a rain jacket stood on the dock in the foreground and talked into a microphone. A light rain did nothing to put out the fire, but a steady stream of chemicals from a fire team made short work of the inferno. The headline read *Foul Play Suspected in the Bombing of a Multimillion-Dollar Luxury Yacht in the Port of Hamburg*.

"Foul play." Goshawk chuckled to herself. "Ya think?"

A glance at the digital timer on the wall indicated there were thirty minutes until she was to execute phase two. She finished the email she was writing and hit send. The encrypted email would bounce between three proxy servers before it arrived in the inbox of a *New York Times* reporter. Contained in the email was a financial trail with evidence that the *Exquisite* was indeed owned by the Russian president. That little detail might make the morning news in the US.

Goshawk unfolded her long legs from underneath her and padded out of the command center and down the long hallway. The corridor was lined with built-in bookshelves constructed from maple and filled with literature and reference books, including several first editions. She ignored the books as she waited for any indication that Max had been released. It was a long shot that their opening salvo might generate the desired outcome.

In the kitchen she busied herself with a whisk and green matcha powder. She first sifted the powder to remove the clumps and added a splash of hot water before using the whisk in a zigzag pattern until a froth appeared. She added more hot water and carried the mug back to her office using both hands.

No messages from Max. Nothing from MI6. Only a thumbs-up emoji from Cindy. She sipped and watched the news stream and waited.

When the digital timer hit forty-eight hours from when Max entered the Hellmann Schlosshotel in Berlin, she used a nail painted in bright white to push the F2 key.

Davos, Switzerland

The dart was silent as it flew through the air and impaled itself in the guard's neck. The soldier, an oversized brute whose tactical gear rode over bulging muscles, slapped at his neck. His knees buckled and he pitched onto his face.

The figure clad in all black scampered along the

driveway without a whisper and ducked into a recessed area the size of a phone booth along the side of the house. From there the intruder raised the dart gun, took careful aim, and fired a second dart that felled another sentry.

The dart gun slid into a custom holster where the backpack rested on webbing against her back before she jumped and swung to the top of a portico and levered herself up to the flat roof. After crouching for a few beats to ensure no one guarded the roof, the cat burglar stole to where a large skylight was inset into the roof. It took a few seconds to use a special cutting tool before a round hole appeared in the glass. The burglar slipped through the hole, hung for a moment by gloved fingers, and dropped silently to the floor and rolled. The dart gun appeared in her hand as she rose on one knee.

It helped her to know the exact security footprint of the house. All the details had been shared with her when she accepted the assignment. This enabled her to avoid the security cameras and the alarm system that protected the doors and windows. There was a skeletal staff of four guards. When the home's exalted owner was in residence, security was much more pronounced. Today the owner was elsewhere, preoccupied with a war, rumored health issues, and budget problems.

Silent as a bird, the intruder crept to the kitchen, where she shot a third guard. She made her way to the cramped security room in the back where a guard watched a football match on his phone and ignored the six security monitors. A fourth dart caused the soccer fan to slump in his chair. While in the security room, she shoved a tiny USB drive into a slot on one of the computers. Her employer assured her the simple action of inserting the USB drive would begin a routine to disable the alarm system and turn off the video cameras. Sure enough, after a moment, the six monitors turned dark. Her employer also assured her that the little virus she just introduced to the system was designed to erase all the hard drives. The cat burglar, a long-time veteran of such capers, took no chances and left the black mask over her face. A few strands of her raven-black hair escaped from under a watch cap.

After she double-checked that each of the four guards were dead to the world, she took a brief circuit through the home to ensure a fifth guard wasn't lurking somewhere. The mission was one prize, and she made quick work of securing the item. After it was nestled safely in her backpack, she decided to search the house. How often did one get to peruse a residence of such a high-profile world leader?

She began in the master bedroom, where she found a fan-folded package of condoms in a bedside table. "Practicing safe sex, bravo," she muttered to herself. The closet held a half dozen suits in black and dark blue. She ran her fingers over the silken wool. The labels were Kiton and Brioni. Two pairs of shoes were John Lobb. The bathroom contained dozens of lotions, shave gels, and hair products, all in brands foreign to her. "Taming that oily skin, are we?" She took a half-used bottle of something called Clarins Velvet Cleansing Milk and stowed it in her pocket. A stall contained a porcelain loo as well as a wall telephone. She rolled her eyes. A vision appeared of the small man barking orders to invade Ukraine while he took care of his business. It made her snort.

She leaped onto the bed and jumped up and down, leaving muddy boot prints on the Egyptian cotton sheets. She considered leaving a turd on the pillow but figured the less DNA in the crime scene, the better. They might investigate her boot prints to find they are common Doc Martens available pretty much anywhere.

The kitchen cupboards were empty of food, and there was the predictable bottle of vodka in the freezer. The prize was in the refrigerator. Near the top, where it was the coldest, sat six gold tins with the name *ALMAS Iranian Caviar* stamped on the lid. She removed the lid of one and used a finger to taste a dollop of the tiny white beads. The salty eggs melted in her mouth, and she stuffed the six tins into her backpack.

She ducked out a side door and pitched the untraceable dart gun into the woods. Four hours later she was in Zurich, where she left the prize in a locker in Zurich Main station before jumping onto a train headed north. As the spring countryside rolled by, she ate her way through one of the tins using crackers purchased in a shop next to the ticket booth.

The caviar was delectable.

———

Undisclosed Location

The green tea was pungent and delicious. Instead of taking the time to craft the matcha, Goshawk brewed her personal mixture of Fukamushi Sencha, Gyokuro, and Longjing in a small pot, which sat at her elbow. She cradled a pottery mug in two hands and savored its warmth and herbaceous-infused steam.

An alert dinged on her computer. She woke the monitor from sleep and found a note in one of her many chat windows. Goshawk used a variety of websites and applications to communicate with her peers and subcontractors. Some were simple chat rooms like Cyber Grape.com where she used a variety of names such as CaramelCamel and KreamyKomodo to interact with fellow hackers. She also used encrypted apps like Signal and WhatsApp to talk with people who she trusted but where she wanted privacy and anonymity. It was one of these private apps that dinged with an incoming message.

You there?

It was from a man Goshawk had only met once in person but who had helped protect her and wage battle against the American NSA. He went by the moniker the Monk, and he was a legend in the hacker space. He was a whistleblower, a leaker of secret information. It was rumored that the Monk was the source of the Pandora Papers, a vast trove of documents that exposed how the rich protected their money and avoided taxes through shell companies and offshore accounts. The International Consortium of Investigative Journalists, a non-profit with members in more than one hundred countries and in over a hundred media organizations, published the information and did not reveal their source. Still, the underground hacker community attributed the leak to the Monk.

Why was he reaching out now? Right in the middle of the negotiation with the Russian president? It triggered alarms in the back of her mind. It was a year since they corresponded, and now, in the middle of what might be their biggest operation yet, the Monk appeared out of the blue. *There are no coincidences.* Isn't that what Max always said? She sipped her tea and waited.

It took a few minutes for the next message to appear.

I need to see you. Remember that deal last year with

NSA? Well, I have news, but I have to see you in person. I can come to you in Paris. Can we meet tonight?

The hair on the back of her neck stood up straight and a knot formed in her stomach. *How does he know about Paris?*

On a hunch, she opened ProtonMail, one of her encrypted email boxes, and scrolled through the inbox. Most of the incoming mail was automatically sorted into folders using bots. Ordinarily she kept her inbox pristine, but because of all the work she put into this operation with Max, it had gone untended. Sure enough, as she suspected, near the top was an email from the Monk.

I have news about the NSA's attempts to find you. Nothing I can pass along digitally. Only in person. Can you meet me tomorrow in Paris? It's urgent. The email was time-stamped twelve minutes earlier.

A moment of panic overwhelmed her until she shoved it aside. *I got this.* An alert dinged. This one was an attack alert. Someone was trying to get through one of her firewalls. It was a garden-variety intrusion, and her security response was automated. Nothing to be concerned about.

Another alert dinged. And another. Her mind flew through the possibilities as alert after alert appeared on her screen. Not since the NSA attacked her defenses had there been such a coordinated attack sequence on her systems.

A niggle appeared in the back of her mind. In the past, the Monk had helped keep her safe from the NSA. *Coincidence?*

For a harried thirty minutes, she checked through her firewalls, proxy servers, and other defenses, and then double checked her security as the attacks increased in volume and intensity. Perspiration broke out on her brow, but she reached a breakthrough when she recognized the pattern of attacks. It resembled a distributed denial of service attack where hundreds and sometimes thousands of servers were harnessed to commit a coordinated attack on a website with the goal of taking it down. By overwhelming the server with traffic, ordinary users would be denied the services of that website. Except in this case, the massive number of basic attacks was designed to distract her and hide one true assault on her fortifications.

Her fingers flew over the keyboard as she fought through the barrage to find the main attack. It would be hidden among all the trash attacks, and since she now realized the intent and style of the attack, she was able to focus.

There.

She sat back as alerts flashed across her monitors. *Think.* The brunt of the main attack was clear in its intent. Find her geographical location, something that was a closely guarded secret among all computer hackers.

Okay, you fuckers. That's what you want? Let's give it to them.

She had enough confidence in her defenses to take a break and go into the kitchen and prepare a double shot of espresso from the automatic machine. With coffee in hand, she returned to her machine and set about reconfiguring her systems to allow a breach. The trick was to make it look like the attacker was smarter than her defense configuration. Let them in, but only allow them access to what she wanted them to find.

The attacker was about to be permitted to find what they were looking for in the form of her electric bill. The bill, with the Paris Board of Public Utilities, used a fake name but her real address. Ordinarily this information was sealed on a cold storage server that was disconnected from the internet. By shifting the file folder that contained her utility bills from cold storage to a well-guarded but purposefully vulnerable server, the attacker would find what they were looking for. Her fingers flew over the keyboard in a race against the attacker.

Done.

Goshawk sat back and waited.

After five minutes, the barrage of attacks slowed until the alerts became fewer in number.

They found it.

She rose, stretched, and guzzled a bottle of water before sitting back down to reconfigure her defenses. Although her security network had held, after this kind of an attack, best practice was to set up a new fortress.

The new defense protocols took her the better part of six hours, during which she fueled herself with a succession of matcha and espresso shots. When she was convinced that her network was secure, she rose from her chair, stretched, and padded in bare feet into a small room off the living area. There were bamboo floors and tall windows overlooking the city, where pale light streamed in from overcast skies. She worked off the caffeine through a twenty-minute high-intensity workout that included push-ups, sit-ups, plyometric drills, and walking lunges.

After she had worked up a sheen of sweat, she used a small towel to wipe her brow, took a swig from a water bottle, and strolled to the command center. Against all hope, she opened the encrypted chat application she used to communicate with Max.

Still no word.

THIRTY-FIVE

Undisclosed Location in Moscow, Russia

Kozov unleashed Leather Vest, and the brawler waded in with relish. Max did his best to take it, but the Taser might have been a better choice.

Leather Vest started on Max's torso and went to work like a boxer in the early rounds, landing jab after jab on Max's ribs, stomach, and back as he curled into a fetal ball to ward off the blows. When he was done with the torso, Leather Vest kicked at Max's arms, which Max curled around his head for protection. He rolled back and forth to distribute the blows to different parts of his body.

After a few kicks at his head for good measure, Leather Vest grew bored. "Stand and fight, you coward."

When Max stayed on the ground, the thug threw up his hands. The two security men, Kozov, and Leather Vest departed.

As they walked out, Max shouted, "What time is it, Kozov?"

Undisclosed Location

The news report on the monitor above Goshawk's head was uplifting. She used a remote control to unmute the sound and crossed an arm over her chest while the other elbow rested in her hand. She tapped a fingernail against the enamel of her tooth as she concentrated on the news report.

On the screen was a BBC reporter with flowing black hair dressed in a tailored suit. She posed on one side of an easel, where a small painting rested. The painting, which was twenty-six by twenty-one inches, was stretched over a wooden frame. A fussy man in a dark and unkempt suit stood on the opposite side from the BBC reporter. The fussy man talked animatedly as he gestured at the painting.

The painting itself was a curious piece. Comprised of blocks and other shapes in beiges, silvers, and grays, there were half a dozen nose-like images among the accumulation of cubist shapes. Along the bottom of the news screen were the words, *Le Pigeon aux Petits Pois, one of Picasso's stolen works, returned.* The reporter explained that the painting, whose name is translated as *Pigeon with Peas* and was worth an estimated twenty-five million dollars, was returned anonymously. A courier entered the Paris Museum of Modern Art and left a cardboard tube with the museum's curator.

After a three-hour interrogation by the Paris Police, the courier was released. The tube had been overnighted to his company with explicit instructions to deliver the package to the museum. Upon examination of the contents of the tube, the curator recognized the lost painting, which was stolen from that very museum in 2010. The man in the unkempt suit, who was an art historian, explained to the camera why he believed the painting to be authentic.

Goshawk used the mute button, took note of the time on the clock, and walked into the living room, where she watched an episode of *Game of Thrones*. When the alarm on her phone chimed, she returned to the office and pressed the F3 key.

Monaco

The woman known by her Instagram account as _sophia_ exited the Allées Lumières boutique and turned right on Av. de la Madone. She was tall and trim, with sharp cheek bones, alabaster skin, and straight black hair to her shoulders. She walked on platform boots that went up her calves and stopped at the knee. Bare thighs disappeared under a short skirt. Her walk was that of a runway model, and in fact, she had strutted along many a runway in her short time on earth.

sophia walked a block before she slipped into the back seat of a white Mercedes with blacked-out windows. She gave the driver instructions in Russian, and the burly man in the dark suit started the vehicle.

As the luxury sedan purred from the curb and merged into traffic, she removed a silk top from inside her jacket and tossed it on the leather seat. No, she didn't pay for it. Yes, she possessed the money to buy it. She had the money to buy whatever she pleased. Shoplifting was a hobby, something to do in an otherwise dull life full of parties, piles of cocaine, and endless shopping.

She held the top to the light and snapped a quick picture with her phone. Last week, _sophia_ celebrated her millionth Instagram follower by throwing a lavish party aboard Dmitry Orlov's yacht while it was parked in Port Hercule, Monaco's main port. The party raged all night, angered anyone who resided in a flat near the port, and resulted in two hospitalizations: one for alcohol poisoning and one for a cocaine overdose. No one in Monaco's government or in Orlov's entourage dared complain. No one wanted to anger _sophia_'s boyfriend.

sophia typed out a brief caption: *Pilfered this little gem this morning #fashionista #workinhard #freeneasy* and posted the picture. A brief scroll through her posts indicated she never revealed her face. The selfies were all with either her head turned, or her face obscured by her hair or the phone. Many pictures showed a bare midriff or a creamy thigh, but there was no cleavage. Her cleavage wasn't deep enough to compete with the rest of the breasts on Instagram. Most of her pictures showed her latest fashion choices, and some were of stolen items. As a result, her images were rewarded with thousands of likes.

The Mercedes glided to a halt outside her flat and she stuffed the silk top into her shoulder bag and stepped from the back seat. The terms of her trust fund were simple. Never mention her boyfriend by name. Never confirm that she was anyone's girlfriend. Be noncommittal about the sources of her wealth. Stay away from the United States. Always remain on birth control. Sleep with no other men. Visit Moscow or Sochi whenever he sent the jet. No Instagramming when visiting her boyfriend. That was it.

As she approached the revolving door that led to her

flat, a sprawling and eclectically decorated penthouse on the top of the Odéon Tower, she was swarmed by a dozen men in white uniform shirts and blue trousers. The blue pants were adorned with a red stripe along the leg and their uniform hats had a red sash. Pistols were raised and the Monaco police sergeant yelled for her to put her hands in the air.

sophia smirked as she set her handbag on the ground and raised her hands. Must be a mistake. Once the police chief found out who she was, the men in uniform would fall all over themselves to rectify the mistake. A top-level police official might lose their job. Her boyfriend owned this town and everyone in it.

The police hustled her into the back of a van. At the police station, she was relieved of her belongings, including her phone, purse, the stolen top, and even her Versace leather platform knee-high boots, and was placed barefoot in a holding cell. This was getting annoying. The last time this happened, and her identification was examined, she was released with fawning apologies. This time she asked for a phone call but was denied. As afternoon turned to evening, which became nighttime, and no one spoke to her, her emotions ranged from indignant to seething anger to glowering to sullen. Finally, she panicked and screamed at the top of her lungs for someone. Anyone. No one showed.

Where are my boyfriend's people?

Paris, France

. . .

The warehouse district where Goshawk maintained her fortified compound was on the south side of Paris in an industrial district that was busy with trucks and forklifts during the day but quiet as a mouse at night. Her building was unmarked, surrounded by a tall chain-link fence capped by thick barbed wire, and unremarkable in every way. Gray, windowless, and four stories worth of metal, the building blended in with all the others in the district. If the fact there was no loading dock caused anyone to scratch their head, they soon forgot about it as they continued about their business. The only visible way in and out of the massive building was a single reinforced metal door along a side street. The windowless door opened with a metal handle and there was a large security camera overhead. Unbeknownst to anyone watching the building, there were dozens of hidden security cameras around the perimeter. It was through these cameras that Goshawk watched the action.

She recognized the utility van parked outside for the past three nights as fake. No humans showed themselves, but it didn't take a genius to figure out it was a surveillance team. A quick search for the plate number indicated the van was stolen. When three men emerged on the night of the attack, her suspicions were confirmed.

It was 2:30 a.m. Paris time when an alert woke her from a fitful sleep. She rose from the couch and tapped the space bar on her keyboard to wake her computer. A grid of gray-green images from the security cameras powered to life and showed three men approaching the side door to her warehouse.

Her emotions fluttered between sadness and excitement, and she rose to make tea. She returned as a bright flash appeared on the monitor that showed the front door.

After she toggled to a second camera view, she settled back and blew on her tea to cool it.

The small door charge exploded, and the team leader drew his silenced pistol and flipped down his night-vision goggles. After a two-second pause to make sure his men were behind him, the team leader kicked at the door and entered the warehouse, pistol held in two hands.

His foot crossed the threshold and stepped onto a concrete floor before he stopped in his tracks, which caused his men to stutter-step to avoid running into him. The team leader spun slowly, his pistol tracing an arc around the interior of the empty warehouse. Through grainy-green night optics, nothing was visible except bare concrete that ran almost the full block. He peered at the ceiling to see massive halogen lamps, each one extinguished. A latticework of metal walkways crisscrossed the ceiling.

"What the—" It was one of his men, who entered behind him.

The sole thing visible in the entire space was a crude twenty-foot by twenty-foot building in the middle of the concrete floor. It was two stories in height and constructed out of two-by-fours and plywood, as if it had been hastily erected.

The team leader made his way across the concrete, alert for traps. There was a door set in the building's side. *Is this where she lives?*

He and his men took one circuit around the building, but there was nothing else in the warehouse. It was empty, and there was a single door leading into the plywood structure.

The team leader put his hand on the doorknob, and after confirming his two men were behind him with their pistols ready, he turned the knob. It was unlocked. With a glance back at his men, the team leader pushed open the door.

———

Her tea smelled of hibiscus and jasmine. Goshawk sat cross-legged in her desk chair and watched on a monitor as the three men fanned out and searched the interior of the warehouse. When one of the dark humanoid-shaped blobs on the screen approached the interior building, Goshawk set her tea on the desk and tapped her tooth with a lacquered fingernail.

———

The team leader walked into the twenty-by-twenty-foot room followed by his two men. If he was perplexed before by the empty warehouse, he was more confused by this room. There was nothing in it except a small ornate table like his grandmother used to have near the door where they put keys and mail.

This table was empty. At least that's what he thought until he approached the table and removed his night-vision goggles. There was a piece of paper. He used the flashlight from his phone to illuminate a sheet of printer paper before he picked it up. His two men approached as he held it up with a sinking feeling.

The paper contained one word.

Boom.

By this point Goshawk had switched to another monitor. This one showed the interior of the small room, where three men stood around a small table.

One man held up the paper, and a split second later, all three sprinted for the door.

Goshawk pressed a key on her keyboard.

A metal-on-metal grating noise filled the twenty-by-twenty-foot room, which was followed by a booming and slamming. The team leader reached the door to find it blocked by a sheet of metal. He pounded on it with a *thud*. The metal was thick. After he pushed on it and made every attempt to budge the door, a pit formed in his stomach. They were trapped.

That's when he noticed a hissing.

As he and his men searched for the source of the hissing, a wave of dizziness and nausea washed over him, and he fell to his knees. Thirty seconds later, he pitched forward, and his chest hit the floor as darkness consumed him.

When a team from the General Directorate for Internal Security, also known as the DGSI, France's counterespionage and counterterrorism agency, arrived at the nondescript gray warehouse in the 13th arrondissement of Paris, they were shocked at what they found. The tip had arrived through suspect channels, an untraceable email to the inbox of the agency's general director, who was peeved at the intrusion. A search of the warehouse yielded nothing except a twenty-by-twenty-foot building made of two-by-fours and plywood.

As one of the DGSI's tactical team approached the door with a battering ram, the door hissed open on its own and a wave of gas wafted out. Gas masks were produced, and the warehouse was aired out before they found three Caucasian men comatose but very much alive.

When the dust settled, the general director marveled at how three Russian thugs on Interpol's most-wanted list were found incapacitated in a warehouse on the southside of Paris. The DGSI was never able to penetrate the vast warren of shell corporations that owned the warehouse to discover its owner's identity. Nor were they aware when, months later, the warehouse was sold to a Scottish oil conglomerate.

THIRTY-SIX

Undisclosed Location in Moscow, Russia

The biggest struggle was not the physical pain he endured from the beating by Leather Vest. Yes, the bruising and aching was painful, but it wasn't the worst pain Max had felt. There was little blood because he had managed to protect his face and neck. And the problem wasn't the austere prison room. The plush cell was much nicer than the root cellar outside London. While the sheets were scratchy and the temperature remained in the sixties Fahrenheit, he was provided ample food and water, and he took his time reading *Anna Karenina*. When he finished that novel, a wide variety of choices awaited him. Nicotine cravings came and went, but he'd grown used to those sensations.

Max's biggest struggle was not knowing whether Goshawk was safe. Was she still executing their plan? Was she still sending their secret emissaries out to carry out each mission? If Goshawk were captured or somehow disabled by the Russian president's legions of hackers, Kozov and Leather Vest would be more aggressive. They might let Leather Vest do more damage. Maybe they would pluck Max's fingernails or something worse. As long as Goshawk remained safe, their plan was still viable.

One of the hardest decisions they had made was to move Goshawk out of her Paris compound. It had taken her years to build up her house-within-a-warehouse and only a weekend to tear it down and move her belongings into storage. Now she was sequestered somewhere no one would find her. *Hopefully.* It gave Max a small level of comfort.

A folded pillow was under Max's neck to ease the pain that radiated from his head. His legs were stretched out on the leather couch and moved as little as possible to prevent shooting pain in his torso. He was deep into Part Two of *Anna Karenina*, where Anna succumbs to Vronsky's advances, when the door banged open. Max braced himself for another onslaught by the giant with the broken nose.

Kozov entered, flanked by the two bodyguards, but Leather Vest was absent. Kozov resumed the position he always took when talking to Max. He leaned against the wall with crossed arms. "You need to release her."

Max swung his legs to the floor and hid the grimace of pain that shot through his obliques. Careful not to crack the book's spine, Max memorized the page he was on, closed *Anna Karenina*, and set it on the table. He held out his hand.

"What?" Kozov's eyebrows went up.

"I need a phone."

Kozov stared at him.

Max shrugged. "Do you want me to do it telepathically?"

The Russian president's right-hand man did nothing. He stared at Max and shook his head.

"I can get her released with one phone call. Otherwise, she's going to rot in that cell for a long time."

"She won't stay in there longer than an hour on a shoplifting charge."

Max pursed his lips. "Right about now the Monaco Public Security are receiving a packet of documents that show how she is laundering funds on behalf of your boss's cronies."

"That's a lie!"

"Listen, Kozov, I'm not making this stuff up. I'm just following the paper trail."

"The paper trail that your father stole!"

"Doesn't make it not true." Max smiled. "He stole it from the kommissariat and the KGB. Without him, we wouldn't have this chance to unwind the whole thing. That benefits your boss." Max spread his hands. "I understand your boss isn't used to losing. He's usually in the position of leverage and everyone gives in to his demands. I'd encourage him to set that aside and think of this as a win-win situation. He's going to get the names of the men who work against him. Men who are actively siphoning Russia's wealth from its borders." Max wanted to cross a leg over the other but didn't dare risk showing any discomfort. "It's not like I'm blackmailing him. He stands to gain a lot in this transaction. I simply require something in return."

Kozov didn't move.

Max stood and stretched. "We haven't begun to hurt him financially. We have records showing a vast number of shell companies and cronies who all hide his wealth. We have a line on where a lot of it is." Max chuckled. "But when his money starts to disappear, and the wealth of his closest friends vanishes, what then?"

Kozov traced a finger along his lower lip.

Max eased himself onto the couch. "You know I have all the files. It's worse than the Panama Papers or the Pandora Papers." Max referenced two document leaks that showed how the world's wealthiest hid their wealth in legal and non-legal tax shelters, shell corporations, and offshore banking. "If you thought I was bluffing before, now you know I'm not. If you thought I was bluffing, I'd be dead right now. The reason I'm still alive is because you need me alive."

Kozov pushed himself off the wall and strode to the door.

"Kozov."

The Russian president's fixer turned.

"He doesn't need this fight right now. Why not eliminate one of the fronts he's fighting on?"

Kozov exited the room followed by the two bodyguards. The door slammed behind them.

THIRTY-SEVEN

Building 311, Moscow, Russia

The Russian hacker team assigned to find the Vienna Archive was scheduled to be at work by 7:00 a.m. seven days a week. When a dozen of the more eager members of the team arrived that morning at 6:30 a.m., they found a new man sitting where Colonel Semenov once sat. This man was taller, his bushy eyebrows remained in a permanent furrow, and he didn't speak.

Wordlessly, the team found their desks and read through individual assignments. Several of them got coffee from the massive urns along the back and exchanged questioning glances with each other. They dared not speak of it here in this room.

None of the computer hackers ever placed eyes on Colonel Semenov again.

———

Undisclosed Location in Moscow, Russia

"How do you intend to transfer the information to us?" Kozov crossed his arms.

The two bodyguards were nowhere in view. The door remained open, but the little red lights on the video cameras above Max's head were off. Fewer witnesses among the staff. Kozov stood along the far wall. A folder was trapped under one arm. Dark circles were under his eyes, and he wore a deep frown. Must have been a rough few days for the so-called fixer, who hadn't been able to fix anything on behalf of one of the most powerful men in the world. No sense in rubbing it in.

Don't over close, his father always warned. Get what you came for and get out. No more, no less.

"Once I have the pardon, and I'm safely back in Europe, you give me a server address. The files will be deposited there." Max closed *Anna Karenina* and set the book on the table.

"What's to prevent you from failing to provide the files if I let you go?"

These guys are dense. Max spread his hands. "I want this deal. It's to my benefit to give you this information. I want these consortium members dealt with as much as you do. If I give you the files now, without receiving my pardon first, and you renege on the deal, my only leverage is to continue to take shots at you and the Russian president. That accomplishes nothing except to distract me from finding the kommissar and shutting him down. Give me the server address and I'll arrange for you to get the information."

Kozov walked to the small table and set the file down

and put an Android phone on top of it. "Make the call and get her released."

Max flipped open the manila file to reveal a single sheet of paper. The header contained the elaborate seal and letterhead of the office of the Russian president. The footer showed the distinctive swirled signature of the man himself. When Max read the text, his blood surged, and he dropped the document on the table. "This isn't what we agreed to."

Kozov shrugged. "You mean it's not what you asked for."

The document pardoned Arina and Alex, but it was silent on Max and Max's father. Between the anger and the pain from his injuries, Max eased himself onto the couch. "No deal, Kozov."

The Russian president's man sneered. "He's never going to pardon you or your father. My strong suggestion is to take the deal. Your sister and nephew will be able to live safely wherever they want in the world. Even return to Minsk or Moscow if they so choose. Your father is dead. And you... you seem to have a bit of insurance." Kozov nodded at the table where the Android phone sat. "Make the call."

Max stood and paced away from Kozov. After all the battles, all the pain, and everyone who had been hurt along the way, he finally had what he wanted. What he'd sacrificed so much to get. What Kate, and Julia, and Spencer had all sacrificed for. What Alex and Arina needed. It was finally time to set aside his personal desires and take the win. He turned back to Kozov. "I need one more thing."

"What could you possibly—"

Max picked up the dogeared copy of *Anna Karenina*. "I'm taking this. I want to finish it on the plane."

Amsterdam, Netherlands

When the alert rang out, Goshawk's knees weakened and she almost collapsed. At top speed, she ran out of the workout room, where she was performing a series of tai chi postures, and into the command center. The alert was a special series of chimes configured to ring when she received a communication from Max. She folded herself into the desk chair and used her toe to send it wheeling across the concrete floor to where a laptop sat on a desk. In the secure chat window was a single word.

Yo.

Sweeter words were never typed. Emotion welled in her throat. Her heart soared and her fingers quivered as she typed back. *Who is this?* She collapsed into laughter. It was a much overdue release. Joy bubbled over as tears streamed down her cheeks.

Max's response appeared on the screen. *Ha ha, very funny.*

Goshawk wiped her eyes and composed herself. *What time is it?* After she typed the safety phrase into the chat window, she held her breath. The wrong answer meant Max was under duress.

Time to get ill.

A deep breath escaped her, and she took a sip from a water bottle. Nothing like the Beastie Boys to make her day. *Where are you? Everything okay?*

I'm in Europe. I'm right as rain. Time to finish this thing. I have a server address for you.

There was one more layer of security. *Tell me.* She held her breath.

A server address appeared in the chat window along with the phrase: *By blood or tears, have not the wise and free wept tears, and blood like tears?* It was a line from Shelley's poem "Ode to Liberty," and Goshawk smiled. The poem was a preset code that indicated she should release the files that detailed the identities of the consortium members. *Give me a minute.*

Also please unwind Monaco.

Goshawk rolled her eyes as she responded. *Bummer, but okay.* It took her a few minutes to execute the preprogrammed routine to send the correct files to the specified server address. While the majority of the Vienna Archive digital files sat in cold storage, the files detailing the consortium members' identities were on a well-guarded server connected to the internet. Pre-staging the files like this allowed her to act quickly. She sent Max the twelve-word seed phrase required to decrypt the files, which he would need to provide to Kozov. Only then did she set in motion the actions required to release _sophia_ from Interpol's custody.

She tapped a nail against a tooth before she typed. *Are you coming to see me?*

His response made her stomach flip. *Soon, sexy girl. Soon.*

The euphoria of Max's release was tainted by a news alert that popped up on Goshawk's computer. She used a service to monitor several hundred keywords, and when one of those keywords appeared in a news article, the service dumped a link to that news article into a web-based feed. Keywords such as *Mikhail Asimov, KGB, FSB, Kate Shaw, Julia Meier, BND*, etc. were automatically monitored. The keywords generated hundreds of false positives, news articles that were of no interest to her. Occasionally the service generated something of interest. That morning, as she sipped tea and scrolled the list of results, one headline stopped her cold.

Infamous Computer Hacktivist The Monk Found Dead

Goshawk set her mug on the desk and read the article. Details were light, but the article outlined the Monk's most famous hacks, including using telephones to steal international calling card codes before the internet even existed to being identified as the source of the Pandora Papers, 11.9 million documents outlining the secret offshore accounts of billionaires, celebrities, and world leaders. The Monk was hailed by Julian Assange, the founder of WikiLeaks, as an international hero for the hacktivist's contributions to "illuminating the illicit secrets of the powerful," and he called the Monk "a beacon of light in the quest for free speech."

The Monk was found dead from multiple gunshot wounds by his housekeeper. Police were able to identify the Monk as Samuel Sampson, an American citizen with a dozen warrants for his arrest and who resided in Montenegro, where there is no extradition treaty with the US.

Goshawk closed the browser and carried her tea to her yoga room, where she worked through a series of sun salutations and remembered how the Monk had sacrificed to help her when she needed it the most.

THIRTY-EIGHT

Kiev, Ukraine

"Sir, the helicopter is ready."

The announcement was by the burly man in the dark suit who stood at the door to Artur Pipenko's office. A curly cord ran from his collar to his ear, and the bulge of an Uzi submachine gun was visible under his suit jacket.

"Thank you, Bogdan. Give me five minutes." Artur Pipenko, a slight man with wispy hair and tiny glasses, resumed his study of a thick document.

Bogdan nodded and assumed his normal post outside his boss's doorway. A lieutenant, who was also well-armed, was across the hallway and watched over the atrium. Bogdan performed a routine radio check with his men and used code words to indicate Pipenko was moving soon.

This excursion was ill-advised in Bogdan's mind. While fighting in the area around Kiev had slowed, the conflict was escalating in Eastern Ukraine. The Russians increased the intensity of attacks, and the pro-Russian separatists waged a guerrilla war against the Ukrainian soldiers. Why his boss insisted on visiting the oil fields in Donetsk was a mystery to Bogdan. It was either bravado or stupidity, but Bogdan's boss was not a man easily dissuaded or intimidated. Artur Pipenko didn't become this wealthy by wilting in the face of adversity—he had become wealthy by taking calculated risks, like joining the Council on Petroleum and Natural Gas in direct opposition to Moscow.

The office door banged open, and Bogdan's boss appeared. Artur Pipenko was a slight man made more bookish by his delicate rimless glasses. The tiny man strode down the hall while he shrugged on an overcoat, and the two security men fell in behind.

"Flight plans are filed?" Pipenko's voice was baritone for such a small man.

"Affirmative. As you specified." In fact, Bogdan had told a small fib. The fib was a white lie, but nonetheless risky. Pipenko was a man of principle, and despite the man's pedigree of illegal business dealings, the executive insisted on following rules like flight plans and speed limits. Honor among thieves. Or perhaps it was rooted in the man's staunch nationalism for his beloved country of Ukraine. Pipenko was proud of the country for what he described as seceding from the Russian Federation back in 1991. Bogdan was smart enough not to share his opinion that Ukraine had sold out to the West.

The procession of three men took the stairs and emerged onto the building's helicopter pad and boarded a black and white helicopter. It was a plush Sikorsky S-76C, also known as the Black Hawk model, an older model acquired used from a Saudi family. The interior was appointed with leather and large captain's chairs, and the chairs showed wear and tear. Pipenko called it patina.

As the bird lifted, a junior member of Bogdan's security team visited the men's room and sent a brief text using a burner phone.

The helicopter used a flight crew of two, and even with the two bodyguards, the large passenger compartment was roomy. Artur Pipenko busied himself with phone calls as the bird accelerated on an easterly course. Bogdan watched the terrain change from the concrete jungle of Kiev to the lush spring countryside. There was no military activity, but the burned-out carcasses of Russian military equipment littered the roadways and dozens of buildings lay in smoldering ruin.

Bogdan's senses were on high alert as the pilot announced they had passed into the Donetsk region. He wasn't sure what he expected to see, a procession of Russian troop carriers or a line of Russian tanks plowing through a field, but there was no visible activity on the ground.

They landed in a field adjacent to a sprawling complex that housed Ukrnafta's Donetsk offices. Bogdan breathed a sigh of relief when a deployment of Ukrainian troops and tanks paraded by. His boss's meeting ran long, and by the time Pipenko reappeared, dusk had settled over the region. The executive's eyebrows were furrowed as he hastened to the helicopter, which meant the meeting went poorly. Bogdan was familiar enough with his boss's moods to let him be, and they took off in silence. The crew had refueled the helicopter at a nearby airfield controlled by the Ukrainian military during Pipenko's meeting, and Bogdan almost let himself relax as they turned west. His head was back on the headrest, which is why he didn't see the missile whoosh at the helicopter until the pilot executed an evasive maneuver.

The surface-to-air missile swished from a dark stand of

trees amid a white plume of smoke. It roared skyward, wavered, and acquired its target. The alert pilot deployed countermeasures and banked left, which threw Bogdan against his harness. Pipenko cursed as his mobile phone flew from his grasp and banged against the aircraft's window. Bogdan knew the curse was because of the interrupted phone call, not because of the threat to Pipenko's life. It didn't matter; it was Pipenko's last phone call. The evasive maneuvers were futile.

The 9M317 missile's proximity fuse performed a calculation and detonated the Frag-HE warhead less than a meter from the helicopter's fuselage. The resulting explosion tore away the bird's lightly armored exterior and fire engulfed the interior. Pipenko and Bogdan died instantly. The wreckage spiraled to the ground, which is what killed the flight crew.

Lisbon, Portugal

Leoniod Petrov gazed at himself in the bathroom mirror and used a pair of tweezers to pluck a hair. As he leaned on the granite counter with two scarred knuckles, he scrutinized his face. A few new lines were in the tanned skin around his eyes. He blamed the recent actions by the Russian president to target members of the Council on Petroleum and Natural Gas, of which Petrov was Number Six. It wasn't enough to invade Ukraine. Someone had provided the identities of the council to the Russian president, and Artur Pipenko's death was being called a casualty of war, but Petrov knew better.

Petrov's tenure on the council had lasted ten years, a

time during which he amassed considerable wealth. Thus far he had somehow survived the assassin's assault on his fellow council members, but now that run was over. A half dozen members of the council, and dozens of others across the other three councils, were now either imprisoned for trumped-up tax evasion charges or were dead.

Time to vanish.

Petrov had resigned his post as chairman of Rosneft, one of Russia's largest oil and natural gas conglomerates, and departed the country. He had no family in Russia, which made it easy to abandon his Russian properties. His liquid assets were secreted away in offshore bank accounts in countries like Switzerland, Portugal, and the Caribbean, out of the reach of the Russian president.

The face that stared back at him in the mirror was resolute. A pronounced jaw, jet-black hair, and an unwavering gaze. He leaned over the counter and used a tiny spoon to snort cocaine into each nostril and rubbed a fingerful of the powder along his gums. After he examined his nose to ensure no white powder remained, he adjusted his cummerbund, tugged on the ends of his ruby-red bow tie, and nodded to the head of his security detail who stood behind him. *One last thing to do.*

"Let's go."

The security man spoke into a cufflink mic and followed his boss into the hotel suite's expansive living area. Outside the plate-glass window, the lights of Lisbon twinkled in the darkness. A form stirred under the satin sheets, and a young woman rose and braced herself on one arm. The sheet slipped aside to expose heavy breasts. "Don't go, Leoniod. Stay here, baby."

"Go back to sleep." Petrov turned his back on the

woman and slipped a thin cigarette case and gold lighter into his jacket pocket.

The girl huffed and flopped onto the sheets and pulled the covers over her head.

Petrov touched his security guard's arm. "See that she's not here when I get back."

With a man in front and a man behind him, Petrov stepped into the hallway and headed for the private elevator that would take him to the party at the rooftop bar.

The party was the kind that didn't make the tabloids. The organizers took extreme measures to hide the event from the public. No media was alerted, and the hotel staff was sworn to secrecy. Paparazzi knew nothing of its existence. The guest list was curated and confidential.

If one made it through the phalanx of black-suited, gorilla-shaped men in the lobby, ascended the elevator rimmed with security cameras, and got through the metal detector and the horde of jar-headed security men on the sixty-third floor, they would find themselves on a moonlit veranda. A kaleidoscope of purple and blue lights winked over a party filled with coifed and beautiful people. The guest list was comprised of tuxedoed men who represented the wealthiest of the oil and gas industry.

A white-gloved steward thrust a glass of Cristal into Leoniod Petrov's hand as he emerged onto the veranda alone. His bodyguards had been relegated to the hotel lobby. Male and female dancers writhed to a pulsing beat on raised daises. A glittering pool, lit by submerged lights, was to his right. Handsome men in dark suits smoked cigars while they talked close to one another's ears to be heard over the thumping bass. Women gathered in groups, admiring gowns, most wishing they had spent more on their rented jewelry. The bathrooms, officially segregated by sex, hosted unisex groups of partygoers who shared their drugs and refreshed their makeup.

Petrov set the Cristal aside and wove his way to the bar, where he asked for a vodka, chilled. As he turned his back to the bar, he sipped the alcohol and savored its sweetness on his numbed gums.

Across from Petrov, a short and rotund man sidled over to the railing that overlooked the city. The man's black suit was tailored, and his patent leather shoes glinted in the blinking lights. Petrov downed his vodka, asked for another, and strode to the railing. "Bonjour, Monsieur Lafleur."

The round man turned with a smile on his fleshy face. "Ah, monsieur, you speak French. My people didn't mention it—"

"No." Petrov changed to English. "That's about all I know."

Lafleur chuckled. "Well, that's more than I know in Russian." Lafleur carried a goblet full of red wine in a pudgy hand. The obese man was the CEO of France's largest natural gas conglomerate, Groupe PetrolTech. Petrov, who represented his own privately held oil and gas exploration company based in Trinidad and Tobago, wanted a deal with PetrolTech. One last deal to shed assets before he disappeared. PetrolTech also wanted a deal, and Lafleur suggested the party as a place to meet away from the eyes of media and corporate rivals. Petrov leaned on the rail, sipped his vodka, and made small talk with Lafleur while the party raged on behind them. When Petrov excused himself to visit the men's room, neither he nor Lafleur paid attention to the two dark-suited men who also visited the restroom.

The party ended when a blood-curdling scream pierced the night. It shattered the eardrums of a man and a woman who were hunched over a mirror of cocaine at the sink. They whipped around and the drugs scattered and the small mirror shattered on the tile floor. A young woman in a tight white dress stood outside a stall, her palms pressed to her cheeks. For the moment, her screams had ended, and she hyperventilated, her chest heaving.

A security guard rushed in to find an older, athletic man with slicked-back hair sprawled over the toilet. A pool of crimson blood that matched the corpse's ruby-red bow tie was puddled on the black and white tile floor next to the bowl. Two holes were in his chest and one bullet hole was in the back of his head.

The woman in the tight white dress ran to the restroom door, her stilettos clattering on the tile, and burst into the party. She stopped, clenched her fists, and let out another scream.

Seoul, South Korea

The Chinese Communist Party operated in mysterious ways, which is why Colonel Wu wasn't surprised when she was contacted by the office of the president through back channels. Zhao Zheng had, of course, placed a bounty on Wu's head in the wake of the London debacle, and the president's emissary offered her a deal. Perform this one task and the bounty on her head would be rescinded.

The security detail for Zhao Zheng, the director of the Ministry of State Security, was unparalleled in terms of its quality and secrecy. This was especially true when the director traveled overseas, as he was wont to do, despite his staff's misgivings. Two private jets filed different flight plans, and the flight crews didn't know if Zheng was on their flight or whether he was on the second jet. A body double was often used, which faked out Zheng's own staff. An armed contingent of four to six highly capable men traveled with the director at all times. When traveling on official state business, the director was protected by the host country's security apparatus, which coordinated with Zheng's own security team.

After Colonel Wu's disappearance and the disaster at the Chinese safe house outside London, Zheng would have changed many of his security protocols. But Wu had two things going for her. One was a vast network of friends in the ministry, officers who owed her, and agents who secretly sympathized with her loyalties. The other was knowledge of Zheng's proclivities, the things Zheng liked to do when no one was looking. There wasn't much. Zheng was a disciplined and principled man. He drank only at official functions and even then drank little. He had been faithfully married for two decades, and he didn't do drugs. If there was any overindulgence, it was fitness. Zheng ran an average of six miles a day. While the director's model behavior was impressive and admirable, there was a single flaw.

Zheng enjoyed a simple indulgence when traveling: a post-run deep tissue massage in the privacy of his hotel room by a vetted masseuse. It was one of the few times Zheng was alone. As one of Zheng's trusted advisors, albeit former, Wu was aware of this indulgence.

Right now, the director was sequestered in a top-floor suite in the Seoul Four Seasons, around the corner from the US Embassy. Wu watched from a van parked across the street as Zheng departed the hotel in a jogging suit flanked by two bodyguards. The massage was scheduled for an hour after Zheng returned from the run. Wu knew this because a friend had slipped her Zheng's itinerary. She smoked three cigarettes while she waited. As the director returned from his jog and entered through the service entrance of the hotel, Wu slipped from the van.

The masseuse appeared right on time. The four armed guards eyed the attractive young woman as she dragged a folding table and a massive duffle. One guard pawed through the duffel and examined the table. Another guard waved a wand over the woman's body and found nothing threatening. One of the guards rubbed massage oil between his fingers to test for poison. The woman's background was already scrutinized, and, in fact, the same masseuse was used on prior occasions by the director. The guards had searched the director's room while he was on his jog and performed a routine scan of the room for any listening or recording devices. There were no connecting doors and only one way in and one way out of the suite.

The masseuse was deemed safe and granted access to Zheng's suite. She zipped up the duffle bag, which was filled with oils and towels and other massage gear, and pulled the folding massage table behind her. A guard unlocked the door and moved aside as she dragged her gear into the room.

When she passed through the suite's door, she screamed. It was a piercing shriek that brought guards running. A gruesome sight greeted the two bodyguards when they burst through the door.

Zheng was sprawled on his back. He wore a white robe, which gaped open at his chest. Blood was everywhere. It covered the beige carpet and the gold upholstery on the couch and two chairs. It had soaked through Zheng's robe in crimson splotches. Blood spatter covered the walls.

As the masseuse belted another scream, one bodyguard tiptoed through the blood and took hold of the director's wrist. There was no pulse, which wasn't a surprise. A jagged knife cut gaped from one ear to the other.

The next day, the four bodyguards of the late director's security team were promoted and reassigned, one to each corner of the Chinese empire. Their respective families were awarded luxurious apartments and their children were upgraded to more prestigious schools.

A search commenced for Colonel Wu, who disappeared without a trace.

THIRTY-NINE

Bath, England

Max stepped from the passenger seat of the Range Rover and was greeted by Tom, the groundskeeper, whose ruddy face was clouded by a frown. A vicious wind blew his wispy hair in all directions, and he tried to tame it with a gnarled paw. The former SAS commando wore a worn barn jacket over several layers of warmth, wool slacks, and a pair of muck boots plastered with mud. The clouds were low, and the ubiquitous English mist made it feel like they were walking through a moist sponge.

Max put an arm around the venerable Special Air Service soldier and turned him in the direction of the house. "What is it, Tom? Why the long face?"

Throughout the many surveillance detection flights between Moscow and the UK, Max thought primarily of two things. One was a warmth that came from finally protecting his sister and nephew. After a year of fighting, he savored the comfort of knowing that at least Arina and Alex were safe. He also relished the idea of seeing Alex.

Tom's feet dragged in the gravel drive. "It's not my fault. I threatened. I pleaded. I asked them to wait one more night. I knew you'd be here today, but they... they left. She said they couldn't wait."

Max stopped and faced the older man. Tall and muscular even in his advanced age, Tom met Max eye to eye. He put his hands on Tom's shoulders. "What do you mean? What happened? Who said..." It dawned on him. "Arina was here, wasn't she? And she took Alex."

Tom nodded. His eyes clouded. "I'm so sorry."

Max's head sagged, and he peered at the ground. *Again. And just when she didn't need to.* The document on official Office of the Russian President letterhead with his signature and seal pardoning Arina and Alex was nestled in his jacket pocket. Max put his arm around Tom's shoulders and guided the groundskeeper along the drive and up the wooden stairs to the front porch. "It's not your fault, Tom." Alex and Tom had grown close in recent months. *Tom misses Alex as much as I do.* "She's his mother, I guess she's entitled."

Inside the farmhouse was warm and dry, and the smell of beef and onions promised one of Tom's wife's famous shepherd's pies. A generous portion of the succulent dish and a few measures of Irish whiskey did little to help the pit in his heart. When the food was gone and the kitchen cleaned, Tom poured a glass of whiskey for Max and produced a bottle of scotch, from which he poured two glasses. "We're going to miss you around here, sir."

Before Max was able to ask what he meant, Callum Baxter appeared in the doorway and accepted one of the glasses of Scotch from Tom. The MI6 officer wore a thick sweater, which was a departure from his traditional tweed jacket with the arm patches. His goatee was trimmed, and he wore a new pair of rimless spectacles.

Max raised his drink. "Those glasses are very fashionable, Callum. Who's the lucky lady?"

Baxter waggled his trimmed eyebrows.

After the three men raised their tumblers and sipped, Baxter tipped his head in the direction of the den, and Max followed him through the door with the Irish whiskey bottle in his hand. The two men settled into leather wing chairs.

"Were you here when Arina showed up for Alex?" Max poured them both another round of the amber whiskey.

Baxter tasted the whiskey before he nodded. "She was in a hurry."

"No one called me."

"You weren't exactly on the grid." Baxter produced a leather pouch and a pipe and proceeded to fill the bowl with pungent tobacco.

Max sipped. Something was off with Baxter's tone. "Was she okay? How did she look?"

"Gaunt but improving." Baxter held a lighter to the bowl and inhaled.

"How did she arrive? Does she have money? Where are they going?"

Smoke curled from Baxter's mouth. "She was cagy. Close to the vest. All she said was that everything was all right and that she and Alex would be happy where they were going. She appeared in a rental car."

"Was she armed?"

Baxter shrugged. "I don't know. I didn't ask. Better for me not to know if a foreign national is walking around England with an illegal weapon."

"Did you track her? I imagine she's taking him out of

England. Have you—"

The MI6 officer put out a palm. "We didn't."

Something wasn't right. It was one thing for Arina to arrive out of the blue and claim her son. That was her right as the boy's mother. But Baxter's dismissive behavior was odd. Max spread his hands. "Spit it out. What's going on, Callum?"

"We've made some decisions. Internally."

Max furrowed his brow. "Who is we? What kind of decisions?"

Baxter took a long drink. "They're mothballing the task force."

Max sat back. "Why? We're barely getting started. I've got tons of intel I can pass along. We can do real damage. Dismantle—"

"There was an internal review." Callum Baxter puffed the pipe. "The Foreign Secretary took a hard look at what we were doing and decided it was too risky. And too expensive. The Davos thing was a serious embarrassment. It set our relations with the Swiss back years. Putting Cindy's life at risk in Berlin. The four dead bodies you failed to mention at the Chinese safe house. The cost to maintain you guys here in Bath. They deemed it too much."

"What about the Zaitsev intelligence? Without me, that Russian would still be selling illegal weapons from his London residence."

The MI6 officer filled his glass with the Irish whiskey. "It didn't help that when we processed the farmhouse where you were held captive, we found the hook in your cell."

"What about it?"

"You said you wiggled it loose in order to free yourself. That hook was solidly embedded in the wooden beam when we got there. Whatever happened in that farmhouse... You weren't being honest."

Max hid his anger behind the glass as he gulped the whiskey. "Can't C—"

Baxter's head shook as he waved the tumbler. "C's hands are tied. For what it's worth, he thinks it's short-sighted, but there are other politics at play here."

"He's cutting his losses."

"So to speak." Callum puffed on his pipe. "I know we've had our differences, but I was in favor of continuing. I argued that the value of the intelligence we stood to gain outweighed the rest of it, but it's way over my pay grade."

Silence engulfed the two men as Max sipped and Callum refilled his pipe.

"We're close on the kommissar." Max set his empty glass on the table. "We're going to take him down. You guys can have the credit."

Baxter shifted in his chair and shook his head.

Max rose and walked out of the room.

London, England

"I'm looking. Trust me." Goshawk's profile was on the laptop screen. The laptop rested on a glossy lacquer coffee table, and Max sprawled on a gray-purple velour couch. The video connection was secured by a VPN.

The hotel suite in the grand Rosewood hotel was more lavish than he preferred. Max had wanted a two-bedroom suite in central London, and this is what Goshawk procured. The hotel's exterior was Edwardian and baroque and originally served as the offices of the Pearl Assurance Company before WW1.

Max cared about none of that. Instead, he racked his brain in a vain attempt to figure out where Arina and Alex had disappeared to this time. Last time, Victor Dedov, a man with means and the skills, had sheltered her. The only clues this time were the silver SUV that picked her up at the Aspen hospital and the white rental sedan she was driving when she took Alex. The SUV was a dead end.

The incessant clacking of Goshawk's lacquered fingernails on a keyboard arose through the video chat. He tried to not let it irritate him. In the last twenty-four hours, Max moved his few belongings out of the cherry farm outside Bath, hugged Tom, kissed Tom's wife on the cheek, and accepted one last ride from the MI6 team. C offered to drop him off anywhere within the 2,400 nautical mile range of the MI6 Learjet. With nowhere else to go, he asked to be dropped in front of the Palace of Westminster near Big Ben.

Baxter accommodated him but admonished him not to perform any illegal activity on British soil. "I won't be able to protect you."

Starting at Big Ben, Max performed an elaborate surveillance detection route around the city that culminated at the Rosewood, where Goshawk reserved a suite under the name Gareth Bale. When Max checked in wearing a ragged beard, black cap pulled low, and black leather jacket, the front desk agent, a comely young lass with straw-colored hair and heavy eyeliner, looked askance at him. Max was clearly not the famous Welsh footballer who played for Real Madrid. He winked at her as she handed him the key. After taking the stairs to the room, he called Goshawk and asked her to find any trace of Arina. For the last two hours, the hacker scoured immigration records, flight manifests, car rental databases, and CCTV footage, but so far had drawn a blank.

"It's a needle in a haystack, hon." Goshawk took a sip of tea. "Find a tall blonde woman who looks like a model and who just happens to be the daughter of a master spy. If she doesn't want to be found…"

An alert dinged in the background of Goshawk's command center, but it wasn't enough to make Max raise his head. When Goshawk exclaimed out loud, he sat up.

"Take a look at this."

He eyed the screen as a video file appeared via the chat's share function. There was a sideways triangle centered in a circle on black. She clicked on the sideways triangle and the video played.

Black faded into hazy light. A small room tiled in white appeared. A cot sat along one wall opposite a table. A metal latrine-sink combination was in one corner. Max leaned close. "Can you make it bigger?"

"That's what she said." Goshawk chuckled as she clicked to zoom in on the image. A slight figure lay on the cot, under a sheet. Curly chestnut-brown hair was spread out on the pillow. Max's gut clenched as Goshawk zoomed so the figure's face was clearer. "Shit. That's Kate Shaw."

The video cut to black before another room appeared. This room was identical to the first, although the furniture was reversed. A woman with dirty silver-blonde hair sat on the cot, her back to the wall and her knees up under her chin. Goshawk zoomed in and the face became Julia Meier.

"There's a message along with the video," Goshawk said. "He wants to make a trade."

"Who does?" Max sat back on the couch and stared at the ceiling.

"The kommissar."

FORTY

London, England

"Let me guess. He wants to trade the Vienna Archive for their lives." Max pinched the bridge of his nose. A horn blared and a siren screamed outside the hotel window where the A40 ran on an east–west course through central London, yet Max heard none of it.

"You got it." On the video chat window, Goshawk typed rapidly. The hacker was holed up in her remote compound.

"How did you receive the message?" Max took a pull from a water bottle.

"It appeared in one of my public mailboxes. That inbox is always full of spam, but I had an alert set to search for a few keywords like Kate Shaw, which is what caused it to ding."

"Can you trace the email?"

More frenzied typing. "Working on it, but don't get your hopes up."

There was a scratch at the door followed by the chunk

of the deadbolt. Max snatched the pistol from the cushion. The door clanked against the safety catch. With the gun level and ready, Max approached the door from the left, away from the field of view through the door's crack.

"Zurgan." The voice came through the crack in the door.

Max relaxed. *Zurgan* was the correct password. After he put the gun into the back of his waistband, Max unlatched the door's safety catch and swung the door open.

A diminutive and disheveled man stood in the hallway. His long gray hair was held back in a ponytail under an olive-drab brimmed cap like Che Guevara's revolutionary army used to wear. Wispy facial hair sprouted on the man's face, but it couldn't hide his wide smile. The smile revealed crooked yellow teeth and more than several dark spots where teeth were missing. His face was the ruddy color of rust merged with a gray pallor that came from decades on the Mongolian steppe. The man wore a canvas work jacket and dirty pants. Underneath the clothing, Max knew, were extensive tattoos of colorful Mongolian battle scenes from the days of Genghis Khan, who was his ancestor.

After looking left and right along the hallway, Max ushered the shorter man into the suite and closed the door, chunked the deadbolt, and activated the safety lock.

The two men embraced. "Badū, my friend." Max grinned. "Thank you for coming."

The Mongolian shrugged. "You called. Here I am."

Last winter, the two men met while incarcerated in one of Russia's toughest prisons. Badū rescued Max during a prison fight and admitted that he was a former agent in Mongolia's spy service and an old friend of Max's father, Andrei. Max and Badū formed a fast friendship.

"Wasn't sure you got the message." Max returned to the

sofa to check on Goshawk's progress as Badū fetched a beer from the mini fridge.

"I have good news and bad news." Goshawk raised her eyebrows. "Which do you want first?"

"The bad news."

"I traced the email."

"That's the bad news?"

Goshawk shook her head. "No, I gave you the good news first."

"What the—" Max groaned. "What's the bad news?"

"The email with the kommissar's message and the video of Kate and Julia originated from the inbox of Kaamil Marafi of the CIA."

"Kate's Kaamil Marafi? That's impossible." Max sank back against the cushions and rubbed his forehead. "Unless he was spoofed. Are you sure someone didn't hack his system to pretend like it originated from him?"

Goshawk tapped a nail against her tooth. "I can't be a hundred percent sure, but Kaamil took a lot of pains to cover his tracks. The email was sent by an encrypted inbox, so I can't see what else is in there. But the internet keeps clues about people's online behaviors. Kaamil is good, but not that good. I was able to trace the originator of the email and that led to his CIA profile."

Max considered the implications. Either Kaamil was compromised or the young analyst from the United Arab Emirates was involved with the kommissar. "What are the message's instructions?"

"I'll put the message on the monitor." Goshawk clicked a few times, and a text document appeared. *Kate Shaw and*

Julia Meier are in our custody. You are to provide us with the Vienna Archive in its entirety or their lives shall be forfeited. Await instructions.

"Either Kaamil is in on this or he's being used. Either way, he's our only lead." Max chugged from the water bottle and glanced at Badū. "Let's pay Kaamil a visit."

FORTY-ONE

Washington, DC

Kaamil Marafi's flat was in a modern glass and brick building on the corner of First Street SE and K Street SE, between the Navy Yard and I-695. The building was called, believe it or not, Parc Parkside, although as Max watched the building from inside a van, there were no parks in sight. A quick Google search on his phone indicated the word *parc* was Old French for a livestock pen. Fitting.

The building had no security to speak of, other than an RFID key fob that each occupant was required to carry. The fob admitted the residents into the underground parking garage and the front or the rear entry. When Badū cased the lobby, after gaining entrance by tailgating one of the building's harried residents, he found rows of mailboxes, a few plastic plants, and banal prints on the wall. Mail flyers filled the trash can and spilled out onto the floor. Residents going in and out were of the millennial and Gen Z variety and included young professionals peppered with a few hipsters. Across the street was an almost identical building, perhaps by the same builder. A Starbucks was on one corner next to an Orange Theory fitness joint. A 7-Eleven sat kitty-corner to the building. Everything you needed within a one-block radius.

Kaamil Marafi's apartment was on the seventh floor overlooking First St SE. His unit was a one bedroom and rented for $3,000 a month. The building's key fob security system was connected to the internet to allow service technicians to login from the comfort of their suburban office, and Goshawk had no trouble hacking into the security system. With a simple script, Goshawk was able to spoof the database and enable a five-dollar RFID key fob from Radio Shack to allow building access.

Max and Badū sat on the van's rear bench seat. The windows were blacked out, and a camera was on a tripod, which they used to watch as residents entered and exited. During their three days of surveillance, Kaamil used the front door to attend an Orange Theory class every morning at 6:00 a.m. At 8:00 a.m. each day, Kaamil drove out of the garage in a small BMW convertible and made the twenty-minute drive along the George Washington Parkway to Langley. The CIA analyst was less precise with his return. They knew from the tracking device Badū had hidden under the BMW's bumper that Kaamil often worked late at Langley. He always stopped on the way home for take-out food and ate in his apartment in front of the television.

Two days prior, Badū snuck into the Emirati's apartment while Kaamil was at work. A detailed search yielded nothing. No weapons hidden around the apartment. No computers or devices. Nothing other than food, clothes, and a few books. The apartment was well-appointed but sterile.

"What's the plan?" Badū bent his head to eat a taco.

Max sipped coffee. "Tomorrow, Kaamil and I will have a chat."

The interior of the van stank of body odor, stale coffee, and onions from the food truck three blocks over, which Badū frequented. Max and Badū sat in the van and reviewed the plan one last time. It was evening on the fourth day of surveillance and Kaamil remained at the office, at least as far as the GPS device indicated. The plan was simple, and it involved Max talking to Kaamil in his apartment while Badū maintained watch from the van.

The laptop dinged with a message from Goshawk. "We got a new note from the kommissariat." This one was as brief as the first one. She shared her screen so Max and Badū were able to read the message.

Send the electronic files of the Vienna Archive to 4534@cim348dm*em&nd.com. Once received and verified, we will provide instructions on where to bring the physical files. You have two hours.

"What kind of email address is that?" Badū asked.

Goshawk smirked. "The encrypted variety."

"Odd though." Max sipped coffee from a cardboard cup. "What's to prevent me from making a copy and handing that over? Or handing over only part of the files? How do they intend to verify?"

"There realistically isn't a way to verify." Goshawk faced the screen. "The only way to ensure they have the originals is to kill you. The next message will be for you to bring the files yourself, which of course will be a trap."

"Of course." Max's eyebrows rose. "But if they kill me, all the files go public, which renders them useless."

"Which means they won't kill you." Goshawk grimaced. "They'll just incarcerate you for the rest of your life."

Max let that percolate around his mind as Goshawk attempted to trace the email's origin.

After ten minutes, when only typing and clicking was heard over the video chat link, Goshawk proclaimed the email as originating from Kaamil's inbox. "Same routing. Same proxies. Nothing different."

Darkness descended on the urban neighborhood. Young professionals walked the streets wearing backpacks and carrying bags of take-out food. Max removed the Glock 9mm from the small of his back, checked the clip, and chambered a round. "Kaamil's BMW is at Langley?"

Badū confirmed it was.

"You see anything out of the ordinary, send a text," Max held up his phone. "An alert will ding if you text me."

Badū nodded.

"Time to pay Kaamil a visit." Max opened the van's sliding door and slipped into the darkness.

The interior of Kaamil's apartment was spacious and decorated with sleek and modern furniture, large works of art on the walls, an elaborate hi-fi system, and a massive television. Tall floor-to-ceiling windows lined the living area and followed the building contour past an interior concrete wall into the single bedroom. The king-sized bed was made, the kitchen was spotless, and there were no family pictures or mementos anywhere. It was a museum, as if someone had recently performed a photoshoot for *Architectural Digest* magazine. The only thing of interest was a duffel bag in the master closet. Max opened it to find three changes of underwear and T-shirts and socks, jeans, a ball cap. He also found a strap of one-hundred-dollar bills, a hundred notes to a strap, which equaled ten thousand dollars. He zipped the duffle and left it where it lay.

A text buzzed on Max's phone. *The BMW just left Langley. You have about twenty minutes if he makes no stops.*

Max went into the kitchen and fussed with the espresso machine until he coaxed out a double shot, which he downed and prepared another. A search of the cupboards uncovered a set of matching dishes from a designer home goods store. The fridge contained a dozen bottles of beer, a leftover Chinese food container, and nothing else. The freezer was stuffed with frozen dinners. Max tossed back the second espresso shot and popped open a beer.

His phone buzzed with a text message from Badū. *BMW entering garage.*

As he was trained to do, Max steered clear of the windows and took a seat in a modern leather lounger in the shadows. Rather than close the blinds, he left them open to allow muted light to filter into the room. He set the pistol on his lap and nursed the beer. From his vantage point, the front door was in view, as was the open living space that merged with the open-concept kitchen. Lights from the apartment building across the street winked on and off in the darkness.

The deadbolt chunked, keys jangled, and the door swung open. Kaamil Marafi stepped in, tossed his key ring on a credenza, bolted the door shut, and reached to turn on the living room lights.

"Leave them off."

The Emirati whirled and his gaze stopped on the espresso machine, which was on.

"Decent espresso, but if you grind your own beans, you'd get a better pull." Max held up the gun.

Kaamil lifted his hands to his waist. At six feet tall, the Emirati filled out the dark-blue dress shirt with a muscled physique. Shirt cuffs were held together with cuff links. An electric-blue tie and light gray suit pants completed the outfit. His black hair was trimmed tight, and a week-old beard covered his jaw. "Max. My gosh you scared me. How did you—"

"Sit." Max waved the pistol at a black leather couch near the window. When the Emirati stayed still, Max increased the volume of his command. "Sit down."

Kaamil walked to the couch and sat. He rubbed his palms on the thighs of his pants. "Max, what are you doing here?"

The sniper rifle was a SAKO TRG 42, her personal favorite. Manufactured by Finnish gunmaker SAKO, who was located an hour north of Helsinki in the hamlet of Riihimäki, the gun had a tan stock and was chambered for the .300 Winchester Magnum. The rifle was kitted with a Leupold scope and a seven-round magazine. Cora would only need one round.

The setup of Kaamil Marafi was her idea, although her boss, the kommissar, had no idea she now waited across the street, sniper rifle in hand. Make the emails appear to have originated from Kaamil Marafi. Put enough security around the email transmissions where Asimov's hacker had enough difficulty tracing them to make them appear legitimate.

Sure, Asimov might take out Kaamil Marafi, thus ridding them of a security risk. Marafi, the Halo Group's longtime mole at the CIA, had served his purpose, and now he was expendable.

The apartment where she waited was dark. Cora had scouted the apartment weeks ago. The home's occupant was on extended leave overseas, so Cora had the run of the place. She pushed the long kitchen table so it was perpendicular to the window. The rifle was set on the table and rested on its bipod legs. She used a glass cutter to make a small hole in the window. One less substance for her bullet to travel through. She had waited this long to take out the famous assassin. Leave nothing to chance.

One shot, one kill. One shot, and her career with the Halo Group was over. But it was time. She had grown weary of the kommissar's antics and unhealthy obsession with eliminating Asimov. Her boss's disagreements with Ashe were a distraction that might eventually bring down the whole house of cards. Cora had alternate plans. Plans to become her own boss. Be an entrepreneur. Independence. Control her own destiny.

Cora lay prone on the table, nestled the rifle's stock against her cheek, and dialed in her scope. The night was calm with low humidity. A picture-perfect setting to kill the most famous assassin in the world.

After which, she planned to disappear. Australia or New Zealand. Let things cool off until she was able to establish herself in Europe.

Until that point Kaamil Marafi's apartment had remained dark, but now a tall shadow moved around the apartment. The shadow had performed a cursory search of the bedroom and living area before it lingered in the kitchen, where she didn't have a good angle on a shot. She needed her target to walk near the windows or snap on a light.

Time to make my legacy.

FORTY-TWO

Washington, DC

Max remained in his chair but aimed the pistol at Kaamil. "Forget about the denials. We know you're working for the kommissariat. We know you're the CIA mole."

Kaamil's eyes widened and he spread his hands. "What are you talking about?"

"It's over, Kaamil. Cut the shit. We have evidence. Did you think we wouldn't trace your emails?"

The analyst's brows scrunched together. "What emails?"

"The emails you sent Goshawk with the videos of Kate and Julia's incarceration. You're good, but you're not that good."

"I don't know what you're talking about. What videos? That wasn't me." Kaamil's face clouded and he rubbed his chin. "Oh, my God. I'm being set up."

"Are you denying it? Are you saying you're not the mole?"

The CIA analyst slumped, and his eyes roamed around the room. "I'm screwed. I'm a dead man."

"You're stuck, Kaamil. Might as well tell me what's going on." Max waved the gun. "I need information. Help me with that and we'll move you somewhere safe, where the CIA can't get to you."

"That's the least of my worries." Kaamil rubbed his hands together. "They'll find me wherever I go."

"The CIA?"

"No." The analyst snorted. "The Halo Group."

"The Halo Group? What's that?"

"Oh, God." Kaamil rubbed his face in his hands. "You don't know?"

"Educate me."

Kaamil stared at the ceiling for a beat. "I'm screwed either way. Might as well." He let out a long breath. "The Halo Group is a defense contractor, kind of like Blackwater. They perform legit operations in war zones on behalf of the US government, but they also have a black ops unit. It's off the books and operates outside the law."

"What does this black ops unit do?"

"Whatever the US president wants."

"Like his personal army?"

Kaamil shrugged. "Or his personal police force. They operate here in the US or anywhere abroad. Missions where the president needs to operate with impunity."

Max's eyebrows rose. "Are you telling me the US president has his own paramilitary group?"

"Why is that such a big surprise? Don't most countries have such a thing?"

"Doesn't seem possible in America. Land of the free. Not the land of the oppressed."

Kaamil shrugged. "Anyway, the head of the Halo Group is the kommissar. One of the heads, anyway."

"One of the heads?"

"The kommissar runs the off-the-books stuff. His partner, this guy named Alden Ashe, runs the legitimate part of the business."

"And who is the kommissar?"

Kaamil shook his head. "No clue. I don't know. His identity is a closely held secret."

Max walked to the kitchen and put his beer bottle on the counter. The pistol remained in his hand, and he kept his eye on the Emirati. Kaamil's head sagged. "Why'd you do it, Kaamil? For the money?"

"I didn't have a choice." Kaamil rubbed his face. "They control my immigration status and threatened to send me back to the Emirates, where I'd be jailed. I can't go back there." The analyst's voice was pleading. "I'll do anything to avoid that."

"So you betrayed Kate?"

"I feel terrible about that." Kaamil moaned. "I can't go back to that jail. They keep the lights off all day, so we were in pitch dark, then they'd leave the lights on all night so there was no sleep. They play horrible loud music day and night. There are random beatings. That place is hell on earth."

"We can help each other, Kaamil. Tell me everything you know about this Halo Group. Sounds like they're my ticket to the kommissar. We take him out and free you from his hold over you."

The CIA analyst leaned back on the couch and covered his face with his hands. "I'm screwed no matter what I do."

"You are in trouble, Kaamil. But if you help me, I'll help

you. You're going to tell me everything you know about the kommissar. Together, we'll find out who it is and put a stop to it."

"Show yourself, damn it."

Cora's palms were dry, and her fingers were steady. The muzzle was an inch from the hole in the glass. Through the scope, the back of one man's head was visible. The man sitting on the couch. The interior of the apartment across the way was murky. The scope's night vision was good, but there was doubt. She believed it was Kaamil Marafi's head, but she wasn't sure.

Patience.

A silhouette in the rear of the apartment rose from a seated position and walked through the shadows. It resembled a tall man's form. As the form walked across the back of the apartment, she tracked it with her rifle scope. Her finger crept to the trigger. She was ninety percent sure the form was Asimov. And if it wasn't, who cared? One bullet in the shadow and she could easily swing the muzzle an inch to her right and take out the second target before anyone reacted. Both men dead.

Her go bag was packed, her apartment was sanitized. The Halo Group might track her, but it wouldn't matter. Her boss didn't take insubordination lightly, but she knew how to disappear. Once Asimov was dead by her hand, her legacy was set. There would be plenty of work as an independent.

Her finger tightened on the trigger.

The shadow disappeared from view.

Patience.

———

Max paced from the kitchen to the front door, where he leaned against the wall. The gun was in his hand. "Are you going to help me, Kaamil?"

Kaamil massaged the back of his neck with two hands. "I'm a dead man."

"Let me help you, Kaamil."

"You have no idea who these people are. They're unstoppable. They will find me."

Max snorted. "No one is unstoppable. When I'm done with them—this Halo Group or whatever they're called—they're finished. There won't be a Halo Group to find you. All you need to do is worry about the CIA, and I can help you hide from them."

———

"There," she muttered under her breath as the shadow reappeared from the kitchen and walked along the back wall. It stopped near the apartment door, which was to the rear of the room, and it remained in that position, leaning against the wall.

The line of sight wasn't perfect. The couch where Kaamil Marafi sat was perpendicular to the window, so the CIA analyst's profile was mere inches in her scope from where Asimov stood. The target's head was buried in the shadows, but his torso was clear.

A headshot was ideal, but a torso shot was okay too. The .300 Winchester would blow a hole the size of a dinner plate in the target's chest. No one, not even the mighty Mikhail Asimov, was able to survive that kind of wound. Besides, preserving the dead body's face helped the authorities with positive identification. There would be no question that Asimov was dead.

Her finger curled around the trigger.

The scope's crosshairs were centered on the shadow's chest.

She breathed in and let her breath out.

At the precise moment of her natural respiratory pause, she pulled the trigger.

Kaamil rose to his feet and put his hands in the air. "Do I—"

A bullet hole appeared in the window, and at the same time, Kaamil's head exploded in a shower of blood and gray matter. The window didn't shatter, rather a small hole appeared and a small portion of the glass spidered. With a ragged portion of his head gone, Kaamil slumped to the ground.

High velocity round. The thought appeared in Max's mind as he dove for the floor.

By the time Max's chest hit the wood floor, the bullet had already exited Kaamil's face and deflected to impale itself in the drywall near the door. Three inches from where Max had stood.

The wind was knocked from his chest as he landed hard on his stomach. He rolled to the living room's corner. Pistol in hand, he heaved for breath and calculated the angles. The shooter was probably across the street in the apartment building identical to this one. Hard to tell whether they were up one floor, down one floor, or directly across. No sense sticking around to find out.

He pushed the credenza out into the living room, so it was between him and the window to offer limited cover. After a deep breath, he crawled to the door, reached for the handle, and yanked it open.

A second later, he was in the hallway and running for the stairwell.

———

The blow landed on her temple just as she squeezed the trigger. She never saw the result of her shot as it veered from her chosen target and blew through Kaamil Marafi's head and embedded itself in the wall near to where Asimov once was. The force of the punch caused her to tumble off the table to the floor, where she landed hard. The rifle toppled on top of her, and she flung it away as she bounded to her feet.

The next strike landed hard on her jaw. She toppled back but pinwheeled her arms and managed to stay on her feet. A third punch hurtled at her face, dead aim on her nose, but she deflected and bobbed her head out of the way. Ordinarily she would pivot and attack while her opponent was off-balance from the missed punch. But when she turned, the attacker wasn't where she expected. Instead her feet were swept out from under her, and she landed on her back and gasped for breath.

An unusual feeling crept along her neck and into the ancient parts of her brain. It was panic, something she rarely sensed in a fight. The feeling that she was outmatched. *Get away.* It was her only thought. *Get out.*

Up on all fours, she frantically scurried away as another

blow crashed into her temple. Stars sprang into her vision as she collapsed to the floor. A sinewy arm wrapped around her neck.

Her last thought before she blacked out was how intricate the tattoos were on that arm.

FORTY-THREE

Washington, DC

"What did you do with her?" Max took a chug of beer. The malty alcohol tasted good after the near miss.

"Do you really want to know?" Badū used chopsticks to shovel noodles into his mouth.

"I guess not. She's off the playing field?"

Badū spoke through a mouthful of lo mein. "She's gone."

Max swigged beer. "How did you know she was there?"

"Routine sweep of the neighborhood with the night-vision specs. Saw the hole cut in the glass. Only shooters cut round holes in windows."

"Lucky for me. Not so lucky for Kaamil."

Badū shrugged. "Not luck." He munched on the noodles.

The two men were holed up in a motel near Andrews AFB across the bridge from Alexandria. It was the kind of place where each room had a door out to the parking lot, the sheets were scratchy but clean, and your neighbors minded their own business as long as you did the same. Max paid cash for three rooms next to each other, and they settled into the middle room with the takeout and a six-pack. The laptop was on with a private networked feed to Goshawk.

"What do we know about this Halo Group?" Max rose and plucked two fresh beers from the bucket of ice, snapped the caps off, and handed one to Badū.

"Not a lot to know." The video feed was on with Goshawk's shared screen, and she flipped through web page after web page. "They're a privately held military contractor. They recruit soldiers from the armed forces, triple their salary, and deploy them on security missions and other operations around the world on behalf of the US government. Unlike Blackwater and other government contractors, the Halo Group's reputation is solid. Not a lot of press releases or news articles. No indication of this black ops group Kaamil referenced. Getting through their network security will be difficult, but I'm working on it."

A man's picture popped onto her screen. It resembled an actor's portfolio shot. Silver-hair, tan skin, white teeth, early fifties. Blue suit with a red tie and an American flag pinned on his lapel. Goshawk resumed her briefing. "This is Alden Ashe, founder, president, and CEO of the Halo Group. Decorated Special Forces veteran with tours in the Gulf including Operations Desert Shield and Desert Storm. He got out of the army at age thirty-five. And then 9/11 happened. According to the bio on the Halo Group's website, Ashe formed the Halo Group twenty years ago, right after the towers fell."

The image of a family portrait replaced the picture of Ashe. It showed Alden Ashe standing next to a striking blonde woman. In front of the two adults stood two little blonde girls wearing matching pink dresses. Minnie Mouse knelt next to the girls, and Cinderella's Castle towered in the background.

"Pure Americana." Goshawk smiled. She clicked, and Ashe's picture disappeared and an image of a beige office park replaced it. "This is from Google Street View. Their offices are out near Dulles airport in Herndon. More in-depth research will require time."

"What are the odds this Alden Ashe fellow is the kommissar?" Max chugged his beer.

"I just got access to their servers. I'll see what I can find."

"Where's he live?"

"Hold, please."

More frenetic clicking while Max shoveled lo mein into his mouth using chopsticks.

"A place called Lake Manassas, about twenty miles from his office in Herndon, Virginia."

Max took a final bite of his noodles and washed it back with his beer. "Shall we go talk with Mr. Alden Ashe?"

Lake Manassas, Virginia

"Took you long enough."

The silver-haired man who spoke was clean shaven, tanned, had a strong jaw, and might pass for one of those adult male models in the clothing catalogs. The kind of guy who achieved a measure of success in life and is now content to hang out on the dock of a lake with a dog or stroll along a beach with a wife who is aging gracefully. Even his name, Alden Ashe, conveyed quiet confidence, the kind of confidence where he excelled at difficult things without working too hard.

Except he twisted his wedding ring in Max's presence. A single sign of weakness. Ashe wore a dark blue suit with a white oxford shirt open at the collar. They were in Ashe's study in a rambling mansion on a few acres thirty-eight miles west of Washington, DC. Outside, the darkness was interrupted only by landscape lighting. Max had surveilled the house until 11:00 p.m. when Ashe's Audi sedan passed through the gate. The rest of the family were nowhere to be seen.

"How do you mean?" Max trained a gun on Alden Ashe as the executive leaned his posterior against a massive cherry desk. Ashe alternated between fidgeting with the wedding ring and crossing his arms. The room was paneled with warm wood, and two walls housed built-in shelves filled with books. Down a gravel road, at the rear of Ashe's property, were horse paddocks, and a few blocks away were memorials to Civil War battlefields.

"I tried to reach you." Ashe glanced at a sideboard with two crystal decanters filled with brown liquid. "I left several messages for you. I used a back channel. A guy I know in MI6 here in DC."

Max filed that away to check with Cindy. "Didn't get the messages. I've been busy." Max waggled the pistol.

"Right. I've seen the news reports of Petrov and Pipenko. Did you know that Zhao Zheng has been replaced at China's Ministry of State Security?"

Max shook his head. "No, but I'm not surprised. Why did you try to get hold of me?"

Alden Ashe let out a deep breath. "The enemy of my enemy is my friend, no?"

"Explain." Max shifted the gun so it was no longer pointed at Ashe, but he held it ready.

Ashe rubbed his face. "I woke up a year ago and realized that I had lost control of my business to this... this... thug. My partner had turned into a monster. Our business used to be a force for good. We made things right in the world. We were one of the good guys." Ashe shook his head. "What started as a onetime off-the-books operation on behalf of the president turned into a full-fledged secret police group at his beck and call. I didn't like it, but I looked the other way. The money was too good, but it all seemed justified. The operations were... well... even though they were outside the law, they resulted in good outcomes."

"What happened?"

"Two things. The first is the off-the-books operations got more aggressive. We were bugging citizens' phones and taking control of their iPhones. Senators who the president wanted watched. I learned of at least two cases where the president used information we found through this surveillance to influence a vote in congress or get a specific piece of legislation passed. Who knows how many more of these operations happened without me knowing."

"What else?"

"What?" Ashe glanced at the sideboard again.

"You said there were two things that happened. What's the other?"

Ashe snorted. "It was you."

Max's eyebrows rose. "Me?"

"You got under his skin. He started behaving as if the only thing in the world that mattered was getting rid of you. He was obsessed." Ashe gave his wedding ring a twist. "The final straw was when he kidnapped and tortured Lieutenant General Vincent Brown. Bluefish. He was looking for any information Brown might have on you. How to get to you." Ashe threw up his arms. "We kidnapped a decorated Marine general and tortured him until he died."

Max pursed his lips.

Ashe shrugged. "Maybe to someone like you, it doesn't matter. You probably don't follow laws yourself. But our operations have always been under the direct authority of the office of the president of the United States. Don't you get that? MacCulloch, I mean the kommissar, acted on his own. On our own soil."

"What did you say?" Max waggled the gun. "MacCulloch? Is he the kommissar?" Max furrowed his brow. "How do I know that name?"

Ashe's shoulders sagged. "He's the deputy director of the CIA." Ashe pushed away from the desk and walked to the sideboard, where he removed his suit jacket and rolled his shirt sleeves. "Drink? You might want one after you hear what I have to say."

"Keep your hands where I can see them."

"Suit yourself." Ashe angled his body so his hands were visible, and he splashed the brown liquid into a crystal tumbler. "We had a good thing going. I run the legitimate operations, which include securing government contracts for protection details and other legitimate paramilitary operations in various theaters where the US government needs deniability. Iraq, Afghanistan, Syria, the Philippines. All aboveboard, all within the law. We compete with Blackwater and others, but so far, we've avoided any controversy. Our record is clean." Ashe walked to the desk and rapped his knuckles on the wood.

He hoisted himself to sit on the desktop and cradled the drink in two hands. "MacCulloch runs the black ops side of our business. It's a spy business for hire or a paramilitary mercenary group available for top dollar. Off the books. Stuff the public isn't comfortable with. Stuff where the US government can claim complete ignorance. Raids in sovereign countries. Assassinations of the government's enemies. Getting weapons into the hands of guerrilla militia. Taking down drug dealers in Mexico where we don't plan to arrest anyone. That sort of thing."

"MacCulloch is the kommissar?"

Ashe sipped and nodded. "That was his other job. Good God, the man has three jobs. Deputy director at the CIA, he oversees the black ops arm of the Halo Group, and he's the kommissar overseeing the councils. No wonder it's all falling apart."

"Explain."

Ashe set the glass on the desk. "It was 1991. The Soviet Union had collapsed. The Soviet states were independent. Yeltsin was weak and permitted the oligarchs to amass a great amount of wealth as the country privatized. During that mess, Donald Regan, secretary of state under Bush forty-one, concocted a hell of a plan. The idea was to infiltrate the new Russian government with a small team who would in turn recruit members of the Russian government and Russian private industry. Take advantage of the chaos going on over there. The original intent was to sow discord and gather intelligence. But it evolved into much more than that. Greed is a potent thing. For those in the Russian government who watched the oligarchs gain tremendous wealth, it was a powerful recruiting tool. Soon the four councils were formed, and money began flowing out of Russia. At first it was in dribs and drabs, but after that, the flow increased."

"What happened?" Max perched a cheek on the arm of a couch.

Ashe laughed. "Your father happened." He picked up his drink and swirled the ice cubes in the brown liquid. "When Andrei came over to our side, the side of the kommissariat, it was a real coup. At the time, he was the highest member of the KGB that we'd been able to recruit. He had grown tired of the KGB's tactics and all the human rights violations, and he viewed us as a way out. He grew through the ranks until he became a trusted member of the kommissariat, the three-man board that controlled the whole mess. Apparently, Andrei didn't think that was enough, and he started gathering all the documents that make up that fucking Vienna Archive. That was the beginning of the end, although none of us knew it at the time."

The pieces began to fall into place for Max. The same chaos that permitted him to languish in Paris as a sleeper KGB operative also allowed the US to gain a foothold in the Russian government. Something clicked in Max's mind. Was his father's act to join the kommissariat treason? Or was it a carefully orchestrated plot to infiltrate the kommissariat in order to expose it or gain intel on the group? Had his father aimed to gather the Vienna Archive documents from the outset? "Now you want out? Out of the Halo Group?"

Ashe's eyes widened. "No. Not at all. I want to clean up the Halo Group."

Max nodded.

"When I got out of the Army, I was at a loss." Ashe shook his head. "Unsure what to do. My whole life was the Special Forces. The missions, the men in my unit, the camaraderie, and the battles. More than a few people approached and asked me to run for something, but politics is a fool's game. When 9/11 happened, I wanted to help. Do something real. We started on a shoestring, and I've made the Halo Group my life's work. I can't bear to watch it unravel."

"Why don't you end it yourself? Turn him in to the CIA director. I'm sure Wodehouse wouldn't appreciate MacCulloch moonlighting like this."

Ashe rubbed his hands on his pant legs. "I have twin daughters. One is a first-chair flute player and a straight-A student. Wants to be medical researcher. The other is the star of her soccer team. I want to live long enough to see them get married and have children. I want to bounce my grandchildren on my leg. I've seen six tours in Iraq and Afghanistan. I've been in combat with bullets whizzing where I make one wrong move and I'm dead. But this is the most scared I've ever been." Ashe gulped his drink. "If I turn him in and he's protected by the president, I'm a dead man." He pushed away from the desk and paced. "Besides, if I turn him in, it will invite too much scrutiny of the Halo Group. The kind of scrutiny we don't need right now. I'm not sure we'd survive."

"What do you have in mind?"

Ashe peered at him for a beat. "I want to make a deal."

"I'm listening."

"I'll give you his location along with any intel I have on how to get to him."

"In return for what?"

Ashe swallowed. "You do what you do best."

FORTY-FOUR

Leesburg, Virginia

"Any word back from the packet of documents we sent over?" Max paced in the cramped hotel room.

To buy them time, Goshawk had sent the kommissar a huge set of electronic files to the encrypted address. "No word. They're probably still going through it all." She chuckled. "It was a lot of docs."

The tiny team had moved from the roadside motel near Andrews AFB to an Embassy Suites near Dulles airport. The larger room afforded them a work area and a kitchenette where they stocked enough food and bottled water so they didn't have to leave the property. Goshawk was on the laptop screen, while Badū lounged on the bed with a paperback and Max noshed on Funyuns, onion-flavored corn snacks in the shape of onion rings that sounded gross but were quite good when chased with beer.

Goshawk and Max reviewed the information provided by Alden Ashe. According to Ashe, Stephen MacCulloch was sequestered in the Halo Group's compound located in Eastern Finland, not too far from the Russian border. It was the same compound, according to Ashe, where MacCulloch operated the kommissariat. The building was an ancient and sprawling castle built in the fifteenth century to defend the border from the Russians. The grounds were hundreds of acres of forested hills and tiny lakes, all surrounded by stone walls twice as tall as a human. The land nearest the perimeter was protected by heat signature scopes mounted to the walls and motion-activated cameras. A team of twenty trained men patrolled the grounds with automatic rifles and teams of dogs. Ashe figured MacCulloch had bolstered the troop strength to guard the captives.

"Said the spider to the fly." Goshawk snorted. "This place is a fortress. How are you going to get in there?"

"Ashe is helping with infiltration. When it's over, he will be staged nearby to take control of the compound."

"Putting a lot of weight on this guy." Goshawk spoke as she typed on a keyboard. "Can you trust him?"

"Probably not." Max flipped a Funyun into his mouth. "You checked him out, right? Straight shooter?"

"As far as I can see."

"What if we kidnap one of his kids as collateral?" Badū set his paperback down as Max handed him the bag of Funyuns. "Or the wife."

"An interesting yet revolting idea." Max grimaced. "Where is his family anyway? The house was empty."

Goshawk, who had hacked into the Halo Group's servers and was reviewing materials she found, also got into the Ashe family's finances. She clicked, and an image of a credit card statement showed on the monitor. "First class flights for three to Seattle two weeks ago. One way." After more clicking, Goshawk leaned back in her chair. "There is evidence her parents live there."

"He must have sent them away for safety." Max snatched the bag of Funyuns and took a handful before tossing the sack back to Badū. "We don't have the time to run an operation in Seattle. What other ideas do we have?"

"I think it's a trap," Goshawk said on the screen. "Once Max gets in there, they close the noose. You can't trust this Ashe guy."

The three grew silent. Goshawk clicked and typed while Max stood off to the side of the window where he was protected but also able to see the street below. Badū picked up his book, found his place, and started reading.

Max turned from the window and picked up the bag of onion snacks from the side table where Badū had set them. "We don't need to kidnap anyone." He popped a Funyun into his mouth. "Badū, you're my insurance."

The former Mongol intelligence officer shook his head. "I'm going with you."

Max finished off the bag of snacks, crinkled the bag into a ball, and tossed it into the trash. "This is my deal to finish. You stay back. Let's go introduce you to Ashe."

The next meeting with Alden Ashe took place in the Manassas National Battlefield Park. Badū accompanied Max but remained on the edge of the tree line as Max approached the former Army Ranger on foot. The former KGB officer and the former US Army Ranger met face-to-face at the end of the stone bridge that spanned the Youngs Branch River.

Ashe appeared wearing jeans, an oxford shirt, and a

light puffy jacket to ward off the morning chill. His silver hair was hidden under an olive drab ball cap emblazoned with ARMY. His face wore a frown. "What's so important that we meet again in person?"

Max kept his hands in the pockets of his leather jacket and remained a few steps away from Ashe. "Preparations are going well. If you can get the plane on short notice, I think we're a go."

"I said I'd take care of it." Ashe creased his brow. "That's not why you called me out here at seven in the morning." The executive glanced over Max's shoulder at where Badū stood twenty feet away near the trees. "Who's that?"

Max tipped his head Badū's way. "That's my insurance."

"Insurance?" Ashe narrowed his eyes, and a moment passed. "You don't trust me."

It was more of a statement, as if it was the first time Ashe had considered this.

Max narrowed his eyes. "I don't like having to say this, but we know where your family is. If I'm walking into a trap, that man, and others, will do what they need to do."

Ashe looked up at the sky where puffy clouds hung against a cobalt blue backdrop. "Do you know the history of this spot?" He turned and waved an arm at a line of Civil War-era cannons across the wide field. "This is where two important battles of the American Civil War were fought. The first and second battle of Bull Run. Both were decisive wins by the Confederates."

Max shook his head. "I don't." The history of these battles wasn't in his Western indoctrination training.

"This bridge was used by the retreating Union army." Ashe pointed at the bridge near where they stood. "This is also the battle where Confederate General Thomas Jackson got his nickname. Stonewall." Ashe strolled and led Max away from the bridge and through a field. Badū trailed twenty meters back. "In the second battle, the Union lost about 14,000 troops and the Confederates only lost about a thousand. This battle was a huge blow to the Unionists and prolonged the war another three years. Experts estimated over a million died during the American Civil War and the country was almost ripped apart."

Ashe's hands were shoved in his pockets. Max's instinct told him to trust the man. That his upbringing, his Army service, and his success at the helm of the Halo Group gave him great pride. Pride in his service, pride in his country. That wasn't an emotion Max was familiar with—it had been decades since Max felt any kind of nationalistic pride—but it gave credence to Ashe's desire to clean up his company.

Ashe gazed out over the former battlefield. "Anyway, living out here among the battlefields of the Civil War reminds me where our country came from, how our country matured, and the sacrifices people made to make this an amazing country." He faced Max. "What MacCulloch has done is despicable, and it turns my stomach. He's tarnishing the legacy of so many heroic men and women who sacrificed everything to build this great country. I'm embarrassed to have permitted it to go on this long. If you need insurance, fine. But rest assured, I'm going to do everything I can to end this chapter of the Halo Group's history and put us back on a track to doing good."

Ashe held out his hand.

After a second, Max took it.

Ashe pumped once and let go. "Godspeed."

FORTY-FIVE

Near the Finnish-Russian Border

High-altitude, low opening. Also known as a HALO jump. Used when stealth is paramount. Very different than a HAHO, or high-altitude, high opening, which is a safer type of jump. For obvious reasons. Ashe arranged for the airplane and crew through a series of cutouts to help prevent word of the operation from getting back to MacCulloch.

The temperature inside the cargo section of the C-130J Super Hercules matched the outside air temperature. Max was clad in an insulated base layer under a black jumpsuit and flak jacket. The cold didn't bother him, and in fact, he welcomed it. The cold meant he was operating. A large, gear-filled duffel was attached to his legs with carabiners, a chute was strapped to his back, and a massive altimeter was affixed to his wrist over his jumpsuit.

For the past thirty minutes, Max had breathed one hundred percent oxygen through a face mask to help flush nitrogen from his blood stream. Jumping at this altitude with nitrogen in your bloodstream might lead to decompression sickness, similar to when a deep-sea diver rises to the surface too quickly. Goggles, a helmet, and a fitted oxygen mask completed his kit.

A light winked green, the jumpmaster held up his fist, and the rear deck opened. The C-130J was flying at 35,000 feet over Eastern Finland. Max stepped out into the inky blackness. The minus fifty-degree Fahrenheit air nipped at him, but Max put it out of his mind and focused on his oxygen canister and the altimeter on his wrist. As he stepped out, Ashe's words rang in his ears. "Once you're out of that plane, you're on your own."

What else is new?

He hurtled at the earth for eight-five seconds until the altimeter read 3,000, as in 3,000 feet above the ground. He deployed the chute, was yanked from the free fall, and glided into a field near a stand of trees. He hit the ground at a run and used a knife to cut away the chute. After he stowed the billowing material in a bag and camouflaged the bag with brush, Max fished his gear from the duffel bag. Flat on his stomach, he inched from the tree line and scanned the castle grounds with night-vision binoculars. Nothing moved.

A new moon was barely visible in the southwest sky. The cloudless night exposed the nine stars that comprise Virgo, and Max knew the moon was to the right of the constellation. The second largest constellation always reminded him of a woman, a maiden actually, in a dress, lying in repose. Virgo represents fertility, which stems from one of the stars, Spica, the brightest star in the constellation, which means "Ear of grain." Max thought of fertility more to mean the woman in repose, but that was his own warped sensibility, he supposed.

The dark night was fortuitous, and he utilized the night-vision goggles, through which a grainy green image of the castle grounds was visible. When Ashe said the only assistance was the C-130 for the HALO jump, the executive meant it. Ashe needed to distance himself as far from this operation as possible. Plausible deniability in case something goes wrong. And so Max sourced his own gear, which included a suppressed SIG SAUER M17 9mm pistol and an Advanced Armament Honey Badger chambered in the .300 ACC Blackout. The rifle was integrally suppressed. Extra magazines were stuffed into his vest pockets.

The grounds were expansive, at over one hundred acres, much of which was covered with wooded forest, rivers, and lakes. Patrols consisted of ATVs manned by teams of two, and sometimes included dogs. But even the patrols couldn't cover all the property.

The stand of trees where Max lay was to the northeast of the castle's main cluster of buildings. The castle itself was a massive structure of stone walls, broad parapets, and tall towers. The HALO jump was his way around or over the perimeter defenses, which included the twenty-foot stone wall, the heat and motion sensors, and the guards on patrol. Nearer to the buildings, the defenses were lax by comparison. Despite the weaker security near the castle, the keep's towering stone walls offered their own defense. How to gain entrance to the castle without being detected? Max waited and watched.

If I had a dollar for every time I infiltrated a castle.

A light winked on in a window high up along one of the walls. The light stayed on for three beats before it went out.

Max noted the time as the seconds ticked by. The light in the window flicked on again. It stayed on for three seconds before it shut off. Max counted to ten. The window remained dark.

Go time.

Max sprinted across the remaining expanse of field and disappeared into a thicket of brush that lined a stream.

———

The only sounds in the cavernous room were the rustle of paper, fingers tapping on keyboards, and the whir of the laser printer. None of the dozen people in white lab coats spoke. A pallet that had been stacked high with boxes of printer paper was now almost empty. Piles of documents lined folding tables. Rolling whiteboards were covered with notes in erasable ink. A sideboard with urns of coffee and food items had been ravaged.

In the middle of the work room, a woman in a white lab coat strolled with her hands on her hips. Periodically she leaned over an assistant's workstation and held a murmured conversation. Her brow was in a permanent furrow, and she pinched at her lower lip. *This was bad. The kommissar wasn't going to be happy.*

At some point in history, this room had housed dirty, smelly, and boisterous men in armor and robes, waving legs of mutton and sloshing mugs of mead. Or at least that's how the woman in charge imagined the place in times of yore. All that was gone now. Polished concrete lay where the dirt floor once was. The rough-hewn tables were replaced with plastic folding tables. Cords taped down with black gaffer tape streaked everywhere. Halogen lights replaced torches and lanterns. Wireless access points dotted the rafters.

Her medieval fantasy faded as her concern mounted. The secret documents her team was assigned to categorize and curate were junk. There were copies of documents already in the public domain from the Panama Papers and the Pandora Papers. Reams of useless documents from Edward Snowden's 2013 leak were included. The woman knew this because she had spent much of her career researching that material. So far, there was nothing new in this cache of files, and there was little relating to the Russian government, the KGB, or the Russian president. After having gone through seventy percent of the files, her conclusion was that they had been duped.

This information was going to make her boss angry.

Speak of the devil. The towering double doors at the end of the workspace banged open and her boss strode through. He was flanked by his personal bodyguard, a man in a midnight-blue suit who carried an automatic rifle.

"Report?" MacCulloch barked.

"We're about seventy percent through the documents," the researcher said. "So far, there's nothing here."

"What do you mean nothing?" MacCulloch's face turned red. He strode to a pile of papers and snatched the top document.

"Sir, it's all documents already in the public domain." The researcher shrugged and held out a thick sheaf of papers. "This is the outline of PRISM, the NSA's program for collecting information from US citizens. Snowden leaked it in 2013 and it's available on Wikipedia." She tossed the document onto a table and picked up another. "This document shows how Ringo Starr hid assets offshore. It's part of the Pandora Papers leaked years ago by the International—"

"I know who leaked those. Why are they here? What

about the Vienna Archive?" MacCulloch waved his arms like he was stretching his shoulder muscles, except he resembled a crazy person instead of an athlete.

The researcher shrugged. "I think it's a ruse. They put together a bunch of junk to keep us busy. We'll see in another few hours, but I don't think there's anything here of value. It's all—"

MacCulloch unleashed a tirade of curses as he whirled and stalked to the door, the bodyguard in his wake. As he yanked open the doors, the researcher heard him issue a command to his bodyguard. "Bring me that Shaw bitch. They want to play with me? I'll show them who they're playing with."

FORTY-SIX

Near the Finnish-Russian Border

It took Max thirty minutes to painstakingly make his way from tree stand to tree stand and close in on the castle walls. In medieval times, the trees and brush would be cleared from anywhere near the castle walls to allow lookouts to see enemy movement. In today's world, the Halo Group had deployed electronic surveillance to the grounds' perimeter but permitted nature to reclaim much of the castle grounds. Covered with mud and smelling of vegetation, Max was frozen in a stand of undergrowth as a patrol trudged by.

Ahead was a towering stone building that resembled a church crossed with an airplane hangar. The gray stone foundation gave way to red-brick walls and a black-tile roof. What windows existed were narrow, perhaps designed to prevent intruding marauders from squeezing through while allowing a capable archer to rain arrows down on the attackers. Max had no intention of gaining entrance to the main castle building through a narrow window.

He used the dense foliage that grew along a creek for cover as he crept along the rocky stream bed and followed the gurgling water until it reached an archway in the stone wall. The castle was built over the water source, and in medieval days, the creek was used to carry excrement, spoiled food, and other human waste away from the castle. With his assault rifle up, Max disappeared through the archway and splashed into the dark tunnel.

Stephen MacCulloch paced the slate floor. "Bring me that Shaw bitch, damn it. And get a video camera. I want them to see exactly how we do this."

The room was like the nave of a church. The arched ceiling was supported by thick wooden beams three stories up. Narrow windows lined each wall. Wall sconces, one between each window, were fixed in place where the torches used to be, and they cast yellow light upward. At one end of the room was a massive riser, like a judge's bench, which was constructed out of heavy maple. Four massive halogen lights, like the ones used at construction sites, were on stands and illuminated a single spot on the floor in front of the bench where the slate tile was covered in a bright red carpet. The kommissar's suit of armor was in the other room, but the broadsword leaned against a massive oak table near to where MacCulloch paced.

Tonight the judges chamber, as MacCulloch liked to call it, was silent except for his own muttered curses. He had received the news of Cora's death, and he reeled from her insubordination. *Damn bitch deserved what she got.*

It was Asimov's game with the documents that made him pound his fist on the table. In a moment of uncontrollable fury, MacCulloch grabbed the broadsword with two hands and swung it so the blade thunked into the wooden table. He wrenched it free and swung it again, and this time the blade clanged against something metal and bounced. He hoisted the weapon a third time and slammed it home. Wooden slivers flew, and the strike shuddered through his shoulders.

The main door squealed open, and his team pushed their captive into the room. Kate Shaw's hair was matted and tangled, dark circles hung under her eyes, and something white and flakey was dried on her cheeks and lips. Her stare was vacant, and her head hung and lolled unsupported. The men were required to carry her as she offered no resistance and no help.

"Get her on the table, damn it."

While MacCulloch caught his breath and leaned on the sword, two soldiers manhandled the captive so she lay faceup on the table, her arms and legs splayed and secured to the wood. MacCulloch gave explicit instructions, and the woman's left arm was secured to the table using several zip ties over her bicep so that her wrist was free. Her wrist was able to flop around, but it was prevented from moving too far. Didn't matter, this would be an imperfect operation. Shock and awe. That's what he was going for.

When he was done, zip ties would serve as a tourniquet to stem the flow of blood. Can't have her dying too soon. One of his men appeared with the suit of armor and helped MacCulloch into it, helmet and all, as another guard set up a camera on a tripod. One of the halogen lights was maneuvered to illuminate the captive and her position on the table. The video camera was switched on.

"Make sure that thing is on, we only have one chance to get this right." MacCulloch laughed and hefted the broadsword and rested it on his shoulder. The weapon's tarnished steel blade glinted in the halogen light. "Is the camera on?"

"Yes, sir. Good to go."

MacCulloch used two hands to raise the sword overhead. Slowly, deliberately, he brought it down and touched the Shaw woman's wrist with the blade. He adjusted his stance to make his feet wider, lifted the sword two feet into the air, and lowered it to the woman's wrist as if he was taking aim. *Time to make Asimov pay.* Adrenaline coursed through his veins, and with a mighty heave, MacCulloch jerked the blade up and over his head.

The blade was high, back in a two-handed swing with his weight centered, when he screamed.

Max squeezed the trigger.

A bullet spit from the integrally suppressed Honey Badger and entered the back of the kommissar's knee. The bullet pierced the chainmail armor, entered the rear of the man's knee, and pulverized the kneecap on exit before it ricocheted off the slate floor and impaled itself in the wooden door trim. Blood, pale bone, white ligament fragments, and metal splinters sprayed the floor.

The kommissar screamed, his leg buckled, and the sword was suspended in the air momentarily before he and it toppled backwards. The sword hit the slate tile at the same time as the kommissar clanged to the ground in his suit of armor.

From Max's position high atop the maple judge's bench, he shifted the rifle and fired. A guard's neck exploded. A slight adjustment to the left and another guard fell. By the time he shifted his rifle again, a third guard reached for the pistol in his side holster and Max shot him before the man's gun came free.

The room turned silent. Odors of cordite, gunpowder, and blood permeated the room.

Metal clanged against slate as MacCulloch wrenched his helmet off and let it fall. "You shot me." He fought and clawed to put himself in a sitting position. "Damn, that hurts." Blood pooled on the slate.

The table where Kate was secured was two feet behind the kommissar. Her head hung and hair obscured her eyes.

"It's over, MacCulloch." Max remained prone on top of the maple bench, a dozen meters from where the kommissar sat. "You're going to bleed out if we don't cauterize that wound."

"It's not over," MacCulloch yelled. His voice cracked, but his voice was strong. "It'll never be over. Not as long as the West is strong and the East is weak."

The kommissar reached out an armored arm and metal scratched on stone as he managed to pull himself a foot to the left. "We'll never let the East rise. Gain any kind of foothold. You think we care about Ukraine? When we liberated Ukraine, we knew Russia would eventually invade. It's an excuse for us to put the boot on the neck of the East. Shut Russia off from the world's financial system and crush their economy. If enough Russians feel the pressure, they'll take up arms against that idiot in office." MacCulloch wedged his gauntleted fingers into a crevice between tiles and pulled himself along the floor. *Screech.*

"You think the world doesn't want the Cold War?" MacCulloch's voice wavered. "The end of the Cold War was the worst thing to happen to the one percenters. You know what the real one percenters are, Asimov?" The kommissar laughed.

A dead bodyguard's pistol lay on the ground another two feet from the kommissar. Max kept his rifle's scope centered on MacCulloch's arm. The steel chest plate would do little to stop the .300 caliber bullet from the Honey Badger, but Max didn't want to kill the man. Not yet anyway.

The kommissar's laugh turned into a squeal. "The one percenters are the top crust of the world's wealthiest. You know how we make our money?" Another effort with his arm yielded six inches. "Defense spending. You know why we need war? To use all the weapons and military equipment so they can sell more to the world's governments. You think we didn't know Russia would eventually invade Ukraine? Who do you think is supplying all of Ukraine's heavy weapons?" The kommissar laughed. It was a high-pitched cackle. "War is good for business, Asimov. War is good for the economy. The Federal Reserve flooded the currency markets with billions of dollars. Sure, it makes asset prices high, but it also makes inflation and devalues the currency. That's bad for people's portfolios. Well, war is one of our saviors. It puts people to work, it converts raw materials into finished products that can be sold. It creates demand." He reached out and pulled himself another six inches.

The pistol was now within grabbing distance for MacCulloch. Max adjusted his aim. "I don't care about any of that, MacCulloch. Why'd you go after my family?"

"Been asking myself that a lot, recently." MacCulloch's voice was weak.

"You pick up that gun, I'm going to put a bullet in your

shoulder," Max yelled. "Why'd you target my family, MacCulloch?"

Screech. MacCulloch reached for the pistol with a quivering hand, found it, attempted to lift it, but dropped it. It clattered to the slate and landed a foot away. "You damn Russians. You think you deserve a place among the most powerful countries in the world. Well, you squandered your gains in 1991 when you dissolved the Soviet Union. Why did you do that? Now your president"—MacCulloch coughed—"Your president wants it back, and he's not going to get it back." He pulled himself over to get closer to the pistol.

"We're Belarusian, MacCulloch."

"All the same." The kommissar wiped perspiration from his face.

"Tell me why you want to kill us, and I'll end it quickly for you," Max shouted.

MacCulloch grabbed for the pistol and Max pulled the trigger. A bullet cracked into the table leg near MacCulloch's arm. The kommissar yanked his hand back from the gun as if it had seared his fingers and laughed. It was a maniacal howl. "Watch where you're shooting, Asimov!"

"Next time, it's going into your arm or your shoulder," Max shouted. "My father is the one who stole all the documents. You could have just taken him out, left the rest of us alone. Now it's all about to end, MacCulloch. Now tell me why you were targeting all of us."

FORTY-SEVEN

Near the Finnish-Russian Border

A door banged open, and two guards walked in. When one of them saw the kommissar on the floor with a puddle of blood surrounding him, he stopped short. The second man recovered faster and yanked his pistol.

"Shoot him, you fools!" MacCulloch bellowed.

Two more guards ran in, and they both pulled their pistols from their holsters.

Max aimed the Honey Badger at the nearest soldier and fired. The guard who hesitated fell with a bullet to the chest. Guard number two fired off wild shots at Max's position. Max slid off the rear of the judge's bench and took cover as two soldiers struggled with the heavy oak table where Kate was secured and tipped it over on its side.

Max peeked over the desk's top long enough to see Kate Shaw hanging on the table, suspended by the zip ties that secured her to the wood. A human shield. The three soldiers took cover behind the thick table and fired wild shots at the desk.

MacCulloch was out in the open. Max considered whether to kill him, but his desire for information took precedent, so he squeezed off four shots that went over the soldier's heads before he ducked into the foot well of the maple judge's table. Bullets plunked into the hard wood but didn't punch through.

"Hold your fire, damn it." MacCulloch's voice was a croak but carried to Max's location. "Get reinforcements in here." More scraping of metal on slate meant MacCulloch had grabbed the pistol. Voices spoke into mobile phones. "The judge's chamber... We have him trapped." More scraping of metal on slate.

They're dragging MacCulloch behind the table to safety.

Max eased from the footwell of the judge's bench and, with his head down, leaned to his left. The bench was gigantic and built to accommodate three people while they sat in oversized chairs and peered over their subjects. Max fired the Honey Badger as he chanced a look around the left side of the bench. His bullets shot wide, as he intended, but it gave him an opportunity to check out the enemy's position.

A trail of blood led along the floor and around the backside of the overturned table, and MacCulloch was out of Max's line of sight. Two soldiers were partially hidden behind the table with their pistols trained at the bench where Max hid. Kate hung awkwardly on the tabletop, suspended from her bonds. An errant shot might kill her. Running footsteps pounded on slate tile on the other side of the far door.

"You're outnumbered, Asimov!" MacCulloch bellowed

from behind the table. "Toss your weapons and come out of there with your hands in the air."

"Let Kate go, MacCulloch," Max yelled. "And I'll spare your men."

A titter of laugher wound though the group. "Might want to be careful with your bullets, Asimov. Don't want a stray round to take out your friend."

"My bullets never stray." The door that Max used to enter the judge's chambers was along the back wall, behind the massive bench, and was exposed to gun fire. Through the door was the inner sanctum of MacCulloch's offices and sleeping quarters. It's how he had gained access to the judge's chambers.

"Surrender now. Do that, and Kate and your mother go free." MacCulloch's voice was weak.

He's losing blood. If I want answers, I need to move fast.

Max crouch-walked to the other side of the desk and fired four shots high as two more men ducked into the room carrying automatic rifles. They upended a desk and took positions behind it while firing lead at the judge's bench. It was now six to one. Seven to one if you counted MacCulloch.

"Last chance, MacCulloch." Max stuck his head out from behind the desk. "Let Kate and Julia go. If you do that, your death will be quick." He squeezed off three shots before he crouch-walked to the center footwell in the bench. There was one chance to escape without exposing himself to gunfire. If it was going to work, he needed to act fast.

"You're deluding yourself, Asimov." MacCulloch coughed. It was thick with mucus. "Toss the weapon and come out with your hands up. You have to the count of five before we hurt Ms. Shaw."

Underneath the wood bench, Max rose to a squatting position while bending at the waist so his back was against the top of the bench. He used his quads and clutched the Honey Badger's handgrip. If they rushed the bench, he would take out as many as possible. *Here we go.*

With a heave, Max rose to a partial standing position. The judge's bench, which was balanced on his back, lifted an inch and he squat-walked so the wooden structure moved sideways. The idea was to shift the desk into a position that covered his escape through the room's rear door.

A soldier barked a command and a volley of gunfire hit the desk. Bullets plunked into the side but didn't punch through the thick hardwood. An ache from the strain of moving the desk consumed his neck, back, and quad muscles, but Max pushed through it. The desk shifted several inches before fatigue forced him to set it down.

"Hold your fire, hold your fire." One of the soldiers had taken charge, and there were whispers among the men.

Max heaved and the heavy judge's bench moved another six inches. *Almost there.* Max took a breath and pushed up with his quads. The massive table advanced another six inches. *Another foot and I can make a dash for the door.*

The scurry of feet on slate and weapons cocking. More whispered commands.

If Max were in charge of the guards, he would direct his men to sneak up on the desk to catch the bench-mover off guard while he was unable to fire his weapon. Max heaved as sweat rolled from his brow and he pushed the desk another six inches. With a final effort, he hefted the desk and moved it another foot.

There.

Back on his haunches under the desk, Max grasped his rifle. Four flash-bang grenades were stowed in his vest, but even the concussive blast can cause injury. He didn't want to risk hurting Kate. In a crouch, he lunged for the door.

———

The room filled with gunfire. Shots plinked off the wall and hit the door. Bullets sang by his head, and one threaded his tactical shirt near his bicep.

Max wrenched at the handle and flung the door open and stood face-to-face with a tall man in a midnight-blue suit.

———

Without waiting for the man in the blue suit to make a move, Max hurled himself through the doorway and around the jamb as bullets buzzed his head.

The tall man in the blue suit moved to the opposite side of the door and the two men stared at each other, their chests heaving. They waited on either side of the open door as slugs chewed the door trim and the drywall in the hallway.

The man in the blue suit was armed with a Glock pistol, which he held in a two-handed grip, barrel pointed at the floor. Perspiration covered his face, and his tie was undone at the neck.

"Took you long enough." Max's voice was low. The man in the blue suit was Miko, Stephen MacCulloch's bodyguard and Ashe's confidant. Miko was the one who signaled Max with the light high in the tower and was quietly rounding up MacCulloch's henchmen during Max's gunfight in the judge's chambers.

"There are twenty men loyal to MacCulloch," Miko whispered. "I got ten locked away. How many in that room?"

"Four dead. Six shooters left." Max caught his breath. "MacCulloch is wounded. Losing blood. A captive is strapped to the table."

Max held up a fist and changed it to two fingers and pointed along the hallway on Miko's side.

Miko nodded once.

Max breathed and waited.

"Hold your fire. Hold your fire, damn it." The voice emerged through the din of gunfire and the shooting stopped.

In a crouch, Max darted across the open doorway and the two men ran down the stone hallway. Two left turns brought them to the main doorway of the judge's chambers, where Max paused with his rifle barrel pointed at the ceiling. When Miko caught up to him, Max moved across the doorway and handed him a flash-bang grenade. Since Kate faced away from the door where they stood, Max calculated that the table would shield Kate from much of the concussive blast.

Miko nodded once and grabbed the handle.

Max nodded and Miko pushed open the door.

Both men tossed their flash-bangs and pulled back as the grenades exploded and smoke billowed.

Max darted in with his gun ablaze while Miko followed on his six, also firing.

———

The flash-bangs did their job. Max shot two stunned soldiers as Miko shot two more. The remaining two soldiers tossed their weapons and stood with their hands in the air. Miko secured the two soldiers' hands behind their backs and put them facedown on the floor, while Max trained his rifle on MacCulloch. The kommissar lay on his side in a pool of blood and dropped his pistol.

Miko used plastic cuffs to secure MacCulloch's wrists in front of him, and Max cut Kate from the table and helped her over to a wall, where she sat with her arms wrapped around her knees.

The kommissar's face was ashen and covered with perspiration. He tugged at the collar of his chainmail suit with his tied hands. "Damn it, Miko. You, of all people."

"Why'd you do it, MacCulloch?" Max crouched in front of the captive. "Why did you come after my family?" Max's rifle was slung across his back and his SIG was in his side holster.

"Go to... hell... Asimov." Spittle formed at the corners of MacCulloch's mouth.

"What do you have to lose now?" Max said. "Might as well tell me. You should have just gone after my father and the Vienna Archive. You didn't have to bring my sister and nephew into it."

"Your father betrayed everyone," MacCulloch spit blood. "He... betrayed his country. He betrayed us."

"I'm not buying it—"

There was a tug at Max's waist. Before he was able to react, a pistol fired, and a hole appeared in MacCulloch's temple.

Max jumped back as Kate stood over the dead kommissar, the pistol held in two hands, its smoking muzzle pointed down. She spit on MacCulloch's face before she stumbled back a step.

"Damn it, Kate." Max took the gun from her hand and helped her back to the wall, where she slumped and gazed at the ground.

Alden Ashe arrived at the castle with a team in two helicopters and took charge. A platoon of soldiers loyal to Ashe secured the compound under Miko's command. Medical personnel treated the wounded while two cooks got busy in the galley and prepared food.

Max found Julia Meier in a cell and helped her into the kommissar's private rooms, where she and Kate convalesced. Food and water were brought. Medical assistance was provided, although the primary damage to both women was not physical.

A dozen men loyal to the kommissar were incarcerated in two cells. What Ashe planned to do with them was none of Max's business. When Ashe and Miko were confident the castle and grounds were rid of MacCulloch's loyal soldiers and the security protocols were back in place, Ashe strode into the room where Max sat with Kate and Julia. The two men went into the hallway.

Ashe wore suit pants, a white oxford with the sleeves rolled up and an askew tie. He gripped Max's hand. "You did me and the Halo Group a great service."

Max shrugged. "Couldn't have done it without Miko's assistance.

The Halo Group's CEO bowed his head. "We're fortunate Miko was equally disgusted by his boss's behavior. He and I have been talking for a year about how to end this.

When a plan presented itself, he stepped up." Ashe let go of Max's hand. "We're in your debt. The C-130 is waiting for you at our airfield, and one of our helicopters will transport you there. Let's stay in touch."

Max nodded as Ashe departed.

While he waited for the helicopter's preflight preparations, Max searched MacCulloch's living quarters. The rooms were small but opulent and poshly appointed. An armoire was filled with custom-tailored suits from Savile Row, silk ties, and pressed shirts. A nightstand contained a sleeping mask and not much else. Under the bed was a small but ornate wooden box. The top was inlaid with hand-carved engraving, and a brass lock held the box closed.

Max used his tactical knife to pop the lock. The inside of the box was lined with red felt and it contained a few items. There were several yellowed pictures of a couple wearing clothing from 1950 or 1960. There was an expired Finish passport with MacCulloch's picture and the name Linus Törni. Trapped in the passport was another picture and it fell into Max's hand.

The photo was also yellowed, but the couple in the image wore more modern clothing. It showed the couple posing for the photograph with the Uspenski Cathedral, a famous landmark in Helsinki, in the background. The man in the photograph was a younger Stephen MacCulloch. His arm was around a woman, who leaned in with her hand on MacCulloch's chest.

The woman in the picture was Julia Meier.

FORTY-EIGHT

Minsk, Belarus

"Run, Alex! Go, go, go!"

Arina's blonde hair was held back by a ball cap and the tresses bounced as she jumped up and down to cheer her son. On the field, two teams of eleven-year-olds scampered to and fro and attempted to kick the soccer ball into the opposing goal. One team wore blue jerseys, while the other wore red. Parents lined the field and encouraged the athletes or smoked and scrolled on their phones.

It was a rare sunny day in the Belarusian capital and the soccer parents took full advantage. A few adults stood, some paced the sidelines, and others sat in chairs. From Max's spot at the top corner of the bleachers, behind and above a group of parents who talked about the latest offenses of their authoritarian president, he had an unobstructed view of the action on the field.

It didn't take long to pick Alex out of the two groups of boys. Max's nephew had sprouted in the past few months, a hint that perhaps he might achieve his mother's height. The blond mop of hair kept getting in his eyes, but Alex's focus never wavered. He dribbled the ball with the deftness of a professional midfielder and took a shot that missed the goal by inches.

"It's okay, Alex! You'll get it next time!" Arina's voice carried over the field, and Alex waved at his mother. Still young enough to not resent his mother's presence. How long would that last?

As the ball bounced back and forth between sides, Max's attention wandered to the man standing at Arina's side. Occasionally his sister put her arm around the man and squeezed him tight. Almost as tall as his sister, he wore his dark hair long. With his pale skin and thin red lips, he resembled an aging rock star. Despite the warm sun, the man wore a jacket to hide a pistol—at least, that is what Max guessed.

The crowd cheered, which drew Max's attention back to the field. Alex broke away, dribbled, and kicked a long shot that bent around the goaltender's outstretched fingertips and flew into the net. Arina pumped her fists over her head, and the man next to her clapped. Alex ran in a long curve with his arms outstretched while his team mobbed around him. A hint of things to come. The boy was a natural.

Emotion welled up and Max bit his cheek to prevent any waterworks. As Alex and his teammates celebrated, Max watched the man standing next to Arina. The man was Alex's father. Maybe one day Max would learn the answer to the mystery. How and why had Alex's father disappeared when Andrei destroyed his own house and faked his own death? And why did Arina hide the fact? And where had he been for the last year?

Arina's sorrow and tears on the night the bomb exploded at their parents' house were real. Did she know her husband faked his own death alongside Andrei?

It didn't matter. Some mysteries weren't meant to be solved. His sister and nephew were safe. Alex was back with his mother and father.

When the whistle blew to end the match, the boys scattered, and Alex ran to Arina's outstretched arms. He hugged his mother and high-fived his father. Alex's father clapped as Alex returned to the team for the obligatory team handshake.

By then Max had disappeared.

———

London, England

The two men met in the middle of a lush field in St James's Park. Behind Max, the fountain in the middle of the lake streamed water in a three-foot geyser despite the rain. It wasn't a hard rain, more like a drizzle, but Max wore an overcoat and a flat cap and held a black umbrella. The rain and fog had chased the pedestrians from the park, and the two men were alone.

C also clutched an umbrella, and they faced each other. "What I don't understand is how an American organization, off the books I guess, was able to penetrate the Russian political and economic system like that and siphon so much money out of the country." C shook his head as rain pattered on their umbrellas.

"Ashe told me it was going on for a long time," Max said. "Since the collapse of the Soviet Union back in '91.

There was mass privatization of industry, and a few oligarchs made off with billions. The Russian government was in complete chaos. The kommissariat offered senior people in the Kremlin, people who missed out on the rush to privatize, a way to profit. MacCulloch was supported by the US government, the Germans, the Chinese, and the Halo Group provided him with his own private army." Max shrugged. "Over time, the secrecy and protocols prevented the Russians from figuring it out."

C pushed his glasses up on his nose. "And MacCulloch's jealousy was his downfall in the end."

Max nodded. "He couldn't let Julia go. She broke his heart when she left him for Andrei, and then Andrei betrayed the kommissariat. Everything MacCulloch believed in crumbled and the need for vengeance took over. He didn't know when to stop."

The rain pelted their umbrellas as C gazed over Max's shoulder. For a moment, the British spymaster was somewhere else.

Max wondered where he went. "Erich Stasko still working for you?"

"He is." C's eyes refocused on Max. "He runs his banking empire from London now, where we can protect him."

"And he and Inge?"

"Still apart but tied together forever by the bonds of parenthood and business." C pursed his lips. "I guess our little gambit with the cabin in Finland worked. Having Goshawk float Riverside as the possible location of the Vienna Archive was genius."

"It was a move right out of my father's playbook." Max had conspired with C and Goshawk to try to root out the suspected mole. They had put Riverside into emails, text messages, and other signals mediums, hoping to uncover the leak. "I was as surprised as anyone when both Kate and Julia fell into the trap." Max sighed.

"Were you?" C's eyes narrowed.

Max shrugged and smiled. "Not the CIA's finest moment."

C shook his head. "It was a step backward between us and the CIA. They deliberately put an asset into our team. It's unforgivable."

Max shifted the umbrella to his opposite hand. "Maybe the new CIA director will mend fences. They have enough to clean up over there now that Wodehouse resigned and MacCulloch is dead. Have they picked a new director yet?"

C shook his head. "Not to my knowledge. Rumor is it will be a bureaucrat from Congress."

"Because that worked so well last time." Max snorted. "And Callum? He fell hard for that woman, didn't he?"

It was C's turn to sigh. "He did."

"How did you uncover it?"

"He self-reported. When the woman disappeared, he figured it out." C shrugged. "He gets points for that, and it probably saved his pension. We took care of it quietly. Maybe he can teach at Cambridge or write a book."

"I'll go see him."

"He'll like that. I suppose various intelligence agencies will keep looking for your Vienna Archive." He gave Max a sideways glance. "Why don't you leak it, like the Pandora and Panama Papers?"

"What's the point?" Max turned his free hand to the sky. "The councils are all disbanded. The kommissariat is dead. As far as the Russian president goes..." Max shrugged. "He'd just find others to launder his stolen money. Besides, there were no real ramifications to those leaks. The Pandora and Panama Papers—all that documentation leaked to the public and nothing happened."

C nodded. "Well, if you need a custodian, you know where to find us. What will you do now?"

Max shrugged. "Alex is in a good place, so maybe I'll help Spencer with the cabin."

C raised his eyebrows and cocked his head. "Are you retiring for good?"

Max smiled.

C chuckled as the men shook hands and parted ways.

They met in a café across the River Thames from where the tan brick and green windowed MI6 building sat. Cindy was able to walk across the Vauxhall Bridge from her office and appeared in a crisp white blouse and tailored navy sport coat. When she hugged Max, he picked up a scent of orange blossom from her hair. She wore it down, off her shoulder, and a simple silver pendant was around her neck.

When she pulled back from the hug, she touched his bearded cheek with her palm. "Keeping the beard? At least it's trimmed."

Max smiled. "Hides the scar."

Cindy's face beamed. "They promoted me. I'm running Baxter's old team."

She hit Max's palm when he held it up. "Well deserved," Max said. "It was time for Baxter to retire."

Cindy grimaced. "It was bittersweet. I learned so much from him, and what happened to him was..."

"It was his fault." Max jabbed the table with his index finger. "He should have taken more precautions. A lot of people could have been hurt. It's a lesson for all of us."

The waiter brought two espressos, each with a sidecar of water, a block of sugar, and a tiny spoon. Cindy plopped her sugar cube into her coffee and stirred while Max sipped his without the sugar.

"What will you do now?" Cindy set the tiny spoon down.

"A lot of people are asking me that." Max shrugged and smiled. "Were you able to look into that one thing I asked you about?"

Cindy's face brightened. "Of course, I almost forgot." She dug into her shoulder bag and slid Max a manila envelope. "It's all in there. Transcripts from the calls, reports filed by the MI6 DC field office. Sounds like Ashe was telling the truth."

Max nodded and slipped the envelope into his own bag. "Why didn't the DC field office pass along the communications to London?"

Cindy put up her hands. "You were off the books, remember? The officer in charge didn't think it was credible. Even if he would have thought it credible, no one would have known who to give it to. It's not like Callum put up a banner that you were on our payroll. Everything is so compartmentalized that the requests eventually died."

"Lots of bureaucracy, I guess." Max grinned. "At least I know Ashe was telling the truth." Max sipped his coffee while he listened to Cindy describe her new office and her team. After two expressos, Max left some cash on the table and followed Cindy out into the overcast day. They hugged, and as Cindy turned to go, she took Max's hand. "Don't be a stranger, okay?"

Max watched her walk to the bridge. She turned and made a wave and blew him a kiss before she disappeared into the throng of suits that crowded the sidewalk.

London, England

Max used a gloved finger to jab at the bell before he brushed the rain from his leather jacket. Thick drops pattered on the sidewalk and thumped against the shingled portico over the porch where he stood. A car splashed along the narrow street, its windshield wipers metronoming. Max shrank behind a pillar as the headlights swept over the house and disappeared. *Instinct, a muscle memory that might never fade, even though I'm now safe. Relatively safe, anyway.* He poked the bell a second time.

"Yeah, yeah. Wait a bloody second." The door opened to reveal Callum Baxter. A dull glint reflected off a shotgun barrel as the former MI6 officer squinted into the darkness. "Christ, is that you, Max?"

"You gonna let me in?"

Baxter held the door open for Max before he leaned the shotgun next to the umbrella bin. "The front door, eh? No more sneaking into my back garden and stomping on my rose bushes?"

Max followed Baxter into the kitchen, where the older man busied himself at the stove. "Tea?"

"You got anything stronger?" Max hid his surprise. At seven in the evening, Callum Baxter wore a dingy white bathrobe over frayed plaid pajamas. Crumbs were caught on his beard, which had filled in around his face and blended in with the goatee. His glasses, when they caught the light, were covered in dust and grime.

Baxter reached into a cabinet and brought out a green glass bottle with a white label. "Only Scotch."

Max wrinkled his nose. "Tea is fine."

Baxter busied himself with a kettle. When the water boiled, the two men took their tea mugs to the kitchen table, a rectangular farmhouse table with a scarred top. Baxter found a tin of biscuits and put them on a plate before he collapsed into a chair. "It's over?"

Max nodded. "MacCulloch is dead."

"And the Halo Group?"

"Still in business. Alden Ashe emerged unscathed, and business is better than ever." Max shrugged.

"You talked with Ashe?" Baxter's bushy eyebrows rose.

"A couple times." Max tried the tea and burned his tongue. "Just to wrap up loose ends. More importantly, how are you doing? You guys catch her?"

Baxter rose to his feet and brought the Scotch bottle to the table, where he splashed a measure of it into his tea. The former MI6 officer shook his head. "She's gone. In the wind." He held up the bottle.

"No thanks." Max held up his hand. "That woman worked you over, didn't she? She built you up, made you feel great, and then tore your guts out."

The former MI6 agent gulped his tea. "Sure did."

"Any assessment on how much intelligence she stole?" Max blew on his tea to cool it.

Baxter's head shook slowly.

"It was bad, though, huh? She provided all that intel to the CIA, and in turn, Kaamil leaked it to the kommissar. A double whammy."

Baxter peered into his mug.

"What are you going to do about it?"

The ex-MI6 officer shrugged. "I'm out. They forced me into retirement. It's Cindy's problem now."

"Cindy doesn't have much to go on. Tall. Brunette in

her forties. Speaks English. Sexy as hell." Max raised an eyebrow. "That describes a lot of women."

Baxter nodded. "She's probably cooling her heels on a remote island after getting plastic surgery and a new haircut."

"Did you ever find out her true name? Her identity?"

Baxter stared at Max for a long spell before he shook his head. "No, never did."

Max stroked the handle of the teacup. "I talked with Cindy. She's doing well. Promoted. Running a team."

Baxter nodded and cupped his tea-Scotch in two hands. "She deserves it."

The two men drank in silence. When Max's teacup was empty, he pushed it aside. "Want me to find her? Take care of it for you? The least I can do for all the help you gave me on this thing."

Baxter drained his cup, rose from the table, and carried the dishes to the sink. He stood at the sink for a long time and gazed out the window at the backyard, where wet leaves glinted in the moonlight.

After five minutes, Max got up to leave. He put his hand on Baxter's arm. "If you change your mind, give me a call."

Washington, DC

A bell chimed when Max pushed open the glass door. A warm waft of loam, soil, and mulch hit him in the face. That was followed by waves of sweet floral scents. The tiny shop was jammed from floor to ceiling with flowers in every color and every variety. There was barely any room to walk down the two narrow aisles, and Max was forced to duck his head to avoid the leaves of a massive ficus tree. Outside, a spring sun peaked through rain clouds. Inside the store, a dampness clung to his skin.

"Help ya?"

The proprietor, a gangly man in his forties with a bushy head of black and gray hair, waved at Max. The man wore a dirt-stained apron and stood behind a small counter, where an old manual cash register sat next to a credit card machine that advertised Apple Pay. Rows and rows of balloons that proclaimed happy insert-your-holiday-here lined the back wall. Saloon-style doors led into a back room, where Max glimpsed more greenery.

Max held out a palm. "I'm looking for someone. Is Kate here?"

"Nope." The man fussed with a bouquet. "No one here by that name."

The saloon doors banged open, and a woman appeared. She wore a soiled apron over a work shirt and jeans. Wild curly hair was held back with a rubber band, and tortoise-rimmed glasses were perched on a pert nose. The woman's cheeks were hollow, as if she were malnourished, and dirt was caked on her fingers and under her nails. She pushed up her glasses with the back of her hand. "It's okay, Ted." Kate Shaw turned and disappeared into the back room.

Max raised his eyebrows at Ted, who in turn nodded his head at the doors. "Tread lightly."

Through the saloon doors was a back workroom that was filled with even more plants and flowers than the front of the store. Kate stood at a long wooden worktable and hacked at flower stems with a set of rusted shears. "What do you want?"

Max shrugged. There was no good answer. "Wodehouse told me that you left the agency."

"And?"

All the words Max rehearsed on the airplane vanished. The apologies, the excuses, the rationalizations. "I don't know, Kate. I was hoping..."

Kate threw the scissors on the table with a *thunk* and turned with her fists on her waist. "Yes, they kicked me out of the agency. I'm out of that life, Max. You won. You and your damn family and that damn Vienna Archive and all of it. You fucking won. What more do you want?"

The saloon doors opened, and Ted walked in. The light glinted off a pistol clutched in his hand. The barrel was pointed at the floor. As he eyed Max, Ted sidled over next to Kate. He was a swarthy outdoorsman with leathered skin and sparkling blue eyes. A strong jaw. The kind of man who was able to start a fire with two sticks, skin a buffalo with a pocketknife, and cook a pot of buffalo curry over an open fire.

Max shuffled his feet. "I was hoping we might... um... I don't know. Get a cup of coffee or something?"

"Do I look like I have time to get coffee?" Kate waved a hand at the roomful of flowers.

Ted caught his eye and shook his head.

It was subtle, but Max got the hint. "Okay. You know where to find me." He pushed through the saloon doors, squeezed by a customer admiring the azaleas, and exited into a spring downpour.

FORTY-NINE

Outside Aspen, Colorado

"She'll come around." The tall and lanky man set a tape measure on a pile of two-by-fours. A tool belt was around his waist and complemented the flannel shirt and jeans. A tattered ball cap with a John Deere logo attempted, and failed, to tame a shock of silver hair. Three days of facial stubble was speckled with gray. Spencer White leaned his butt on the deck railing.

"I don't think so." Max's boots crunched in the gravel. A heavy spring snow had fallen and coated everything with a fluffy whiteness, but a strong sun warmed his skin. Max crinkled a sack and withdrew a long bottle of reddish-amber liquid. He held it out to Spencer, who waggled his eyebrows as he read the label.

"Eagle Rare." Spencer grinned. "And the seventeen-year variety. This stuff is twenty-five hundred bucks. If you can find it."

"Goshawk's skills finally came in handy." Max chuckled

as he admired the construction work. "The cabin is looking good, Spencer."

Indeed, the building was impressive. The old cabin had burned to the ground the previous winter, the victim of Ruslan Stepanov's attackers who almost succeeded in kidnapping Alex. The new cabin was expansive, made of massive tan logs held together with white mortar. An A-frame comprised the second floor while a full wall of windows looked out over the pond and the valley. A stone chimney pierced the steep roof. A deck surrounded the front and sides, which is where Max found Spencer working on the railing. "This place looks like it belongs in a magazine."

Spencer White, the former CIA Special Activities Division operative, took the bottle and led Max inside to the cabin's great room. A three-story stone fireplace covered one wall, and the windows offered an impressive view of the valley. Max's boots tracked in the construction dust as he followed Spencer into the half-completed kitchen. Great slabs of silver granite covered a center island, which is where Spencer set two tumblers. The former CIA operative held up the bottle.

Max put his palm out. "You do the honors."

Spencer pulled the tiny red tab, which caused the foil to separate. He yanked the cork and put the bottle to his nose. "Ah, perfection." Spencer took a swig straight from the bottle and grinned. "Smooth." He sloshed a measure into each glass and handed one to Max.

They clinked glasses.

"To freedom." Spencer sat back and drank.

"To freedom." Max sipped and let the warmth trickle down his throat. Ripe cherry, vanilla, and oak swirled on his tongue as he swallowed.

The men walked out to the deck where two Adirondack-style chairs sat overlooking the pond and the valley below. A fire pit sat in the dirt near the porch, and Spencer arranged cordwood over a pile of kindling. "Got a light?"

Max tossed him the Zippo with the Belarusian flag burnished on the side, and Spencer used it to light the fire. There was a time when the metallic *clink* of the Zippo's lid opening combined with the bourbon would have triggered a craving for nicotine. *No longer*.

After they sipped and sat in silence, Spencer poured more of the bourbon into each glass. The sun dipped past the tree line, and they moved the chairs from the porch to be closer to the fire.

"Ted is a decent man." Spencer poked at the fire with a long stick and a plume of embers rose into the sky. "I operated with him in Afghanistan. He'll take good care of Kate."

A pang of jealousy arose in Max's chest. He pushed it aside. *Move on*.

Spencer sat back, picked up his glass, and looked over it at Max. "How are Alex and Arina?"

"They're good." Max sipped. "Back in Minsk. Alex is the star of his football squad."

"Are you going back there?"

"Nah. He's better off without me around. He's got his two parents. Doesn't need me kickin' around confusing everything."

Silence passed. The fire licked and crackled. The sun crept across the southern sky. A hawk soared in lazy circles in search of dinner. A clump of wet snow thumped to the ground.

The level of bourbon in the bottle was at half-mast when darkness overtook them. Spencer rose and put two steaks on a grate over the fire and tended to them with a survival knife. When they were charred and pink and juicy, the two men chewed in silence. It was pitch dark when they were done, and the only light came from the stars and the roaring fire in the fire pit. Smoke and flying ash swirled.

Spencer tossed the paper plates and leftover gristle into the fire. "She'll come around."

Max stared into the glowing embers. "I don't think so."

FIFTY

Paris, France

The taxi was a Japanese EV, complete with the *TAXI Parisien* sign lit on the roof. There was no *Uber Go Home* sticker, and the turbaned Sikh driver nodded as Max tossed his bag into the rear seat and slid in next to it. The price was the equivalent of $80, and Max winced.

"Inflation and gas prices." The Sikh shook his head. The car glided away from the curb and joined the throng of traffic on the A1 pointed southeast into the city.

It's an electric vehicle, for bloody sake. But Max kept his mouth shut.

Max thumbed the window down and let the spring air wash over him. As always, a cacophony of smells swirled. There was a tinge of paint thinner, the scent of floor wax, and faint acrylic, which reminded Max of the city's rich bohemian history in art. Those smells were familiar. There was also a mixture of floral and grasses. Spring in Paris.

Blaring horns interrupted his homecoming reverie, and he closed the window.

It was a thirty-minute drive to the destination Max gave the driver, which was in the center of the city. As the cab left the highway and turned onto city streets, Max rolled the window down again and soaked up the sounds of the city. There was a repetitive pounding from a road construction crew. A lorry's engine growled. An Italian motorbike screamed by.

Home.

His adopted home, anyway. The city where he spent several years on assignment with the KGB prior to the fall of the Soviet Union and with the FSB after the formation of the Russian Republic. The city where he used KGB funding to establish his jazz club, La Caravelle, as a cover. The city where he fell in love with, and betrayed, the American spy named Katrina.

The taxi let him out at the Pont de l'Archevêché, a narrow bridge over the Seine, and he hoofed it across to the Square Jean XXIII, a small but vibrant park. The Cathédrale Notre-Dame de Paris arose on the far side of the green space, its French Gothic architecture an abrupt contrast against the soft landscape of the park and the azure blue sky. A crane towered over the structure while sections of the cathedral were covered in sheeting as part of the restoration from the recent fire.

He turned into the park and strolled the broad sidewalk next to a trimmed hedge that separated the green space from the river. As he approached the stand of cherry trees in full bloom, he stopped and inhaled. Floral and fruit filled his senses. Today the sand pit beneath the trees, usually popular with young children, was empty. A jogger wearing tights and listening to earbuds ran by, but otherwise he had the park to himself.

A bench beneath the pink blossoms faced the river. He sat and placed his bag next to him and closed his eyes. For the first time in a year, there was no threat to his life, no threat to his family, and no threat of surveillance. It was as if he had set down a massive backpack full of rocks. Somewhere a baby wailed. A mobile phone rang. A tourist barge sailed by on the river, the tour guide explaining in a metallic voice how the fire consumed the Notre Dame cathedral. It all soaked in, and he breathed deep.

When he opened his eyes, he let his gaze linger on the Eiffel Tower. Known locally as the *la dame de fer*, or the Iron Lady, the immensity of the tower was always surprising. It rose 324 meters into the air and dwarfed everything around it. While the metal structure dominated the skyline, it felt out of place. The iron latticework of the tower reminded him of the industrial East, not the enlightened West. For a city that produced the elegance of Degas, Rodin, and Monet, the sharp metal was a foreign monstrosity. Except it always reminded him of home. And the Parisians loved la dame de fer, so the structure inherited the beauty around her.

After he had his fill of the cherry blossoms, Max walked west, skirted the cathedral, and crossed the river south on Pont Neuf. From there it was a brief walk to Saint-Germain-des-Prés, the famous neighborhood filled with the best cuisine in Paris. It was also where his jazz club was located, or the jazz club he used to own.

When he had agreed to work for the CIA, which felt like decades ago, Kate helped him sell the club to Della, his manager. At seventy-plus years of age, the heavyset and ever-cheerful Creole was the brains behind the operation, and she deserved the place. Since then, there was no news about how the club had fared. It was probably boarded up.

La Caravelle was on the edge of the famous neighborhood, with a veranda that overlooked the river and offered a view of the Pont des Arts, a bridge over the Seine known for the love locks attached to its metal grillwork by strolling lovers. In 2015, the city was forced to remove over a million of the locks for fear the weight might collapse the bridge. La Caravelle was shuttered during the day and sprang alive late at night when the snare and the trumpets and the piano started.

As he rounded a corner and stepped out to cross the street, La Caravelle appeared. Max stopped short. A taxi blared, and Max jumped back onto the curb. He didn't know what he expected to find upon returning to Paris. There was no communication between him and Della, partly by Max's choice and partly because he was busy. Max assumed the club went on like it always did, attracting world-class jazz bands and providing the city's elite with a place to be seen. A small part of him was afraid there might be a *For Sale* sign on the building, but he wasn't prepared for what he saw.

The long, squat building itself was unchanged, painted a dark forest green that appeared as a soft black at night. The wine-red awnings with the name La Caravelle in cursive remained, but that was where the old building gave way to the new. Jutting up to the building and running east to west, someone had built a long wooden deck along the river complete with elaborate trellises and pergolas covered with flowing greenery and bright flowers. Under the pergolas were tables covered in white cloths and silver cutlery. Black-frocked waitresses serviced tables filled with well-heeled Parisians. When the traffic cleared, Max crossed the street and stared in wonder at the open-air restaurant.

Every table was filled. Women in white silk and gold jewelry held wine glasses filled with straw-colored liquid that glinted in the sunlight. Men in colorful leisure shirts and heavy watches laughed and chatted. Midway along the deck, an elaborate arch covered in white blossoms served as the entryway. Dozens of people milled around on the street outside. Max sidled over to a group of women. "Is this place any good?"

The women all tittered. One waved her lacquered nails at him and spoke in French. "You must be from out of town. Everyone is talking about this place. They don't take reservations. It's an hour wait. The chef was just awarded a Michelin star."

"What's a Michelin star?"

The women cackled and one of them rolled her eyes. Max walked along the building and tried the front door. It was locked. He continued around the back, vaulted over the fence, landed next to a dumpster, and came face to face with a large Black woman. Her silvery hair was held under a cap and a black apron was stretched over a wide bosom. She held a mobile phone to her ear, and her eyes widened at the appearance of the bearded man before her.

He smiled.

The phone dropped to the ground, and she enveloped him in a massive bear hug.

"Hi, Della."

"Bonswa, Max. Where you been?"

The same greeting every time. "Home, Della. Had to go see my sister."

Doubt clouded her face. "Everything okay at home?" The fat rolls on her arms jiggled as she held Max's biceps.

"Yes, Della." Max winked. "Everything is all right."

A tear formed in the Creole woman's eye, and she let go of his arms. "Are you back for good, *zanmi*?" It was her pet name for Max, the word *friend* in Haitian Creole.

Max shrugged. "You obviously have things under control. I hear someone gave you a Micheline tire."

Della's laugh echoed off the wooden fencing that formed the bar's delivery and recycling area. She took his arm and pulled him through the back door and into the kitchen, where new equipment gleamed and a large staff of white-frocked cooks bustled. "That don't matter. But here..." She stopped and dipped a spoon into a large bowl, where a serious blonde woman frantically whipped the contents. "Taste."

Max tasted and a medley of flavor flooded his mouth. "Delicious. What is it?"

"It's called mousseline. Egg yolks, butter, lemon juice, cream." Della pulled him into the tiny office and rummaged through stacks of papers, files, receipts, invoices, and bills of lading. "Here." She thrust a document at him and bustled out of the office to the kitchen, where she barked orders and clanged pans.

The document was six pages in length, held with a single staple, and covered in grease stains. Its corners were tattered. It was the bill of sale for the restaurant, which was dated about a year ago and was written in French. It was vaguely familiar. After he flipped through it, it became clear the document was the bill of sale that Kate had helped him with. The document was supposed to transfer ownership of La Caravelle from him to Della for the price of one euro. Max was so distracted back then he didn't remember reviewing the contract.

He paged through it. On page four was the sale amount,

and he confirmed it was for one euro. He flipped to the last page where the signature blocks were. His illegible but distinctive signature was in its proper location, dated a year prior. The block where Della was supposed to sign was blank.

"Della!" He hastened out to the kitchen, where she chopped green onions with a chef's knife. Her movements were a blur, and the onions ended up in perfectly proportioned little round dials. "You forgot to sign."

She set the knife on the aluminum table with a clatter and stepped around to where he stood. With a flourish, she snatched the document and ripped it to shreds, which she pitched into a blue recycle bin. When she resumed chopping, she winked at him. "Welcome home, *zanmi*."

A dozen serious men and woman in white frocks bustled about the kitchen. "At least tell me we still have jazz in the evenings around here, or are we running this Michelin tire food thing at night also?"

She shrugged. "Of course, we have jazz. Guess who the headliner is tonight?"

A list of famous jazz performers scrolled through his mind. "Don't tell me. Sonny Rollins?"

"Rollins is ninety years old. I don't think he's flying from New York to play at your little club."

"Our little club, Della." Max listed a few other acts, all of which elicited an eye roll from Della.

"Wait. Don't tell me."

Della nodded.

The upstairs apartment at La Caravelle was unchanged from when he last stayed here. What was it? Ten months ago? A tiny kitchenette, a small bedroom, a closet, and a nook for sitting. That was it.

He tossed his bag onto the small table and opened the safe, where he found stacks of euros and the restaurant's ledgers. He sipped tea and familiarized himself with the last year of the club's business. After six months of lackluster performance, Della had opened the restaurant portion and the revenue took off. So did the expenses. The twelve white-frocked chefs weren't cheap. Max whistled as he examined the numbers. Decent profit margin, though. Della took a small salary. *Time to fix that. She deserves more. Way more.*

Downstairs he found the crew turning the main room from dining into a lounge. The old stage remained, along with the Steinway Salon Grand. A young man assembled a drum kit while a crew performed a sound check. Max sat at the mahogany bar and the bartender gave the surface a wipe and set out an ashtray.

Max pushed the ashtray aside. "Bourbon, neat." He crossed his legs and sat angled with a view of the stage.

The bartender, a slender woman with a nose ring who wore a white oxford shirt, black tie, and black apron, put her finger to her chin as she surveyed the row of bottles under the mirror. She pulled a green bottle with a white label. "We have Scotch. Will that work?"

"I'll have a burgundy instead." Max made a mental note to talk to the bar manager about the liquor selection. He sipped the red wine and watched as the band finished their set-up. Customers streamed in, and soon the main room was filled with patrons.

The lights snapped off.

The crowd quieted.

The bassist plucked a string and the thumping pulsed Max's heart.

The shadow of a tall woman appeared, and a stage light flicked on to illuminate her stark white hair. She wore a white backless gown that flowed to the floor and revealed a body full of tattoos. As the base thumped, she clung to a microphone on a stand using both hands. Her eyes were closed, and she started in on an Irving Berlin classic called "What'll I Do."

The bartender refilled Max's wineglass as he fixated on Goshawk's face. Her eyes were closed as she clung to the mic and purred the lyrics. When the last note died away, the applause was thunderous. Goshawk caught Max's eye and smiled.

One of Max's father's quotes popped into his mind. Andrei had a quote for every occasion and sometimes he liked to adopt other people's quotes for his own. This one, Max knew, was by the author C.S. Lewis.

Isn't it funny how day by day nothing changes but when you look back, everything is different?

Sylt, Germany

Max eased the SUV onto the side of the sandy highway and set off on foot down the beach. Julia expected him soon, but he wanted to walk. *Breathe in the salty air and enjoy the warm sun.*

He kept the beard to hide the scar, but it was trimmed, and his head was freshly shaved. The air was warm enough to allow a T-shirt and jeans. He carried no weapons and was getting used to the feeling of safety. Of relative safety. He found a trail through the decrepit pillboxes that remained from World War II and stepped onto the beach.

A ten-minute walk south brought him within view of Julia's home. She had sent a picture of it, and Max compared the image on his phone to the real thing. The house was a neat brown rectangular structure about the size of two shipping containers. A greenhouse was situated to the north side, and there was a small deck with chairs for watching the ocean. Dunlins, small tan-and-white wader birds with long bills for digging bugs out of the sand, milled along the beach and darted in and out of the water. Max found Julia in the greenhouse.

She accepted a hug, and the two adjourned to the porch, where Julia served Max a Kölsch beer and herself an iced tea.

"How's your health?" The dunlins scurried around the beach near the water's edge.

"I'm fine, Max."

Max examined her as she stared out to sea. Julia Meier had aged in the past weeks since her rescue from the compound in Finland. The wrinkles were deeper, the hair was whiter, and she moved more deliberately. *Lack of purpose takes a toll, my son.* The phrase was uttered by his father one day in reference to getting old, and it stuck in Max's mind. They sat in silence as the waves washed up on the sand and the dunlins darted to-and-fro. After he drained the beer glass, he removed the picture of Stephen MacCulloch and Julia from his pocket and handed it to her.

She took it and stared at it and her fingers quivered. "That was a long time ago." A tear formed in Julia's eye and rolled down her cheek. She wiped it away and handed the picture back. "Kate did us all a favor. Some memories deserve to remain buried. Get rid of that."

"People deserve closure, too." Max put the picture back in his pocket. "Let me guess. MacCulloch was your source at one point. You two fell in love. Around the same time, you were in love with Andrei. You dumped MacCulloch in favor of Andrei. This entire thing was about a love triangle."

Julia gazed out over the blue-gray ocean. The waves were gentle, and sea grass waved in a light breeze. "More like a spy triangle."

"Something tells me Andrei and MacCulloch would call it a love triangle."

That was all Julia said about the matter. Max stayed for a couple of hours and helped her in the greenhouse before giving his mother a hug. "I have to get back to Paris."

Julia hugged him back and wiped away a tear. "Come visit, anytime." She stood on the deck with her hands shoved in her pockets and her silver hair fluttering in the wind.

As he walked down the deck steps to the beach, he turned and waved. "I'll be back, don't worry."

"When?" Julia's voice carried over the sound of the waves.

He trudged down the sand and called over his shoulder. "Soon enough."

IF YOU LIKED THIS BOOK ...

I would appreciate it if you would leave a review. An honest review means a lot. The constructive reviews help me write better stories, and the positive reviews help others find the books, which ultimately means I can write more stories.

It only takes a few minutes, and it means everything. Thank you in advance.

-Jack

AUTHOR'S NOTE

It's with great elation and some melancholy that I pen this note while I sit in the Basalt Public Library overlooking a vast marsh of green reeds, bouncing butterflies, and darting hummingbirds. The field is lush from the large amount of rain we've had this summer, and the river is hidden behind tall grasses. A few charred tree trunks from the 2018 Lake Christine forest fire are visible on the far ridge.

The Basalt Public Library is a fitting place to look back on the last eight years and six novels. It all started here on the double-wide brown Formica table between sections 364 and 698 in nonfiction. This is where Max Austin came to life and where he did battle with Nathan Abrams and Wilbur Lynch. This is also where I met friends like Kristin, who was laboring on her PhD dissertation. The homeless man with whom I waited each morning for the library to open is gone, however. I hope he's okay.

The view is the same and, miraculously, I still weigh the same, despite the constant stream of peanuts and M&Ms that power my writing. For some reason, they took away the tissue boxes and replaced them with hand sanitizer. We've endured two presidential elections, a worldwide pandemic, war, and a forest fire that forced me and my wife to evacuate our home. Jill and I have been fortunate to enjoy good health and life-changing travel, and I completed an Ironman triathlon, which was on my bucket list. As the pandemic started, I switched writing locations to my home studio where I have a larger monitor and a more ergonomic keyboard but a lesser view. Through it all, Max has accompanied me (and you) for the ride.

That ends here. With *Endgame*, the six-book series is complete.

In 2014 I set out to write a three-book thriller series in the tradition of *The Lord of the Rings*, where the main story arc continues over multiple books. You may not know this, but *The Lord of the Rings* is actually six books contained in three volumes. The main storyline of the fate of the ring and the fellowship doesn't culminate until book six. I hoped to write my series in eighteen months and move on to a new project. Eight years and six novels later, here we are. I guess Max had more story to tell than I realized.

Many of you have asked what the future holds for Max. I honestly don't know. All I can say is writing is in my blood. It's also tattooed on my arm.

So stay tuned, dear reader. And thank you, from the bottom of my heart, for accompanying me and Max on this journey. It means nothing without all of you.

Jack Arbor
Basalt, Colorado
August 19, 2022

ACKNOWLEDGMENTS

I think it was Jimmy Fallon who said, "Thank you, hard taco shells, for surviving the long journey from factory, to supermarket, to my plate and then breaking the moment I put something inside you. Thank you." It reminds me of the novel writing and editing process where, despite endless eyes scouring the manuscript, there is always one more thing to fix.

In my quest to produce a fitting end to Max's six-book journey, I have an endless list of people to thank. The credit goes to them, the errors are mine.

First and foremost is my wife, Jill, who suffered through endless story discussions over tofu fried rice and Singha beer at Phat Thai in Carbondale.

Second is my scrupulous editor, Martha Hayes, who is directly responsible for the smooth-as-silk prose. In addition to being my editor, Martha has become a trusted advisor and a friend, and Max would be lost without her.

Third, I'd like to thank Bruce Zellers, my high school history teacher, who without knowing it, instilled in me a rich curiosity for events of the past. Although history is a set of lies agreed upon, according to Mr. Bonaparte, history also plays a large role in influencing the events of the present. Max's story wouldn't be this rich without the enormous influence of his father's actions.

I'd also like to thank Robert Slayton, Professor Emeritus

in the Department of History at Chapman University, who keeps me honest with regard to weaponry and ammunition.

I continue to be blessed with a distinguished and preeminent group of advanced readers who take time out of their busy lives to read an early version of the manuscript and send me comments. This time around, several of this group used the story to help distract themselves from the ravages of Hurricane Ian and managed to send me notes even though their electricity was out or their homes were severely damaged. I remain grateful.

Among them, in no particular order, are Judith DeRycke and MJ, Katherine Robinson, Keith Kay, Preston Trotter, Claudia Adkison, John Rozum, Jen Close, Bill Hess, John Bailey, Stephen Robinson, Bill Prescott, Wahak Kontian, Amy Degnan, Holly Smyth, Donna Van Meer, Linnea Firenze (LiLi), Sandra Neubaum, Thomas Tenhula, Julie Gautier, Don Payton, Chris Chase, Karen, Flannery, James Slater, Vince Gassi, Bruce Bean, Terri Sones, Mark Tiras, Joames Rutherford, Buddy, Phil Taylor, Scott Koopman, Thomas Tursick, DC aka Emilee's Grandpa, Andrew Klein, Ron Mateas, Gregg Backemeyer, Tim Dickenson, Donald Payton, Robert Nulph, Ron McDaniel, Brian Sillivan, James Farmer, Ed Spotts, Ken Sanford, Scott Barnett, Eric Nichols, Sharon Cameron, Julie Petrovic, George Donnelly, Andy Perla, Marry van Oers, Karen Lawrie, Portia Shao, Joel Kaufmann, Neelima Bhatia, Carrie Salomone, Lee Gregory, Bart Bloom, Anna Haas, Gail Romero, Shay Morton, Lynnea Linquist, Bob Vilardi, Wayne Barnard, John Bilancione, David Potts, Chris Oerman, Kathy Mischka, Susan Boyle, Lynette Bean, Dennis Martin, Hugo Ernst, Marjan Glavac, Antoinette Brewster, Tamar Meskin, Lynn Makris, David Skinner, Bruce Borstein, Ron Powers, Herlinda Bryant, Michael

Bugosh, Nancy Jamison, Lynn Nix, David Woytek, Melody Paquin, John Maxwell, Kimberly Mars, Karen Lamiero, Scott Barcza, Gary Ritzman, and Terry McEachern. If I forgot anyone, or spelled anyone's name wrong, please accept my sincerest apologies.

I remain in awe of the insights and detailed nuances picked up by this group of dedicated readers. Without them, *Endgame* would be a lesser novel.

JOIN MY MAILING LIST

If you'd like to get updates on new releases as well as notifications of deals and discounts, please join my email list.

I only email when I have something meaningful to say and I never send spam. You can unsubscribe at any time.

Join my mailing list at www.jackarbor.com.

ABOUT THE AUTHOR

Jack Arbor is the author of seven thrillers featuring the wayward KGB assassin Max Austin. The stories follow Max as he comes to terms with his past and tries to extricate himself from a destiny he desperately wants to avoid.

Jack works as a technology executive during the day and writes at night and on weekends with much love and support from his lovely wife, Jill.

Jill and Jack live outside Aspen, Colorado, where they enjoy trail running and hiking through the natural beauty of the Roaring Fork Valley. Jack also likes to taste new bourbons and listen to jazz, usually at the same time. They both miss the bagels on the East Coast.

You can get free books as well as prerelease specials and sign up for Jack's mailing list at www.jackarbor.com.

Connect with Jack online:
- (e) jack@jackarbor.com
- (t) twitter.com/JackArbor
- (i) instagram.com/jackarbor/
- (f) facebook.com/JackArborAuthor
- (w) www.jackarbor.com
- (n) newsletter signup

ALSO BY JACK ARBOR

The Russian Assassin, The Russian Assassin Series, Book One

You can't go home again...

Max, a former KGB assassin, is content with the life he's created for himself in Paris. When he's called home to Minsk for a family emergency, Max finds himself suddenly running for his life, desperate to uncover secrets about his father's past to save his family.

Max's sister Arina and nephew Alex become pawns in a game that started a generation ago. As Max races from the alleyways of Minsk to the posh neighborhoods of Zurich, and ultimately to the gritty streets of Prague, he must confront his past and come to terms with his future to preserve his family name.

The Russian Assassin is a tight, fast-paced adventure, staring Jack Arbor's stoic hero, the ex-KGB assassin-for-hire, Max Austin. Book one of the series forces Max to choose between himself and his family, a choice that will have consequences for generations to come.

The Pursuit, The Russian Assassin Series, Book Two

The best way to destroy an enemy is to make him a friend...

Former KGB assassin Max Austin is on the run, fighting to keep his family alive while pursuing his parents' killers.

As he battles foes both visible and hidden, he uncovers a conspiracy with roots in the darkest cellars of Soviet history. Determined to survive, Max hatches a plan to even the odds by partnering with his mortal enemy. Even as his adversary becomes his confidant, Max is left wondering who he can trust, if anyone...

If you like dynamic, high-voltage, page-turning thrills, you'll love the second installment of The Russian Assassin series starring Jack Arbor's desperate hero, ex-KGB assassin-for-hire, Max Austin.

The Attack, The Russian Assassin Series, Book Three

It's better to be the hunter than the hunted.

A horrific bombing rocks the quaint streets of London's West Brompton neighborhood and Max Austin finds himself the target of an international manhunt the likes of which the world hasn't seen since the hunt for Osama bin Laden. The former KGB assassin must put his fight against the Consortium on hold while he seeks redemption.

As Max chases the bomber from the gritty streets of London through the lush Spanish countryside and into the treacherous mountains of Chechnya, he's plunged into a game of cat and mouse with a wily MI6 agent determined to catch Max at all costs.

Can Max find the terrorist and clear his name before it's too late?

The Attack is the third installment in The Russian Assassin adventure thriller series that pits Max Austin against his arch-enemy, the shadowy consortium of international criminals that will stop at nothing to kill Max and his family. If you like heart-pounding, page-turning thrills, grab this adventure starring Jack Arbor's grim hero, the ex-KGB assassin-for-hire, Max Austin.

The Hunt, The Russian Assassin Series, Book Four

Friends are the family we chose for ourselves.

A man on a mission to save his family. A friend missing and presumed dead.

Max Austin is no stranger to mortal danger and hard decisions. But when the former KGB assassin is confronted by the choice to rescue a friend or save his family, he'll have to dig deep to keep those he cares about alive.

Haunted by a mysterious shadow that dogs him at every turn, he journeys through the treacherous Turkish desert, the harsh confines of Washington, DC, and the dirty alleyways of Cyprus searching for clues from his past. Along the way, he finds himself a step behind his adversaries who are intent on eliminating Kate Shaw before she can reveal her secrets. This time, failure in Max's quest will mean death for his friends and family alike.

Will he find Kate Shaw, or will this be Max's last mission?

The Hunt is the gripping fourth installment in Jack Arbor's Amazon bestselling series, The Russian Assassin, staring his stoic hero Max Austin. With a barreling pace, lovable characters, and unputdownable action, you'll see why Arbor's books sell like hotcakes and why readers clamor for more.

The Abyss, The Russian Assassin Series, Book Five

Every betrayal begins with trust.

A man fighting to save his heritage. A race to find a secret cache of documents. A deadly family secret revealed.

It's Christmas eve. Max and Kate are convalescing in the snowy woods of Colorado when violence strikes. On the run again, the ragtag family must trade their deepest secrets for safety.

Tormented by mysteries from his past, Max learns the truth about his father's treachery. A vast cache of documents that expose the inner workings of the Russian government are hidden from sight. The CIA, MI6, China's Ministry of State Security, and other clandestine groups are hunting for the secret archive along with Max's mortal enemies.

In a race against time, Max visits the grandiose ski resort of Chamonix and escapes a fateful train ride through the South of France before trekking across the treacherous borders of southern Russia. Deep in the heart of Siberia, Max must confront his past to decrypt his father's mysteries before his enemies beat him to the prize.

Will Max uncover the Vienna Archive and reverse his family's fortunes before it's too late?

The Abyss is the fifth installment in Jack Arbor's Amazon bestselling series, The Russian Assassin, staring his stoic hero, Max Austin. With a breakneck pace, endearing characters, and endless action, you'll see why Jack's books fly off the shelves and why readers holler for more.

Cat & Mouse, A Max Austin Novella

Max, a former KGB assassin, is living a comfortable life in Paris. When not plying his trade, he passes his time managing a jazz club in the City of Light. To make ends meet, he freelances by offering his services to help rid the earth of the world's worst criminals.

Max is enjoying his ritual post-job vodka when he meets a stunning woman; a haunting visage of his former fiancé. Suddenly, he finds himself the target of an assassination plot in his beloved city of Paris. Fighting for his life, Max must overcome his own demons to stay alive.

ENDGAME
(A MAX AUSTIN THRILLER - BOOK SIX)

This book is a work of fiction. The characters, incidents, and dialogue are drawn from the author's imagination and are not to be construed as real. Any resemblance to actual events or persons, living or dead, is fictionalized or coincidental.

Paperback ISBN: 9781947696129

Copyright 2022 by Jack Arbor and Ajax Media Group, LLC. All rights reserved. No part of this book may be used, reproduced, or transmitted in any form or by any means, electronic or mechanical, including photocopying, recording, internet transmission, or by any information storage or retrieval system, without the express written permission of the publisher, except where permitted by law or in the case of brief quotations in critical articles and reviews.

Requests to publish work from this book should be sent to:
jack@jackarbor.com
Edition 1.0

Published by High Caliber Books

Cover art by: www.damonza.com
Bio photo credit: www.johnlilleyphotography.com

Made in United States
Troutdale, OR
04/25/2024